There was a clatter, loud in the angry silence, as a ̶ ̶ ̶ was flung open and troopers of the Bodyguard marched in: two files of them, armed, and wearing full battle armour. Rynert the King walked between them to his seat at the head of the table; and he alone of all the high-born in the Hall wore a sword. It was a *taipan*, with a faint curve to it which told of great age, and like the dirk beside it at his belt was unrelieved vermeil even to the metalwork of hilt and scabbard. Note was taken not merely of the weapon's presence, but of the colour chosen for its mountings. Some of the lords who had been at Baelen Field recalled Kalarr cu Ruruc, and in that recollection found little of ease or comfort.

Rynert wasted no time on preamble; he laid both hands flat on the surface of the table and said simply, 'Aldric Talvalin, my lords.'

'What of him, my Lord King?'

'He must die.'

Also in Legend by Peter Morwood

THE DEMON LORD
THE DRAGON LORD
THE HORSE LORD

THE WARLORD'S DOMAIN

Peter Morwood

A Legend book
Published by Arrow Books Limited
20 Vauxhall Bridge Road, London SW1V 2SA

An imprint of Random Century Group

London Melbourne Sydney Auckland
Johannesburg and agencies throughout
the world

First published in the Legend imprint in 1989 by
Century Hutchinson Ltd.
This Legend edition 1990

Printed and bound in Great Britain by
Courier International Ltd, Tiptree, Essex

ISBN 0 09 958910 9

For Diane,
This book,
This world,
And all the others.

*With thanks to Liza Reeves and Jean Maund
for a light hand with the blue pencil.*

PREFACE

Horse Lord.

Demon Lord.

Dragon Lord.

Aldric Talvalin has been all of these already in his short life.

It was a life which began four days after his twentieth birthday, when his world turned upside down.

He was born the youngest son of three to the High-Clan Lord of Dunrath, Haranil Talvalin, and as that youngest son he stood to inherit little: horse, weapons, armour and his family name. There would be those who regarded that last as most valuable of all. Certainly it was valuable enough to wipe out the family.

Across the ocean to the East, the Drusalan Empire had expanded for a hundred years. Once expansion ceased and became consolidation, the Imperial Grand Warlord, commander of all military forces and – nominally – answerable only to the Emperor, could see his own position coming to an end along with the constant warfare which had created it. For all that those of the Sherban dynasty had long been no more than the puppets of their own self-appointed military dictators, there were enough powerful men and women in the Empire to assure the Warlord's fall from favour; and there would be many, many people waiting for that day.

It was the Warlord who chose High-Clan Talvalin, isolated as they were in the north of Alba. They would be long dead, and an Imperial military intervention to keep the peace would have responded to the request of his own agent Duergar long before the King in Cerdor could react; his only possible reaction would simply further justify the need for a Drusalan force in Alba . . .

The plan would have worked perfectly . . . except for Aldric, who survived the massacre by being elsewhere at the time. He swore a great oath to avenge himself on the slayer of his family and the destroyer of his clan, not knowing then of any deeper significance behind the killings, and not caring even had he known. That Duergar Vathach was a sorcerer served only to add insult to injury.

Aldric escaped death twice that day in the fortress of Dunrath, once by an unpunctual return home and again when the arrow intended for his neck transfixed his shoulder instead. Yet still he would have died from cold or loss of blood somewhere in the snowy wastes where flight had taken him, had he not been taken in, hidden and healed by Gemmel. That Gemmel Errekren was another sorcerer . . . served only to add irony to kindness.

The young man and the old passed from wariness to friendship to fosterling and foster-father. Many years before, Gemmel had lost his own and only son to the Drusalan Empire, killed for no more reason than Aldric's father. It seemed grimly appropriate that he should gain another son from the same source. Aldric's education became that of someone his countrymen would have called a wizard's whelp – an education far more advanced than their minds could have grasped. It was education to survive.

Aldric survived. Duergar Vathach, and the plans of his master, did not.

That was the beginning of a long hate-affair between the Grand Warlord and Aldric Talvalin; and for many months Aldric was ignorant of having done more than keep the oath he had sworn in his own blood to his dying father. That ignorance continued during a mission for King Rynert of Alba to the fortress of a rebel Overlord on the borders of the Empire, for Rynert had no more scruples than his enemies about fomenting unrest. Except that this Overlord was insane, and his son was using the Alban monies to dabble in sorceries which even Aldric had preferred to leave alone.

The mission, a task born in respect and honour, ended in betrayal and death. Within a matter of weeks Aldric's ignorance – at least of his King's duplicity – had been washed away in a welter of blood. Rynert's planning had gone further than he had told his vassal, and the young lord found himself handed over to the commanders of the Emperor's faction, bought and paid for with treaties of aggressive non-aggression against Alba.

These men, all high officers – among them the Chief of Secret Police and a general who was foster-father to the new Emperor just as Gemmel had been to Aldric – intended to embarrass the Grand Warlord by stealing away a political prisoner from the one prison in the Empire from which no one had ever escaped. To enhance that embarrassment, and to show Alban support for their stance and activities, Aldric was to come with them – whether or not he agreed.

The rescue was successful, the escape was not. There were more deaths: Drusalan . . . and Alban. Dewan ar Korentin, Captain of King Rynert's Bodyguard and Aldric's friend, had been outraged at the way he had been handed over like a piece of merchandise, and had accompanied Gemmel in an attempt to save his friend's life. He did – but at the expense of his own. Dewan died at the hands of Commander Voord of the Secret Police, the man whose cold, precise brain had formed the plan to kill the Talvalins more than four years earlier.

Dewan's death bought Aldric more than life; it bought knowledge: of names, and places, and reasons. But not, even then, a full awareness of Voord's hatred.

Its price is higher still, waiting to be paid, waiting to be learned, in the black places, the shadows beyond nightfall, the heart of darkness that is

THE WARLORD'S DOMAIN . . .

PROLOGUE

There was a pavement of white marble beneath him, treacherously slick under a covering of trampled, dirty snow, and the wind that slashed at his face and body was edged with such a cold as more fortunate men might only dream of.

Pain, and the gaudy spattering of blood across cracked milk-white marble. Snow falling, drifting, a white shroud across a leaden winter landscape. Out of that stillness, the sound of tears and a buzz of glutted flies. The smell of spice, and incense, and huge red roses. . . .

The marble paving-slabs where he knelt hurt his knees; he didn't know whether that came from the shattered stone or from the crushed and dented armour encasing his legs, and in any case such a small annoyance was entirely swallowed up in the thin, hot pain – both present and anticipated – of the dirk-point which pricked skin a finger's breadth below his breastbone.

'Heart-line,' said the voice of Esshau the weapon-master in his ears. 'Here, young sirs, in, upward and a half twist of your blade for a quick kill. Or for suicide.' Esshau, a stocky, dark, sardonic Prytenek who had been his model and his hero for years, had never dignified the act of *tsepanak'ulleth* with its formal title. He had never called it other than what it was. Esshau had disapproved of waste, and had made that disapproval outspokenly plain. Only his talent with weapons and in teaching their use had kept him employed at Dunrath. . . .

Why Esshau? He's been ashes ten years now . . . ?

Why not? You'll be joining him soon enough – though he'll not like the way you chose to do it.

Blood runnelled between the crooked claws that had been his fingers; he could see its vivid spots on the marble

10

paving, and soaking into the snow. But for all there was so much, he couldn't smell it. A deep breath drew only the winter's chill into his lungs, and riding on it the unseasonal scent of roses. With snow inches deep on the ground, there should have been no such smell . . . yet it was there, impossibly strong, incredibly sweet, a perfume that made his senses swim like wine.

Issaqua. . . .

A rose as red as blood, thorned with demon fangs. Hungry. Eager. Vengeful. . . . And waiting for its due and proper gift of death.

O my lady, O my love. . . .

He dared not look at her, for fear that the sight of her face would steal away the courage and the small store of determination he had gathered together, to help him . . . do what he was about to do. To give a gift freely, rather than see it stolen. To die a willing victim, in the full knowledge that with that death others would have life.

He drove the *tsepan* home, and agony consumed him.

Liquid heat flooded his hand and wrist, making his palm slippery, preventing him from giving that twist to the knife which would speed him on his way. For a moment he could taste his own blood rising in his throat. For a moment he could see her face, shock-white, appalled. *I love you though I leave you, my sweet lady*, his look said; there was neither time nor strength for the luxury of a spoken word. *Think kindly of me now and then.* . . .

And he could see that other face, thin, fine-featured, pale as the death that had refused to accept him; still unable to believe, rejecting what he saw even at this moment when denial and rejection lost their meaning. That face, all the faces, all the world, slid sideways into a black mouth that reeked of roses.

Oh Lord God, why don't they prepare you for how much a tsepan *hurts . . . ?*

And then there were no more faces and no more thoughts, but only fire and snow and blood and darkness, and the darkness filled the world, and devoured him, and he died. . . .

ONE

Go past the Mountain and through the valley, the old man had told them.

That much was easy. *En Kovhan*, The Mountain, was a huge and shadowy triangular bulk on their right side as they rode south. The sword-hand side, the old man had said. Aldric had thought his tone and choice of words were ominous then – and downright threatening now. Yet the country seemed soft, gentle, its contours smoothed by millennia of slow-turning seasons until it was very different from the harsh outlines of *Glas-elyu Menethen* in Alba. Very different indeed. Even now in the depths of winter an occasional patch of green still showed through the snow; none of those greens were the sombre pine-dark of the Jevaiden, and he was thankful for that at least. Thankful that his memories were allowed to rest, this once.

Then Kyrin eased her grey gelding to a standstill and rose in her stirrups, looking swiftly from side to side, and all the old wariness came back to Aldric with a rush. He realised that his hand had closed on his sword-hilt with neither intention nor conscious command. It was enough to make a man embarrassed.

'It's beautiful,' she said, turning after a moment to look at him for some sign of agreement. And that was all she said.

'Yes.' He made himself say it, made himself relax, made his fingers unwind from Widowmaker's braided leather grip. Aldric grinned a sour little grin. *You're jumpy*, he thought, silently critical. But another, unbidden voice inside his head said, *and with good reason* . . .

They were in the valley now, with forested slopes rising steeply to either side – but Aldric was only too well aware that they weren't steep enough to inconvenience a mounted ambush, nor so thickly wooded that archers would be unable to shoot. He stared suspiciously at it, watching the evening drawing in, stretching out fingers of shadow from the deeper shadows underneath the trees.

'We're going to be late,' said Kyrin. There was disapproval in her voice.

'But I sent a message. We're expected. And anyway, it's not my fault.' That came out defensively, as a protest, no matter what he might have intended for it. 'If we'd had a map . . .' He left the rest unfinished, knowing quite well that Kyrin would add whatever else she felt was necessary. He wasn't disappointed.

'If.' She stared at him a moment, then shrugged. 'Yes. Quite . . .'

To be called to conference at all during the holiday season was undesirable, and an imposition. To be called to conference at midnight, in winter, with snow on the ground, was little short of scandalous and scarcely to be borne. The Alban Crown Council assembled with poor grace in the corridors of the Hall of Kings, exchanging irritable mutters – and then were shocked even beyond scandal by the words of the very junior officer-of-Guards who appeared before them with discomfort written in large letters on his face.

'My apologies, my lords,' he said, ducking a perfunctory bow towards them, 'but you must leave your swords with me . . .'

There was silence for perhaps a minute, murmured disbelief for maybe as long; then noisy outrage. Never since the Clan Wars five hundred years before had any Alban royal councillor been asked to give up his blades before a meeting. The right to keep and bear arms in the King's presence was a privilege seldom granted, and one guarded most jealously by those who held it. To be requested, no matter how courteously – though flanked as he was by six fully armoured troopers, the young officer's

14

request was no more than a nicely-worded order – to give up that privilege was tantamount to insult. Alban clan-lords were *not* insulted, even by their King; and that a king would dare the risks – which history had proven to be very real – of giving insult singly and collectively to so powerful a group of men suggested that the matter for Council attention was far more delicate than they had been led to believe. The thought occurring simultaneously to several brought a sudden silence to the group.

Lord Dacurre moved first. Old, gruff and well-regarded, he knew that from the instant his age-mottled hand lifted towards his weapon-belt all eyes were on him. That wrinkled, sinewy talon paused for a moment near the hilts of *taipan* and *taiken* as he considered the impli-cations of what he was about to do. Aymar Dacurre had been adviser to three kings in his long life, but a personal friend of only two. This present ruler, Rynert, seemed incapable of either engendering or returning warmth. But he was still the King. Dacurre looked at the other lords one by one, his gaze slow to move away from each face. Just as slowly he unhooked the longsword and its shorter twin from his belt, offering them both, sheathed and hori-zontal on open palms, to the young officer. 'These blades,' he said quietly, 'are seven centuries old. Respect them as they deserve.' Then, over-shoulder to his companions: 'My lords, best do it. Then perhaps we'll find out *why*.'

They filed into the great vaulted Hall, every man among them irritable and on edge. There was an uneasiness not merely about themselves and the situation, but about the very place in which they were to meet. Its echoing empti-ness was not so well lit as was customary, most of the scant illumination coming from the great log fires which spat and crackled in the nine hearths lining the walls, and from the few oil-lamps set along the length of the table whose polished surface was the only bright thing in a Hall over-full of shifting shadows. It was a long refectory table of dark, waxed oak, lined with chairs for the twenty-odd *kailinin-eir* and with long-stemmed cups and flagons of wine arrayed across its surface like soldiers on parade. Such furnishings were used for Councils in the Drusalan Empire – but never in Alba, where men were presumed able to control their passions without the need to surrender their weapons, or to sit behind a table so that its timbers might serve to keep them from one another's throats. They stared at the offensive gleam of wood with expressions ranging from disdain to unconcealed outrage; it was just another facet of the evening's strangeness . . . and something more to be stored away in the memory of men to whom a reckoning would have to be made, sooner or later.

There was a clatter, loud in the angry silence, as a door was flung open and troopers of the Bodyguard marched in: two files of them, armed, and wearing full battle armour. Rynert the King walked between them to his seat at the head of the table; and he alone of all the high-born in the Hall wore a sword. It was a *taipan*, with a faint curve to it which told of great age, and like the dirk beside it at his belt was unrelieved vermeil even to the metalwork of hilt and scabbard. Note was taken not merely of the weapon's presence, but of the colour chosen for its mountings. Some of the lords who had been at Baelen Field recalled Kalarr cu Ruruc, and in that recollection found little of ease or comfort.

Rynert wasted no time on preamble; he laid both hands flat on the surface of the table and said simply, 'Aldric Talvalin, my lords.' And after that he said no more until someone – sitting quite still, he didn't even turn his head to see who spoke – made the necessary request for elaboration.

'What of him, my Lord King?'

'He must die.'

Full night was upon them. There were stars overhead, clear and bright in a freezing cloudless sky, but there was no moon. In the starlight, Aldric could see the pale glim-

16

mer of Kyrin's face as she turned her head towards him, and the paler cloud of breath that she released in a little sigh of annoyance; but he couldn't see her eyes, and that was probably just as well. There would be accusation in them, and for all that their expression would probably be diluted by the sardonic humour he employed himself on far too many occasions, it was an expression which he didn't want to see at all.

'We're lost.' The Valhollan accent made her words come out even flatter than such words usually would.

'We're close. I'll ask someone; they'll be bound to know—'

'—that we're lost . . . ?'

'No!'

'No?'

'No. And besides, we *are* expected.'

'Oh yes, of course. I was forgetting. But I'd feel better about it if you weren't trying so hard to convince me of it. And yourself. But all right – ask. Someone. Anyone. If you can find them awake . . .'

There came at last a time, as the night dragged on, when Aldric's temper began to fray. Despite careful directions from a number of locals – some of whom he had plainly woken from a sound sleep – he was still no closer to finding the steading that he sought.

'If they're making game of me . . .' he muttered between his teeth.

'What if they are?' Kyrin, dozing in her saddle with one knee crooked around its pommel to keep herself from falling, yawned sleepily. 'You're the foreigner here. *Inyenhlensyarl*. Just as much as me, for once, and with as few rights. Maybe fewer. I'm not . . . not an enemy. But even so, I think they're being friendly enough, in a back-handed way.'

'?' Aldric made an interrogative noise in the back of his throat that couldn't be dignified as a question.

'I think they don't want to disappoint you. They're telling you what you want to hear – directions to a hold – rather than what they know – which is that none of them have any idea of how to find it.'

Aldric looked at her and through her, and this time it was as well *his* expression was hidden by the darkness. But the way in which he spat on to the ground was plain enough for them both.

A few uncomfortable minutes passed in a silence broken only by the slow tramp of weary horses. Then Kyrin coughed politely and pointed; Aldric knew about the pointing, because he could hear the rustle-and-creak of mail and leather as she stretched out her arm, and the glitter of stars reflecting off the metal.

'Now what?' he said, and for the first time in that too-long night, Kyrin heard real tiredness in his voice instead of the increasingly forced bright optimism which had annoyed her before she realised what it was.

'We're passing a gateway,' she said, noting absently that her voice was as weary as his.

'Which we've already passed five times tonight, I think. In both directions. So?'

'Don't you think that maybe we should try asking there?'

'I've had enough of. . . .' Then he coughed, sounding just slightly apologetic. 'All right. One more . . . just this one. And then I'm sleeping under a tree.'

'Or a bush.'

'Or the rock I feel as if I crawled from under. But I'm going to sleep somewhere . . .' and Kyrin actually heard him laugh.

The frozen pounded earth of the road gave way to a gravel track which crunched noisily beneath the hooves of pack- and riding-horses. The buildings to which it led were in darkness, without even a doorway lantern, and Aldric reined back uneasily. 'I'm not sure about this,' he said softly.

Kyrin could detect more than tiredness in his voice this

time; there was an uncertainty and a tension which had come from nowhere, for no reason. Leather creaked faintly in the midnight stillness as he twisted in his high-peaked saddle, trying to see her face or maybe only read something encouraging from her half-seen outline. Other than a drift of breath, silver in the light of winter stars, he could see nothing. And she knew it. 'Aldric . . . what's wrong? It's just a house like all the others . . . isn't it?'

'I . . . Yes. I think. But I've got – call it a feeling – about this one. There's something not right – as if we're being watched.'

'Oh.' The pause which followed went on too long. 'Are you going to sit on that horse all night – or do you want *me* to hammer on the door?'

'Light of Heaven, no! I'll do it. You stay where you are. And be careful.'

'Of what?'

Her question, or maybe his answer, was lost in the crisp double thud as Aldric's boots hit the gravel. He straightened his back, tugging at his furred and quilted clothing to neaten it – and to conceal the half-armour that he wore beneath – then walked to the door of the house and raised his gloved right hand to tap politely on the wood.

Polite or not, the knock never landed. The door jerked back from his descending knuckles, and the glare of a suddenly-unshuttered lantern made him flinch away, shielding eyes dilated by darkness from an amber-mottled purple glare that just now was all that he could see. Even then Aldric might have drawn blade on pure defensive reflex had it not been for the subliminal image which had scorched beyond even the lightborn blindness . . .

The image of a crossbow, levelled at his chest.

There was a cacophony of barking in his ears, and Kyrin's stifled cry of shock far out on the edges of the uproar. Then everything went quiet. Except for the sound of someone laughing . . .

★　.

Rynert's statement came out so flat, so unembellished by any intonation, that there were several at first who thought their ears had deceived them. Even when reaction manifested, it was muted by the shock of what they had just heard. If only by default, Lord Dacurre found himself the spokesman once again.

'*Mathern-an* . . .' Rynert favoured him with the courtesy of a swift glance. 'Lord King . . . *why*?'

'I am the King: I could say, because I command it.' Rynert did not smile as he spoke, and it became starkly plain that there was no subtle joke in what he said. He leaned back a little, steepling his fingers together in the old gesture and studying his silent lords over their entwined tips. 'But say rather: because his recent . . . activities . . . have brought us closer to war with the Drusalans than I care to contemplate; because he has made more free with the Art Magic than any honourable Alban lord has ever dared to do in all our history. And because he has caused the death of my own Captain-of-Guards.'

That last stirred them more than anything else had done, for those whose business kept them close to Cerdor had noticed Dewan ar Korentin's absence this past month and more; but had not – given the man's rank and position – cared to make more enquiries than the listening to rumour would allow. Those rumours current had told of a mission for the King; of secrecy; of importance both personal and political. They had told of enough to discourage the asking of incautious questions. But they had never told of anything like *this*.

'How . . . how did this happen?' No one councillor seemed to have asked the question aloud, yet it was so much to the forefront of every mind that it might well have taken shape out of the air.

Rynert told them: of the simple task of carrying friendship-messages which Aldric Talvalin had perverted to suit his own designs; of his interference in Imperial policy for as-yet-undisclosed purposes; of the killing of two Drusalan Overlords at Seghar and the setting up of another; of the constant thread of sorcery running through every report about him; and now the apparent destruction of part of the Imperial city of Egisburg. It was this which had cost ar Korentin his life: no accurate information had so far filtered through, but the rumours – oh, there were always rumours – were concerned with the kidnap of an important personage under the guise of a rescue, the murder of a highly-placed political figure, and it seemed now almost certain that in trying to restrain further such excesses Dewan ar Korentin had met his death.

Rynert deplored his own lack of foresight in allowing that particular young lord to be his emissary to the Drusalans, for all Aldric's persuasiveness. He was to blame for everything, since he should have realised at once that it would have been tantamount to letting a wolf negotiate with sheep. . . .

. . . And it proved the power of his impassioned rhetoric that not a single one of his Council saw a trace of the ridiculous in the sprawling and traditionally inimical Drusalan Empire being described as helpless against one young man. Too many of them had memories of Aldric's single-minded pursuit of vengeance, and the blood retaking of his usurped ancestral fortress. Many of their relatives and friends had died in that short, savage campaign, and just for the present they forgot that more had been at stake – for themselves and for all Alba – than one man's personal satisfaction. The only thing they chose to remember, and of which Rynert chose to remind them, was who seemed to gain most profit at the end of it all. The same man who had then apparently washed his hands of his comrades' blood and gone about his own affairs.

Aldric opened his eyes a fraction and at the same time raised both his hands, open and palms outwards, to the level of his ears. The laughter continued, breaking off only when a dog – how many dogs, for the love of Heaven?

– growled again and was silenced with a sharp word of command.

He was beginning to see them now, through the dance of glowing streaks inside his eyes, and seeing them was not a comfort. Two leggy Drusalan guard hounds sat back on their tail-less haunches and regarded him with fanged, tongue-lolling grins which had nothing humorous about them.

Aldric had met Drusalan hounds before; and the memory was not a pleasant one.

'All right,' said a voice that was still thrumming with mirth, 'I recognise you. Haranil-*arluth*'s youngest. Don't worry; this thing isn't even loaded.'

The woman's hair had been steel-grey. It was silver-white now, gilded by the lamplight, and she was wearing a staid and all-enveloping sleeping gown rather than travelling furs and fine woollen broadcloth; but for all that Ivern Valeir looked very little different from the last time Aldric had seen her, in the courtyard of Dunrath when she and her husband had come to sell their fine horses to his father, six years and a lifetime ago.

Except perhaps for the guard hounds . . . and the crossbow.

He swallowed once or twice, trying to clear the constriction in his gullet which felt like his heart half-way between his mouth and its proper place, then endeavoured without much success to fit a wan smile on to a face turned white as paper as he gave her the most courteous bow he could summon in the circumstances.

'You invited me, lady,' he said, and for a wonder there was neither tremor, nor anger, nor accusation in his voice. 'I sent a letter to your husband, asking that I might at last accept the hospitality you both offered, that time in Dunrath when my father paid you for the horses. Unless, of course, I've made a mistake?' That crossbow was still cradled in her arms and Aldric, ever prudent, did not for an instant believe what she had said about it.

'No mistake.' She quirked an eyebrow at him. 'You

22

were invited, yes. Expected . . . well, call that one *yes* as well. But earlier.' Ivern looked up at the sky and rather pointedly – thought Aldric and Kyrin both – at the post-midnight configurations of the stars that glittered there. 'Much, much earlier.'

'He – *we* – got lost.' Kyrin's explanation did not please Aldric much, but he kept his mouth shut and let her talk. 'We woke up most of the province trying to find you. And even then the finding was by accident . . .'

Ivern shifted the lamp and looked out into the darkness of her own courtyard. That smile was back on her face as she flicked an amused glance between Aldric and his lady. 'Ah. So,' she said, plainly trying not to laugh. 'I *see* . . .' She probably did, at that; those eyes were like Kyrin's in their ability to look far and deep. 'That sort of "earlier" wasn't what I meant, my dear, although it's true enough. I meant years, not hours – before Ansel, my husband, died.' She saw a muscle twitch in Aldric's face, and shrugged to dismiss the matter. 'Oh, but that was years ago as well. Now, there are stables and a guest annex behind the house. Once you've settled your animals, come in. You'll have to chop some firewood for the stove, young man, but you look as if you'd be good at that. And then something warm to drink, and a talk, would do us *all* good. Although I think a good night's sleep right afterwards would do you two most good of all. . . .'

'There you have it, gentlemen,' Rynert said when the tangled, bloody tale was done. The outrage vanished from his voice like frost from glass, so that once again his words came out without inflection, expressing his preferences neither one way or the other. He sat still now, frighteningly so, as immobile as a corpse freshly dug to sit at the head of the table, and with eyes as blank, seeming neither to blink nor to breathe, as patient as a cat waiting at a mouse-hole. But waiting for what? Which of them was the mouse?

Except for the few who had met Aldric Talvalin face to face and refused to believe that the man they knew was capable of what they had been told, there was not one among the councillors who found his behaviour other than appalling. High-clan lords were accustomed to the wielding of power, and to utter ruthlessness if such was required; but – to those who were convinced – this was excessive. To the others it was simply stupid and that, rather than the shocking violence, made it unbelievable. A capability for ferocity, and for the foolishness of impulsive action – that was one thing. This was another. And they all found Rynert's reluctance to give them a lead . . . uncomfortable. Unnatural, and unlike him. Usually he would hint, if only by unconscious shifts of posture and expression, at which direction he hoped his council's vote would take. Not that such hints would have swayed their decision; this was Alba, not the Drusalan Empire, and clan-lords were followers of their own persuasions rather than another man's implicit – or indeed explicit – views. Yet Rynert's blank, uncaring face was so unlike the subtly mobile features which they thought they knew – especially after his first blunt declaration – that private speculation made them feel more uneasy than deliberate, diametric opposition to the King's openly stated, carefully reasoned command. And such a lack of interest as this, in so grave a matter as they had been told of, was most unsettling of all.

'Lord King.' Hanar Santon rose and bowed. He was youngest of all the clan-lords present and most recent to his title, his father not half a year dead by formal suicide in the *tsepanak'ulleth* ritual. But he spoke no more than the brief formal salutation, for when he straightened from his bow it was to stare at eyes with no more life in them than wet pebbles, and the other, unsaid words congealed in his throat so that he fell silent.

Rynert gazed at him with a sere, level stare like that of a painted ikon. Lord Santon could have borne a shrivelling glare of anger, outrage or condemnation, for that at least

24

would have indicated some emotion. But this . . . was as if he did not even exist.

None of the others tried to speak after that. They were also feeling that their existence had been called into question. Had there been some sort of *feeling* up and down the Council table, one or other of the lords might have felt roused to put some question of his own – the question which had formed in every mind by now: *Why were we summoned here at all . . . ?* But without that feeling, that passion, that emotion – without *something* – it seemed better to them all that the oppressive silence remained unbroken.

'So.' Soft-spoken though it was, Rynert's single syllable had all the impact of a stone dropped into a still pond. Though the King had not moved one iota from his straight-backed posture, there was as much power apparent to all as if he had sprung to his feet and struck the table with a clenched fist. His face, however, was calm.

And if that was *calm*, thought more than one of his lords, then *calm* is what we call a house with all its doors and windows boarded shut.

'If it is your desire, my lords,' he continued in that placid voice so unlike his own, 'then I give you an hour in which to consider. In private.'

There was no mistaking his words and the small movement of his hands for other than a dismissal – and one which was welcomed by many. What seemed to be happening in King Rynert's mind was rapidly becoming both something his lords wanted no part of, and something they wished to discuss amongst themselves. They rose almost in unison, made their obeisance – and followed the King's Bodyguard out of the Hall as quickly as their dignity allowed.

Rynert watched them go, sipping red wine from the cup before him, then drained the cup at a single draught; and only when the door clicked shut behind the last did he release his held-in breath in a long, slow hiss through teeth that had involuntarily clenched shut. So tightly shut that as he became aware of the reaction and released the pressure, he knew that tomorrow his jaw muscles would ache.

'All alone at last.'

The voice came from behind him and though Rynert had expected to hear it at some stage of the night, to have it come without warning from the shadows at his unguarded back was still enough to make him jump. He regained control of the reaction almost at once, and when he turned to face the darkness it was an unhurried, seemingly unworried movement. Even though his hand *was* on the hilt of his sword. . . .

'Where is the other this time?' the voice continued. 'Your bodyguard?'

Rynert slid a chilly smile across his face and even as his facial muscles moved, could not have said how much of the coldness was for effect and how much was genuine. 'I no longer need him.'

'How nice for you.' The *taulath* emerged – seemed almost to condense – from the shadows where he stood, dressed in a grey so dark that it was almost black and yet not so dark as to lend his shape a definite outline. Only his eyes were visible; his head was covered by a hood, his hands by gloves and his feet by soft boots that made them noiseless as the paws of a cat.

The Shadowthief held no weapon, and there were none sheathed or holstered anywhere in plain sight – but Rynert knew that this didn't mean the assassin was unarmed. Far from it. . . . The sinister presence was making his heart pound in his ears again, and though it shamed him there was sweat on his brow; he didn't betray its presence by wiping it off, and hoped that with the light at his back the telltale beads would be invisible.

'You came here at my bidding,' the King snapped. 'So be about your business.'

'I came here at my choice,' the *taulath* corrected, 'and it is your business too, King of Alba.' His tone was gently reproving, a deliberate reminder of what Rynert had chosen to forget. 'So tell me, what *is* your business this time? Theft? Espionage? Another killing . . . ?'

There was a silence as the King stared at the mercenary assassin, angry – and yet in the circumstances unable to be properly outraged – that an honourless person would presume to guess his employer's intentions. Rynert let it go no further than a glare, for if this *taulath* was the same one as he had dealt with before, any observation concerning honour or the lack of it would be returned with interest, and the discussion would degenerate into a nasty scene. As for the *taulath* himself, his eyes blinked mildly and his whole body posture radiated unconcern over what Rynert did or did not say and do.

'Yes.' The King took his hand from his sword and sat down again, arrogantly, with his back to the hooded man. 'Yes, indeed. Another killing. And no mistakes.'

'Rynert, Rynert. . . .' The *taulath* padded around so that they were once again face to face, sat down on the corner of the table and nonchalantly swung one leg to and fro, seeming to admire the fit of boot and smoke-dark leggings. His voice and phase of language were both excessively familiar. 'Now really: were there any mistakes last time? Or the time before that?'

Another silence and a glare were Rynert's only replies.

'There. You see. So – who will it be?'

Rynert told him and gave – sketchily – the same reasons he had elaborated to the Council. The *taulath* whistled thinly, whether in feigned or genuine surprise, and didn't speak for several seconds.

'A friend, once,' he said eventually.

'How so?' Rynert's question came back with an unmistakable snap to it.

'Simple.' Behind the mask there had to be a chilly smile. 'You're trying so hard to convince yourself that you're doing the right thing. Too hard.'

'When I want your opinions . . .' Rynert began in a soft, dangerous voice, half out of his chair with one hand back on his sword-hilt. The sentence died there, for the *taulath* hadn't moved a muscle, was still sitting there, watching with a calm deliberation that was somehow more ominous than any matching move towards a weapon. As if he didn't care because he didn't need to care; as if he felt certain that he, alone and empty-handed, could take Rynert to pieces any time he chose.

'I offered none. Reasons concern neither me nor mine, except through idle curiosity. Very idle. What does concern me is the fee.'

'As agreed.'

'Listen to the man. That was agreed before I knew who – and how much – you need . . . ah . . . want him dead.'

'What do you mean . . . ?'

'All your understated and yet so passionate concern for the honour of Alba, put in jeopardy by this one man; your fears for the political repercussions of his actions; and your outrage over his use of sorcery and the death of your Captain-of-Guards. Magnificent, Rynert – and meaningless. You forget, I think, our last discussion . . . and the last mission performed for you.'

'That has nothing to do with what brings you here,' snarled Rynert, slamming his fist against one arm of the chair.

Once again the *taulath*'s voice seemed to smile, although the eyes glittering through the slits in his mask were as cold and humourless as flint. 'Let me refresh your failing memory. There was the matter of stealing certain things from the wizard, Talvalin's foster-father – things like that portrait. A simple enough matter, and reasonably inoffensive even if not quite the way to treat a guest in your house. But to give all that information to the Drusalan Secret Police . . .'

'What of it?'

The *taulath* shrugged. 'Tell the truth, Rynert, if only to yourself. After what you did, no matter what high-sounding reasons you produce, once he learns of all this Aldric Talvalin will be . . . annoyed. And you're afraid that you know what form that annoyance might take. So

28

you want him killed, before he considers doing it to you. And what's one over-mighty nobleman more or less?'

'And when do mercenaries take it upon themselves to advise a king?' asked Rynert, his voice dangerously devoid of tone.

'Consider it a part of the service. Now, about the fee. Twenty thousand marks, in the usual division: half now and half on proof of completion.'

'You're joking!' Even as he uttered the protest, Rynert knew well enough that the *taulath* meant what he had said. Just as Rynert knew that he would pay it. It angered him that a mere hired killer should have given so precise a summation of the truth, and caused him to wonder if any of the councillors had made a similar judgement. If they had. . . . He crushed that line of thought into the back of his mind. Alban Crown Councillors were advisers to the King; but they were also noblemen in their own right and anything which impugned their dignity or honour was likely to be something they would regard as a personal insult. Deliberately or otherwise, Rynert had already offered enough veiled insults tonight for one more to be too many. His chest hurt, a grinding insistent ache that seemed always with him now, no matter what his personal physicians did.

The *taulath* was gazing equably at him when his thoughts came back to the here-and-now. As equably as the blank-masked face permitted, anyway, and with an air of smug satisfaction that neither the mask nor the featureless dark clothing could conceal. 'And don't tell me that you've come here without the money, my Lord King; you've never done so before.' He slid soundlessly from the table, all business now. 'Talvalin. Where can I find him?'

'I . . . don't know.'

The *taulath* stared at him, not believing his ears. 'If I had known what you were going to say, Lord King, the price would have been far higher still.' Then, gathering himself together somewhat: 'But you must have some intimation of his last whereabouts, surely?'

'The Drusalan Empire . . . probably,' Rynert smiled faintly, 'as far from the city of Egisburg as he can get.'

'He was involved in *that*?'

'He was directly responsible for it.'

'Then small wonder you want him out of the way. If he'll do that to his enemies, who knows what he might do to an ex-friend . . .'

'I told you before—'

'—And I decided not to listen. Oh, I and my people can find him for you, King Rynert – and kill him for you, too – all for the price I asked before I found out how much work was involved. But I'll expect some small favours afterwards. Nothing costly; just immunities and pardons. As many as needed, and as often as needed.'

'Feel free to leave now.'

'Haven't you forgotten something?'

Rynert looked at the dark silhouette, thinking how utterly inhuman it looked, and reached inside his tunic. The *taulath* tensed, relaxing only when Rynert's hand came out holding nothing more aggressive than a roll of treasury scrip. He looked at the sheets of paper as if they were poisonous, then peeled off ten and flipped them disdainfully towards the assassin, with exactly the same gesture as a man might make when flicking something foul off his fingertips.

'These are good?' the *taulath* said, looking at where the scrip-sheets lay at his feet and as yet making no move to pick them up. 'You know I prefer coin.'

'And I prefer what I prefer. Take them or leave them.'

The assassin took them; but lifted each sheet from the floor with such elegance that whatever loss of dignity Rynert had intended was quite absent. 'They had best be good, Lord King; I'm not beyond going to work on my own account.'

'Get out,' said Rynert. The *taulath* watched him for a moment, not moving, then began slowly backing towards whichever window or unguarded door he had used to get in. When the man paused, evidently on the point of yet another dry little observation, Rynert's patience snapped. 'Get away from me!' he screamed, springing from his chair and drawing his sword with a rage-born speed and energy he hadn't known that he still possessed.

And on the instant of his scream, the doors burst open and Rynert's guards came running in. Hard on their heels were the noblemen of the Alban Crown Council, all now armed with their newly-recovered swords. Still crouched in a fighting posture that was made foolish by his wide eyes and shock-gaping mouth, Rynert stared at them only to find that none of them were staring back at him but rather at the place behind him where he had last seen the *taulath*. There was a soft laugh from the mercenary, still in plain view for just that instant too many, then silence as he took his leave as quickly and quietly as he had arrived.

'Rynert.' Hanar Santon spoke it: just the name and nothing else. He was looking now at the roll of treasury scrip still resting on the arm of Rynert's chair, and had plainly drawn his own conclusions from all that he had seen.

The King coloured and his hands clenched into fists. 'I have a title, my lord,' he said.

'No, not now.' Santon shook his head; it was less a negatory gesture than that of a man trying to clear his mind of confusion. 'My father took his own life because he felt that he had failed you, yet you repay his memory with this. You have no title, Rynert; you've forfeited that. And duty, and respect, and honour. I defy you, man. I offer you defiance and I challenge you to change my views.'

In the dreadful stillness they could all hear how harsh and rapid Rynert's breathing had become. The quick flush of rage had drained out of his face and left it white as bone. 'What about the rest of you?' he asked at last.

Heads turned imperceptibly towards the man whose

31

seniority of age, rank and respect made him their chosen spokesman. Lord Dacurre looked at them all, then walked to the King's Chair and leafed through the roll of scrip-sheets. They fell through his fingers to the floor like leaves in autumn. 'Lord Santon speaks for us all,' the old man said. 'You must give an explanation, or—' Dacurre drew the sheathed *tsepan* from his belt and looked at it for a moment before setting it down on the chair's cushion, '—do as Endwar Santon did. The choice is yours, Rynert *an-Kerochan.*'

Rynert the Crooked. No one had called him that in twenty years, and right now it was a name which referred to more than just his twisted body. The King began to tremble; his heart was kicking inside the cage of his ribs like something frantic to be free. Black and crimson spots dancing across his vision all but hid his treacherous, self-seeking councillors from sight, and a stabbing pain was running like hot lead down his left arm. Rynert swayed, then caught his balance with an effort.

'I choose death,' he said, steadily and with all the dignity that he could summon. He took a single step forward and the hall reeled about him as agony exploded in his chest. Rynert's sword clattered on the tiles as he dropped it to clutch at the left wrist of an arm that felt on fire. Sweat filmed his pallid skin as he clenched his teeth to hold back a cry that was more shock and outrage than pain. His physicians had first warned him of this long ago, and many times since then; a warning he had ignored, like so much else over the years. A warning he had no more cause to heed . . . not now.

The pain faded, not vanishing but gathering for a fresh assault, and all of Rynert's world narrowed to a single point of focus: Lord Santon's face. It wasn't smiling, or gloating, or satisfied; that he could have accepted and understood. Instead its expression was one of pity and regret, that the illusion of what Hanar Santon had thought his King had been, the lord to whom he had given his duty and respect, should prove to be frail flesh prone to failings after all.

Rynert did not want pity and suddenly hated Santon for daring to consider it. Releasing his throbbing arm, the King bent low and grabbed for his fallen sword, gripped its hilt and cut savagely at the young lord's face. Cut at the expression of pity, to cleave it off.

Santon reacted to the attack as he would to any such, instantly and without conscious thought. He drew his own *taiken* from its scabbard and straight into a simple parry that deflected Rynert's blow – and continued through to a cut of his own. . . .

Rynert's sword-point lowered, relaxing; then his fingers slackened their grip and the blade fell chiming to the floor again as both hands pressed against his belly and the long straight slash now crossing it from one hip to the other. Everything was suddenly so still that it seemed the very night noises had paused to listen. 'That was stupid,' he said after a moment, although no one could be sure if he meant his own or Santon's thoughtless actions. Blood ran through his fingers and made a glistening puddle on the floor.

Rynert stared at it and then sat down, heavily and uncoordinated, on the steps of his throne, looking at each of his councillors in turn through eyes that were already glazing. 'Who will stop the *taulath* now, my lords?' Rynert said, and smiled a horrid smile that let blood dribble from his mouth to make a dark red beard across his chin. 'If anybody even wants to. There are the Talvalin lands, after all; among the richest holdings in all Alba . . .' He laughed, a sound like a wet cough. 'Protest what you will to each other, gentlemen, but don't trouble me, I pray you. Unless I misread you all most gravely, I leave this land the gift of such war as it has not known for half a thousand years. Make me a liar . . . if you can.' Again he smiled and again blood leaked between his teeth. 'Now leave. I'm dying and I'd as soon do it in private.'

Nobody moved. They stood in silence, watching him.

Rynert watched them in his turn for a few moments with a faint look of amusement on his bloodied face. 'I did what I did because I was afraid to die,' he said finally. 'I'm not afraid any more. You can only fear what you have a chance to escape. My choice . . .' The mocking humour drained from his face as the last blood and the last remnant of life drained from his body, and King Rynert of Alba fell sideways and was dead.

There was a funereal stillness in the shadowy Hall as the lords of Alba's Crown Council stared furtively at one another and at the corpse huddled on the floor, and then there were footsteps as someone at the back of the group turned and walked swiftly away. None of the others looked to see who it was; that would have meant admitting too much, both to themselves and to their erstwhile colleagues: that each man among them also wanted to leave and be about his own suddenly urgent affairs, and that each among them wished that he had been first out of this room with its abattoir smell and its cloud of unspoken accusations.

One by one they left, treading softly for respect or caution, or with the slapping footfalls of those who didn't care what the others thought. At last there was only young Lord Santon and old Lord Dacurre, standing on either side of the blood and the body, one with a sword in his hand and the other with something close to regret on his face.

Dacurre looked at the blade with its smeared stain and shook his head. 'He was dying before you hit him,' the old man said.

'What do you mean? How do you know?' Santon blurted out the questions, not wanting some sort of worthless comfort just because Dacurre had been his father's friend.

'Rynert was never a strong man. Some illness in his childhood . . . His heart tore in his chest, from rage, or fear, or shock, or a score of other things. I knew it when I saw it in his face. I've seen it happen before; it might well happen to me, now that I'm old. But that,' he indicated Santon's *taiken*, 'didn't kill him. It just made matters quicker.'

'And harder to prove.'

'To the others, maybe. Not to me.' Dacurre looked up and down the Hall, found it empty even of guards and muttered something savage under his breath. 'Gone to grab what they can. Bastards!' Then he cleared his throat in irritation at himself. 'I'm sorry, boy. Forget I said that. It's their prerogative, when the King dies . . . unexpectedly. Whoever follows might not care to employ them again, so they have to make the best of it . . . Tradition.'

Santon looked at him blankly, not really understanding.

'Clean your sword and sheathe it,' Dacurre told him, suddenly brisk. 'We've got things to do.'

'What?' Then understanding dawned. 'Oh. Him. Why?'

'Because . . . Because he was the King once, and because he's dead now, and because there's nobody else. Just us. No matter what he was or did, he's entitled to the decencies at least. So straighten his limbs and close his eyes, and find something to clean his face.'

The old man bent over the body of his King and tugged at the dead weight with both hands, then swore disgustedly as the corpse made a sound that was half-belch and half-groan; a smell that was a mingling of blood and wine pricked at the air and Hanar Santon jerked two steps backwards, whimpering and jamming his knuckles against his teeth. 'Come along, help me here!' Dacurre snapped, and then saw how the colour had leached from the younger man's face. 'Oh, he's dead all right. I just moved him wrongly – squashed out whatever air was left inside him . . . which I wouldn't have done if you'd given me some help. . . .'

Santon shivered, finding himself still unaccustomed to sudden death and the aftermath of slaughter. He had not witnessed his father's formal suicide, and the other two people whose deaths he had attended had taken their leave of life peacefully and in bed. 'Will there . . . will there be a war?' he asked, trying to concentrate on something – *anything* – else.

'Eh?' Dacurre rubbed his hands together in a useless attempt to get the blood off them. 'I don't know; I truly don't. And to be honest with you, my young Lord Santon, I don't much care. Though I suspect we'll find out. Lift him. Carefully now – I said *carefully*! You opened him up, don't finish it by spilling him all over the floor.'

Santon's mouth quirked with nausea at the prospect and he looked away from the gaping wound. Nobody had ever warned him that the culmination of his *taiken* training would result in this. A decorous smear of red, perhaps, but not . . . He shuddered. 'What – what about Aldric Talvalin then? And the *taulath*? I mean, with the King dead . . .'

'I don't know how to contact assassins or call them off. Or where to find Talvalin.'

'So what will happen?'

Dacurre shrugged as best he could and gestured with a jerk of his chin at the body they both carried. 'Something like this, I fancy. Except that I can't guess who it will be. Come on, boy, hurry it up. Dammit, these were my best formal robes once and it feels as if he's leaking again. . . .'

TWO

The angled shafts of sunlight were golden with suspended dust, but he couldn't see . . .

The warm air was heavy with the scent of mint and roses, but he couldn't breathe . . .

He was trying to break free, but something far, far stronger than himself was holding him down so that he couldn't move . . .

'Aldric . . . *Aldric* . . . !'

And there was waking, and sanity; awareness that he was no longer alone, no longer helpless. Awareness that . . .

'It was only a dream, dear heart. Only a dream.'

Aldric stared at the fluttering, new-lit candle flame and watched his own limbs as a shudder racked through him. The flame's reflection gleamed back at him from skin entirely sheathed in clammy sweat. The sweat that comes with fear. 'A dream . . . ?' he echoed, ashamed of the tremor in his voice, and took three slow, deep breaths to calm himself, making them last so that he wouldn't have to think of anything else for a while.

'I didn't think it was the kind of dream you'd want to continue. By the look of you I was right.' There was concern in Kyrin's voice and in her eyes. Concern for more than just her lover scared awake in the night by a bad dream; because both of them knew that Aldric's dreams had an ugly habit of coming true. She had lived through the last part of one nightmare already and had no wish to see another.

Aldric looked at her and recognised the source of her worries. He dragged an uneven smile from somewhere and plastered it across a mouth which didn't want to wear it just now. 'You were right. Oh, how very right . . .'

Kyrin was watching him, waiting for whatever he was going to tell her – if he was going to tell her anything at all. There was a cup of watered wine in her hand, and Aldric reached out for it with a hand far steadier than it had any right to be.

'I must have been tangled in the bedclothes,' he said and took a long drink, staring over the rim of the cup at the sheets twisted like ropes around his legs. 'They were holding me down . . .'

This most private nightmare Kyrin knew already. She alone. He had told her of it a long time ago because he had known, somehow, that she would listen and more, that she would understand. Only someone he loved and who loved him in their turn *could* understand.

When he had been *aypan-kailin*, a teenaged warrior cadet, sex to Aldric and the others of his age was an occasional experiment between the very closest friends, another facet of a complex adolescence in the near-monastic environment of training barracks. Like the other small and private pleasures of which the training and the tutors had no part, it was one with sharing secrets, sharing a purloined bottle and sharing the same miseries as the rough wine wreaked its revenge . . . Until one hot afternoon in the deserted tack-room of Dunrath's old stables when all of that had changed. That was when Aldric, aged sixteen and cleaning harness during a solitary punishment detention, learned the meaning and the pain of rape from the prefect who was supposedly supervising him.

From that time forward there had been no real friends, only 'acquaintances' distanced by distrust. There had never been anything approaching love for other than family, who saw nothing more than a quiet, introspective younger son growing even more withdrawn and silent, and sometimes there had been no love even for himself. Not long after the rape he had gone out quietly into a cloudless night and made an oath to the watching stars – and to the One who watched beyond them – that he would never hurt anyone as he had been hurt.

And four years afterwards, it no longer mattered anyway. That was when Duergar Vathach's murderous plotting on behalf of the Drusalan Empire had turned his whole world upside down, and his family were gone, and he was first a landless wanderer and then a wizard's fosterling, and the vengeful nature he had fought so hard to keep in check became instead something to encourage. Not merely a spasm of ferocity that was an attempt to make himself feel clean and regain a little of his self-respect, but something to be nurtured as an honourable obligation in a killing matter. They were all of them, all killing matters nowadays . . .

'What have you to say for yourself, *Hautheisart* Voord?'

Etzel, Grand Warlord of the Drusalan Empire, erstwhile paramount commander of half her armies and – until Emperor Ioen had shown himself capable of independent thought – power behind the throne, spoke softly, but his eyes and his face betrayed the anger that his words did not.

'*Woydach*, I did all that you asked of me. I did my best.'

'In the past, *hautheisart*, your best has been a deal better than it was this time. Indulge me. Explain in your own words exactly what went wrong.'

'The long version, *Woydach*, or the short?'

'Try the short. Save the long for later . . . when I decide if you have a later.'

Voord's head jerked up sharply at that, and he stared first at Etzel and then at the two armoured guardsmen who flanked the Grand Warlord's chair. It was a high-backed, wide-armed seat, that chair, not a throne for the only reason that no one had yet applied the word to it, and it was set on a raised dais of four steps so that Etzel could look down on whoever was standing in the main body of his audience chamber – or sitting round-shouldered on an uncushioned, uncomfortable wooden stool with his hands clasped between his knees as Voord was doing. There was enough room behind and to either side of the chair for maybe ten guards; that there were only two now was more an expression of Etzel's contempt for the man on the stool than for any more practical reason, even though the pair who remained were among the dozen or so in the Bodyguard who had been invariably seen in Etzel's presence for the past three years. They were his sword and his shield, one to protect him and the other to ensure that those he commanded to die did so without delay.

Voord looked at one and then at the other, at the armour they wore and the weapons they carried, but could see nothing of the faces shadowed by the nasal, peak and cheek-guards of their black and silver helmets. Neither moved to return his scrutiny or even to acknowledge his existence, but stood instead like carven images of war. And the death war brings.

'You read my written report, *Woydach*. It was Aldric Talvalin – the one who was the hinge of this stratagem. He was the cause of my . . . my lack of success. His actions were not those anticipated, and consequently the possibility of his behaviour was not included in our planning. He—'

'He acted in a fashion you at least might have expected, Voord,' Etzel interrupted. 'Had you thought about it, which from all the evidence gathered here,' he laid the flat of his hand on a thick dossier resting across his knees, 'you did not. Careless. Foolish. And potentially ruinous. I dislike having ostensibly secret plans made public, especially when that public includes my enem—, ah . . . political opponents.'

'It won't happen again.' Voord's voice was still calm and he spoke as though stating an incontrovertible fact rather than the clichéd feeble excuse he himself had heard – and ignored – on so many occasions. 'You know me too well.' He stared again at the shadowed faces of the guards. 'All of you . . .'

'I know you very well indeed,' said Etzel, 'just as you know me. And you are no longer of much use, Lord-Commander Voord, having lost your place of rank in the Emperor's Secret Police.' No threat, not even the delicate threading of menace through the words – just a pronouncement, like that of laws, or policies, or sentences of death. 'Deputy to Bruda himself, sir! Do you know how many years, how much gold, how many lesser spies were sacrificed to make you secure in such a position, to make you trusted, to make you privy to the secrets that might be of use to me? I doubt it!'

'Ah, but I did.' His pride dented now, Voord straightened his back, planted fists on hips and glared, no longer looking so much like a schoolboy being chastised. 'And I worked long hard hours on my own studies, to make all the efforts of others that much more worthwhile.' *Platitudes*, said his mind. *Why bother?*

'Yes. Your studies . . . I know about them. Less than I might do, but more than I want.'

'You yourself gave me permission—'

'And you overstepped the bounds of that permission. You overstepped so very many things, Voord, that I am at a loss where to begin.'

'Try,' said Voord.

The *Woydach* looked at him strangely, for his tone was not that of a man with any great concern in his mind. 'As you wish. Show him.' Etzel made a peremptory gesture with one finger.

His left-hand-side guard stepped down from the dais and crossed to the three canvas-sheeted bundles lying by the wall, bundles which Voord had been carefully refusing to notice since he had first been summoned into the audience chamber a full half-hour past. He was noticing now; indeed, he was staring most intently both at the soldier and at what he had been sent to uncover.

'Proceed,' said Etzel. The guard stripped back the first sheet with a flourish and stepped to one side, folding it neatly as he went.

'Books?' said Voord, pushing an edge of scorn into his voice. 'You're taking me to task over books? I had thought I deserved better treatment than that!'

'And I had thought, *Hautheisart* Voord, that you were possessed of more intelligence than to meddle with such books as these! Shall I list them?'

'No need; I know their names well enough myself.' He did indeed: there was a small fortune's worth of rare volumes strewn every which way across the floor, and their subject matter broke enough of the Empire's stringent sorcery laws to gain him a death sentence twenty times over. Except, of course, that he had been granted official licence to study the Art Magic without penalty, let or hindrance. Until now, apparently.

'You know the statutes concerning magic as well as any, Voord,' said Etzel softly.

'I was given immunity from the law.'

'Show me.'

Voord began to say something, then decided not to waste his breath and showed his teeth instead. There was nothing else to show. All of the agreements and arrangements had been made verbally, and he cursed himself for a fool that he hadn't seen where such an oversight could lead. 'I haven't any written papers,' he said finally, 'as you well know. Congratulations on a well-laid plan, *Woydach*. What now?'

'You're a dangerous liability, Voord. You always were, but until now you always had a degree of usefulness to offset it.'

'Not any more, eh?' said Voord, angry and at the same time far too cheerful for a man in his position. 'So you're going to dispose of me and pretend I never even existed. All because of a few books. I'd have expected more from you, Etzel; I really would.'

'If you want more, *hautheisart*, I can show you more. A great deal more.' The soldier who had uncovered the books turned his head, anticipating the command that was no more than a gesture of a crooked finger, and uncovered the other two bundles on the floor.

The things within the bundles were still recognisable as human, but after what had been done to them, only in the same way that a roasted fowl can be recognised as a bird – and for exactly the same reason. It explained the faint savoury smell which had been prickling at Voord's nostrils since he entered the audience chamber. But it did not appall him as it did the Warlord Etzel. For all that he had not expected to see them here, Voord knew who as well as what he was looking at; they had been beggars, grubby street urchins whom nobody would miss, taken and prepared as sacrifices – or would have been, had Etzel not gone prying into matters that were not his concern.

Voord smiled thinly at the Warlord. 'Dinner?' he said. 'Surely not without a table?'

Etzel looked at him as he might have stared at some vermin which had pushed out of the dirt beneath his feet. 'You are a foul creature, Voord,' he said, 'and my only lack of understanding is in why I failed to see it years ago.'

'Perhaps because it was more useful to be blind. And I defy you to deny that I was useful. I did as you bade me do, my lord, by whatever means were in my power to offer to your service; it is no fault of mine that you do not have Alba in your grasp, or Vreijaur, or Marevna the sister of the Emperor. I did as I was able to do, and was crippled for my pains!' He held up the wretched twisted talon which was all that remained of his left hand, flexing what little movement it still had so that the dry skin and the crippled sinews made an audible, anguished creak.

Etzel's shudder was plainly visible. He refused to look at the two cooked corpses that he himself had commanded brought here, and seemed reluctant even to look full at Voord. 'Just tell me one thing,' he said. 'Why this?'

'It was necessary. Required. It was,' Voord waved at the heap of books, 'written . . . there. I obeyed the writing.'

'You're good at obeying orders, aren't you?' said Etzel.

'It was part of my training.'

'I see. Then I order you to die. You're a dirty creature, *Hautheisart* Voord, and the Empire which I plan to build will be a better place without you.'

Voord looked from one guard to the other, unperturbed. 'Another bloody empire-builder,' he said quietly, as if to himself. 'Soon this Empire will be so full of them that there'll be no room for ordinary people.'

Etzel ignored him. 'My guards will help you on your way. Goodbye, *hautheisart*. Give my regards to whatever foulness pays you heed.'

'Do it yourself, *Woydach*.'

'Even in the face of death you keep your insolence. Voord, in another, better life you would have been a fine soldier. You two.' The blank, armoured faces of Etzel's guards swivelled fractionally, like automata, to regard the man who gave their orders. 'Kill him. Here and now.'

'Killing matters?' said Kyrin. 'You never really need to find a reason. Not from what I've seen.'

She was sitting at the foot of the bed, pouring wine by candlelight, and Aldric smiled faintly at the domesticity of it all. If he never truly had a reason before, he most certainly had one now, more even than the requirements of honour. A worthwhile reason. The defence of his lady, as the old songs said – the lady he wanted as his wife.

And then she turned and looked straight at him, and her hand came up in a warding gesture. 'Don't say it, Aldric. Don't even try. We had this discussion before, remember?'

'Yes, I remember. That first night, in Erdhaven. But we didn't finish it – at least, not to my satisfaction. And everything that happened between then and now. You left me – but then you came back. That tells me enough. We should finish with all this nonsense, all this running about doing the King's bidding, for God knows he owes me

44

peace and more after what I've done for him this past few months!'

'When we go to Drakkesborg—' Kyrin began to say. Aldric looked at her, then raised one eyebrow.

'What gave you the idea that anyone was going anywhere?'

'You did. It's not the King's bidding any more, is it?'

'Gemmel-*altrou* is my father, and I have duties and obligations to discharge. Stealing back the Warlord's Jewel for him is—'

'He set a spell of compulsion in your brain, man! To *make* you do it.'

'And he took it back. This is my decision, nobody else's. Kyrin, I owe him my life!'

'So you're going to Drakkesborg to look for some blasted jewel that *might* help the old man to go home – wherever home for that one is – even if it might get you killed.'

'Yes. But might, not will. The Warlord Etzel doesn't know me, and—'

'I'm coming with you, if it's as safe as all that. We took our last leave from one another like . . . like a claw from flesh. We won't be parted again.'

Aldric, sitting cross-legged, bowed slightly. 'Lady,' he said very, very softly, 'I love you. When you went away, I missed you so very much.' He looked at the candle's spike of flame as though he was watching something through a window, then back at Kyrin. 'You make me whole, *Tehal'eiyya* Kyrin, my lady, my loved. But understand this. What I'm doing *is* dangerous; it scares me. I would as soon not be afraid for you as well.'

Kyrin watched him silently, neither talking nor needing to talk; just looking – at his face, at his eyes, and at what she had seen in them during the quiet times when they lay in one another's arms and looked at each other, as lovers were allowed to do. She had seen then what she was seeing now: the complexities of much troubled thought; an innocence that had never truly left him, despite all that had befallen, despite the mask of weary cynicism that he hid behind; the echo of a loneliness that was all but gone; and the joy when he looked straight at her with that expression in his eyes. Kyrin met that intensity once again, a glowing warmth like the gaze of Ymareth the Dragon, and wondered as she did so – just a little – how darkness could be so bright.

'No. My lady, I want. . . . To turn, and see you. To listen, and hear you. To reach out, and feel your hand in mine. I need you – as I need sunshine, or fire in winter. As I need food, and air. And honour. . . . But wants and needs have to be set aside sometimes and this is one of those times.'

Kyrin's slender fingers closed around Aldric's outstretched hand, squeezing hard. 'I need you as much as you need me. My good lord and my own beloved, however could I not? When you go through the gates of Drakkesborg to . . .' – she hesitated a little, then made a sound that might have been an unborn laugh – 'to be so damned honourable again . . . I'll be with you. You go – and we both go.'

Aldric just stared at her, then raised her hand to brush against his lips. 'I could almost pity the Drusalan Empire.'

Kyrin's fingertips traced the scar running along his cheekbone. 'Be more specific: pity the Grand Warlord. I suspect that he'll need all the pity he can get.'

The left-hand soldier drew his shortsword and took a pace forward, and the right-hand soldier followed suit – then leaned across the still seated Grand Warlord to stab a handspan of steel into his erstwhile companion's neck, so that the man collapsed with a clatter of armour and a spurting of blood to die on the steps at Etzel's feet.

Voord smiled, a minute quirk of his thin mouth which betrayed as much relief as anything else. He looked weary and a little sick, as any man might who had faced the imminence of his own death so early in the morning and seen it set aside. 'Command them again, *Woydach*,' he suggested. 'Maybe they didn't hear you the first time?'

The Grand Warlord said nothing, but as a horrid suspicion formed in his mind so tiny beads of icy sweat formed on his upper lip. 'How long?' he asked, surprised by the calmness of his own voice.

'Hault, it's been four years in the Bodyguard for you, yes?'

'Nearer five in the regiment, lord,' said the soldier. 'And three of those in the Warlord's personal guard.'

'I have always believed in advance planning, *Woydach*,' said Voord quietly, 'especially when I could never be sure that you might find my past usefulness an embarrassment and myself someone to be rid of in haste and without ceremony. Thus . . . Directly I gained a little power and influence, I prepared this . . . ah . . . insurance against unforeseen events.' He nudged the dead guard's fallen shortsword with the toe of his boot. 'It seems to me that neither my time nor my money was wasted.'

'So you knew all this time that you were safe?' Etzel's mouth curled into a sneer. 'It explains your bravado rather better than the unlikely possibility of some real courage.'

'Not that you'd believe me, or that I worry whether you do or not, but no – until Hault made his move I couldn't be certain that I was not alone. Not that I need be concerned one way or another . . . not any more. Hault, come here.'

The soldier took the few steps necessary to reach his true commander's side and saluted Guards-fashion with a snap of the still-bloody shortsword across his chest that sent a nasty little spattering across the floor. 'Sir?'

'Show him. Now.'

'Sir!' Hault saluted again, then brought the sword down from the salute and straight out into a thrust. It went into Voord's flank in the soft place just under his ribcage, met nothing more resistant than internal organs and came out the other side as a repellent peak in the *hautheisart*'s tunic that tore just enough to let its point glitter briefly in the

47

lamplight. Voord gasped and went more pallid even than his normal complexion; he gasped again as it was withdrawn, but not loudly enough to drown the sucking sound as entrails reluctantly released their grasp on steel.

There was no blood, and only two small rips in a previously undamaged military tunic betrayed that anything untoward had happened. 'Uncomfortable to feel,' said Voord, panting slightly, 'and unsettling to watch, but having a tooth pulled is more painful.'

'Father of Fires . . .' Etzel choked out the oath, then covered his mouth and gagged.

'That One has nothing to do with it!' snapped Voord, suddenly and unreasonably savage. 'Or with me!' And then, more controlled and so softly that he might have been speaking to himself: 'The Old Ones give me more than stories to believe, and my sacrifices in Their name reward me with more than the stink of burnt beef or the babbled second-hand benedictions of some disinterested priest . . .'

Woydach Etzel looked up at the windows of his private chamber and beyond them to the low, cool sun of winter noon. He knew that he was soon to die, and though the certainty of that knowledge took away his fear of death as he had seen it leave so many at the foot of the scaffold steps, what remained and was enhanced by his familiarity with Voord was a terror of the manner of his dying. And because of that, because nothing he might say now could make his situation worse or better, there were the questions that he wanted to ask no matter how useless their answers might now be. About belief in tales to frighten children, and Voord's strange, twisted fervour; about the why and the how of such sorceries as even the darkest of old stories only hinted at.

As Voord crossed to the books that were strewn across the floor and squatted down as though to begin putting them to rights, Etzel drew breath to ask the first of all his questions, but it caught in his throat when Voord turned to face him. He was holding one of the books, cradling

48

its opened weight like a child in his arms while his mouth silently shaped words from its handwritten pages, and his speculative gaze at Etzel was that of a butcher sizing up a joint of meat. 'Hault,' he said without looking at the guard, 'go outside. Let nobody in. Don't come back until I call you. Understood?'

'Understood, sir.' There was something terrible about hearing Hault's relief at being sent away, and about the haste with which he left the room.

Etzel wanted to look after the soldier, to take this one last chance of escape as Hault went through the door and out into the world where none of this had happened and where he, Etzel, was still a man of power and influence, but he was unable to tear his eyes away from Voord's corpse-pale face. The *hautheisart* was muttering something in the hasty monotone of a priest hurrying through the familiar part of a boring litany, but Etzel could still make sense from the slipshod tumble of syllables and that sense turned his belly sick within him.

'. . . call upon thee O my lord O my true lord O my most beloved lord O Granter of Secrets I pray thee and beseech thee hearken now unto thy true and faithful servant . . .'

The book was balanced on Voord's right forearm now, leaving his left hand free to creak drily as he spread the remnants of its fingers, obscenely aping a priestly sign of benediction. '. . . O Dweller in the Pit Jewelled Serpent Flower of Darkness I give now unto thee this offering this blood-offering this life-offering O Lord Devourer . . .'

Voord's voice stumbled on the words of the invocation and began a gasp he couldn't finish. Some Power beyond that of its withered sinews was straightening his hand, twisting it from the curled and broken claw it had become five months before into a poised fork of bone and leather, twisting it with such violence that it took away his breath and even his ability to scream.

It was Etzel who closed his eyes and screamed, but only very briefly and in a small, lost voice before the thing that

49

had been Voord's hand reached out and pulled his face off.

Woydach Etzel, erstwhile Grand Warlord of the Drusalan Empire and would-be maker of emperors, was grateful for the shock that stopped his heart an instant later and permitted him to die. . . .

When Voord's nausea had faded, all that remained was the tremble of realisation that his offered sacrifice had proven so acceptable that the Old Ones had used his hand to take it for themselves. Their gifted power of deathlessness was freshly renewed in his body, the corpse of an enemy lay at his feet and the insignia of still more power glittered about that corpse's neck.

En sh'Va t'Chaal was its formal name in the inventories of State Regalia; *t'Chaal*, the Jewel, so much a symbol of the Grand Warlord that it had been incorporated into the sigil and cresting of the rank. Voord stooped to fumble with the catch of Etzel's collar of office, undid the snap at last and lifted the Jewel from the puddle of blood and slime where it had lain . . .

Then swore at the sudden freezing chill of the thing, stabbing through his leather glove, and all but dropped it again. Glove or no glove, had the Jewel not be crusted almost an inch thick in frozen gore it would have taken the flesh off his hand. Voord's studies had taught him about many objects which radiated such appalling cold, but none of them were things that any Imperial-race Drusalan of the Central Provinces would wear openly around his neck. Cautiously he lifted it higher, and even the slight warmth from his exhaled breath was so different in temperature from the Jewel and its bloody casing that the crust shattered and fell away in tiny splinters of crimson ice. Small wonder that it was mounted in so elaborate a framing of gold filigree and fine velvet, for no man born of woman could wear such a thing against his skin. Looking at it more closely, and glad in his heart of hearts to have something to distract him from the sights and the smells that went with violent death, Voord wondered from what mine the gem had come and how in the name of the Dark it had *been* mined.

It was rectangular, and small enough to rest comfortably in the palm of his hand had he been fool enough to place it there; colourless in itself, but cored with green and a delicate cobwebbing of gold that seemed to lead out to the minute gold studs which crowded three of its edges. Voord breathed on it again, watching as the warm exhalation in that warm room became first cold-weather mist and then a heavy downward roll of white smoke that tinkled faintly with the ice-crystals in it. Whether it was man-made or demon-made was of little consequence to Voord right now. All that mattered to him was that he was alive when he had expected to be dead, and that the confirmation of his ultimate promotion dangled from his fist.

Securing the collar around his neck was difficult with only one usable hand – the left had retracted back into the crippled talon to which he had grown accustomed – but he managed the task at last. It was heavy, and for all the filigree and velvet he could feel the coldness of the Jewel seeping through into his flesh. Nor was the Grand Warlord's seat as comfortable as he thought it might have been, when he sat down in it and tried to relax his nerves from the jangling tensions of the past few minutes.

And now *he* was Grand Warlord. He had aspired to the position for years, from the time when his first promotion had proved how one man might rise more quickly than others equally capable if he was that much more ruthless – and had the proper support. There would be no questioning of his right, not once the soldiers of the *Tlakh-Woydan* regiment had been thoroughly sweetened with gold. Apart from the occasions when they had themselves seen fit to take a hand, the Bodyguard had shown small interest in who – or what – carried the title of Grand Warlord. Just so long as they were accorded the respect, the privileges and the high pay they regarded as their due, the regiment had as little interest in the political

51

machinations of those who struggled for places at the top of the heap as they would have in the squirmings of a bucketful of crabs.

The air in the chamber stank of blood and sweat and he looked at the mess of death – shivered slightly, wondering: *Was it worth all this?*

The unaccustomed self-doubt startled him. Of course it was. A little killing, something to which he was more than accustomed, and let him become the most powerful man in the Empire, stronger than Lord General Goth and his whelp of an Emperor, backed by elite military forces and by powers that no other man would dare to call upon or challenge.

The question now was, what to do with all this new-found power . . . ?

Voord looked around the room again and knew quite well what he was going to do with it, at least for the next few minutes. 'Hault,' he called, 'get in here.'

The soldier came in at once, so quickly that Voord might have suspected him of listening outside the door – except that Hault was beyond all such suspicion since the man would have listened as a matter of course, just as Voord would have done, and had done in similar circumstances. Information gleaned from the wrangling of senior officers could prove useful in all sorts of ways to an ambitious subordinate, and if there was one characteristic shared by the men of the Secret Police on either side of the Empire's political divide, it was ambition. Whoever they claimed to serve, the foremost was always themselves.

Hault would have been well aware that he had been sent away so that he could with perfect truth deny that he had witnessed murder done. He would have been expecting to see Etzel's body on the floor when he was summoned back, for a trooper serving with Lord-Commander Voord – or who was acquainted with any man who had – knew of the *hautheisart*'s predeliction for dreadful violence as the final solution to almost any problem. But from the expression on his face as he rolled the corpse over – an expression fortunately shadowed for the most part by the peak and cheek-plates of his helmet – even he had not expected a response quite so drastic as *this*. 'At your command, sir,' the soldier said in a flat voice meant to conceal what he was really thinking.

The attempt failed; Voord knew the men who served him far too well for their collective peace of mind and now was no exception. 'Call some servants, have them get this garbage out of my throne room, summon Tagen and five men and take that bloody disapproving look off your face *right now*.'

Hault flinched. That 'my throne room' had not been lost on him. For diplomacy's sake he went through the full sequence of an Imperial parade salute and carefully changed his acknowledgement of the order from 'sir' to *Woydach*. It seemed to Voord that the man was even more grateful to be dismissed this time than before. The notion brought a smile of sorts to the new Grand Warlord's thin lips that would have made Hault hurry even faster to get out.

No matter what they said about me then, they'll sing a new song now. To a tune of my own choosing. Voord sat back in the uncomfortable chair, determining privately to have it replaced – or at least re-upholstered – and then closed his eyes and let his mind wander far away from the here and the now.

They were pleasant memories, perhaps the only truly innocent pleasure that he still possessed. Voord seldom indulged in reminiscence; it was a sign of softness, of weakness – and a waste of valuable time in so busy a life as he lived now. But just once in a while he deliberately let the defences slip, to try to remember how things used to be. The trying had slowly grown more difficult over the past year, almost as if those few pleasant recollections were being rubbed off the slate of his memory. Maybe the things that he had heard said behind his back when the speakers thought him out of earshot held more accurate observation than the veiled insults or crude jests they seemed. Perhaps he was going mad after all, losing his mind a piece at a time. It had never been like this before. . . . Before. Voord took care never to let that thought go any further.

He had been born not far from Drakkesborg, and on clear days the lowering citadel at the heart of the city had been visible on the horizon. His father Eban had served there, first as an ordinary soldier and then, with accumulated merits and good conduct awards, as a serjeant and an officer. One of the images that still remained, one of the very few that were as clear as the very first time, was that of *vosjh'* Eban sitting in the kitchen with his parade harness on the big table in front of him, encircled by the admiring audience of his family as he clipped the paired silver bars of *kortagor* rank in place for the first time. And that was as high as he had gone despite all the other merit marks that he gained in the rest of his career. A short career. Of the wife and four children who had watched him apply the shiny new insignia, not one could have dreamed that in ten more months their father would be dead of the lung fever contracted during urban patrol on a particularly cold, wet night. That he was buried with the partial military honours due an officer who died as a result of duty but not active service was small comfort. Nor was the meagre pension due the dependants of an officer dying in such circumstances of any real use to a widow with a growing family. Voord – third child, only son and already listed for entry in the Service – had two long years before he entered barracks to wonder what a bowl of porridge would be like if he had salt and honey and milk to stir into it, enough to taste and even some to spill. Or to eat it only when he wanted to and not because that was all his mother could afford. What was most frightening was the way his mouth forgot the flavours of other food, even that of the thick, rich oatmeal of cold winter nights, and could remember only the dismal taste

54

of the thin gruel. The hungry time had been Voord's first step towards acquiring high military rank, regardless of arm of service or specialisation, just so long as its duties did not include late-night patrols in dirty weather. And even now, nine years later, he still loathed the taste of porridge plain and unadorned . . .

The servants who mopped blood from the tiled floor at Voord's feet and carried out the slack-limbed corpses were no strangers to the task, since Warlord Etzel and at least two of his predecessors were accustomed to order executions in the perfunctory manner of men swatting flies, and have the killing done at once where they could see it. They went about their business of swabbing and lifting and dragging with lowered eyes, taking care not to see things they were not expressly directed to see, not even noticing that one of the bodies they took away was that of Etzel. Any servant in the Warlord's citadel who noticed such things out of turn was one who was soon dragged away himself.

Lost in his own thoughts, Voord didn't even see them; he noticed only that the floor became clean and the room cleared of all unpleasantness except for his precious books. He looked down at the fat grimoire resting now in his lap, and stroked it as another man might stroke a cat. It and the others would soon be restored to their locked cabinet, and the cabinet itself moved to the *Woydach*'s luxurious living apartments. *Soon* – his fingers caressed the sleek black leather of the grimoire's cover – *very soon* . . .

'My lord?' Hault spoke from the door, reluctant to come any closer to Voord than he had to. 'My lord, *Kortagor* Tagen is here.'

Voord favoured him with a sleepy, heavy-lidded look; his lazy touching of the black book did not falter by so much as a single stroke, and he seemed to gain some sort of comfort from the contact. 'Then send him in, idiot!'

he said. 'You should know not to keep my close friends waiting. And Hault . . . ?'

'My lord?'

'What else is on your mind?'

The soldier said nothing, but the corner of his mouth quirked in a way that might have suggested either amused surprise or startled apprehension. Had he been standing closer Voord could have been sure, but the muscle spasm had at least confirmed as correct what he had heard in Hault's voice. Certainly it did his own reputation no harm at all . . .

'Yes. Something else. I can read you as easily as this book, friend Hault.' His eyes opened a little wider and fixed Hault with an interested stare. 'Probably more so. What goes on that I should know about?'

'You have a visitor, *Woydach*. Or rather, there's a man asking for *Eldheisart* Voord. I don't think anyone's corrected him so far, not until you give the word.' Hault's bearded lips stretched into a kind of smile, a baring of teeth rather than anything much more humorous. 'Though most of those who might tell are already wrong themselves. The news hasn't travelled yet.'

'So. Then once I'm done with Tagen, send him in alone.'

'He's alone already, lord.'

'Ah. What kind of a man is he, then, this visitor looking for me at the rank I held six months ago? Old? Young? Rich? Poor . . . ? Describe him.'

'Elderly, my lord – at least fifty years; comfortable, by his clothes. Comfortable, but not wealthy. He looks,' said Hault disdainfully, 'like a successful merchant.'

'I grow intrigued. Go on, go on, let in *Kortagor* Tagen to see me and then bring in your comfortable merchant – but be sure to search him first. Just in case of accidents, eh?'

Hault gave Voord an odd look at that, not understanding such caution in a commander who had proved so graphically that he had nothing to fear from weapons.

Watching him as he went through a salute before leaving the room, Voord could see the thoughts and questions chasing one another across the soldier's face. He grinned, quickly and privately, then wiped the expression from his face before anyone might see it and draw the wrong conclusion. No matter that steel could do him no permanent harm, its passage through his flesh still hurt more than he had been willing to show before witnesses, and he saw no reason to risk discomfort for the sake of such precautions as any high-ranked officer would be expected to take; and besides, the habits of the many years before the Gift were hard to break.

Tagen and his five troopers came to heel-stamping attention just inside the doorway and gave Voord the full salute due to his rank with all the precision and ceremony of the Bodyguard regiment to which they nominally belonged. Tagen looked much as the men and women on Voord's personal staff always did; young, broad-shouldered and handsome in *Tlakh-Woydan* half-armour, with the wary eyes and expressionless faces of those friends considered intimate enough to share in the secrets of Voord Ebanesj.

He and Voord had been together since Officer-School; the younger man had recognised even then – because Voord had explained it to him – that he was in the company of a star determined to rise no matter who or what was cremated in the process. Impressed, Tagen had remained with him, surviving where others had not during a meteoric career which had been politically upward and morally downward all the way. During those chaotic years they had shared everything – food and wine and women, bed and bloodshed, advantages and enemies. Nowadays the advantages were many and the enemies few – Voord's connections with *Kagh'Ernvakh* had seen to that – but there were still some names remaining on the list. In such killing matters Tagen had long since abandoned the allocation of innocence or guilt. That was Voord's affair;

he just followed orders . . . except when the matter
became personal.

'*Tagen, sh'voda moy. Yar vajaal dath-Aalban'r Aldric
Talvalin?*' Tagen nodded. Of course he remembered.
'*Inak dar Drakkesborg'cha. Slijei?*'

Tagen's impassive face split in a broad grin. This was
one of the personal matters. Because of Aldric Talvalin,
he had been ordered to kill his very good friend Garet;
Commander Voord had given the command, so he had
done as he was told – but he hadn't enjoyed following his
orders as much as usual. Because of Aldric Talvalin, he
had been promoted only a single grade after the affair at
Egisburg, instead of the three grades he had been promised; Commander Voord had been very sorry, but of
course Tagen had to understand that since he had failed
in his duty . . . Tagen understood very well. He understood that he was being made a scapegoat for the Alban
and though he and Voord had made it up later – because
it hadn't been Voord's personal decision to restrict the
promotion but just something which had to be done –
Tagen had put Aldric Talvalin at the top of his own
private list of names and faces. Work to do in his spare
time, so to speak. To discover that the Alban was more
than just his own concern, that Commander Voord wanted
him dealt with as well, and to be told of it in the Vlechan
dialect which they both shared was a delight.

'*Slij'hah, hautach*! His head only, or do you wish other
parts also?'

'No! No, Tagen. Understand me clearly. All of him . . .
and unharmed. To me, here in Drakkesborg. *Viaj-chu,
slijei?*'

Tagen was disappointed, and didn't trouble to keep the
emotion hidden. It had been just the same that last time
in Tuenafen, when Garet was still alive. For some reason
they hadn't been allowed to hurt the Alban, and Commander Voord had even kept the woman Kathur all to
himself. It wasn't fair, and it wasn't like the Commander
to be so selfish; after he had finished questioning or

punishment, they were always given their turn. Maybe he was getting soft. Tagen glanced up at him, wondering, then looked quickly away and squashed the thought down into the back of his mind where not even the Commander could see it. Or maybe – a happier notion – he wanted the Alban here to play with him in comfort. Yes, that would be it. Commander Voord wasn't getting soft at all; he just wanted to enjoy all the luxuries he had worked so very hard to gain.

'Yes, sir. I understand quite clearly now. But sir, if he resists—'

'Then you overcome the resistance.'

'I know that, sir. But in Tuenafen when the action squads went out you gave us drugs to put him to sleep when we caught him.'

'Soporifics, yes, I remember that. Go on. What's the difficulty? Do you,' Voord smiled thinly, 'not use drugs any more?'

'That's not the problem, sir. You know that.'

'Then,' and Voord's smile vanished as if it had never existed, 'get to the point.'

'Sir, I'd rather he wasn't put to sleep this time.'

'I said *unharmed*, Tagen. And I meant it.'

'But sir, please, just something for him to remember Garet by . . . Just a few minutes, that's all I'd take.'

'We all miss Garet,' said Voord wearily, his tone that of a man who had been through all the permutations of this argument before, 'and there'll be plenty of time for mementoes, but I gave you an order. Obey it.'

'Yes, sir.' If he had dared, Tagen would have let his voice sound sullen, but he had learned through painful experience that he could not do that to Voord and expect to get away with it. Instead he did as usual, tucking away his anger with all the other thoughts and ideas that he didn't want the Commander to know about, keeping them safe until he could let them out. When that happened someone died, but there were always chances to relieve his feelings in the line of duty, and anyway the people who died were Enemies Of The State – Commander Voord always made sure of that. Tagen liked the way the Commander said *Enemies Of The State* as if they were written in big letters, because it meant that the people Tagen killed were more Important than the enemies ordinary soldiers killed. He knew that because Commander Voord had explained it to him.

'Where is he, sir, and how do I find him? The usual way?' Tagen always made sure to ask that before the Commander told him how; it sounded better when people could hear you had been thinking for yourself. He knew he wasn't clever the way Commander Voord was clever, but he could talk well about weapons and armour and mountain-climbing and feats of strength and all the things that he was good at if he was given a minute to think of what to say.

'The usual way. Contact the *tulathin*, pay them what they want and find out what their spy-net knows. Then go and get him.'

'And if he's not alone, sir? The usual again?' Tagen was hopeful, because if he was finding out things from the *tulathin* then this business was a secret, and there was only one good way to keep a secret.

'Yes. Leave no witnesses. Go do it, Tagen. Dismissed.'

The *kortagor* and his squad clanked through another salute before they faced about in drilled unison and left Voord alone again. He was smiling a little, but nothing like the grin which Tagen had been wearing, a happy expanse of teeth similar to those of an attack hound offered fresh raw meat. Voord always felt slightly inadequate when dealing man to man – or man to doom-machine, which was how it often felt with Tagen. The soldier, intimately close and twelve-year-faithful friend though he might be, seemed sometimes no more than a weapon in human form, an intelligent petrary missile to be launched against one's enemies, and no more capable of recall. There had been

60

times before, as there would doubtless be times again, when Voord had cause to wonder what would happen if the need arose to call him off, and whether Tagen would pay heed to any countermand without the presence of the man he had called 'The Commander' for eleven years regardless of existing rank. Turning him on was easy; he reacted to the phrase *Enemy Of The State* as an oil-filled lamp reacted to a burning taper, but so far as turning him off again was concerned, Voord had no idea how to snuff out Tagen's fire once it was lit.

He relaxed a little, and was wondering whether to call for wine or just get out of this damnably uncomfortable chair and fetch it for himself when Hault reappeared in the doorway. 'Engeul Gernai, my lord,' the guard announced, stepping aside to let a stocky man into the room and continuing to speak without regard for how this new listener might receive the words. 'I searched him myself. He's clean.'

The man was indeed as unimpressive as Hault's earlier disparaging description had suggested. He was small and balding and prosperous, if prosperity meant a roll of fat around the waist. For all the fatness there was a haggard look about him, as if he had missed several nights of sleep. But he wasn't the class of person who usually requested to see a senior *Kagh'Ernvakh* officer; more often it was the Secret Police who wanted to have words with people like him.

'Well?' Voord was getting tired of being stared at and he was also growing hungry. 'Well,' he said, 'what do you want?'

'I wanted to see you, sir,' the man said hesitantly, plainly afraid of the company he had asked to enter, 'I'm a merchant. Of Jouvann.'

Voord blinked, bored already. If all this creature wanted was some sort of licence to sell his wares, then why in the Name of Darkness had he been allowed to get in here and waste important time which could be spent in doing other things, like eating. He lifted one eyebrow wearily, wondering if the change of expression would be noticed or if he would need something rather less subtle – like having the merchant beaten out of the citadel – and it was as if that single eyebrow was the floodgate that released a stream of babbling.

'I sell wine, my lord.' Gernai made the announcement as if it meant something important. 'All the wine of the Empire and the Provinces, and some excellent spirits. You may buy from me by the single bottle, or my merchant company can provide for the needs of any gentleman's cellar. At present I can offer you Seurandec, Brightwood, Briej, Hauverne Kingswine – where I can give you both a three-year and a seven-year vintage, one to offer to acquaintances, my lord, and the other to keep for yourself and your friends – red and white Teraneth, and—' The man's flow of words tailed off as Voord held up one hand for silence.

'You don't need to speak to me, Gernai. From the sound of it, the castellan would be more your man. But I'm curious; why did you ask for *Eldheisart* Voord?'

'I used the name and the rank I knew, my lord. Are you not that man? My apologies for wasting my lord's time . . .'

'Your information is several months out of date, man; several months and several promotions. You address the new Grand Warlord of the Empire!'

'Oh, I see.'

The Jouvaine merchant sounded much less impressed than Voord had expected him to be. And there was something else, something niggling that he couldn't place just now. One of those annoying little matters which nag at the back of the mind, evading sleep until the answer comes just before dawn. Voord tried to dismiss it, but the question would neither become clear nor go away.

'But are you the same *Eldheisart* Voord that I was told to find, my lord . . . ?'

The man was persistent at least. 'Yes, I am, was, whatever,' Voord snapped. 'Come to the point of all this before

I have you thrown out.' And what *was* the matter with . . . ? His accent, that was it. 'You have a Jouvaine name. Why don't you have a Jouvaine accent?'

'My lord is wise—' Engeul Gernai began, prelude to some oily flattery, and was cut short when Voord interrupted with none of the studied courtesy he had been trying to maintain.

'What goes on here?'

'My lord sounds afraid.' The man calling himself by a false name made a forceful gesture with one hand and uttered a grunt of effort like someone lifting a heavy weight. Behind him the tall doors of the chamber quivered once from top to bottom and slammed shut with a heavy boom. The double clank as both bolts shot home into their reinforced slots was almost an afterthought in the wake of that huge noise. 'My lord is well advised to fear.'

'Your accent is Vreijek,' Voord said.

'I never had the knack of simulating other voices, Lord-Commander Voord. How did you come by the new style and title anyway? Your usual method? Never mind. I didn't come here to see the Warlord; I came to see the officer who was Imperial Military Adviser to Lord Geruath Segharlin – the man who was so friendly with my daughter . . .'

'Ar Gethin.' The crows were coming home to roost with a vengeance.

'Yakez Goadec ar Gethin. Her name was Sedna. She was beautiful . . .'

'Who told you to ask for me?' There was threat here no matter what Hault had said – he would be dealt with later – but Voord was still little enough concerned to have some room for curiosity.

'Another of your women, Voord Ebanesj. Another of the many, boys and men and girls and women, whom you used for your own purposes and twisted up and threw away. Kathur the Vixen sends you greetings, and says you should have killed her.'

'So I should indeed.' Voord looked at the fat little

Vreijek and stretched his mouth into a smile like a snarl. 'That error can be remedied more easily than the slut will believe possible.'

'Kill. That's all you know, Voord – just as that was all you could think to do when my daughter found out the truth behind your scheming—'

'Scheming? *Scheming*? Yak'ardec ar Gethin, you have a mind like a playwriter! Twisted enough to give challenge to Osmar himself, I think.' Voord had been sitting up very straight in the harsh Warlord's chair; now he allowed himself to relax, unconcerned, innocent of whatever accusations this stupid old man was flinging about like seeds at planting-time. 'Listen to me, merchant, father and' – a glance at the still shut and bolted doors – 'passable sorcerer, I had nothing to do with your daughter.'

'Had you not, then? So why is she dead and you alive and higher than you were?'

'I am being patient with you . . . very patient. More patient than my custom with irritating provincials and far more patient than your manners deserve. Now shut your mouth and listen, because I'll say this only once: I did not kill your daughter. I barely knew your daughter. She was the mistress of Crisen Geruath, son of the local Over-lord, while I was no more than Imperial Adviser for the Segharlin and Jevaiden Military Districts. There was no love lost and almost no communication between—'

'Liar. *Liar*! I had expected more courage from you, or at least more originality. If you were Imperial anything at all, then why do I find you in a position of such authority here in the *Woydek-Hlautan*, the Warlord's Domain where the Emperor's mandate is ignored? Answer me that!'

'Ah.' Voord's slouch of studied relaxation froze as if a poisonous reptile had appeared in the room – or one of those reptilian lesser demons of far-too-close acquaintance. 'You prepared your arguments quite well, ar Gethin, didn't you?'

'Yes, I did. It was stopping my ears to what I learned that I found hard. Your name appeared at every turn, and each time it appeared there was more blood on it. Crisen Geruath is dead, his father the old Overlord is dead, Prokrator Bruda who was your senior officer while you pretended to be a member of the Emperor's Secret Police – he's dead, too; Kathur you raped and broke with your fists . . .' Yakez was working himself into a passion that would end in one of two ways; either he would attack with whatever that cretin Hault had let slip through his search – Voord's right hand moved inside his tunic and found the knurled-steel grip of the slender dagger that went everywhere with him – or he would break down . . .

Fingers still tight around the dagger-hilt, Voord watched dispassionately as the old man dropped on to both knees and folded over his own anguished sobs. There was an exposed place the size of a florin coin on the exposed nape of ar Gethin's neck, and Voord was torn between driving his knife-blade into it or using the pommel to stun so that the Vreijek could be sliced to dripping shreds later and at leisure. He debated too long for either chance, because the old man straightened abruptly with more energy in his short fat frame than anyone of such a shape had right to own.

Someone . . . several someones were hammering at the outside of the door, jolting it on its hinges and making the wrist-thick bolts clatter derisively. Apart from the noise, they were producing no effect. Yakez Goadec ar Gethin stood up very straight, and for all that he had to tilt back his head on its thick neck, he looked Voord in the eye. 'There are so many things that I would like to do to you,' he said, 'but all of them would end in death. Kill, die, death, that's all you know, that's your only solution. Voord, I am no sorcerer. I learned only the two spells: one for the door, to let us have this little chat without interruption, and one other. Because I looked at what was left of Sedna when you and the thing you conjured up were done, and I read the books in her locked library cabinet . . .' – Voord's narrowed, watchful eyes

65

went wide – 'and I decided to be merciful. I decided to take death away from you.'

He reached into the money-purse strapped to his belt and pulled out its lining in a chiming shower of coins. A lining that was fine, smooth leather, as fine as the binding of the book that still rested on Voord's lap. The same leather, even to the grain . . .

'*NO!*' Voord's voice soared to a scream as Yakez flung the flap of woman's-leather at him and he felt it strike his face, felt it stroke against his cheek as warm and soft as the innermost skin of a lover's thigh. The scream was drowned by a monstrous crash as the doors, their bolts snapping back in response to the same gesture which had first locked them, flew open under the weight of shoulders pressed against them.

Tagen was first in, his regulation shortsword already clear of its sheath and lacking only something to cut. Voord supplied that something; flinging out his hand, he pointed at Yakez as the small man smiled up at him and roared, 'Take that one!'

Whatever the meaning of the order, no matter what words were in it, Tagen heard only the words which he had always heard in a command uttered with that urgency. His balance shifted as he ran forward, the fist holding his sword swung back, reached the high point of its swing and came whirring down. He didn't hear what the small man was saying, or make sense of the Commander's frantic shout, but saw only that his target neither dodged nor ducked, and corrected the arc of his sweeping stroke as much by deadly reflex as intent.

'And my death will seal—' Yakez had begun to say.

'Don't hurt him, you damned—' Voord had begun to shout.

But the sound of Tagen's sword as it sheared off the Vreijek's head made a thick, wet nonsense of all the words. Blood splattered everywhere, over the steps, on the newly-scrubbed floor, on to Tagen's armour and all over Voord's feet as Yakez Goadec ar Gethin's severed head smacked against the stone between them.

The torso didn't remain upright the way they sometimes did; it didn't stagger, sway or even reel, but slammed straight down after its own head under the impetus of the blow. Breathing hard, Voord looked at it for perhaps a hasty count of five and then glared at Tagen.

'I said *no*, Tagen. You disobeyed my direct order.'

'Commander, I heard you cry out and I saw this one in a threat position. If I had waited, he might have—'

'Enough. It doesn't matter.' *Small use having a perfect instinctive killer like this one and then expecting him to behave like someone normal* . . . 'Be about your duties.'

The itch was just a tingle on his skin, an irritating need to scratch. Voord's wave of perfunctory dismissal became an unembarrassed raking of his ribs that was such a relief, that felt so good . . . until his fingers sank to the knuckles in the sorcerously healed stab-wound that suddenly reopened in his side. He looked down and saw it, and went chalk-white with shock. Then the pain hit him, all the rending anguish of a sword-thrust in the belly, so that his back arched convulsively and a reflexive jerking in the muscles of his legs sent him tumbling from his seat down on to the bloodied floor.

There was no blood of his own, only the gash with his hand in it and the sickening wash of agony that was worse even than when he gave the use of his left hand in sacrifice to the Old Ones. Voord had thought his maiming was the most terrible pain that he had ever borne until this moment.

He was wrong. Even as he squirmed on the blood-greased tiles, first one hole opened in his head and then a second in his neck; the ragged punctures left by Alban *telek* darts. There was a crater of splintered bone above his right eye, and beneath his chin the clearly visible cartilage of his gullet had been perforated so that even his screaming sounded strange.

Some of the soldiers who had come running to the

rescue choked, and retched, and fled, while others remained but clenched their teeth and gazed in every direction but at the man they had thought to save . . . who, pierced by wounds that should have killed him three times over, still writhed and shrieked and tried without success to die.

THREE

The sword was red oak, straight and smooth and polished, and it had been in his hands since the grey time just before dawn. More than two hours of striking-practice, with only enough rest breaks to prevent his muscles from cramping in protest as they blurred the sword through cut and thrust, parry and block, or brought it to those snapping stops which required as much control as any sweeping stroke.

He had spent years learning how to be lethal with a sword. Years of focusing the force of a strike; years of learning how to bring steel edge and human anatomy together with an executioner's rather than a surgeon's skill; years of learning how to deliver the classic cuts with no thought for what they did.

To face a human being perfect in the eyes of the Power which had made it; and to strike it with a sword perfect in the eyes of the smith who had forged it, in a movement perfect in the eyes of the master who had taught it. From the sum of all that perfection, *defeat* left only food for worms.

And what – or Whose – was the purpose behind such a consequence as that . . . ?

Aldric looked at the wooden *taidyo* braced in his hands. Even now, ostensibly relaxed and with his thoughts turned inward, he had adopted the ready posture of mid-guard-centre, a stance from which he could develop three separate killing forms. He breathed out through his nostrils, the breath drifting away in twin plumes like smoke on the cold air, and lowered the weapon's point with slow deliberation to the ground. Only then did his gaze shift to the left, to where *she* awaited his attention; and all at once the winter's chill ground through the glow of well exercised muscle. He shuddered, just once, but with such violence that it brought both rows of his teeth clattering together.

The *taiken* lay an arm's length from where he stood, resting on an austere sword-rack of unvarnished pine. Black lacquer, black leather and black steel, all a stark contrast against the snow and the cross of straw-pale wood.

Isileth.

Widowmaker . . .

The blade, in its many-times-refurbished mountings, was twenty centuries old. Aldric looked at her, as he had often looked before, and wondered again in silence: *How many widows? How many lives? How much blood have you drunk in your two thousand years of life, my cold mistress?*

She would drink his blood, given the chance. Or Kyrin's. Or anyone's. For all the courtesy that they were granted, *taikenin* were never so proud as the men and women who carried them. Whether of prince or of peasant, any death – *all* death – served as their nourishment. He leaned his weight on the *taidyo*, driving it down through the churned snow between his feet and into the dirt beneath, and decided that this morning at least he would leave Isileth at rest within her scabbard.

'Brooding again, are you?'

Aldric jerked sideways to face where Kyrin, well wrapped in a deeply-hooded, fur-trimmed over-robe against the snow that hung in the leaden sky, came stepping delicately through last night's ankle-deep fall. He hadn't heard the sound of her feet, and her voice had made him jump; this in itself precluded any denial of her gentle accusation. Even though he tried.

'I was thinking; that's all.'

'Just another word for what I said.' She lifted a towel and his black leather jerkin and shirt from where they were draped across the picket fence. 'Ivern and her people; they still wonder about you. About us both.'

'Let them wonder,' he said and returned the *taidyo* to

70

its canvas sleeve amongst his other practice gear. With it he seemed to set aside his sombre mood; or at least return it to whatever locked compartment of his mind he kept it in. 'The less that people know, the less they can let slip.'

Aldric shrugged hurriedly into his clothes and then – with the merest shadow of a bow – took Widowmaker from her rack and slung the scabbard's strap across his shoulder, but instead of hooking it into a proper combat position on his weapon-belt he left the longsword loose against his hip. The hip farthest from Kyrin.

There were stories about Isileth Widowmaker, and while he was not prepared to credit an inanimate piece of metal with such a thing as jealousy – not even a blade of her profound antiquity, no matter what the stories said – yet he was not about to take foolish chances. Aldric had seen too many strange things for that.

Kyrin looked from his face to the black longsword, and then back. 'Still brooding, as I said. About last night?'

'And bad dreams? No. That was in the past.'

'So the past doesn't concern you. Aldric-*an*, you're a high-clan Alban. The past always concerns you. I swore an oath once – and as a high-clan Alban you above all should understand how closely a sincere oath can bind – to use my ability and my judgement for the benefit of the sick . . .'

'Are you suggesting that I'm . . . sick?' Something unpleasant hovered in the way he asked it.

'Not sick . . . not like that. But you're hurt; you're in pain. And I don't want you in pain, not ever. I want you rid of the old wounds, the ones that never healed. Time it was done with once and for all.'

'I don't need any help.'

'No? Not even when you tear at yourself, rip those ancient hurts wide open again every time they have a chance to close? I've watched you do it, Aldric, and it's an ugly thing to see. You're bleeding inside, man – and you're the only one who can't see it!'

71

'I'm a killer, lady. A killer, not a healer. And all the good intentions in the world won't change that fact.'

'So then why blame yourself for Dewan?'

Aldric looked up at her – a sharp, over-quick movement of head and eyes. 'Because Dewan died when I was too slow to—'

'No. He died because he'd seen the alternative. He gave himself for . . . for me. And for you. For both of us. Dewan died because he gave his life for ours. At least do him the courtesy of not debating his choice.' She had never dared speak to him like this before – but it had to be said. That, and gentler things, like: 'How much use would living be for me if you were gone?'

Aldric said nothing for several minutes. There was real anger in his eyes, smouldering there like red coals, and for one frightening moment Kyrin thought that she had gone too far. Then the eyes closed briefly, squeezing tight, and when they opened again the moment was gone. 'As little use,' he said softly, 'as my life would be without you.'

'So. You see.'

Aldric smiled at her, a wintry skinning back of lips from teeth. 'Oh yes, I see very well,' he said, his voice clipped and quiet.

'You were born and brought up *kailinin-eir*. Even if you choose to deny that heritage, the culture behind it is unchanged. Vengeance and blood-feud were – still are – accepted. Traditional. Just as killing *yourself* is an accept-able, traditional thing. *Tsepanak'ulleth*.' She was pushing, bringing the unsaid into the open.

'But why haven't you done it, Aldric? All the deaths, all the guilt, all the grieving. Why haven't you rid yourself of them? Why do you . . . not just live with them, but treat them as honoured guests in the house of your mind? Because that's the way it looks to me. Why – when you've got your way out here?'

She touched the black *tsepan* at his belt with one finger, a brief, careful contact as if with some dainty, deadly creature that was, for the moment only, tame and safe. 'You haven't used it, Aldric. Tell me why not.'

Aldric let her hand withdraw to a safe distance, then gripped the lacquered hilt of the Honour-dirk and eased its three-edged spike of blade clear of its sheath. He stared in silence for the longest time at the weapon's bitter point. For so long, indeed, that Kyrin thought he might refuse outright to answer . . .

Or worse, in one of those sudden spasms of fury, try to do what she had so scathingly suggested was permitted him to do. With the shadow of that fear rising in her mind, she reached out swiftly to lay a hand across his wrist. Not restraining it, not yet, but at least reminding him of her presence. He looked at her, full in the face, and again their eyes met; and now hers were worried and apprehensive while his had gone introspective, cold and emotionless as chips of ice.

'Why not?' he echoed, speaking more to himself than to her. 'Because I always thought my life was of more use than my death. While I was still alive I could set wrong things to rights. Justify myself to people. To you. To myself.' The *tsepan* went back into its scabbard with a whisper of steel and a small, solid click.

Greatly daring, Kyrin reached out and took it from him with an unvoiced sigh of relief. It was only when that dagger was out of his reach that she stared him in the eye and let a little of her fear escape as anger.

'Justify yourself?' The question snapped out, harsher than it might have been, long patience at the end of its tether. 'Then why *don't* you?'

Aldric merely inclined his head in the beginnings of a bow. 'Because whatever way I chose to do it, I truly had no reason until now.'

He pulled the square-faced gold ring from where he had always worn it on his right hand and slipped its warm metal on to Kyrin's finger. 'This will keep the place until I buy another just for you,' he said.

Kyrin looked at the ring on her finger and felt her eyes

sting with the threat of tears. She stared at the *tsepan* in her hand as if she had never seen it before. The time was not long past when she wouldn't have dared to touch the Honour-dirk, much less make observations about the rightness of its use. That she had done so now, like the glimmer of gold on her hand where none had ever been before, meant something.

Didn't it . . . ?

Kyrin glanced back at Aldric, and a half-born word faltered on her lips as she realised he wasn't listening or even looking at her.

Instead he was staring up towards the high hills to the east where the beams of the late-risen sun speared through a crack in the heavy sky. They were blurred and robbed of their full strength by the falling snow, but there was still enough power in the light to bleach sky and snow together to a blinding glare, like the mouth of a furnace but without any heat at all.

'Company,' said Aldric, his voice turned flat and unpleasant. Kyrin followed the direction of his gaze, squinting at the brilliance, and although her vision was shot with streaks and sparkles of phosphorescent purple she could see quite plainly what was wrong.

The six riders on the hill-crest sat very still on their tall horses, long dark shadows streaked across the snow before them, no movement but the white breath of men and animals drifting on the breeze. They were half a mile away with the sun at their backs, but even without seeing their faces Kyrin doubted that they were dinner guests. 'Who are they?' Her words were not so much a question as a wondering aloud, but Aldric answered anyway.

'Not friends,' he said, his voice taking on the terrible calm that she recognised from other times and other places. 'If they've got a long-glass, they'll know we've seen them. Is anyone around the steading except us?'

'No – Dyrval's up at the farm and Ivern went off to market before I—'

'Good. Into the stable: tack-room first. Saddle up in

case we have to run for it. Then get some of my gear –
both *telekin* and the great . . . no . . . the shortbow for
you. A half-sheaf of arrows should be enough.' He
squinted at the distant horsemen again and shrugged.
'No armour. Not visible, anyway. Willowleaf tips in case
there's mail underneath.'

'I'll ask you this again,' said Kyrin, following him
towards the stable door. 'Who are they – or who do you
think they might be?'

Aldric took his eyes from the still-unmoving riders just
long enough to give her a nasty sort of smile that showed
far too many of his teeth. 'An accurate list would take far
too long,' he told her, and there might have been just the
merest touch of bitterness in his voice as he said it. 'Let's
just say that if they're looking for Ivern or the others
I'll be grateful, and if they're looking for you I'll be
surprised. . . . And if they're looking for me without evil
intentions I'll be downright astonished. Here they come!'

The horsemen were moving, walking their mounts forward in a leisurely fashion, but after what Aldric had said
– and what he had only hinted at – Kyrin would far
rather have seen them riding away than coming any closer.
Except that they *were* coming closer, and leisurely or not
there was something in the way they sat their horses that
made her uneasy. Even at such a distance she could see
how they rode. She had seen Aldric fork a saddle that
same way, menacing and businesslike, straight-legged,
feet braced against long-leathered stirrups, spine braced
against high, curved cantle, reins gathered together in one
hand to leave the other free for weapons.

The stable and tack-room were gloomy at the best of
times, and seen through eyes which had been staring
straight at the sun they were as black as a wolf's throat.
They saddled both riding and pack horses more by touch
and memory than by sight, and Aldric at least made a few
false attempts at it if the sounds of clattering and an

occasional oath meant anything. 'You can use a bow, can't you?' he asked out of the darkness.

'Yes, I can.' If Kyrin's voice had an irritable edge to it, that was probably due more to nervousness than because she had to make an effort to keep her *of course I can* unspoken. The weapon was pushed into her hands a moment later, with an untidy bundle of wooden staves and feathers and leather straps that she guessed – rightly – were arrows and a bow, a shooting-glove and a bracer.

'*Telek*,' said Aldric, looming out of the shadows with a spring-gun in one hand. He broke it and spun its cylinder, then snapped it shut and worked the lever. The weapon's mechanisms clicked and the sear engaged with a small, solid noise. 'There. It's loaded and cocked, so don't put a dart through your own foot; that trigger's got a light touch. Inside thirty feet, just point and squeeze.'

'I know. I *know*!' Kyrin took the spring-gun and felt its weight dragging at her hand, a crooked shape of wood and metal that was somehow far more sinister than a sword. She hefted the *telek* a few times and looked at Aldric's outline in the gloom. 'But what happens if they aren't enemies . . . ?'

'That's their misfortune, isn't it?' he said, his voice deadly calm. The voice of a man who had grown tired of being hunted all across the country by one faction or another. The voice of a man who had had enough.

'So you'll shoot from cover, without warning. Like an assassin?'

'Not like an assassin. Like a man outnumbered six – no, sorry' – she detected the glint of a tight smile in the way he corrected himself – 'three to one. And I'll wait until I'm sure.'

Kyrin didn't reply, and Aldric could sense her disapproval without needing to see the stare and the compressed lips. He shrugged and laid a hand to the door. 'But if you really want, there's one way to find out. I just hope they aren't good shots. . . .'

'That's not fair!'

'All right, it's not. But we have to get out of here anyway, or risk them firing the place. I don't like the prospect of being trapped inside a burning building again . . .'

Kyrin looked sharply at him, wondering about the story behind that 'again'. Before she could say anything the door kicked at Aldric's fingers as something smacked into it and an instant later dug into the floor, tearing a hole in the planks and letting a narrow shaft of daylight transfix the darkness of the tack-room.

'Of course, there are other ways,' he said blandly, 'especially if they have crossbows. Convinced?'

'Convinced. They don't have to come in at all, not if they've got enough ammunition?'

'Tell me about it,' said Aldric, and nipped a splinter from the pad of his thumb with his front teeth. 'Which is another reason why I don't want to stay here.'

'But if they can already hit the door—'

'Luck. Or accident. Probably . . .' That hesitation disturbed her more than any further words of explanation. 'Or they've moved faster than I thought. Get down. Flat on the floor.' He hooked the tip of his own greatbow under the door's hasp, muttered something under his breath and pulled, hard. Nothing happened. Again, and again nothing. A third time, much harder—

—And the door jerked back, flooding the tack-room with light and a heavy swirl of the snow that was falling now in earnest. Five crossbow bolts flicked through the sudden opening and hammered into the back wall with a sound like a demented carpenter at work, almost too fast for the individual strikes to be counted. But not quite. 'Go!' yelled Aldric.

Even before Kyrin was clear of the floor, he had stepped into the doorway with an arrow already nocked to his bowstring, spotted a possible target, flexed, drew and loosed all in one quick movement.

The sound of the arrow's impact was mostly that of splitting timber, and five of the raiders burrowed for deeper cover. The sixth uttered a yell, shot his newly-loaded crossbow into the ground and swung out backwards into the yard, nailed through the thigh to the door behind which he had crouched to reload and shoot. He was still yelling, outraged as much as hurt, and with good reason for both sensations; nobody had thought to tell him that at such close range a wooden door was no obstacle at all even to ordinary arrows – and he was facing armour-piercing points.

Aldric knew the drawbacks of a crossbow: they were murderously powerful, but because of that slow, cumbersome things. He had used them himself in better days, but only for hunting. Against a target able to shoot back, they were a liability during their lengthy reloading cycle without something solid to hide behind. Something much more solid than a door of thin-cut end-grained planks . . .

And then the arrow pinning the raider's leg in place tore free and released him to fall sideways into the trampled snow of the courtyard where, fighting forgotten, he used both hands to staunch the outflow of his blood. For all that his clothing was that of a peasant or a forester, unremarkable and instantly forgotten, the wounded man was wearing other garments underneath and had taken the trouble to conceal his features with a hooded mask. Both the mask and the close-fitting second suit of clothes were of some fine fabric grey as smoke.

Aldric and Kyrin tumbled together into the relative shelter round the corner of the stone-built stable and crouched there, panting. 'Oh Lord God, we're in trouble,' he said between gasps. 'They're *tulathin*. Assassins.'

'*Real* assassins?'

'Professionals.'

'We're in trouble.' There was a pause, then: 'But who hired them?'

'Damned if I know.' Aldric was already belly-down in the snow, squirming for a better position, with the seven-foot bow clamped crosswise between elbow-joint and biceps. 'I'll ask that question later, if I'm alive to ask or they to answer' – he ducked as sparks and sharp-edged fragments sprayed from stone when another crossbow bolt probed at their shelter and went humming off at a crazy angle – 'because I don't think taking me alive is part of their contract.'

A thread of crimson oozed down Kyrin's face from a gash left by a splinter, and she pressed a fistful of snow against it to staunch the bleeding. 'Or anyone with you,' she said, initial surprise becoming grim belief in all that he had told her these past weeks. All the fears, all the precautions, all the things which she had nodded at and agreed with, if only out loud but never in her heart.

Matters were different now, face down in the snow with her face stinging, weapons in her hands and the occasional intermittent buzz or metallic smack of passing bolts as a constant reminder that she was going to have to hurt or be hurt. Kill or be killed. Kyrin looked at the coldness in Aldric's face, a coldness which had nothing to do with the snow-melt soaking him, and shivered at the sudden grim reality of it all.

For just a moment she wanted to be sick, right then and there on the ground before her face; then the feeling passed into no more than a clammy shudder in her guts, and she braced her own bow across her arms as he had done and wriggled after him in the crushed snow of his wake.

Ivern's steading might have been designed with defence in mind, and if it had been built in the past ten years there was no 'might' about it. Except for the wooden doors, the stone buildings were sturdy enough to absorb a point-blank strike from anything that mounted raiders could have carried. The layout of house, annex, stables and outbuildings was such that there were no positions from which a missile weapon could dominate more than twenty feet in any direction; a range so short that leaden slingshot slugs or Army-issue weighted throwing darts would be of more use than the slow-to-reload crossbows – the kind of range at which Alban *telekin* excelled.

'Our one advantage is,' said Aldric quietly as he paused well short of a corner, 'that a *telek* doesn't need reloading after every shot.'

'So what about the bows?' Kyrin touched her own shortbow with the tip of one finger. 'Keep them or put them aside?'

'Keep. We might get a clear shot somewhere. But this' – he indicated the ominous corner with a jerk of his head – 'is likely to be *telek* work.' He was breathing fast, and Kyrin could see the flutter of a rapid pulse in the hollow of his throat as he half-turned to lean his own bow and bundle of arrows against the wall.

Aldric went round the corner in a half-roll and a flurry of snow, *telek* levelled at where a target might most likely be. There was no one there, but enough footprints marred an otherwise smooth snowdrift to suggest that someone had been, and recently.

'Do you mean we have to kill them all?' whispered Kyrin in his ear. 'Couldn't we drive them off?'

'How?' The monosyllabic reply was bitter. Despite his well-feigned confidence he doubted that the pair of them could win unaided against five *tulathin*, let alone chivvy them away like a pack of annoying cur-dogs. Rather than kill all of the remaining assassins, it was more likely that the *tulathin* would kill them. Aldric looked sidelong at Kyrin, at the way her teeth nipped nervously at her lower lip, at the softness of her face, and privately decided that killing would be all that would be done to her – even if he had to make quite certain by doing it himself. He was angry at letting her get involved in this, putting her life at risk because of . . . whoever of the far-too-many in his past had sent this execution detail after him.

'Look there.' Kyrin spoke very softly, pointing with her *telek* at what had drawn her attention. A little puff of something that looked like smoke was trailing into view from beyond the hay-barn, and even as they watched, it was joined by a second. 'Fire? Or breath?'

'Doesn't matter. It's not one of us; that's enough.' A swirl of wind-driven snow slapped Aldric in the face, making him flinch. 'Stay here. Mind your back. I'm going round that way' – he jerked his chin at the other side of the barn, – 'and if he comes out first, kill him.'

'What if—'

'Just make sure it's him, not me.' He left his greatbow where he had propped it against the wall, winked at her – though that could have been a flake of snow in his eye – and moved quickly out of sight.

Kyrin stared for several seconds into the whiteness, fixing his vague outline in her mind just in case of accidents, then returned her attention to the barn. The snow flurries were dying away into a heavy, steady fall like those she remembered from back home in Valhol, hard to see through and almost hypnotic to watch. She considered the *telek* for a moment, then thumbed its safety-slide into place, shoved it through her belt and set an arrow to her bowstring.

Better the weapon you know than the weapon you just claim *to know*, she thought with a crooked little smile. At least Aldric hadn't asked her whether she would be able to put an arrow through another human being. Her answer might have shocked him. These people were trying to kill her, and had only themselves to blame for the—

How the man had crept up behind her was all too plain, with the falling snow deadening both sight and hearing, but the only reason why he hadn't shot her in the back must be that he'd spotted she was female and was minded to a little fun before he finished her off. That was his mistake. For all that he was a *taulath* and a professional assassin skilled at killing people, he had small ability at attempted rape, especially when the subject of his unwelcome attentions was more than just a frightened farm-girl.

He got as far as wrapping his left forearm around her throat and – instead of jamming a dagger under her ribs as the neck-pressure suggested he might do – began pawing at her breasts with the other hand. Mauled, out-raged, but still very much alive, Kyrin dropped the bow and its nocked arrow and reached up with both hands.

She snapped his little finger like a twig, then wrenched the pain-loosened forearm from her neck and used it as a lever to hurl her attacker to the ground. The *taulath* landed with a jarring thud on his tail-bone and the back of his skull, an impact that knocked even the uncompleted scream of pain out of his lungs as no more than a grunt.

'Bastard!' hissed Kyrin, clawing the *telek* out of her belt.

'I'll gut you for that, bitch!' the man snarled back with his first regained breath, rolling over with a shortsword gripped in his uninjured hand and already clear of its sheath. Kyrin froze – because the words and the accent were both Alban.

That shocked hesitation was almost enough to kill her, for it let him regain his feet, his balance and enough time to lash out the beginning of a cut with the *taipan* shortsword – also Alban, she could see that now – which would have taken her face off. The pause when time went slow was almost long enough for her to die, but not quite. Her *telek* snapped back on line and jolted in her hand to put a single lead-shod dart into his eye.

Kyrin's heart was beating too quickly and too loudly by far, seeming almost to advertise her presence, and there was an acid queasiness in her stomach which came not from the killing but where the killed man came from. The implications of *that*, already running through her brain, were too ugly to be believed and too urgent to be kept secret for longer than it took to find Aldric again – some-where out there in the snowstorm, not knowing that the men he stalked were his countrymen, trained as he had been himself and most certainly more ruthless. They were people he might hesitate to kill for one reason or another, as she had almost hesitated, whereas to them he was a job of work, payment on completion and no more.

She was not so panicked that she was about to do something stupid; but whatever she did, she would have to do it fast . . .

The man lying at Aldric's feet wasn't dead, but he would likely wish he was when he came to his senses and the egg-sized lump at the back of his head made its presence felt. Shooting the assassin would have been as easy, but given the chance of choice Aldric had left him alive. Why, he didn't know. But he wasn't about to correct the error by killing a helpless enemy, good sense though that might have been.

Instead he came very close to killing Kyrin as her anonymous shape appeared out of the falling snow. His *telek* was levelled and his fingers were already putting four of the necessary five pounds' pressure on the weapon's long trigger before he saw just who it was aimed at and twitched the muzzle to one side.

Kyrin's face was pale enough already, and the experience of staring down the bore of a weapon whose power she had had demonstrated barely seconds earlier was enough to leave her as white as the falling snow.

'*Doamne' Diu!*' he snarled. Alone, things would have been easier, since with Ivern and Dyrval and all the others away from the steading, anyone else would have been an enemy and could be dealt with as such. Despite, or maybe because of her courage, Kyrin tied his hands by refusing to hide. But there was another way out, if the snow continued to fall as heavily as it was doing now; a way out in the most literal sense.

'Back to the stables. The horses are ready to go; we'll mount up and get out of here while the weather holds bad.'

'You mean *run?*'

'*Escape* sounds better. We're still outnumbered—'

'Barely! They'll be easier than the others—'

'No, dammit! I know more about *tulathin* than you do. We've been lucky so far—'

'There's no such thing as luck!'

'Then we've—' His patience gave way at last and he grabbed her by the arm. 'Argue later, for God's sweet sake. But right now, *move!*'

Kyrin opened her mouth to say something savage; then the focus of her eyes moved from his face to a place behind him and her heel hooked round behind his knee so that they both went tumbling sideways. Two bolts from the three crossbows she had seen in the instant they were levelled went scything through the snowy air where they had stood and exploded sparks and splinters from the hay-barn wall. And that left one.

As Aldric rolled from the fall and back to his feet, Widowmaker came from her scabbard with a whisper of steel on wood . . . and then froze half-way to a guard position as the man with the last loaded crossbow walked forward slowly, enjoying his moment of absolute superiority. Behind him, the other two slung their missile weapons and drew shortswords for what would now be only butchery.

'Aldric Talvalin,' said the first *taulath*. He spoke excellent Alban, with a Pryteinek accent, so that Aldric glared hatred. The man's crossbow wasn't aimed, but pointing nonchalantly at the ground . . . for now.

'Keep the girl safe,' said the hateful Alban voice behind the hood. 'Girls are for dessert.'

'Sweets are bad for you,' said Aldric, deliberately using the highest form of the Alban language as an unsubtle insult. It was the way a clan-lord would address a beggar, if the clan-lord deigned to communicate with more than just his riding-quirt.

The *taulath*'s crossbow came up, steadied, sighted on Aldric's forehead . . . and loosed. Blue fire exploded unsummoned from Widowmaker's pommel-stone and enveloped her blade in the instant of the missile's flight.

The longsword shifted to guard in a flicker of hot blue-white light, and emitted a shrill metallic screech as her edges met the accelerating crossbow bolt and sheared it point to nock in two. Aldric hid disbelief behind a hungry feral grin and whipped the blue-burning *taiken* through to an attack posture—

And then there was a slap of impact and the centre of the *taulath*'s hood went explosively concave. As his companions dived for cover, the assassin took a single tottering step backwards and fell. Aldric matched his movement with a raking stride forward that slammed his heel square into the centre of the masked face, then brought Isileth Widowmaker down with all his force on to the crown of the hooded head.

The *taulath* lay quite still in the snow, split to the middle of the chest, crumpled and bloody and somehow smaller now. The other *tulathin* were nowhere to be seen.

'What – what happened?' Kyrin had spent the past few seconds face downwards in the snow, displaying good sense for what Aldric considered was the first time in far too long. 'I thought you were dead!!'

'Exaggerated rumours.' Aldric's sardonic smile was not a particularly pleasant thing to see, especially since it was spattered with the dead man's blood. 'Now, quick and quiet: to the stables.'

'I said what happened?'

'Slingshot.' He augmented the laconic answer by turning her hand palm-up and dropping into it what looked like a small egg. Kyrin glanced down – then made a shocked little noise as she realised exactly what he meant, dropped the still-bloody lead slug into a snowdrift and scrubbed her smeared hand hard against the leg of her riding-breeches. The slug had been completely round when it left the sling, but now it was slightly flattened – because a human skull can always put up some resistance, even to a slung lead shot . . .

'Who killed him – not you?'

'I wish . . .' Aldric pushed open the stable door and

led the way in with the muzzle of his *telek*. Apart from agitated horses, the place was empty. 'No, I just made sure. He shot at me, and then that thing took part of his head off. The other two got out of sight; they're still out there somewhere.' He swung up into Lyard's saddle, leaving one foot free of its stirrup so that he could lean sideways, *kailin*-style, along the horse's neck, and looked back at Kyrin. 'So are the others, the *tulathin* in white who killed him.'

'More *tulathin*? Friends of yours?'

'Just more assassins. They didn't want the first squad to kill me – that's the only good thing about them. As for what *they* want, I think it's me again. Alive, this time.'

'No encouragement to stay.'

'All right, you win.' Aldric laughed, a harsh bark of sound with something of a tremor in it even now. 'Let's *go*!'

They rode out of the stable and the blizzard closed around them in an icy, impenetrable curtain of white, whirling around black horse and grey, roan pack-pony and bay. It struck their faces like chilled feathers, enfolded them, sifted across their tracks and bleached the vagueness of their outlines until not even the trained eyes of a *taulath* could have told which mass of white was horse and which was rider, and which was merely drifting snow.

And by the time one or other of the *tulathin* had both time and safety enough to look, those looked for were gone.

FOUR

There was confusion in Cerdor.

To those who had lived there during the past thirteen days, it felt as if there had never been anything except confusion in the city, ever since the King had died and all his lords save two had fled back to their own lands. It had little to do with that death any more, regardless of what the rumours said, but had a far more sinister source that even rumour was reluctant to touch upon: the uncertainty of powerful men.

Granted that King Rynert's death had been the first cause of all the trouble, still it had stemmed less from his passing than the manner of it. That had been interpreted not merely by uninformed second- and third-hand sources but by men who had been there in person as the action of an overly-ambitious and haughty clan-lord – Hanar Santon – slighted over some matter by the dead King. That the truth of the matter was very different had no significance now, for the error had gathered its own momentum and was impossible either to disprove or to stop for all that its consequences were already spreading across Alba like plague-marks covering the face of a once beautiful woman.

There had been no meeting of the Alban Crown Council since that night, not even to vote on their establishment of a Regency to rule the country – Rynert having failed to leave an heir. Most of the lords present at that last fateful meeting were now watching each other from the dubious safety of their respective citadels, setting to rights the fortifications which long years of peace had allowed to fall into disrepair and mustering enfeoffed lesser lords to their defence. None would listen to reason; not since they had seen what they thought was Reason conversing with a hired assassin and moments later slashed open and slain on the steps of his own throne . . .

'At least there are no declarations of faction yet.' Hanar Santon patted the sheets of despatch reports together, aligning their edges with punctilious neatness for the tenth time since their delivery half an hour before.

'Yet.' His companion's voice was without inflection, neither echoing nor squashing Hanar's optimism. 'That doesn't mean anything, either way.' If there was cynicism in the statement, it was not the studied art practised by younger men. Aymar Dacurre had had many years of experience in which to get his practice right. The old clan-lord had as much faith as anyone else in his fellow men; he simply didn't anticipate it without proof.

'But you heard the names, didn't you? Powerful high-clan-lords, all of them.'

Aymar sighed. *These children*, he thought. *They learn history, but they never learn from it*. As if the mere fact of being high-clan-lords was enough to absolve them of blame for anything. . . . It was all written down in *Ylver Vlethanek*, and the Book of Years was being echoed far too closely for Aymar Dacurre's comfort. The same postures of pugnacious defence had been adopted five hundred years before, and by the ancestors of the same men who were adopting them today. Those disagreements had become the Clan Wars, and so far as Dacurre could see it would require very little force to push the present situation over into a repetition of the conflict which had left such a bloody stain on Alban history. But now there was another factor to take into account, a factor which the old lords had not needed to worry over and which their descendants either failed or refused to consider. The source of the push: the Drusalan Empire.

If what Aldric Talvalin had said was true – and Dacurre had seen no reason to disbelieve the young man's words whether they were heard at first hand or related through his foster-father Gemmel – the Empire had been casting speculative glances towards its neighbour for some time. What galled most was the reason behind it all; not expansion by conquest, or even simple acquisitiveness, but simply so that a bureaucrat could continue to justify his function.

The military dictator who styled himself Grand Warlord had lost most of his influence in the Western Empire when the new Emperor Ioen had belied his youth and revealed that he possessed a mind of his own, rather than the collection of thoughts and opinions borrowed from the Warlord like so many of his predecessors. The Emperor had negotiated peace – or at least pacts of mutual non-aggression – with all the countries on his borders by revoking the unpopular provincial annexations that were the source of so much unrest. He and his advisers had taken what at first seemed considerable loss of face until it became clear that they had lost nothing. More, they had gained the respect of many on all sides who had grown weary of the constant brutal round of rebellion and suppression in provinces seized for no better reason than that their and the Empire's frontiers ran together for longer than a given minimum distance. But without war, the position of *Woydach* became superfluous, and Warlord Etzel faced redundancy, loss of rank and power and privilege – and the long-leashed vengeance of all those who had survived the trampling of his rise to power.

The danger had become clear almost five years ago, during an insignificant incident which had exploded into scandal and slaughter with the resurrection of a long-dead sorcerer and the butchery of all save one of Alba's foremost high-clan families, the Talvalins. The idea behind that had been for the Imperial legions to intervene, as they had done before in other places, to restore 'equilibrium and peace' as the then-Emperor interpreted the term; an intervention whose payment was invariably the province or country which it liberated. That had been the first indication of what was to be a constant threat just beyond the horizon, and one which had lately grown still more significant.

During the course of the past year, after acrimonious exchanges at all levels of the Imperial Senate, the Grand Warlord had split away from the Emperor's 'pacifist' faction and had retired to the old capital of Drakkesborg. There he had set up an Eastern Empire, *Woydek-Hlautan* – the Warlord's Domain in the guttural Drusalan language – whose political aims were those of the old emperors of the Sherban dynasty rather than those of their milksop descendant: bring unity by the swiftest means. Swiftest of all those means was force of arms and of course, while the 'Empire' was at war, it required a supreme military commander, a Grand Warlord, once more.

Alban foreign policy had never been particularly subtle or ingratiating where the Empire was concerned. Lord Dacurre knew that much even before he had begun working his way through the Archive records of past Council meetings. He could remember several occasions when his had been the sole dissenting voice against the condoning of acts of piracy against Imperial shipping – and to his shame, the two meetings where he had agreed that arms and financial support should be tendered to insurrections in the Imperial provinces now freed by Emperor Ioen's policy of conciliation. At least he'd been able to prevent the issue of letters of marque, which would have been equivalent to a secret declaration of war on the Ocean-Sea; Cernuan and Elherran privateers were not the most controllable of auxiliary troops, and he had said as much, to the great offence of Lord Diskan of Kerys in Cerenau.

And then other things had started coming to light, like drowned corpses during a spring thaw and smelling about as sweet. Aymar Dacurre had discovered things in the Archive which had never been mentioned by the late King Rynert, for all that they had been written down by assiduous *hanan-vlethan'r* – the court recorders who noted everything of significance for all that their writings were often edited later. These records were not edited, and it galled

Dacurre to realise that had his fellow councillors seen what had been written there, they would not now be peering at each other and the rest of the country over ramparts. What he had seen, and what he had read, had been the truth behind Rynert's version of what Aldric Talvalin had been doing in the Empire, and in Seghar and – most significantly of all – in Egisburg where Dewan ar Korentin had died. Considering such things, he was astonished that the Imperial threat had not materialised already in the form of warships off the Alban coast, and that non-appearance had given him cause to wonder what Aldric was doing in the Eastern Empire – or *to* it – that might keep its ambitious Grand Warlord so busy.

'Hanar,' said Aymar Dacurre, 'you are my grandson.'

Hanar Santon started very slightly at that. He had known it all his life, but had never heard it spoken aloud except by his mother, Dacurre's second daughter. The explanation for the silence had involved such words as 'favouritism' and 'respect' and, most of all, 'honour', so he had never pursued the matter. To hear it now from the old man himself was something of a shock, for they had moved to first-name terms only in the past ten days or so.

'My grandson indeed,' the old man continued, 'by an excellent and honourable father. And despite the difference in our ages, my friend. But, Hanar, you are also sometimes such an innocent that I despair of your ever seeing sense.'

Santon blinked and licked his lips. He didn't know where this might be leading, but in the company of a fire-eater notorious through three generations of Alban nobility he was ready for the worst. 'Sir?' he ventured finally and braced himself for whatever blast he might have provoked. There was none.

'All this talk about high-clan lords. When you have some free time again' – and Aymar laughed both at the thought of free time and at the expression on young Santon's face, since free time for either of them was less likely than honesty in Imperial politics – 'you should go back to your histories and read for yourself how much grief those who style themselves *ilauem-arlethen* have caused down the years. Enough, and more than enough. But first, and now, read this.'

The Court Archive skidded down the table and came to a stop almost exactly where Aymar had intended that it should, in front of the younger man. That its passage upset Hanar's painstakingly sorted sheaf of notes and reports bothered him not a whit; there would be plenty more of those before the day's work was done and locked away from prying eyes.

'Read it?' The Archive was a good handspan thick, for all that its leaves were thin and the writing on them small. 'You mean, now?'

'Not all of it, boy. Just look at the pages I marked; you should find them of interest.' Aymar drew across another bundle of papers and inked his writing-brush with care, then glanced at Hanar from beneath his fierce white eyebrows. 'But read them carefully. You may well learn more than your tutors ever taught you . . .'

'Feeling better now?'

Chin-deep in the hot bath-water, Aldric stirred a little but made no reply other than a faint sigh of contentment. Eyes closed, with a pillow of rolled towelling behind his head, he both looked and sounded asleep.

Kyrin wrapped a warmed towel around herself – there were plenty more draped over a rack in front of the fire – and padded across the room to look down at him, telling herself that she was only making sure whether he was indeed asleep or just very relaxed, and that he was in no danger of slipping so far down into the tub that he might inhale some of the water. For all that, the making sure took several minutes of close study rather than the cursory glance it might otherwise have required. 'You've lost too much weight with worrying about things that you can't help, my love,' she said quietly in her own language, and then smiled. 'But you're still good to look at. Very good indeed.'

Whatever opinion Aldric might have expressed, the loss of weight was true enough and beyond argument. His face was leaner than it should have been, and the body which in her memory was broad-shouldered, square and strong was now an incomplete sketch of that remembered image, with all the big muscles defined like a surgical anatomy and ribs and pelvis stark under skin which lay too close to the bone.

'You need to stop all this errand-running,' Kyrin said. She spoke in Alban now, still reluctant to disturb him and yet half-hoping he was awake enough to listen. 'You need to stop concerning yourself with all the troubles of the world and find yourself some peace instead.' She turned away and shook her head sadly. 'I just wish the world's troubles would leave you alone to do it.'

'Do what?' Aldric's voice was lazy, an effect of the vast heat of the water, but lacked the dullness of someone recently asleep.

Kyrin looked at him and raised one eyebrow. 'Oh – so you weren't asleep at all.'

'I wouldn't dignify it by calling it sleep.' He raised one hand to rake back damp hair from his eyes, very slowly and carefully since in water so deep and hot a sudden movement might cause a spill and would certainly cause discomfort. 'But I wasn't much awake either. What were you saying?'

'Nothing much.'

Aldric gave her back the raised eyebrow – now his own were visible – and added a little to the delivery. 'You never let me get away with a response like that, so why should I let you? Tell me about nothing much.'

Kyrin exchanged her damp, cool towel for a fresh one, warm and dry, and told him just how very much the nothing much involved. 'And neither of us knows,' she finished, with anger starting to edge her words, 'who those

93

assassins were, or why they came looking, or who sent them. But they tried to kill you all the same!'

'They tried to kill you as well.'

'Just because I was in the way, or with you, or a witness.'

'Quite. And whose fault is that?'

'Oh, damn you!' Her anger flared and faded like the plume of sparks that billowed up the chimney as a log collapsed in the grate. 'If I thought you nitpicked for any reason other than to tease me, I'd . . . I'd. . . .'

'Drown me in the bath-tub?'

'And maybe I will yet.' Kyrin glanced at Aldric as he climbed from the water. 'We stay here tonight. What about tomorrow?'

'Another inn, closer to Drakkesborg.' He lifted one of the towels and scrubbed at his hair for a few seconds before elaborating a little. 'I'm in no hurry to get there.'

'Then why go at all? Why not go home to Alba?'

Aldric raised both his eyebrows. 'The old song, eh? Yet you were the one who said they knew the whys and wherefores of my going.'

Kyrin shrugged and smiled faintly. 'A girl has to try these things every now and then.'

'You don't like Drakkesborg?'

'I've never been to it. I'll go there with you, but . . . but I don't like the sound of the place.'

'I do. Imperial Drakkesborg, the City of the Dragon. But with a name like that, I'm biased anyway. And the place does have a few good things about it – theatres, for one.' He hitched at the towel wrapped around his waist which was trying to slide floorwards, draped another cape-wise across one shoulder and an outstretched arm, then cleared his throat in a portentous sort of way and assumed a dramatic pose.

'It pleases me to see the joyful season that is Autumn,'

he declaimed, rolling the words around his mouth like plum-stones:

94

For it swells the fruit upon the trees
And makes the harvest rich and tall.
And it pleases me to hear the song of the birds
Who make their mirth resound through all the woods.
And it pleases me to hear the song of silver trumpets,
And it pleases me to see upon the meadows
Tents and pavilions planted,
And the flowers of silken banners
And the raiment of fair ladies.
And it pleases me to see ranged along the field
Bold men and horses standing tall
Come from afar to make pretence of war . . .

Then the more important of the two towels gave up its struggle to hold on to Aldric's hips and slithered to the floor despite his frantic clutch, and Kyrin dissolved in helpless giggles.

'Oren Osmar's *Tiluan the Prince*,' he explained carefully, trying to keep his face straight. 'It's not really like that. At least, not exactly. . . .'

'Nothing else at all?'

'Nothing, my lord.'

'Very well.' Lord Dacurre looked tired and far older even than his seventy-three years. 'You may go. Dismissed.'

The trooper saluted crisply – more crisply than he had done before the dead King, and with more respect – then snapped around and walked from the room. Dacurre watched him go. 'I appreciate the lasting peace,' he said quietly, 'but I could almost wish that something would happen. With my fellow lords, or even with the Drusalan Warlord. Anything. Just so that I could do something about it, rather than sit here and do nothing at all.'

'You're doing far more than you need, just sitting here.' Hanar Santon had sat quietly while the soldier handed over his written report and delivered the verbal observations that went with it. Dacurre – and through his example, Santon – placed considerable value on what was thought and said, the kind of information that seldom passed from a man's mind on to paper, no matter how much of his inmost thoughts he might have tried to write. It was listening to what was said and what was felt that was of real use. Both men had often wished there was some way to glean the same knowledge from within the Drusalan Empire as they were able to obtain from inside the walls of Alba's citadels. 'Tell me, Aymar,' Santon glanced casually at the new report, then set it aside and stared at the old man, 'how much sleep have you been getting?'

'Enough.' Even as he said the word, Dacurre knew that he was wasting his breath. Hanar Santon was no more a fool than anyone else who had seen him today, and Aymar knew that trying to deceive the young man was pointless – especially since he had managed perhaps eight hours of sleep in the past seventy, and it showed.

'Of course. Then the reason you fall asleep in your chair must be other than weariness.'

'Yes; you're forgetting about boredom.' Both men grimaced at the joke which had long ceased to be funny. The luxury of enough idleness to feel bored was something they had both forgotten in the days since the King was killed.

'Boredom?' It was the standard response, but spoken now in the dull voice of a man exhausted. 'What's that?'

'It's like sleep, except you don't close your eyes.'

'Oh. Mythic vice.' Santon smiled wanly and flipped open the report again, staring at the neat script as if it no longer made any sense. He shook his head like a man walking into a cobweb. 'What day is it now?'

One look told Aymar that this was not another joke but a real and rather desperate attempt to regain a faltering hold on reality. 'Sixteenth of the twelfth.'

Kevhardu tlai'seij, de Merwin, in the formal reckoning. Rynert had been dead twenty-one days now. A lifetime. Long enough for a country to begin to die, except that the threat against its life had done nothing. And neither Dacurre nor Santon could understand the reason why. The old man stretched, trying to ease kinks in his spine which hadn't been there three weeks ago. He wasn't meant to hunch over a deskful of paperwork all day; neither of them was. But with no one else in Cerdor willing or able to do the work, somebody had to. Dacurre wished it didn't have to be him.

The knock on the Council-chamber door brought both men out of their private thoughts with a perceptible jerk, even though neither would have admitted to being startled. Whoever was outside, it was not the usual chamberlain with his diffident rapping, not unless the man had managed to get drunk in the few minutes since he had ushered in the cavalry trooper. This wasn't a polite single knuckle but a pounding fist, and Lord Dacurre knew urgency when he heard it. Caution and the memory of Rynert laid one hand on his *taipan* shortsword, twisting the weapon's safety-collar from the scabbard, before he glanced at Hanar Santon and gave the command to 'Enter!'

Both of the big doors were pulled open and seven guardsmen piled into the room with weapons drawn. Their cutting-spears made the spokes of a wheel whose hub, a handspan from each of the encircling blades, was a slim man who wore ragged grey and a tightly-buckled constabulary restraint-harness which dragged his crossed wrists up his back and almost between his shoulder-blades. Once his garments might have been a close-fitting suit with gloves, boots and hood all uniform with the tunic and breeches, but now he was clothed more in bruises and tatters than anything else. The guards had plainly borne King Rynert's fate in mind, and had been zealous both in their arrest and the subsequent search-and-subdue procedure.

'Well!' Dacurre covered his astonishment with a mono-syllabic exclamation which might have been amusement, or interest, or recognition of a familiar outline. 'We would have met before, except that I recall you were in rather a hurry to leave. I think we can chat more comfortably this time, don't you?'

Aymar Dacurre had all the detestation of any high-clan conservative for the *tulathin* mercenaries, and added to that a loathing of this particular specimen of the breed if – and Aymar had no reason so far to doubt it – the battered figure before him was the root source of all Alba's present troubles. 'You should not have come back.'

'Let me, gran—, my lord!' Santon was on his feet, equanimity and silence washed away by anger. 'I owe this *thing* for all the dirt clinging to my name and to my Honour. Let me deal with him myself.'

'Hanar, be quiet. You sound like Talvalin.' Dacurre's soft-spoken warning was more than most men were permitted, and Santon knew it. He subsided back into his seat, glowering and drumming his fingers on the sheathed *taipan* on the table in front of him but saying nothing else aloud.

Dacurre inspected the small bag laid on the table before him by the serjeant commanding the squad. It contained the results of a stringent body search: small, flat knives, a garrotting-cord, various lock-picks – and a tiny vial of thin glass which the old clan-lord rolled to and fro between finger and thumb, watching the heavy, oily movement of the fluid sealed inside. Then he stared at the *taulath*. 'You are already a dead man. And the law says this: the manner of your passing is in my hands and not,' Dacurre set the poison-vial, carefully aside, 'by your own choice.'

'Yes, old man, I know the formula.' The mercenary grinned without humour. 'I should have had that . . . choice tucked in my cheek where it belonged, and where your soldiers hit me. There would then have been no need for threats and such unpleasantness. But I'd as soon die an easy death as a hard one. So – what do you want to know?'

For a moment Lord Dacurre ignored the insolence and turned his attention instead to the guards. 'You two, bring a heavy chair and secure him in it. You, get one of the Archive clerks. You, call the steward; have him bring wine and food. You others, watch this reptile; if he moves, cripple him.' Dacurre settled back, satisfied that at long last there was activity of a sort, then glared at the guardsman ordered to fetch food who had reappeared in the doorway and looked confused. 'Yes, what?'

'My lord, the steward wants to know for how many?'

'Two, man! Two – and as many of your guardsmen as feel dry or hungry. I'll want your names afterwards – to mention favourably when I report this to your commander.'

'And what about me?' asked the *taulath*.

Dacurre stared at him, as a cat might stare at a mouse giving cheek from under the paw that caught it. Then he smiled, and not the studied smile of cruelty but something strangely tolerant for a man so capable of anger. 'Why not? For sheer nerve alone. All right, guard, get on with it.'

'He was captured in the Hall of Kings, my lord. And he was limping before we touched him.' The serjeant-of-Guards sounded just a little defensive about the state of their prisoner; that sort of mistreatment was usually the prerogative of the Drusalan Secret Police. 'Otherwise we couldn't have taken him. He's a skilled fighter, for all he's one of *them*.'

'Do I hear admiration, serjeant?' asked the *taulath* with an annoyingly arch smile. The soldier glanced sidelong at his prisoner and disdained to reply.

'All right,' said Hanar Santon, 'enough of this. Never mind whether you admire him or not, serjeant; I presume his . . . present condition is a result of that so-admirable skill.'

'Yes, my lord. Taking him alive was harder than killing him, but after what happened I thought you and my Lord Dacurre would want information rather than a corpse.'

'Commended, serjeant.' Santon sipped at a cup of wine and stared at the *taulath*. 'Your prisoner, Aymar. I still want to kill the bastard.'

'Patience. Now, you.' Dacurre returned his full attention to the man strapped in the chair. 'What name do we call you?'

'Call me Keythar,' said the *taulath*. 'In the Drusalan language it means—'

'Fox. Yes, I know that. And it isn't your name at all, is it?'

'Of course not.' The man called Fox smiled slightly. 'But that hardly matters, does it?'

'No.' Dacurre mirrored the smile exactly. 'I suppose not. But from your accent you're as Alban as I am – and I'll not speak Drusalan unless I have to, Fox.'

The *taulath* shrugged indifferently. 'It's a label, nothing more. I stopped caring about such niceties years ago.'

'A pity you are what you are; there must have been some good in you once.'

'Do I hear admiration, Lord Dacurre?' asked Hanar Santon quietly.

Dacurre looked at the younger man. 'No. Regret. You'll recognise it when you're as old as I am. Now, Fox, why did you come back to the Hall of Kings when you must have known the King was dead?'

'Well, that's the question, isn't it? Who says he's dead except those who benefit?'

This was a response that startled not only the two clan-lords but the guardsmen as well, soldiers whose duties required them to overhear many things and react to none of them. Some of these soldiers, however, had seen the ripped corpse carried from the Hall three weeks before, and the discovery that a *taulath* – one of those renowned for knowing secrets – was ignorant of just how dead a disembowelled man could be, came as a surprise.

'You really don't know?'

It might have been the tone or the wording of Dacurre's response that brought it home, but all the muscles of

Fox's face twitched as he realised just how wrong he had been. 'Ah. And I thought that the tales were spread as part of some subtle scheme to provoke unsteady clan-lords into rash action . . . or something like that.' He laughed harshly, at himself as much as at the discovery of his mistake. 'It would seem, Lord Aymar Dacurre, that old-fashioned directness is something my people must learn to consider all over again. I, they, all of us were thinking in curves and spirals; thinking in straight lines is unfashionable in modern politics.'

'You still haven't explained why you came back.'

'That one, the guard with the red beard – have him empty the belt-pouch he took from me. You'll find out.'

The pouch held what Dacurre had expected it might: leaves of scrip drawn on the Crown Treasury, each with the red and black sigil stamps that indicated a nominal face value of one thousand Alban marks. They were crushed and twisted as if someone had begun to destroy them and then thought better of it. Dacurre unfolded one of the ragged bundles of paper and looked at it, nodding as he saw where the problem lay. 'Rynert's authorisation,' he said. 'These are useless.'

The *taulath* nodded, and smiled a thin-lipped smile that showed how much he was pretending not to care. 'As you both know, I've been out of the country,' he said. 'One of my people here tried turning that garbage into coin. I found out when I got back. So here I am.'

'Trying to get your fee in silver,' Dacurre finished for him. 'Or get the value of it from Rynert's hide. A pity that he's dead.'

'Don't think I wouldn't have done it either,' said the *taulath*. 'I . . . we . . . have our principles. We don't like to be cheated.'

'Not cheated,' Hanar Santon corrected. 'Outmanoeuvred. You should have tried to get your money before you killed Aldric Talvalin, not afterwards.'

'I said cheated, and I used the word correctly.' For all that he was battered, bloodied and trussed like a bird for the oven, Fox was very much on his dignity – as much dignity, at least, as two high-clan-lords would give a mercenary killer credit for possessing. 'Talvalin isn't alone, and—'

'Tehal Kyrin, too? You cold-hearted butcher!' Santon's voice went shrill with rage and as he came out of his chair his shortsword was slicing from its sheath again. 'This time I *will* kill you!'

'Sit *down*!' Dacurre glared at the younger man, then shook his head at the impatience of the younger generation. 'Hanar, just every now and then why don't you stop and think before you make a fool of yourself?'

'I don't know what you mean . . .'

'Evidently. Think, I said.'

'But you heard him – he said—'

Dacurre sighed. Once again the facts would have to be spelt out for Santon's benefit. It wasn't that the boy was stupid, far from it, but like his father before him once an idea got itself lodged in a Santon mind a team of horses wouldn't shift it. 'He said that Aldric isn't alone. Present tense; doesn't that suggest anything to you? That perhaps he isn't dead either?'

'Oh. I see . . . now.'

Fox had remained quiet while the two lords wrangled, but when Dacurre looked towards him again he shrugged as elaborately as his bonds allowed. 'The girl doesn't concern me – and didn't then; she wasn't a part of the contract and I wasn't paid to deal with her. If she'd been in the way, well . . .' Another shrug. 'But your dear King said nothing about a bodyguard.'

'Bodyguard?' Aymar Dacurre blinked in surprise. This didn't sound like the lethal swordsman he knew – or thought he knew. 'Aldric Talvalin doesn't have a bodyguard. Never had one, so far as I know.'

'He's got one now: six Drusalans. And you might be interested to know' – the *taulath* Fox smiled like his namesake – 'they're just as much *tulathin* as I am.'

Santon glowered at him, wanting to believe one aspect

of the mercenary's statement but unwilling to trust the other. Before the Light of Heaven, Aldric was capable of doing such a thing, as he had proven himself capable of so much more, but while sorcery had a certain dark glamour to it the employment of *tulathin* was just dirty. It wasn't part of the Talvalin style. 'How do we know that you're telling the truth about this?' he demanded. 'How can we believe you about anything?'

'My Lord Dacurre,' said Fox, 'tell him the reason why.'

Aymar didn't turn his head to address Santon directly, even though he could sense that he was being watched for a reply. Instead he gazed at the *taulath*. 'Because,' he said softly, 'you believe me.'

Fox nodded. He believed completely and without any of the many doubts his own subtle and tortuous mind could conjure up, because this old, white-bearded balding man held the dwindling duration of his life by a thread. If Lord Dacurre was unconvinced of anything that he was told, he would go searching for what he thought was the truth with all the means at his disposal. His Honour bound the promise of brief death; that same Honour bound the promise of a death that would be screams and anguish from the beginning to the ending of it.

'And because of your belief in me,' said Aymar Dacurre, 'I choose to believe in you. Hanar, he is speaking the truth as best he can. There are matters here I do not begin to understand, and matters beneath them that I have no desire to understand. Talvalin is alive. Good. But unless, being alive, he is doing something to keep Grand Warlord Etzel safe at home, his life or death is of small importance here.'

'Etzel is dead.'

The silence that followed on Fox's words was such that all in the room except for the *taulath* might have been struck dead themselves. Hanar Santon and the younger guards had known the name of Warlord Etzel as a kind of bogeyman rather than as a figure with any reality, political or otherwise, and to be told of his death was a greater shock in its way than to learn of the death of a parent. Dacurre was simply relieved. He knew that other and more complex feelings would soon take over, but just for the present Fox's news came as a tonic to offset the weariness of so many, many sleepless nights.

It was only a matter of minutes before the first niggling suspicion cut into his private euphoria. 'But how did you come to know this, when you knew nothing about Rynert?' he demanded, and fixed the *taulath* with a quizzical stare. Fox matched and returned it with as much added expression as the reflection in a mirror.

'I heard about it through my usual sources of Imperial information – sources which have little interest in Alba even when they have nothing else to occupy their minds. What occupies those minds right now is the new Warlord's behaviour. You might find it encouraging. He hasn't been seen in public since it was announced eighteen days ago that he had assumed the rank and style of *Woydach*. From the commands that issue from the citadel in Drakkesborg he seems more intent on recovering those provinces which have seceded from the Empire over the past few years than in pursuing Etzel's old policy of war against Alba. Either way, he's secure; and so, it seems, are you. Assuming that my sources are correct, of course, and that you can get anyone in this country to believe the word of a *taulath*.'

'Never mind that,' snapped Dacurre, never at his best when someone else presumed to guess at what he might be thinking. 'I'll make them believe.'

The *taulath* Fox inclined his head, gazing at nothing in particular; then he smiled a uniquely chilly little smile as if at some private and unpleasant joke. 'Of course you will. Alban clan-lords always pay attention to what *tulathin* say, when it comes second-hand from one of their own. Except that they're not paying attention to anything you say at all right now, are they? Oh, and before you think to have it beaten out of me, the new Warlord is a man called Voord . . . late of the Secret Police. You might well know his name already . . .'

Dacurre and Santon looked at one another. They knew the name indeed; they knew, too, how closely Voord's actions in the past few years had intertwined with the military and political fate of Alba – and with the making of a notorious swordsman and sorcerer from the honour-fixated survivor of one of Alba's oldest families. When they had at last learned all that there was to be known about the situation, it had seemed to both of them that Fate had woven opposites together for the sake of entertainment: life and death, honour and magic, Aldric Talvalin and Voord Ebanesj. What the end of the skein might be, neither man felt qualified even to guess.

The *taulath* who called himself Fox sat still and silent now. He had said all that there was for him to say, freely and without the need for violent persuasion, and all that remained was for Aymar Dacurre to keep his promise. There was not – nor since his capture ever had been – any chance of reprieve or escape; the *taulath* understood that and waited quietly to die. Once the two clan-lords finished their hasty whispered discussion, the short time of waiting was over.

Hanar Santon nodded once to Dacurre and stood up, more calmly now than on the past two occasions when he had surged out of his chair fired with the desire to kill. There was no longer hot blood in what he did, but the vast impartial weight of the Law.

'Man-called-Fox,' he said, 'Aymar Lord Dacurre is satisfied with your . . . assistance. The law has given us your life, and even if we were inclined we could not return it. What we return, by the command of Lord Dacurre, is your choice of means to take your leave of the life held forfeit. So choose.' Santon remained standing, but said nothing more.

The *taulath* looked at his judges and shrugged. 'Why say, when you both know already.' He was staring now at the vial Dacurre held in finger and thumb. 'That way.'

'In wine?' offered Dacurre. It was courtesy, not curiosity, which prompted his question, for by tradition someone about to die either by legal execution or by their own hand in the *tsepanek'ulleth* ritual was accorded more respect than their crime or their rank might have warranted. It was not, and never had been, a matter open to question.

'No, just in my mouth. The broken glass cuts, you see, and the venom enters the bloodstream . . .' There was a glint of cold amusement in Fox's eyes at the way young Santon winced.

Dacurre did not afford him that pleasure, but the old man's lips went very thin. Poison had played its part in the shaping of Alba, but it was a part lacking in any honour. 'You will forgive me,' he said, 'if I ask you to put your head back and allow me to drop this . . . this choice of yours from a distance safely away from your teeth and any splinters of glass you might consider surplus.'

The *taulath* laughed aloud, very softly but with real rather than gallows humour. He had the look of someone who appreciated the black joke. 'If we had met in another place and another time, my lord,' he said, 'I think I might have liked you – enough at least to grant you the same favour you grant me.' He tilted back his head and opened his mouth as a child might when being dosed with medicine, received the pellet and crunched it like a sweet.

'How long?' Dacurre asked.

'My lord, I thought the questions were finished.' Fox grinned, and there was blood on his teeth; slivered glass glittered between them like diamonds. 'And anyway, I don't know. Nobody does for certain. The herbalist who distils it says "quite fast", but he hasn't used it so what does he know?'

Fox chuckled – then gasped, his eyes going wide as his whole body spasmed against the straps holding him into the chair. It passed, and he relaxed enough to grin that bloody grin again. 'Perhaps he does know some—'

Another convulsion drummed his heels against the floor, and whatever he had been about to say was lost in the chattering of his teeth. There was sweat on his face as the clench of muscles calmed to an irregular tic in all his limbs, but he was still grinning though by now it was more the rictus of a naked skull. 'Uncomfortable,' Fox somehow contrived to say, 'but not really painful. Better than a *tsepan* any—'

His jaws clicked shut and cut the words off short as a final spasm killed him.

FIVE

There was rioting in Drakkesborg.

Its cause was straightforward enough; even in the second-wealthiest city in the Empire – and there were those who quibbled even at that qualification of 'second' – prices double and even treble those of bare months past were not to be borne. Such inflations happened every once in a while, the consequence of poor harvests, but never before had the merchants dared such market-place piracy as they were attempting now, and never before had the Grand Warlord allowed them to get away with it once the matter had been brought before him by citizens' deputation. Ironarse Etzel, they called him in the lower city – that and other, coarser things – but it could never be denied that here in Drakkesborg at least he always had time to hear complaints and problems. Until now.

The majority of rumours could be easily discarded; too high-flown for belief, most of them, and the remainder unlikely at best. But the fact remained that *Woydach* Etzel had been neither seen nor heard from for close to three weeks now, and that was where informed speculation took the place of rumour. There were those who said that speculation was just rumour in a finer coat, but they were the same bandiers of semantics who listened eagerly to the latest piece of gossip – or rather, educated opinion – and contributed their own thoughts to whatever the opinion had concerned. All in the most elegantly turned phrases, of course.

The business of these shocking prices, for one thing: nothing to do with poor harvests, at least not this year since the harvest had been if not spectacular then certainly more than adequate. No, the problem this time was the Emperor's intransigence. A mere child, truculently refusing the advice of elders and betters that had been quite adequate for his father and brother. A shame that Ravek had died so suddenly – he would have made a much better Emperor, certainly more tractable than Ioen who was so eager to dance to the tune of his chief military commander. *Coerhanalth Goth*, wasn't it? Nothing but a common soldier. All his fault, probably. Dividing the Empire down the middle like a wheel of cheese, what way was that to run a country? And he was probably responsible for the trade sanctions behind these price rises. A Lord-General, eh? Maybe – but not a gentleman.

And so it went on. Etzel, the story went, was closeted with his own chief military men, organising a strategy to recover the Western Empire, remove Ioen from subversive influences, and very possibly bring the secessionist provinces back into the Imperial sphere of influence – although this last was scoffed at rather, for Etzel himself had let it be known that if places like Vreijaur and Jouvann were unwilling to remain a part of the Empire, then he would be unwilling to invite them back when they discovered the error of their ways. Although the man really should have taken the time to listen when that company of solid wide-waisted worthies had brought their petition to the citadel, or at the very least come out to receive it with his own hand rather than sending a lackey of no matter how high a rank. To be busy was one thing, and quite understandable; to be discourteous was another thing entirely.

That was what had sparked the riots, more than the prices or the scarcities or the rumour-mongers: the notion, seized on by people of the lower sort, that if they were to gain any satisfaction they would have to find it themselves. Reasonable requests had turned swiftly to demands, then threats, and before anyone with authority to stop it could do anything the stones began to fly. Market stalls were torn down and torn apart, the traders who owned them were pelted with the broken fragments and with their own expensive produce – as much of it as remained after the looters were done with it – and though no injuries more serious than black eyes and bloody noses had so far been reported, it was only a matter of time before Authority reacted and someone was killed. At least, someone among those who were still capable of dying. . . .

'Giorl, please – none of that matters now. Just do something . . .' The Grand Warlord of the Drusalan Empire lay on his back and panted like a dog with the effort of uttering coherent speech rather than the wordless whimpering which was all his mouth could usually form during these sessions. The woman he addressed – or more properly, pleaded with – paid him small heed and continued her gentle probing of his wounds. If her hands were gentle, the expression on her face was not.

'I'm doing it, damn you! But I still want to know what bloody horse-doctor put these bloody stitches in.' The voice was angry, yet curiously dispassionate, that of a skilled artist outraged by needlessly sloppy work. 'And why they rotted out before the wounds healed. Because I have to find the fragments, good my lord, before you start to rot as well. Another. And this one needs to be cut free, too. Here. Swallow this; all of it.' The stuff in the cup was a liquid mingling of sweet and bitter, she knew, and knew how hard it was to choke the fluid down, and how long she had to wait before it took effect. Not long, that much was certain. '*Schii'ajn nahr kagh-hui dah* . . .'

Her words became a soft monotone of curses in half-a-dozen languages as she selected something small and glittering from the flat metal case beside her. Voord braced himself, trying to blot out what was about to happen by staring at her clean white browband and the locks of red hair that feathered over it. He had always found Giorl attractive – the attraction of the unattainable since, being married and that unusual thing, faithfully so, she had invariably rejected his advances with more or less good humour – and never more so than when he watched her work. Perhaps because he had never been the subject of that work. Even today, filled with pain and soporific drugs, the sight of her preparations and the first chill touch of an instrument had brought immediate, blatant arousal. That drained away perhaps three seconds later when, despite the soporifics, he began to scream.

Giorl Derawn knew that she was many things to many people: a good wife with a good husband, rare enough these days; a good mother to her daughters and to the third child on the way which she hoped would be a son; a good – indeed indispensable – servant of the Grand Warlord whoever he, she or it might be; and never mind the good, she was the best cutting-surgeon in the city of Drakkesborg.

She had often wondered why. Most surgeons were men, nowadays, and the old freedoms for working women were being eroded by the military society in the Eastern Empire, but nobody had ever dared to question her skill. Maybe it was her ever-increasing knowledge of anatomy, or her ability to distance herself from the work in hand whatever that work might be – to filter out the reactions and the noises and see only the area of flesh on which she worked – or her lack of emotional concern about the pain involved. It was a part of what she did, that was all, and her customary response to questions, arguments and pleas was simply to remember and invoke what giving birth was like.

At least it was nothing like this. She had seen many, many human bodies reduced to glistening tatters; but she had never before seen wounds that refused to bleed, or heal, or kill. Giorl did indeed want to know which of the Bodyguard's regimental surgeons had cobbled Voord back together; but this had little to do with her anger over what looked more like clumsy sailmaking than sutured wounds. She wanted to find out what the injuries had looked like when they were fresh, and she had a suspicion that they had been no different from the way they appeared right now. At least he had stopped screaming.

At last Giorl finished and straightened her back, grunting slightly as her muscles made known their complaint right up her spine. Tweezering out the shreds and fragments of rotted sutures was not, perhaps, as noisy, nerve-racking or downright nasty as many of the things she had done, but she could still think of a great many things that she would sooner have been doing. Caring for her youngest daughter was one of them; the child had been unwell for the past couple of days, feverish and off her food. The instruments clinked faintly as she returned them to their padded clamps in the metal case.

And Voord groaned faintly as she stood up and turned to walk away from him.

Giorl froze in mid-stride, not wanting to believe the sound and yet knowing she had heard it. '*Teii-acht ha'v-raal*,' she swore, very softly. 'Father and Mother and Maiden make it not so.' The prayer must not have been heard, for when she looked back over her shoulder it was so: Voord was still alive.

Any drug whose purpose was to induce the peace of anaesthetic sleep was a systemic poison which could, in a sufficient quantity, induce the far more permanent peace of death. That had been Giorl's intention, anyway. The poppy distillate which she had given Voord had been of such a concentration that it should have stopped his pain and then his heart in a matter of a few minutes. However, it had done no more than render him a little drowsy, and that drowsiness was already wearing off to let the pain come back. Such a thing was medically impossible; but then, his continued survival of such obviously fatal injuries was just as impossible, and he had survived those for twenty days. Both impossibilities stared at her with agonised eyes and hoped silently that she could do something – *anything* – to help.

Giorl concealed her shrug and returned to Voord's bedside, wondering what in the name of Hell she *could* do. The most obvious thing to do, she had done already; and it hadn't worked. As for the alternatives . . . Giorl looked at the gaping holes in Voord's face and body and wondered what the alternatives might be. And if there were any.

'The stitching helped.' Voord's weak and shaky voice cut through her indecision. 'When they were closed, the . . . the wounds didn't hurt as much.'

'Stitches don't work,' said Giorl gently. 'You've seen already. If these don't heal – and I've seen they don't – then the severed tissue will just outlast the sutures the way they did today and you'll be right back where you were when I came in . . . and facing the same prospect. Your choice.' Voord cringed visibly. 'But maybe if you told me how these happened' – inside her head Giorl was smiling grimly as, like it or not, she slipped into the surgeon's customary bedside manner – 'I might be able to work out what to do about them.'

Voord met her steady gaze for a few seconds, then very pointedly turned his face away, stifling the moan that the movement provoked.

'That won't help. Don't forget, I'm good at getting questions answered.' Giorl saw a shudder raise gooseflesh on his naked skin. 'I'm good even without using pressure, so why not talk about it? Eh?' She reached out one hand and laid it gently on his chest, absently noting the movements of heartbeat and respiration – both over-fast – as she did so. 'Talking might help for all sorts of reasons, Voord Ebanesj.' The rapid rise and fall of his rib-cage faltered as he held his breath, whether in reaction to the use of his full name or hearing a voice that had honest, if merely professional, sympathy in it. And then the words all came tumbling out.

Aldric and Kyrin rode into Drakkesborg late in the afternoon, through the main gate in the western wall, the Shadowgate, with the fast-setting midwinter sun at their backs stretching their own shadows long and dark across the snow. The guards at the gate seemed preoccupied with other matters than the searching of baggage, and after the most cursory of inspections were quite willing to accept impressively signed and sealed scholarly passes at face value, without any curiosity as to why two foreign 'scholars' should be so well armed and armoured. Or perhaps the guards knew perfectly well why anyone would want to have weapons and battle harness close at hand. Neither the Empire nor its cities were especially peaceful places, and right now Drakkesborg was no exception.

After a period of 'not noticing' the riots in the hope that the outburst of initially justified protest would burn itself out, notice had formally been taken two days earlier by Authority in the shape of the city's Chief of Constables. Warnings had been posted after the first day and read aloud by official criers at the height of the second day's trouble. Nobody had paid the criers any attention, except to pelt them with offal and with serious snowballs – frozen, and cored with chunks of broken paving.

Notice had progressed to action fairly rapidly after that. Ten squads of troopers from the urban militia had moved out of barracks at first light, and by mid-morning they had restored order of a sort in their own inimitable fashion. It was only because of lenience prompted by the Midwinter holiday season that no lives were lost, but there were aching skulls and broken limbs enough to suppress the fire of civil disobedience in even the hottest head. So complete was that suppression that by the time Aldric and Kyrin were cleared to enter the city, Drakkesborg was restored to at least a veneer of normality – for all that the veneer was not quite thick enough as yet to make them feel entirely comfortable . . .

'I told you, didn't I?' Kyrin's voice was low; the things she was saying were not the kind of things she wanted overheard. 'I said I didn't like the sound of this place. And now we're here, you say that you don't like the feel of it. Very perceptive, Aldric my love. But just a little slow.'

Aldric smiled to himself at her unease – a thin smile, without amusement. He had been wondering how long it

114

would take to come out, and was too much the gentleman to make comment about how she had come to be in the city in the first place. 'At least the passes worked,' he said mildly.

'They got us in, dear. I'd feel happier if I was convinced they'll get us out again.'

'Marevna made certain that they showed no bias to either faction.'

'Meaning you get picked on by both, not neither. I for one would like to get in off the street, with a bolted door between me and whatever's been going on here.'

'Faction fights or something. Tuenafen was like this and—'

'I don't want to know what happened, Aldric.' Kyrin was growing more twitchy with each passing second, regardless of the way ordinary people went about their ordinary business around her. Or perhaps because of it, and because of the way it failed to ring quite true. 'I want to find a place where I can avoid it if it happens again. Now, where?'

That was the problem. Neither knew much about Imperial Drakkesborg apart from their own preconceived opinions, and opinions were of small use in suggesting where to stay, much less how much they would be expected to pay for the privilege. Enough, and more than enough, most likely; the cost of a room for the night had increased steadily and steeply as they approached the city, and the risk that they no longer had sufficient coin to live on had become a nagging worry at the back of Kyrin's mind. However, the problem seemed not to concern Aldric.

'I have no idea where. But first we need some cash money.' He spoke with nothing like the gravity their situation warranted, and Kyrin looked at him as if he had left good sense behind.

'Just where do you plan to find it? Buried in a snow-drift? Or will you just use the Echainon spellstone to conjure it out of a handful of gravel?'

'Don't be sarcastic, love, it doesn't suit you.' As he spoke, his face became an icy mask that warned her she was going just a little bit too far. 'And don't mention It. Not here. Just . . . don't. I know the Imperial coinage isn't worth a lot, but there are some limits.' Aldric reined Lyard to a standstill and glanced at the citizens walking past, looking for the mode of dress that would indicate the sort of person he sought. 'There. That's the kind of man we need.'

He indicated a passer-by whose noble curve of belly and rich robes might have produced a cheerful demeanour, but whose face had more the appearance of someone who lived on pickled lemons. Kyrin followed the direction of his gesture, then pointedly raised her eyebrows as Aldric dismounted and began a brief, one-sided conversation. He was doing most of the talking – none of which she could make sense of through the background buzz of other people – while the fat man's responses were a mixture of monosyllables and silent head movements. His sour expression had deepened when he was accosted about his presumably lawful occasions by a complete stranger who had both a foreign accent and a sword, but as Aldric continued to speak in what, from his frequent grins, must at least have sounded pleasant, the man's eyes became a touch less flinty. As he pointed out what were presumably directions, Kyrin could see the movement of facial muscles trying to assume the long-forgotten configuration of a smile, but only succeeding in suggesting that the last meal of lemons was fighting back.

Aldric saw the man on his way with a courteous half-bow and an inclination of his head that Kyrin noticed was covering a chuckle, then swung back into the saddle. His grin was very wide and white, and seemed somehow to be stuck in place. 'Silly old bastard,' he said pleasantly. 'You try to be charming and what do you get?'

'Do tell,' said Kyrin. The question didn't really need an answer that she could provide.

'Information. Old vinegar-face wasn't exactly chatty,

but at least he told me what I wanted – where to find some money.' Heeling Lyard into a leisurely walk, he swung the big courser around in the direction his informant had indicated.

'How much money?'

'Enough,' he said over his shoulder, 'to make the question of what we'll have to pay for a room one we don't need to worry about.'

'Are you feeling all right, Aldric?' It was only half-way to a joke, because there was nothing in the baggage they could sell except for the two ponies which carried it, and he knew as well as she how little else they owned that could be turned into coinage. As an urgent heel in grey K'schei's ribs brought her level, Kyrin could see that his wide grin had relaxed to an ordinary smile.

'Oh yes.' He stared over Lyard's ears and kept on smiling. 'I feel just fine – and so will you, soon.' He flicked one finger at the tooling of his saddle as if chivvying a fly – except that there were no flies in a Drusalan winter. 'Listen: once there was a man who was asked to do a favour. It was the sort of favour that—'

'Come to the point, will you! What so-crafty scheme have you got to pull out of your sleeve this time, eh?'

'Not a scheme, and not a sleeve. Scrip and saddle are the words you need. There's a letter of credit sewn into the welting just here' – again the fly-swatting flick – 'and we're heading for the mercantile quarter of the city to find the guild which honours it.'

Kyrin blinked, then grinned, then laughed aloud. 'You! I should have guessed! Your sour friend was a merchant, then?'

'No friend of mine, love. Yes – and a wealthy one.'

'He didn't look to enjoy life much.'

'Each to his own delight in life. I've found mine.'

'I know.' She leaned over, reaching out to touch his hand. 'And I'm glad.'

Aldric returned the pressure of her fingers, the pinkness about cheeks and ears not entirely a result of the cold air.

He could still be very shy, sometimes, about the most innocent public displays of affection; and Kyrin could remember other times when he was not shy at all.

'One thing you didn't ask.'

'Mm?'

' "How much is the credit letter worth?" Unless you're not really interested.' With finger and thumb he eased the letter itself from the saddle-stitching – it was superfine parchment, rolled small as a quill – and waved it in front of her nose before tucking it into the deep cuff of his glove.

'Uh, no. I mean, yes. I mean, how much is the credit letter worth?' She could tell already, from the glitter in his eyes, that he wasn't carrying small change.

'Does a value of thirty thousand deniers make you feel a little happier? Because that's what we have, if we need it.'

Tehal Kyrin, Harek's daughter, had suffered many shocks and surprises since she took up with this young Alban nobleman, but she had never been the butt of jokes and wasn't pleased at being used as one right now. Then, as he began to explain the system which made the letter work, a system which her own family had used in their foreign trade dealings, she realised that he wasn't joking after all.

'But why so much?'

'No more than a precaution. I'd sooner have more available funds than I'd ever need to call on than be without enough – especially with the direction the Empire's currency has been taking of late.' He extended an index finger, then stabbed it towards the ground. 'Downwards all the way. At least bullion gold is still reliable.'

'However did you get so much? I . . .' Kyrin hesitated, not sure how he would take what she was about to say, then ventured the observation away. 'I never thought you were so rich.'

Aldric seemed to find her confusion funny rather than offensive. 'What you mean is that you never dreamed you'd see me with more than a handful of silver to my name. Eh?' Somewhat shame-faced, Kyrin nodded. 'Uh-huh. Well, all you need is to remember what my name is . . . and the rank, and the style, and the title that go with it: *Ilauem-arluth inyen'kai Talvalin.* Once in a while it's pleasant to find all of that's worth more than just a point of aim for other people's weapons.'

'You're doing this the usual way, with guild authority over existing funds?'

'Only about one-third of what was available.' Aldric smiled crookedly. 'I didn't want to be greedy.'

'Oh, Heaven forbid. But if you've had a falling-out with Rynert the King, then can't he take control of your treasury?'

Aldric shook his head; he'd already considered that risk. It was why his negotiations were with Guild Freyjan rather than with a smaller guild working on a less usurious rate of interest. Guild Freyjan's interest, at least where he was concerned, wasn't merely on him but in him. They liked to take care of their investment at both ends of the trans-action; and only if Rynert had gone completely insane would he dare locking horns with a merchant guild cap-able of bringing all trade both in and out of Alba to a dead stop. 'He might risk commandeering the gold I didn't pledge to the guild – if the other lords allowed him to set that sort of dangerous precedent – but if he stole what Freyjan's regard as their own property until I surren-der the credit note, then they'd lay such trading sanctions on Alba that he'd be forced to back down within a week.'

'Very clever. I applaud you.'

'Quietly, or people will wonder.' He reined in and winked at her as he slid from Lyard's saddle to the snow-sprinkled ground. 'And we don't want the people in here to wonder any more than they have to already.' The elab-orate crest of Guild Freyjan worked in brass above the door told Kyrin plainly enough what 'in here' was. She nodded at him and patted her gloved palms together very softly, then followed him to the ground.

119

They secured both pairs of horses to the hitching-rail which Freyjan's had so thoughtfully provided for their equestrian customers, dropped a coin or two into the upturned palm of the liveried guild servant whose duty it was to make sure that the animals weren't stolen or their gear interfered with while their owners were away, and went inside House Freyjan. Inside was lit by good quality oil-lamps, and managed to convey an air of unruffled efficiency which Kyrin supposed made those who came through Freyjan's doors feel that their money was not being put to flippant use. All that efficiency served only to give everyone they met a few seconds' free time in which to look at them, either with frank curiosity or in the more indirect way that passed for manners. Aldric was long since used to the sidelong glances which people directed more or less covertly at him; the black and silver clothing which he preferred was a statement of faction in the Drusalan Empire, indicating his support for the *Woydachul*, the Grand Warlord's party. The menacing presence of a combat-slung longsword probably had something to do with it as well.

'Sir, milady?' The speaker – he was using Jouvaine, but then in the worlds of art and literature, diplomacy and its bastard cousin finance, who didn't? – was hardly the sort of man Kyrin expected to see in a mercantile house. Mid-twenties like Aldric, or a little younger, he towered over both of them and from the set of his face was torn between curiosity and a definite dislike of the fact that they were both wearing swords. For his part, he was wearing not only a sword but a small repeater crossbow, and half-armour besides; though the fact that everything was marked with the guild crest made it all right . . . more or less.

'Cash conversion,' she heard Aldric say, sounding more authoritative then he probably felt. 'Credit scrip to Drusalan florins. Cipher code authority *kourgath*.'

'Sir.' The word had a definite 'so *you* say' feel about it, but the guard was courtesy personified as he gestured them to comfortably quilted chairs set by a table which bore a dish of nuts, dried fruits and other small-foods on the same tray as goblets and a flagon of wine. Aldric glanced at the hospitalities and gave a perfunctory nod which managed to suggest that he had expected nothing less, then settled down to take his ease until whoever was to speak to him came out and did so.

The man who emerged was moving with more brisk enthusiasm than the guard's studied lethargy might have suggested was available in the whole building, but then – small and tubby though he might have been – this newcomer evidently knew what that particular code authority was all about. Gossip travels, even in merchant banks. He bowed nicely to Kyrin, deeply to Aldric, sat down and let it be known that after the customary procedures were complete he was at their disposal for as much cash as they cared to handle. At the usual rate of interest and currency conversion charges, of course . . .

'It seems to me,' said Giorl severely once Voord's confession had run its course, 'that you're lucky to be even this much alive.'

'I don't know what you mean.' Exhausted from the pain of injury, the pain of surgery and the soul-wrenching effort of telling everything about his present situation to the one person in the Empire he least wanted to know about it, *Woydach* Voord was content merely to lie still on the thin, hard mattress of sponge-clean leather and be glad he wasn't hurting more than usual.

'I mean that instead of just these mortal wounds which neither heal nor kill you, what about being trapped in a body which had truly died and was decomposing all around your still-living awareness of it? At least you have the good fortune to be reasonably intact.' Giorl polished one of her surgical probes on a piece of soft cloth and studied it incuriously. 'But from all I've heard, the high stakes in sorcery demand a high price. I'll stick to more natural skills, thanks very much. Now, about these cuts and all the other mess . . . you say that closing the wounds eases the pain?'

'Yes, damn you, I've said so already!' Voord would have shouted at her had the strain of producing anything above a whisper not begun to squeeze his entrails out of the holes in either flank. He collapsed back again, panting and bathed in sweat. 'Yes. Close them . . . please.'

'Sutures won't work, the dermal layer outlasts them; we know that much already . . .' Giorl was talking more to herself than Voord, the words mostly medical terms, no more than audible thought and not making much sense to a layman even in his full senses, never mind one who was delirious and almost insane with agony. 'Yes, yes,' she said after a while, emerging from her muttered reverie, 'we could try that, it would at least create no further harm . . .'

'What are you talking about, woman?' Voord stared straight up at the ceiling and tried to control his temper and impatience, because losing one or both did nothing except cause him more pain.

'Silver wire. I could use it to close the cuts and repair the remains of the other damage. It wouldn't rot, and it wouldn't react against your body tissue.'

'Silver wire.' He repeated the words as if tasting them. 'Have you done this before?'

'No.' The blunt frankness of Giorl's reply was supported by what else she had to say. 'And I haven't tried to heal a man who ought to be three weeks dead, either – just before you ask.'

The sound Voord made was like a cat being sick. Only Giorl, more familiar than anyone else in the city with the sounds humans could make under great stress, could have identified it as a laugh. 'Do I win the match?' she asked.

'Only half the points,' said Voord. 'You're forgetting who I am.' He grinned at her, a horrid expression like that on the face of a five-day corpse. 'The Grand Warlord deserves gold wire at least.'

Giorl stared at him, then laughed softly at the determined, ironic attempt at humour. Suffering seemed to be doing something to improve the Voord she knew, changing him inside, maybe even making him into a better person more able to appreciate the difficulties of others. Or maybe not. But it would be an interesting development to watch. 'Of course, my lord,' she said, still laughing just a little. 'Gold wire indeed, my lord. And would my lord also care for little jewels where the ends of wire are twisted together . . . ? Of course,' Giorl continued after a moment, 'I can't use pure gold wire. Too soft. Where would I find silver-gilt?'

'Send one of my body-servants to the fortress armoury. They should have what you want.'

'What I want, *Woydach*, is to go home. There are other things that need doing.'

'Afterwards. I come first.'

Giorl kept the obvious comment to herself and spoke to a summoned servant instead. Once the man had gone about her business, she returned her attentions to Voord and to the confidences he had imparted to her. She had never met a sorcerer before, and apart from curiosity had never really wanted to. Giorl disapproved of users of the Art Magic – not in the same way as the Imperial Courts of Law might do, but simply because in her experience there was already trouble enough in the world without bringing in more from Outside. Voord's present situation was a case in point. The thought of living this horrific half-life was enough to make even her skin creep, and the one way to hope for escape was a route along which she would guide him only with the greatest reluctance.

'Have you considered,' she said at last, 'trying to shake free of this curse by the . . . ah . . . same means as it was laid on you? Have you attempted to reverse the spell?'

'Yes, and no.'

'Mother and Maiden, man, why not?'

Voord's teeth showed as his lips twitched back in an expression somewhere between rueful smile and snarl of

123

impatience. 'Because,' he said, 'no matter what it says in children's stories, sorcery is rather more than just the waving of a wand. To grant power, it needs power. And the sorcery I need takes more than most. I couldn't do it and survive the strain, not like this, except that . . . that now, "not surviving" might mean something worse than death. I'm afraid to die and find I'm still alive . . .'

'There should be enough here to keep us comfortable,' said Aldric, hefting a money-purse in the palm of his hand.

'After the trouble they put you through, I should think so.' Kyrin was still feeling somewhat ruffled by what had been so lightly introduced as 'customary procedures', the way Guild Freyjan had checked and investigated everything to do with Aldric before parting with anything more substantial than good manners, and that he himself had been completely unconcerned did only a little to calm her down.

The cipher code was only the first step. After that, and with the big guard in close attendance, had come comparisons with what was presumably a description prepared and circulated by the Guild House in Alba; comparisons that were ticked off a list like a housewife shopping in the market. Height, weight (there were slight problems with *that* one), eye colour, visible scars, seals and similar means of identification and finally, comparison through lenses of thumbprints made on glass.

When first setting up this financial arrangement back in Alba, Aldric had provided two-score and some-odd prints of each thumb on small strips of glass, one for each of the Houses set up by Guild Freyjan to manage their affairs. These had been sent out together with a copy of the identification chart and would be utilised, they had told him, to make certain that the person attempting to make use of Talvalin money was the person entitled to it. He had provided a fresh thumbprint today, on another

124

strip of glass, and they had both watched while one of the Guild's experts in such matters had compared the prints, first side by side and then with the new overlaying the old, looking for points of similarity or difference. Only when that had been completed was Kyrin able to detect real warmth in any Guildsman's smile. And more important still, the guard had been dismissed.

Apart from finally getting to use his own money, Aldric also gained some advice – free, for a wonder; there were few enough things in a Guild House that didn't have some sort of price tag – concerning lodging-taverns in the city. From the shape of him, the Guildsman who provided the information was most likely recommending not only which tavern had the best rooms for the best price, but the best food for any price. That was all right; neither Kyrin nor Aldric had ever known each other to be averse to a good meal . . .

'It's getting late, m'love. Let's get to where we're going.'

'Good.' Kyrin hunched down into the deep fur lining her hood and watched as a single snowflake dropped like a feather from the evening sky. 'He made it sound a good place to stay, at least.'

'And eat. I'd say he—'

The woman came running down the street towards them, stumbling, skidding on the snow that traffic had packed down between the cobblestones and screaming, always screaming. Her words were Drusalan, more or less – maybe a local dialect or something of the sort – but whatever the reason, she was ignored. More than ignored: ostentatiously rejected. People returning home on foot the short distance from where they had been shopping in the mercantile quarter of Drakkesborg, merchant families of quality who had town houses hereabouts, actually turned their backs to her, pretending that neither she nor her frantic shrieks existed.

Not understanding anything but the poor woman's distress, Aldric shot a glance at Kyrin; it was returned augmented by a shrug that said plainly *your choice*. Kyrin suspected that she knew only too well why this woman was being treated as an outcast, and if Aldric didn't know now was hardly the time to educate him. That need for a decision, and reasons to help make it, were perhaps what prompted the Alban to knee Lyard sideways, blocking the street. No matter how crazed she might be, the woman was at least sane enough not to attempt barging past a pack-pony linked by leading-reins to sixteen hands and a good many pounds'-weight of coal-black warhorse.

'What's the matter?' Aldric asked it courteously; more courteously than he needed, for by her dress the woman was a servant and thus several classes further down the rigid Drusalan social scale than even foreigners. What he got in reply was a slipshod babble of words which, after the first sentence had helped his brain lock into some sort of understanding, were not blurred so much by dialect as by a mind skidding along the edge of desperation-born hysterics.

'*Hnach-at, keii'ach da?*' This time when he repeated the question it slashed out like a whipcut, in the clipped high-to-low mode that any armed and mounted man could use to a woman on foot, except when that woman was without doubt Princess Marya Marevna, sister of the Emperor . . . or Tehal Kyrin with a sword across her back.

It acted as he had hoped, like the slap across the face of any hysteric, to restore at least a degree of coherence. 'Muh-muh-muh,' was all the woman managed at first, but that was more a result of her frantic run along the street than anything else.

She clutched at his stirrup-iron, face red and sweaty despite the evening chill, and gasped breath into her out-raged lungs. Finally, as calm as anyone might be after such exertion, she looked up into his face and said in better Court Drusalan than he expected to hear, 'My lady's little daughter lies dying, lord. I . . . I ask humbly, of your courtesy – help me.' Her grip on stirrup and booted ankle tightened as her control slipped a little, and all the

126

forced courtliness of her language dissolved in the anguish of one word. '*Please . . . ?*'

'Oh, God . . . Kyrin? You know more than I do about these things.'

'No promises.' She spoke softly, and in Alban. 'But go with her. I'll – I'll see what can be done.' *And*, she looked the thought at him but kept its sound to herself, *what* you *can do, my dear . . .*

Giorl, equipped with pincers and long-nosed pliers instead of her more usual surgical equipment, and feeling more like an armourer than a physician, had almost finished her task when the knock came at the door. Without being told, one of the servants – who took care to remain well out of earshot when the *Woydach* had company – moved from his at-ease position to the great steel bar that ensured privacy, and only then paused to await instruction.

'Tell him to open it,' said Voord. He spoke with difficulty through teeth clenched tight shut, because neither the mild soporifics nor a large quantity of distilled alcohol had done anything to alleviate the pain of Giorl's metalwork until she completed her operations on any given injury. Even after she was done, all he had to be thankful for was that the wounds once closed faded to a dull discomfort rather than the white-hot pain when they gaped open; and now only the sword-stabs in his flanks remained to be sewn shut.

'The Warlord commands: let the door be opened.' Giorl spoke the few high-mode words over her shoulder without either turning round or slackening the grip of her fingers and thumb on the layers of skin, muscle and subcutaneous fat through which she was threading an alcohol-doused gilt wire. Any loss of concentration and it would be all to do again, something for which Voord wouldn't thank her. It was strange work, more mechanical repair than healing, and despite the pain it was plainly causing Voord it was like neither of the two skills which made her so important in the city of Drakkesborg.

Three men came in. They had evidently come directly from outside the building, for newly fallen snow was still piled deep on the hoods and shoulders of their Army overrobes, while inside the military mantles – Giorl paused in her work to stare until a whimpering groan from Voord reminded her of the task in hand – they wore the all-concealing garb of *tulathin*.

Only when the biggest of the trio put back his face-concealing mask did she feel a little more at ease. He at least was a man familiar enough to any who had known Voord Ebanesj in the past few years: the man called Tagen, who was Voord's closest friend, confidante, body-guard and some said lover. Certainly his presence indicated that the other two were friendly – so far as anyone could claim that a *taulath* was friendly.

'Tagen, I told you to take five men,' said Voord, and for all the weakness in his voice he overlaid the trembling frailty with menace. 'I see you and two others. What happened?'

For all that she couldn't see them, Giorl was conscious of the various servants in the room taking as hasty a leave as good manners would permit. Certainly Tagen said nothing until the sound of the great door closing made it plain that he and his people were alone again. She, of course, remained – not only because the work she was performing on Voord's tattered body was not something he would allow her to leave unfinished no matter what the circumstances, but Voord and Tagen were both well aware that Giorl Derawn had already heard so many secrets that one more wouldn't make a deal of difference.

'What happened, sir, was that he wasn't alone.'

'The woman?' Voord sat up with a jerk, then lay back gasping as Giorl glared at him and continued to stitch. 'I told you about the woman; I warned you before you left Drakkesborg that he wasn't travelling alone, so what went wrong?'

'When we found him, he was being attacked already. You wanted him alive, so we killed as many of the others as we could, but by the time we were finished he had gone. There was snow falling, tracking was a waste of time, so instead of trying to follow we cleaned up our own mess, took the bodies out of sight into the forest for the wolves to deal with and left the steading where we found him as the owner would have wanted to find it. That's what happened, sir. We lost three; the others were very good.'

'The others . . . Tagen, what were they? Mercenaries or hired bodyguards who had turned on their employer, or just plain bandits that you interrupted?'

'They were *tulathin*. Just like us.'

Voord swallowed this piece of information with as much reluctance as if it was a mouthful of rotten meat, staring at the ceiling and no longer reacting to Giorl's attentions, in a manner that she found unsettling. What she was doing – the same thing that she had been doing this hour or more – was hurting no less; he simply wasn't noticing it any more. 'And what about the target? You said he got away. Surely you went after him when you finished covering your tracks – or had he covered his own too well for that?'

'Sir, I said already – he didn't cover his tracks, the snowstorm did. Even if we had gone straight after him we would have lost him just as quickly as—'

'As you did by doing nothing whatsoever!'

'Certainly he's still alive, sir.'

'Oh. And what makes you so sure of that? Knowing it's what I want to hear, maybe?'

'The *tulathin* say so, sir.'

'Ah. Wonderful. I'm utterly convinced.' Voord jerked and made a whining sound down his nose as Giorl sealed the last-but-one-loop of wire with a quick rotary twist of the pliers. Patient stared at surgeon, surgeon gazed at patient, and no emotion was transmitted either way.

129

'Almost done,' said Giorl. 'I could leave the last until you've finished talking . . .'

'No, not when I'm just getting used to the notion of constant pain. Get on with it, and get it over with. I might be needing you for other matters.'

'*Woydach'ann*, you told me that when I was finished here I could go home. My daughter is sick. She needs me. She—'

'Can wait. Enough. Finish. Now, Tagen, tell me how this remarkable mess could have happened when I trusted all the planning to yourself and the *tulathin*? What went wrong?'

'They, and the three who died, have worked for you and for *Kagh'Ernvakh* this year or more. But they remain what they first were, *tulathin*. A clannish lot, regardless of their hired loyalties. Most importantly, they have a net of spies and informants all over Alba and the Empire.' Tagen walked a little closer, seeming either deliberately or unconsciously to be distancing himself from the two *tulathin*.

'What I suspect happened,' he continued in the same careful monotone, 'was that someone else wanted Tal-. . . him dead, and hired *tulathin* of their own. Both ours and theirs obtained their information from the same source, went to the same place and . . . well. An unfortunate coincidence.'

Giorl finished off all her sutures by braiding a scrap of soft leather into the wires, so that the sharpened ends would not catch on clothing or other skin. She was listening to all that was being said, but without any great attention since there was a feeling about the whole business which suggested she would soon be hearing about it over and over to the point of boredom.

'Is that what they told you?' Voord's voice had lost most of its emotion, as if he had seen sense and regained full control of his temper. 'Or was it an opinion you formed yourself?'

'Something of both, sir.' Tagen stiffened fractionally,

seeing what Voord was driving at. 'Though they did take great pains to tell me their view of the situation, and wasted no time about it either. Sir.'

'And was that all they told you?'

'Yes, sir.'

Voord took a long swallow of the drug-laced spirit that waited in a cup beside his bed. A dribble of the stuff ran like purple blood from one corner of his mouth as his lips quirked in a sort of smile and Giorl, seeing it, knew that whatever suffering had done to him it had not erased the mind-set of the man with whom she was familiar.

'And tell me, Tagen – again, in your opinion – was this *all* that they told you all that they knew?'

'Yes, sir.' And then that deadly pause. 'I believe so, anyway.'

'So.' Voord raised himself on one elbow, brows furrowing a touch as the ache of old/new injuries nagged at his nerves but came nowhere near the stabbing anguish of before. 'Guards! *Guards!*'

Soldiers sprinted into the room with gisarms at the ready. None of them knew why they had been summoned, just that when it was the new *Woydach* who did the summoning then it was as well not to keep him waiting. They stamped to attention, weapons ready at port-arms, and waited for orders. As usual, they didn't wait long.

'Those two,' said Voord, indicating the startled *tulathin* who had just now realised how horribly things were going wrong, 'are to be prepared for stringent interrogation. No, repeat no, preliminary questioning is to be carried out. By my command. Take them away.'

Even through the noises of armoured men moving in formation and the voices raised in protest, Giorl heard Tagen's breath come out in a sigh of pure relief. His Commander was evidently in one of those moods where listening to reason wasn't a priority, and at such a time not even long-time friendship was a protection.

'My lord,' said Giorl, even though she knew already that it was a waste of breath, 'your wounds are closed to the best of my ability. May I hold you to your promise and go tend my daughter now?'

'Of course not.' Voord swung his feet to the floor and stood upright unaided for the first time in several days. He chuckled and reached for his clothing. 'Aren't you forgetting what *I* pay you for, Giorl Derawn? All this doctoring is what you do for other people. For me, you extract secrets.'

'But I only have my surgeon's instruments!'

'They're sharp; they hurt; they'll do. After all, it was a leather-working knife that first time. So improvise.'

Giorl shrugged. The sooner she was done here, the sooner she could get home and take care of Mal, because the poor child really was *not* well . . . 'All right,' she said, all brisk now because that was the best way to be in present circumstances. The small, bright steel things clinked softly in their sprung clips as she closed the case and picked it up. 'I wasn't really listening. Those two . . . ?'

'They claim they've told me everything,' said Tagen helpfully.

'Oh, that old chestnut,' said Giorl wearily. 'Well, then. Let's see if they're sure . . .'

SIX

Aldric and Kyrin followed the woman as closely and as quickly as they – encumbered by four horses, and two of those laden with baggage – could follow someone on foot who knew the layout of the busy streets and was moving with a speed born of panic. There was little opportunity to say much either to her or to each other, which was perhaps as well. Once again there was the unpleasant spectacle of other pedestrians looking, recognising and then deliberately snubbing, and even though Aldric seemed not to notice – or betrayed nothing of it if he had – Kyrin was disliking the situation more and more.

The place to which the woman led them was a town house typical of the well-to-do area of an Imperial city. Kyrin had seen a similar style before, in Tuenafen; it presented to the world the usual featureless outer wall, a wall broken only by the house doorway set square in front up a small flight of steps. There was no stable entrance; those who could afford to live in this part of town could easily afford the rent of space elsewhere for carriage or horses, and had enough servants in the house to fetch conveyance when it was needed. Rather than leaning out over the street in the way older houses did, this – like the others to either side – was set well back. There was a high hedge to either side, thickly capped with snow, to maintain a degree of privacy from even its nearest neighbours. Kyrin pursed her lips and nodded, seeing still more apparent confirmation of her doubts – but like her other private thoughts, she kept this one quiet; right now, except in the matter of medicine, her opinions were not required.

The elderly man who came out as the horses clattered to a halt had evidently been waiting for the woman to return. It was equally evident as he held the bridles while

Aldric and Kyrin dismounted that he had been weeping, and his renewed tears and prayers of gratitude as they went past him and into the house were either genuine or remarkably well acted.

And the mist of pain met them just inside the door; it was like an acrid flavour tasted by the mind but not by any other sense, and it was of such intensity that it made them both hesitate on the threshold. 'Dying of what?' Aldric wondered aloud for the first time.

Kyrin remained silent. Her own past experience as a physician's aide had taught her all the odours of a sick-room, and for all that a deal of this was born of immediate suffering much more of it seemed an echo of older agony. She glanced at Aldric, carefully sidelong from the corner of one eye, but saw nothing to indicate that he detected any of that strata of past pain. What she felt now merely reinforced what she had seen in the street and what she had guessed from that sight, seen before in her own coun-try: people ignoring, people not caring, people taking the opportunity for a deliberately blatant insult. Never mind that it was in the better part of town, never mind its neat, clean exterior, never mind the servants. They were his servants, and this was his house. The hangman's house . . .

'What in the name of Heaven . . . ?' The servant woman had run off towards some inner room, leaving them alone. Aldric had opened a door, looked inside – and now was staring at the racks of stoppered bottles, the shelves of jars, the cases of small glittering instruments – mostly metal, some of glass – all looking wickedly sharp.

Kyrin peered in over his shoulder and sucked in a breath between her teeth. She had expected something of the sort, iron and leather engines of brutality, but these were too . . . too subtle. Too delicate. Not the hangman's house, then. Someone more skilled, more sophisticated. She felt the fine hairs lift on her arms and at the nape of her neck as a shudder like an icy needle ran down the core of her spine.

Alba's legal system was unlike that of Drusul and Valhol, having no place for the use of torture, and Aldric plainly didn't recognise the blades and needles for what they had to be – implements not for the relieving of pain but for the causing of it. Kyrin was reluctant to explain, but was drawing breath when hesitation, sense and caution were each and all drowned out by the sound from deeper within the house. It was a scream, thin, wavering and very weak – the sound of a child in pain.

We have to get out now, at once, she thought, hating herself for it, and grabbed at Aldric's sleeve to pull him away in the grace-time while nobody but servants knew that they were there. And then it was too late, for the woman was back and there was a man with her.

He too had been weeping, but now was blotting at his eyes with a cloth and trying to recover something that approximated dignity with which to greet his guests. Kyrin stared hard at him, trying to read from his face, his eyes, his stance, anything at all that would confirm he was an evil creature undeserving of their help or sympathy. She read only desperation and an aching, helpless grief so that no matter what suspicions she still harboured, the fear that they had come too late still twisted deep inside her like a knotted cord drawn tight.

'Of all days,' the man said in a voice that was almost flat calm and trembling with the effort of staying so, 'of all days for me not to know. Of all days for her to be gone and for me not to know . . .'

He blinked at them, seeing a man in black and silver and a woman in grey and blue, both with sword-hilts rearing above their shoulders, looking in the dim light and their hunched furs more capable of taking life than saving it, and clenched his fists until the knucklebones gleamed white through the tight-drawn skin.

'Sir, madam,' he said with that same dreadful calm, 'I thank you. I apologise for troubling you. But swords will not . . . not save . . .' His lip quivered, he turned his face away in an attempt to regain the control that was slipping so fast and only one word escaped him: 'Help.'

Aldric turned his head slowly to stare at Kyrin, wondering why she had already held back far longer than he would have thought her capable of doing in this circumstance. She tried to meet that stare and had to look away. *You took an oath.* The voice in her head was her own, and yet so heavy with accusation that it was not hers at all. *You didn't quibble then. Why do it now? He can't believe that you're just standing here. Tell him why and walk away, maybe he'll understand – or do what you swore to, that night by starlight. But either way, be honest . . .*

Kyrin tugged back her hood, heedless of the snow that fell from it to the floor, and began to walk rapidly down the corridor in the direction from which the man had come. She heard another rustle and thump which told that Aldric had just followed suit, and smiled a swift tight smile which creased little lines into her face. As she opened the door at the end of the passage and saw the bed whose size made the tiny body writhing feebly in it look even smaller and more helpless, the smile went away. 'Your servant-woman told us about the child,' she said. 'Now you tell me. How long has she been like this, and where is the site of the pain . . . ?'

The sight and sound of someone being decisive and knowing – or even just seeming to know – what to do was enough to start the man talking; and once started, he seemed unable to stop until he was rid of all his hopes and fears. Most was just background noise to Kyrin – she had more important things requiring her attention than to hang on every word – but she listened closely enough to hear symptoms described and thus guess at causes . . . as well as having her own mistaken notions set to rights.

It became plain that the man, Ryn Derawn, was neither a hangman nor a torturer, except maybe of speech. He was a jeweller and goldsmith, a self-styled artist in the precious stones and metals, and a happily married man with a loving wife and two fine daughters. The younger child, Mal, had been troubled with fever and an upset stomach these two days past, and only that morning had been dosed with an infusion meant to relieve it. His wife had given the medicine herself, just before she went out to work . . .

. . . And at first it had seemed to help. Then the complaints and crying had turned to screams so harrowing that Ryn had sent a servant with Lorei his elder daughter clear across the city to stay with relatives until all was over. One way or another. And still there was no sign of his wife's return . . .

'Why, man. What could she do?'

Ryn smiled wanly. 'Everything,' he said. 'Giorl's the finest surgeon in Drakkesborg.'

Kyrin was too intent on the second stage of her examination to waste time or breath on comment, but Aldric could almost hear her eyebrows going up from where he stood. He had already told her what the conventional Alban attitude would be to women who were involved in medical practice, and there was no reason to believe that the Drusalan Empire would be any less straitlaced in the matter. And that was just where physicians were concerned; surgeons, who not only touched bodies but opened them up and rummaged about inside, would be regarded even more askance. Small wonder that the servants from this house were treated as if they were involved in something dirty . . .

She shook her head and dismissed the annoyance to a part of her mind where it wouldn't interfere with the business at hand. That part of her mind was already almost certain about what was wrong here, and just one more test would prove it. Kyrin laid the tips of her fingers on Mal's lower belly, half a palm's width below and in from where the child's hip-bone was visible, and pressed down barely enough to indent the skin. It was more than enough. Mal's eyes and mouth went wide and she screamed. The little girl's shriek of agony had two effects: it confirmed Kyrin's diagnosis . . .

137

. . . And it provoked Aldric, outraged by the sound, to snatch away her hand with excessive speed and violence, and to snarl something viciously angry at her for causing the child unnecessary pain. Kyrin stared at him, then at the flattened blade of his right hand, and realised with something of a start that the oversight of not explaining what she was about had almost earned her that hand across the face.

Almost, but not quite; and if he *had* hit her Kyrin knew she had only herself to blame. Ryn had flinched from the scream and the pain which had provoked it, but he was evidently familiar with – or had been told about – this apparently brutal but very proper and accurate test for an inflammation in one particular part of the bowels. Aldric was *not* familiar with it, had *not* been told and had laudably – if barely – restrained himself from reacting to what must have looked like casual and thoughtless probing.

'Thank you,' said Kyrin, and if her voice was shaking who could blame her; she knew better than most the power in a focused strike from that particular right hand. 'For not hitting me. I should have warned you.'

Aldric's hand was relaxed now, and he had released his grip on Kyrin's wrist, but he still looked uncomfortable and embarrassed by all that had happened.

'I had to make sure.'

'That she was in pain?' There was confusion rather than sarcasm in his voice. 'We knew that much already.'

'But not why. I know now, and what we can do about it. There's a little tag of tissue, a useless afterthought called an *appendix*, in everyone's guts; not even my master knew what it was for, but he knew what it sometimes did. This.' She gestured down at Mal, who had sunk back into an uneasy muttering drowse until the next spike of pain came to disturb her. 'This infant's *appendix* has somehow become inflamed or infected, and that test was the final proof. Either we cut it out, or it bursts. And if it bursts, she dies.'

'One of the guardsmen in Dunrath fell sick with that,' said Aldric, 'and my father's physician cut it out of him.'

'And . . . ?'

'He lived – long enough to be proud of the scar, and long enough for Duergar Vathach's people to kill him.'

'But he lived. I want this child to live.'

Kyrin eyed him thoughtfully, thankful that he couldn't read what was going on in her mind right now. At least she could stand by and take over if she had to – but hopefully that wouldn't be necessary. She took the plunge.

'And I want you to help. Please . . .' The expression on Aldric's face changed and he opened his mouth to protest, then shut it again. 'Ryn Derawn, listen to me. I don't dare move your daughter in case her *appendix* bursts, so we'll have to work here. There will be mess. Be ready to change the bed – including the mattress. Order clean linens brought here so that we can wrap the child and shift her out of here immediately we're done. Then go to the kitchen and have water put to boil – lots of it.'

'Lady, both the bath and kitchen coppers will be bubbling by now.' Ryn gave her a feeble smile. 'It is midwinter, after all.'

'Better. Then do this: take the biggest pot that has a lid, fill it with the boiling water, have your cook put in salt to four parts in the hundred, then put the lid on and keep it on while the pot is brought up here.'

'As she says, there's going to be a mess. But a hot, clean mess.' Aldric sounded very brisk, but there was an edge to his voice that Kyrin hadn't heard before.

'Quite so.' Kyrin gave him a funny look, but said nothing else until Ryn was out of the room and about his various errands. 'Now *kailin-eir* Talvalin, what's biting you? Afraid of a little blood?'

'No. But there need not be any.' He unhooked the cross-strap of her scabbard and let Widowmaker slide from across his back, then raised the longsword until her pommel was between them. A thread of blue-white fire coiled deep within the crystal that had been set only recently into the *taiken* hilt, shifting slowly as oil patterns on water. 'You're forgetting the Echainon stone.'

'I am not, and I was not. But I will not let you use it.'

'Why not? You've seen that it works! We both have!'

'On open wounds, Aldric. I haven't yet seen it cleanse foul matter from deep within a body. Because of that, and because of other matters, I can't and won't trust it on this child.'

'What other matters?'

'Because of where we are . . . as you continually remind me. Obvious sorcery would not be such a good idea here in Drakkesborg.' *And because you place too much reliance on that thing already. That, and the sword it's mounted in. I wasn't happy when you put the spellstone there. Not happy at all.* 'You see?'

'Yes. Yes, I see.' He unhooked Widowmaker and wrapped her in her belts, then laid the weapon to one side. 'I see much better than I thought. So what do you want me to do?'

'Help me select the proper instruments.' Kyrin walked to the door, paused and glanced over her shoulder at him with a smile around her eyes if not quite on her lips. 'You might discover uses for sharp steel that not even your weapon-master ever taught you. And better uses than you ever thought possible. Come on.'

The place was not the torch-lit stone cavern of an ordinary torture chamber; one of Giorl's predecessors had seen to that when he (or had it been another *she*?) redesigned what was now the citadel's principal interrogation room. There were glazed white tiles on the floor, the walls and the domed ceiling which made the room look like the inside of a skull, and it was illuminated by lensed oil-lamps so that there were no shadows in which the eye could find shelter from the machinery squatting in the centre of the floor over an array of inset gutters that could be flushed with clean water whenever they became choked.

Giorl glanced about, making sure that all but her most final preparations had been completed, paying small heed to the two men who had been given over to the embrace of the machines. Behind her, Voord eased himself carefully into one of the observation chairs where the Questionmaker and the Recorder were already sitting, and pressed offered plugs of soft wax into his ears. The acoustics deliberately created by the room's lining of tiles were not something anyone chose to experience. Those who contributed, of course, did not have that choice or any other.

Besides the officials and the Subjects, there were two assistants who – with mops and swabs and styptic powder – kept clean the areas where Giorl walked and worked. She nodded acknowledgement at them, and allowed one to help her put on the waxed silk smock and cap, then the apron and the long gloves of fine oiled leather which kept *her* clean.

'My lord *Woydach*,' she said, 'will you at least send someone to bring back news of my daughter's health?' It wasn't a demand – she did not make demands of the Grand Warlord – and as a simple request it was refused.

'You should be finished with this soon enough,' Voord said flatly. 'And then you can go to see for yourself.'

Giorl gazed at him, a speculative stare which had unsettled better men than Voord Ebanesj, but then they had not had the twin safeguards of rank and knowledge to protect them.

'Understand me, Giorl, if it was possible I would go myself, but I need whatever information these two have seen fit not to tell me, and if they're left alone now, knowing what they know, they'll concoct some story or—'

'Try to cheat you in some other way, yes.' Giorl spoke in the weary voice of one who had heard the same explanation offered on many other occasions to many other

141

people, and hadn't been convinced then either. 'Very well. But if you used sorcery there would be no need for all this.'

'Aren't you forgetting that sorcery is illegal, and that I've learned I can't trust it, and that if it *was* permitted then there would be no need for you and because of what you know there would be no way in which I could let you leave this citadel alive . . . ?' Voord rattled off the clauses, not threatening her because all the threatening had been done most effectively a long time ago, but just reminding her of her present situation.

'I was not forgetting,' Giorl said, and turned from him to her assistants. 'That one.' She pointed to one of the *tulathin*, fastened naked to an iron chair by neck and waist and thigh, by bicep, wrist and ankle. At present it merely held him fast, but various levers, probes and oil-soaked wicks built into its structure could make it much more than just an ugly, clumsy piece of furniture. The man glared horror and hatred at her, but Giorl had seen worse and in any case intended him no harm just now. 'Fit the clamps and the mirror panels. If he can see and understand what I can do,' she told Voord over one shoulder, 'maybe I won't have to waste much time in actually doing.'

Voord said nothing. He was leafing through the small book that always stayed in here, a book as sinister as any grimoire, the accumulated wisdom of generations of interrogators and generations of pain. Various levels of torment were listed in its pages, set out in the language of bureaucrats the world over. Like the neutral titles of the participants in this abbatoir – *Questionmaker, Recorder, Subject* – it was an arid pedantry of instruments and applications and durations intended to place comfortable distance between the reader and the reality of what he read. What Voord read was a handbook of anguish.

Metal clicked and rattled as the clamps were slotted and locked into position. Adapted from a mechanism for performing delicate surgery, once they were secure the *taulath* in the chair could neither move his head nor close his eyes. That effect had been the original intention of the physician who had invented the device, but not in such a circumstance as this. The prisoner could look only at his companion and at what was being done to him, for once the mirror panels were in place even turning away his eyes would show only a reflection of the bloody reality. There was a choking-pear in his mouth, forcing it into a straining gape which at the same time muted any sound of encouragement he might make to a snuffling grunt, and other than what went on inside his own mind he was unhurt.

The assistants stepped back to let Giorl inspect their work. She checked locks and straps and grub-screws with the same dispassionate concentration as she had been giving to the setting out of her own surgeon's instruments – for none of the delicate devices that were her speciality were ever kept down here with the heavy equipment. They stayed at home, and were cared for along with the tools of her other, later trade.

'The questions are decided,' said Voord, his consultation with the Questionmaker at an end. 'Proceed. Begin with . . .' pages rustled for a moment. 'Twelve.'

Giorl paused an instant, recalling what Twelve entailed as she might have recalled the steps of a complex surgery, then lifted the medical instrument which most closely approximated to what she would normally have used for torment Twelve, shifted her mind away from any concern for the trembling human being trussed before her and set to work . . .

The two knives, the curved tongs and the three needles – all carefully threaded from a new wax-sealed packet of stitching-gut – which Kyrin had chosen were all laid on a metal tray and covered with a white cloth by the time Ryn and a servant returned with the salted water and the clean bedding. She had also picked out several long strips of a soft, loose-woven cloth and two bottles, one filled clear and one with a straw-coloured liquid. From the expression on his face, Aldric had expected her selection to be much larger and more complex, and he seemed almost disappointed with the simplicity of it all. For her part, Kyrin knew that he would soon be grateful there was nothing more elaborate to handle.

With his sleeves rolled up past the biceps like hers, Aldric was watching her preparations with far more apprehension than Ryn; he looked, indeed, more like the sick child's father than her father did. 'Cheer up,' said Kyrin, and saw him twitch, 'this is a fairly quick and simple undertaking. You shouldn't be more than a few minutes about it.'

'*I* shouldn't . . . ?' His voice, in the Alban language, was no more than a whisper, and it was clear that only force of will was keeping it free of a horror that would have needed no translation. 'Just what in hell are you talking about? I can't do this – I don't know how! You're the physician's aide, you do it!'

'Aldric, my loved, I can't.' This was the crunch. This was for his health as much as for the child's, but if he learned she was lying to him . . .

'Why not, for all Gods' sake?'

'Because my oath forbids it.'

'*What*?'

' "I will not cut – but shall leave that to those trained in that Art." ' She spoke not in Alban but in Imperial Drusalan, loudly enough for Ryn to hear what she was saying, and looked to him for confirmation of it. Aldric looked too, but he was hoping more for a denial; he didn't get one.

'I know that oath,' agreed Ryn. 'A shortened version but the truth, near enough.'

Kyrin folded back the cloth from the instruments and moved their tray a little closer. Aldric stared at the tiny knives and didn't move, seeming to the casual or uninformed eye to be considering how to begin. Only she was close enough to see the terror in his eyes; they were fixed, unblinking, watching the bright lamplight shift and glint in the polish of edges and on the points of needles. She knew that he was seeing dead faces reflected back from the burnished metal – faces whose lives he had stolen away with a blade in his hand.

And now, thanks to the hasty planning of the woman he loved and who loved him, he was being asked to cut again, not now for death but for life; and maybe to close at long last the raw lacerations in his own mind. It was a dreadful thing to be wounded so deeply and for so long with a wound that never healed, and if trickery was part of the cure then Tehal Kyrin had a clear conscience about its use.

Moving with the easy speed of long practice, Kyrin set about preparing Mal for surgery. She started by opening the door and all three windows so that a breeze of chill fresh air began to flow through the room, then extinguished all the lamps and angled the bedroom mirrors to reflect light from the door and windows instead. Had he been concentrating on Kyrin rather than on his inner fears, Aldric might have wondered why; except that both reasons were explained the instant she opened one of the bottles and began soaking a cloth in its straw-yellow contents. A heavy, sweetish scent flowed through the room, so intense that it was almost visible, and Aldric shook off his own private thoughts with a jerk of his head and a muttered oath.

'What in hell *is* that stuff?'

'A distillate . . . and an important one. Pungent, poisonous and explosive, hence no lamps and open windows, but this stuff will keep the child asleep and out of pain until you're done.' She made a pad of the sopping cloth, folding it once and then again before laying it over Mal's mouth and nose, then removed the stopper from the second bottle, poured clear liquid into a ceramic dish and began washing her hands. The nose-pricking smell of twice-distilled grain spirit mingled briefly with the heavy odour of the sleeping-drug. 'Now you wash,' she said, shaking drips from her fingertips, 'while I clean what we'll need.'

Aldric's eyes followed her hands as they lifted the small metallic things that clinked when they were laid into yet another spirit-filled dish until they should be needed, then dutifully scrubbed his own hands and arms up past the elbows with the same chilly, fast evaporating liquid. Kyrin glanced at him, wondering if the slight shiver she saw was a result of the cold breeze or the cold alcohol or what her old master called cold feet. She doubted it of this particular man, but it was so very hard to be sure . . .

Then Mal whimpered even through the drug-deepened shadows, and Aldric's teeth came together with a click that was audible clear across the room; Kyrin had the first knife out of its spirit-bath and ready just in time for his hand to snap out and receive the handle slapped into his palm.

'Where do I cut?' he asked, and his soft voice was without any trace of tremor.

Kyrin breathed a sigh of relief, not caring any more who heard it, and pressed her fingertips against Mal's neck, counting the beats of the little girl's pulse. Still too fast. 'Wait,' she said. The rapid fluttering began to slacken its pace, became something like normal for the first time since Kyrin had felt it, then grew slower still. A touch on the eyelashes drew no response. The pad over the child's face was almost dry, and Kyrin moistened it with more of the sleep-drug. She dipped another pad of cloth into a dish of clean grain-spirit and wiped it gently across Mal's belly from hip-bone to navel, waited until the sheen of alcohol had dried and then drew a single marking stripe. 'Cut there,' she said, 'and – and cut as well as you know how.'

She saw Aldric's throat move as he swallowed hard. But she also saw him balance the knife in his hand as an artist might balance a brush, with as much authority as her master had ever shown in all the years that she had watched him work, and as she readied a swab she saw him make the first sweeping cut . . .

. . . The blood felt very warm, tickling Giorl's skin as it wandered over her face in four distinct and separate threads: one from just above her right eye, another down her cheek, a third coming out of her nose and the last dribbling from her slack-lipped mouth.

She moved a little, whimpering because moving hurt. At least Ryn wouldn't be back for some hours yet. She had said as much to Terel, let him know that he had time, just before he . . . She brought one straddled leg under her body and a ragged spike of pain rammed up into her belly, reminding her – as if she needed the reminder – of just what he had done. All that mattered now was that she would have time to clean herself up and think of a credible story before Ryn came home. Clean her body, anyway. Cleaning her mind of the past quarter-hour would not be so easy.

But he's Ryn's friend! she thought wildly. *He's been to our house before, he's eaten here, drunk here, even slept here when he and Ryn were working late. I* know *him!* Known him, and yet plainly not known him well enough. Oh, wonderful hindsight that let her see now the truth behind his frequent visits to the house, his excessive Jouvaine courtesy with all its kissing and embracing – no matter that he was as much a Drusalan as they were, yet he was a well-travelled man and the affectations had looked well on him. She had treated his over-familiar hands and mouth as ostentatious worldly wisdom, or as the slightly off-colour joke it sometimes seemed to be. And oh, the compliments, both private and in Ryn's own hearing, about how lucky her husband was and how jealous he, Terel, was of his old friend, and how if she ever wanted to run away from home she could run straight to him. All with a grin and a laugh. That was all it had seemed to be and perhaps all it was, then; and all it should have remained. Giorl didn't know why the boisterous friendship had turned so sour. Probably no rape victim ever did.

Her bottom lip was split and one of her teeth felt loose. Hardly surprising. She had bitten, until Terel had . . . had persuaded her to stop.

That man used to play with my daughter, thought Giorl, and went cold inside. Lorei had been five, already becoming beautiful. *But never alone. Never, ever alone, even then. Oh, thank you for that much, Lady Mother, thank you . . .* She had not cried in pain for herself and for her own hurts, but she cried now in gratitude for the safety of her child.

Ryn had been told only of a fall downstairs. Mal was his child, *their* child. She had claimed the three barren years a consequence of the 'fall' and Ryn, bless him, had believed. During those years she had made sure to take the proper drugs against conception until she was quite certain that Terel had given her no more than pain and filthy memories . . . and until Terel himself was just another of those memories.

Hatred had brooded in Giorl's mind for those three years, but nothing had come of it until the day when Lorei came in and told how she had met Uncle Terel in the street, and how he had spoken to her for the longest time and had been so nice . . .

For two days Giorl had been quiet and withdrawn. On the morning of the third, she reached a decision. With Ryn off to deliver some finished work, Lorei at her lessons and Mal left with a trusted neighbour, she had gone down to Ryn's toolbox and stolen the leather-working knife he used to cut soft skins into coverings for his buffing-pads. And then she had gone looking for Terel.

He hadn't been hard to find, for all that he no longer visited their house – because of a friendship-breaking quarrel over their shared business which Giorl was certain had been staged just for that purpose. But he had kept his own place on the other side of the city, and opened his own goldsmith's shop as if to prove he no longer needed any partnership. Giorl had thought of dressing up, of wearing cosmetics and letting him believe that she had been taken with his prowess. The thought had been rejected; he was not so much of a fool as to be taken in. And using that sort of deception would leave her no better than the man who had pretended to be her husband's friend.

For all that he *had* been taken in, deceived by nothing more than his own arrogance and pride. Terel had invited her indoors with all the old overblown courtesies, bowing low and kissing the back of her hand like a courtier. He had even started to seduce her, smiling, purring, showing her his house and especially its fine bedroom, plying her with wine the whole time as he had not troubled to do before when brute force had been so much cheaper. That was when she had smashed the wine-jug against the side of his head. He had recovered consciousness tied spread-eagled to the posts of his own ostentatious bed, gagged by the whole apple she had rammed past his teeth and secured with her silk scarf.

Then Giorl had taken out the knife.

She and Terel had learned many things that stinking afternoon: that men plainly knew no natural pain like the pain of bringing a new life into the world; that rape was much more than just an over-rough display of affection – and that it was possible to peel a human being like a ripe fruit . . .

For those few hours Giorl had been insane, and only when the madness and the hatred drained away and let her see what she had done did all the good memories replace the bad. How she and her husband and Terel had laughed at jokes, and gone to the theatre, and worried over lack of work then seen it all come right at last. How Terel had made Lorei a little jewelled bracelet for her naming-day, the one Giorl had thrown away and claimed was 'lost' and replaced with another gift that had never quite been the same . . .

She was still crusted with drying, flaking blood, still holding the knife and still crying bitterly when some instinct brought two off-duty constables and their drinking companion into the house. The officers had seen only the knife and the mess on the bed, and had arrested her at once, but their companion – much more than another policeman – had been more interested to note that the mess was still alive.

And that was how it had begun. *Either you can do it to them at our instruction, and comfort yourself with the knowledge that they're all criminals anyway – or we'll have someone do it to you and your entire family, because we know you're a criminal, too.*

Ryn had heard it all from the constables' non-police comrade, an *eldheisart Kagh' Ernvakh* named Voord, and though it had taken her lovely husband a long time to come to terms with what his friend and then his wife had done, he had recovered something like equanimity at long last, accepted that she was now in the service of the State and left it all at that. Giorl had just one long-cherished and most unladylike ambition: to be a physician. Now that she was employed in activities far less ladylike than healing the sick, some unnamed person in Drakkesborg citadel spoke words – and likely some threats – on her behalf. It was an annoyance that her success in examination stemmed less from her long, hard studies than from that anonymous patron; and from her extraordinary knowledge of anatomy gained in the bloody chamber.

It was still more annoying to learn that she earned more by carving an interrogation Subject like a dinner joint than she ever would by restoring an operation patient to full health and strength. There was also the small matter of her own expendability. Voord had said it himself: she wouldn't be allowed to leave the citadel alive if *Kagh'-Ernvakh* lost their hold on her. Giorl, however, had taken some steps in that direction herself. The insurance, if it could be termed such, took the form of hundreds of sensitive facts filtered from the screams in the questioning room, written down, multiply copied, and held by various people instructed either to open or to forward them elsewhere if Giorl Derawn should either vanish or die of anything other than undisputed old age. It might work, and it might not; there would be no way to tell until the time came to try. And that time was not quite yet . . .

There was less blood than Aldric usually saw when he brought a blade and a body together; but then, there was nothing usual at all about this situation. For all that Kyrin had talked about the clinical detachment of physicians, Aldric knew perfectly well that he was deeply involved in what he was doing. It was as much a matter of his personal honour as any of the ancient *kailin*-oaths.

'Gently,' Kyrin said, 'as if you were cutting silk on a table you didn't want to scratch.' Aldric nodded silently, astonished by both the sharpness of the knife's edge and the steadiness of his own unaccustomed hands.

A bare touch of the blade was enough. The offending organ burst from the incision as if it had a life of its own. Kyrin brushed past him and began to do rapid things with a length of suture and another of the ceramic dishes. She stitched and tied, then stitched some more and drew the stitching tight. 'The other knife,' she said, and pointed. 'Cut there. Now.'

The second knife came to his hand as Isileth Widow-maker came from her scabbard, and he sliced off the foulness with something of the same grim satisfaction as delivering a perfect *taiken* cut . . . except that this time nobody would die.

Kyrin continued to pull the stitches tight. They were, quite literally, a drawstring to keep the infected and the healthy separate.

'Now the water.' She was talking to Ryn, who had done the best and wisest thing he could and stayed out of their way. 'Make sure it's not too hot, then use it to flush out the wound.' Ryn came forward with the pot of water,

151

cooled by now to little more than blood heat, and sluiced it carefully into the incision.

'Save the rest,' said Kyrin. 'Wash it out some more as I suture up to the skin.'

She was working with the curved needle and length of gut just now lifted from their bath of alcohol, sewing membrane and flesh with tiny neat stitches that were very far from the hasty, clumsy wound-closures Aldric had seen employed by some military surgeons.

He watched for a brief moment before glancing at his hands. There was blood on them – but good blood, this time. Living blood, not dying blood, if the smile Kyrin had given him was a true judgement. They wouldn't know for a while yet, but at least he – *he* – had done something with a blade that wasn't part of slaughter.

Kyrin tied off the last suture and wiped all clean with a spirit-soaked pad. All that remained of the incision was an assymmetrical criss-cross of stitches, and those were being covered by a swathing of bandages just as the child stirred. The pad over Mal's face had been dry for some minutes now, and since then she had been breathing the heavy fumes of the sleep-drug out of her lungs without its being replenished. It would be a while yet before its effects had worked out of her bloodstream, and in that time the intrusion of steel and stitches into flesh would be a poppy-muted ache.

'Ryn,' said Aldric gently at Kyrin's prompting nod, 'wrap up your daughter in these clean blankets and take her somewhere warm.'

The man said nothing more than his 'Thank you,' in a voice so faint that the words were barely there at all. But it was more than enough for Kyrin. She watched through bright-blurred eyes as Ryn lifted and wrapped his limp little burden and hurried her quickly to another bed in another room.

'Will she be all right?' asked Aldric after Ryn had gone.

'Wha . . . ? Kyrin straightened from her slump against the wall and tried to listen to him. 'I hope . . . yes, I think she will. Strong child; healthy. Her mother will check, of course, but I doubt even the best surgeon in Drakkesborg would find fault with how you did in these circumstances. Or any others, damn it! You were wonderful . . .'

She threw her arms around him and hugged him tight, then backed away slightly and looked at his face. 'Anything wrong with that?'

'Not with what I did, especially if it all works out—'

'Which it will!'

'But I don't like the idea of us being quite this noticeable.'

'Ah. I see what you mean.'

'This *is* Drakkesborg, don't forget.'

'Love, you remind me every few minutes. How *could* I forget? So you think we should just . . .' Kyrin waggled her fingers in a walking kind of gesture.

'Yes. Very quietly. There's nothing further we can do for Mal now, is there?'

'Not really. She'll heal in her own good time; we can't speed up the process.' She glanced at the crystal set in Widowmaker's pommel as Aldric returned the longsword to his belt. 'At least, not without attracting even more attention to ourselves, huh?'

Aldric smiled crookedly and covered the spellstone with his hand. He made a small sound of affirmation, nothing more. Now that all the tensions and worries were past he was tired, dog-tired after a day that would have been busy enough without this little side excursion into the world of the cutting-surgeon.

'All right then,' he managed at last. 'Let's slip away before anyone comes back and wonders who we really are.'

'And get something warm inside us,' Kyrin suggested.

Aldric's mouth twitched indecisively, half-way between a rueful smile and a quirk of disgust. 'I'd as soon not think about warm insides right now, thanks very much,' he said; then looked down at his hands, clean now, as if seeing life-blood in the truest sense still on them. 'But I deserve a drink, at least.'

'You deserve a hero's toast, my dear,' said Kyrin, linking her arm through his as they walked softly towards the street. 'And I'm buying . . .'

SEVEN

'Where is my son?'

There had been a time, an instant ago, when Aymar
Dacurre and Hanar Santon had been alone in the Hall of
Kings, working over new reports or collating old ones.
There had been a time when, except for the crackle of
fires in the nine hearths and the rustle of papers, the Hall
had been silent. That time was past, ended when Gemmel
Errekren stepped from the core of a howling spiral of
azure flame and dismissed the clamouring blue fire with
a single strike of his staff against the echoing floor.

The sound of Gemmel's thunderclap arrival had broken
two windows, and the blast of icy air arriving with him
had blown a week's worth of paperwork from the desk-
tops and sent it swirling in a blizzard of disorder almost
to the ceiling. And it was obvious to both the Alban lords
that Gemmel didn't care.

'I ask again,' he said, for all that it was a demand
instead, 'where is my son?' The old enchanter took a step
forward, then paused and sent a green-eyed glare up and
down the Hall of Kings, a glare that started fierce and
finished rather puzzled as he took in the reverberating
emptiness, the lack of the usual guards and the white cloth
covering the High Seat. 'And where is Rynert the King?'

Dacurre looked at Santon; Santon returned the look
and added a raised eyebrow to it. 'You don't know?' the
younger man asked. 'Nobody told you on your way here?'

'I wouldn't be asking if I did,' said Gemmel irritably.
He smiled an enigmatic little smile. 'And I didn't meet
anyone on the road I travelled.'

'Quite so.' Aymar Dacurre was doing his best not to be
over-awed by Gemmel's presence, but the overflow of
power that sleeted from the dragon-patterned black stave

in the enchanter's hands made that exercise in control something of a strain. 'You seem . . . well, out of touch with current affairs. Rynert the King is dead. Twenty-three days now. Long enough even for a wizard to learn what goes on in the capital city of his country.'

Gemmel gave none of the looked-for signs of surprise at the news of Rynert's death. Instead he repeated his enigmatic smile, the smile of a man who knows more interesting things than he's ever likely to be told. 'But Cerdor isn't my capital, and Alba isn't my country. I have been in my home, which I have never regarded as Alban sovereign territory . . . and about my own affairs. Yes, Lord Dacurre, I am indeed out of touch with the events of this world.' The way in which he put emphasis on *this* sent icy-footed spiders running up and down Dacurre's back. 'Now, my lord, I grow tired of repeating myself, but . . . where is my son Aldric?'

'Son?' echoed Hanar Santon, then quailed as Gemmel stared at him with a gaze that seemed for just an instant as hot and crazy as a goshawk's, sighting down his blade of nose – and down the suddenly-levelled Dragonwand that looked to the young lord more deadly than any more familiar weapon.

'Now don't *you* start,' Gemmel warned. 'I've had this from better men than you, so . . .' – the old enchanter drew in a long calming breath – 'just don't.'

'*Ilauem-arluth* Talvalin is somewhere in the Drusalan Empire,' said Dacurre. 'Doubtless, like yourself, about his own affairs.'

'Why . . . ?' said Gemmel; but the word was soft enough for both lords to know that it didn't need an answer, at least no answer that they could supply. And then he struck the black staff against the floor so hard that it drove into ceramic tile as if into a loaf of stale bread. 'No.' He spoke with the voice of a man denying that which cannot be denied; Dacurre had heard it often enough. 'Not the Jewel. Not alone. I released him from that charge . . .'

'Jewel?' Hanar Santon stood up slowly and carefully, not wanting to attract the same level of attention that was still sending after-shock trembles down his limbs. 'Gemmel-*purcanyath*, do you mean the . . . the *Warlord*'s Jewel? The Regalia?'

'Yes, I do.' Gemmel both looked and sounded flattened. 'I was going to recover the bloody thing myself – in my own good time. And now he . . . When did you hear of this?'

'Two days ago.' Dacurre had put his animosity aside as he might have taken off a garment; he knew well enough that he was no longer looking at a sorcerer but at an elderly man whose son (Aymar glossed over the inaccuracy as easily as Gemmel had done) was unexpectedly going into danger in an attempt to do some favour for his father – though he found Gemmel's use of the word *recover* worthy of curiosity. 'If it's any solace, the . . . informant made it quite clear that Aldric is as capable of taking care of himself as he always has been. But may I ask the reason—'

'You may ask,' said Gemmel, too shocked to put any snap into what he was saying. His preoccupation with other matters was evident just from that. 'At least he's carrying enough documentation to let him travel freely anywhere within the Empire's borders . . .'

'So where's the problem?' asked Santon. 'Except of course for the fact that he'll have to steal the Jewel. Voord's hardly likely to hand over the insignia of his rank.'

'Voord? What about Voord? What are you saying?'

'You won't have heard,' Dacurre said. 'It's not even public information in the Empire yet. There's a new Grand Warlord: Voord Ebanesj. We know of this one – he was in the Secret Police, and probably achieved his promotion by the usual method.' Lord Dacurre drew one thumb across his throat. 'He's been a thorn in Alba's side for a long while, but now he seems more taken up with his own concerns.'

'The name is familiar enough,' said Gemmel with venom in his voice. 'What worries me is that Aldric won't know of it. And Voord knows him.'

'Gemmel-*purcanyath*, Voord has known of the Talvalins for a long time; he was the one who planned Duergar Vathach's spoiling-raid on Dunrath and—'

'Was he indeed? Then damn him for it!'

The Dunrath affair was past, all that Voord *had* done was past and there was no passion in the way that Gemmel spoke of it. All his concern was for what the Grand Warlord might do in the days to come: a concern that was not political, not patriotic, but purely emotional. He had lost the son of his own blood to the Drusalan Empire and its Warlord – he was not about to lose the son he had adopted in the same way.

No matter that Aldric had the same documents as Gemmel carried, declaring them scholars and guests of the Empire, Aldric also had things that Gemmel lacked: enemies who knew him by sight. Enemies among the Secret Police – and now an enemy not only highly placed but in the very place where Aldric would be going. Unless he learned the truth very soon, he would walk all unwittingly into what was an unpremeditated trap.

There was Ymareth the Dragon – but Ymareth was also about its own affairs and no longer obedient to Gemmel's summons. The recollection of the last discussion with his monstrous creation was still something close to nightmare. Maker-that-Was, the dragon had called him, angered by the way he had tried to make use of Aldric by laying a spell into the young man's subconscious so that he would do . . .

What he was doing now, unbidden. Gemmel had lost much honour by that spell, and the removal of it had not been enough to bring his honour back – or his control over the dragon, which amounted to the same thing. A control based on honour was all very well when that being controlled could make no comparisons; but he had also given Ymareth the faculties of reasoning and judgement and that had been his downfall.

Gemmel had attempted to set matters right by commending Aldric to its protection, as it had once been constructed and given life to protect him – but what Ymareth had gained instead was freedom, and freedom of choice. It had provided awesome assistance in Egisburg and seen them safely on their way; then heeled over on one vast wing and flown out of sight. Ymareth was still out there somewhere; but wherever that somewhere was, it was not close enough for Gemmel to dare include the black dragon in the plan he suddenly, desperately, had to put together.

Whatever plan that might be . . .

Giorl's grim talent with blade and pincer was such that it required no more than twenty minutes – during which the unharmed *taulath* in the chair witnessed his companion suffer three full torments and a fourth barely begun – before he made it quite clear, despite his bonds and the choking-pear stuffed in his craw, that he was entirely ready and willing if not yet able to talk. Directly the interrogation assistants made him able, all manner of interesting things came pouring out, the words tumbling over one another so fast that the Recorder's flying pen was barely able to keep pace.

Woydach Voord listened to the stream of secrets and betrayals, editing out the occasional blubbering plea for mercy as being irrelevant. 'Quite fascinating,' he said, speaking as was customary to the Recorder and the Questionmaker but loudly enough for the *taulath* to hear. 'To learn so much so fast, I would have thought we might need something like,' he looked towards Giorl, 'Thirty-seven.'

In response to his cue, she administered Thirty-seven to the other Subject, so that for a short space conversation became impossible. Voord distanced himself from the

159

noises that echoed within the tiled and spattered chamber. He could see only the movement of mouths as both men screamed and begged and spilled out everything they knew in the hope of making Giorl stop or prevent her from shifting her attention. *They aren't breeding* tulathin *as tough as they once did*, he decided. *The hiring-fees should be reduced*. Then the Questionmaker tapped him on the arm and showed a fresh list of questions based on answers to the first set and augmented by various matters which had been revealed unasked.

Voord nodded; there was already enough information to provide excellent leverage on certain of his lords and generals, who until now had seemed pure as the snow and quite free of any handle he could employ to bend them to his will. Not any more . . . He smiled, lifted a pen and marked the questions of particular interest, then looked up as the first Subject lost consciousness and the room returned to reasonable quiet.

The Drusalan Empire had long ago considered the various aspects of torture as a means of gathering information; there were those who said that the victim would answer any and all questions with whatever his interrogators wanted to hear, just so long as they would stop. Another school of thought insisted that if a man was put under sufficient stress his mind could no longer formulate convincing lies to protect himself or his associates, and the only thing left for him to tell was the truth. Voord was of a third persuasion: that everything a Subject said, whether pressed or not, should be noted down and collated with known facts, and that pressure should then be applied to discover any deviation from the recorded testimony. It was wryly known as the *let's just make absolutely certain shall we* method of interrogation, and the best way of all was with two Subjects, playing one's pain against the other's fear of it. Of course, even then the information had to be cross-checked – in the appropriate fashion . . .

'Leave that one be for now,' said Voord. He glanced again at the list of questions, and then at their ultimate source sitting shivering and immobile in his iron chair. 'Get me confirmation of these instead.'

As the implications of the Warlord's words sank into his fear-fuddled mind, the other *taulath* began to thrash to and fro, trying impotently to break free of the padded steel bands holding him in place. 'I want you to consider Question Seven,' said Voord's voice over the rattle of unyielding metal, 'concerning what you mentioned about *Hauthanalth* Cohort-Commander Tayr. Help him remember with Chair, ah . . . Chair Three. But don't light the heating-wick until I tell you.'

Voord watched with mild curiosity for a few minutes as Giorl's assistants operated screws and levers – he and she both considered Chair torments a deal too crude for her personal involvement – then returned his attentions to the newly-corrected question/answer sheets which the Questionmaker had given him.

He gathered together the various other papers which had resulted from the interrogation and got to his feet.

'Enough for now,' Voord said briskly, patting the papers together. 'Clean up.' He met Giorl's unspoken question without blinking, and nodded. 'Yes, and finish up. I'll not need to interview either of these two again.'

'My lord *Woydach* . . . ?'

'Yes, Giorl, you're dismissed. And thank you for good work.' Voord laid a hand against his side and felt no more than a dull, hot ache. 'In both respects, I hope the child will soon be better . . .' But he was speaking only to the assistants; their chief was already gone. He shrugged and followed her out.

'But what about us?' demanded Aymar Dacurre.

'I told you before, my lord,' said Gemmel. 'This is not my country, and its concerns are not my concerns except in the matter of my son.'

'And what of his concerns, Gemmel Errekren?' snapped Hanar Santon. 'You seem to forget that he's a high-clan lord and as such has certain obligations, certain duties—'

'You mean that he should mobilise the Clan Talvalin troops, lock himself up in Dunrath-hold and snarl like a manger-dog at every other lord who dares approach? I doubt he'd see the need to bother.'

Dacurre looked at the enchanter and said nothing. Gemmel was right. None of his fellow clan-lords had acted towards Aldric in any way that would incline the young man to return. When Rynert had sent him off to the Empire on whatever crazy mission had been in the dead King's mind – and Dacurre didn't have all of the details even now – those of the Council lords who might have taken Aldric's part had remained silent, so that the only voices heard were those of men glad to see him gone. Some of course were merely conservative old men expressing conservative opinions – but there were others, Lords Uwin and Gyras especially, who even then had had an eye on the Talvalin lands. Scarcely a memory that would make either Aldric or his foster-father look on the present troubles of those lords with anything but a sense of poetic justice long delayed.

He began to wonder, as he had done more and more frequently in the past few days, whether it would not be better – or at least more practical – for himself and Santon to abandon the echoing corridors of the palace where they had done little good that any of them could see, and simply run for the shelter of their citadels as everyone else had done. So far no one had moved to use the situation either for advancement or for profit, but once the last two stable influences joined the rest on the edge of anarchy, falling over that edge would be only a matter of time. Probably their flight alone would be enough, either through misinterpretation or because someone like Diskan of Kerys chose to regard it as deliberately provocative.

If only someone, anyone, had sufficient courage to leave the doubtful safety of fortress walls and come here to talk, that would be enough. But – Dacurre smiled grimly – Aldric Talvalin would be the only man other than himself and Santon who would dare to do it . . . the only man crazy enough. All the others would do just as they were doing now. Nothing. He glanced towards Hanar and nodded.

'Very well then,' the young lord said. 'Go find him, wherever he is. Go help him. And afterwards ask him, ask our friend if he would have helped us had he known. But I refuse to ask for aid from *an pestreyr-pesok'n*, a petty-wizard with no notion of what honour means.'

Gemmel's back stiffened. If Santon had pondered for a week he could not have come up with an argument as powerful. His words sounded uncomfortably like those used by Ymareth the dragon, with their accusation of lost or lacking honour and their disdain of everything the enchanter thought himself to be. There had been a time, not so very long ago, when the notion that he might have been swayed by the same arguments these people used on one another would have been a joke, and not an especially good one either. But now . . . To live with them was to live by their rules, like it or not. Each in their own way. Aldric and Ymareth had taught him that much.

'What do you know of wizards and their doings, Hanar Lord Santon?' he asked softly. 'Or of what *I* do, and know, and am?'

'Enough to understand what a reminder would do to your so-haughty pride, Gemmel,' replied Aymar Dacurre.

'We both of us know Aldric,' Santon said. The anger was gone from his voice, as if it had never been there at all – or had been skilfully feigned. 'My . . . my grandfather' – Gemmel looked sideways and lifted one eyebrow – 'knows him as one lord knows another, and as the last son of a good friend. I knew him less well than I might have done, but enough to understand what kind of man you must be for him to call you *altrou* and *father*.'

'So. A nice trap, nicely baited, nicely sprung. A most symmetrical stratagem indeed.' Gemmel didn't trouble to sound bitter about it. There was a very pretty elegance about their web of words that he would appreciate – later, when the sting of it wore off. 'Very well. You shall have my help. Enough of it, at least, that the country will remain at peace while I attend to . . . shall we say, family matters?'

Dacurre and Santon nodded their agreement to the enchanter's terms, knowing them to be far better than any other proposition of the many they had considered and discarded; but when Gemmel laughed they looked nervously at one another, wondering perhaps too late what they had started. They were not kept long in suspense.

'Understand this,' said Gemmel, twisting Ykraith the Dragonwand from where it was embedded in the floor. 'If the giving of that help delays me so that harm befalls Aldric or his lady Kyrin, then the civil war you fear will be no more than a soft summer breeze beside the havoc I shall wreak in Alba. And remember for the future, gentlemen: I do not like traps.'

Power came roaring from the spellstave in a flare of light and noise, and when it faded he was gone.

Voord found Tagen waiting for him in the corridor outside, with another bundle of reports. 'The riots,' he said, saluting, 'have been suppressed.' Then he glanced at the interrogation room door as it swung shut, catching the muffled sounds of sawing and of running water. 'What about them?'

'Suppressed as well. But useful enough beforehand.' Voord exchanged the interrogation data for the riot reports, glanced at the topmost page and rolled them into a tight, disregarded cylinder. 'Tagen, get that lot to the appropriate people and resurrect Talvalin's picture and description. It should go out at Gold-One priority to the Chief of Constables, the Captains of city guards and of the urban militia, and to the *Eldheisart Kagh' Ernvakh*. Mark it Distribution Code Prime.'

Tagen digested the jargon reluctantly. He had small patience with this new efficiency that was no more effective than the old method of doing things. From the way all that would have sounded to a layman, the Commander was declaring war on everything and everybody not inside the city walls; but Tagen knew well enough that when all was said and done, the fancy wording and dramatically coloured message pouches that went with it meant no more than the traditional routine of delivering a message personally and leaving a threat of dire consequences if the results were any less than perfect. Still, that was the way the Commander liked to do things, and it wasn't Tagen's place to quibble. Besides which, he could understand Voord's desire to get Talvalin down here for a chat; he wanted very much to be there when it happened.

'You really think he's coming here, sir?'

'Yes, Tagen, I do. Wouldn't you?'

'Sir!' Tagen's chest swelled at being asked for an opinion. 'Yes, sir, I do think so. He owes you as much as you owe him, if I may make so bold. And he must think he has a chance, or he'd have run for home once he had the opportunity.' Tagen paused as his thought processes ground over another possibility. 'But maybe he did run. After all, he ran when we caught up with him, so . . .' The thought ran out of ideas.

'So, I'll have put the city on guard for nothing?' Voord finished for him.

'Not for nothing, sir. I spoke to some of my people in the Regiment and they think . . .' Tagen drew himself up very straight. 'May I have the Commander's permission to speak frankly?'

'You have it.'

'Sir, the Bodyguard Regiment thinks that you should apply yourself with vigour to matters of state in the *Woyd-ek-Hlautan* before all of the Domain goes to rack and ruin.' Tagen said it all in a breathless rush and remained rigidly at attention as Voord looked at him with an expression of faint disbelief.

'Most interesting,' he said. 'Soldiers with political opinions. And who are these opinionated persons?'

'Sir, you said that I could speak frankly.'

'But not speak treason.'

'It isn't treason, sir.'

'It certainly sounds like it, *Kortagor* Tagen. But what word would you employ?'

'Concern, sir.'

'Indeed? Explain.'

'Sir, the Bodyguard Regiment exists to protect the Grand Warlord—'

'Except when they kill one to replace him with someone they like better, of course.'

'Not you, sir. Since you claimed the Jewel, you've been lavish with both gold and honours – none want to see you replaced. And once it's known who or what we protect you against, the form of protection becomes more obvious. In this instance it begins by my bringing you this warning.'

Voord leaned back against the wall, wincing just a little as one of his wounds strained against the gilt wire holding it shut. 'Bringing me a warning,' he repeated. 'Of a danger to my life, presumably. Why not simply obliterate it instead?'

'Not even the Bodyguard can kill high-ranking Army officers without permission, sir.'

'Ah,' said Voord. 'So it's that, is it?' The requests that he come out of seclusion and set about being a ruler had increased in volume and vehemence over the past eighteen days or so, during seventeen days of which he had been incapable of coherent thought, never mind ruling the bloody Domain. 'And what do the Bodyguard's informants think that these high-rankers are planning, eh?'

'Several things, sir. Rumours are vague, but it seems that several would try to take advantage of the Emperor's offered amnesty, to turn their coats and join with him. Some others, supported by their troops, are supposed to be planning to set themselves up as Overlords – petty dictators, really – in the outlying areas of the *Woydek-Hlautan*. Maybe twenty men in all.'

166

'And they really think they can succeed in this?' marvelled Voord, smiling slightly.

'Yes, sir. Because first they plan to assassinate you.'

Only three weeks previously Voord would have laughed aloud at the thought of the surprise awaiting anyone who tried to kill him. He didn't laugh now. Instead his mind curdled at the prospect of maybe twenty blades ripping into him . . . and neither dying nor healing afterwards.

'Congratulate your informants for me, Tagen,' Voord said in a slightly unsteady voice. 'Tell them there will be gold and high favour for the first man to bring me confirmation of all this . . . intrigue.' He cleared his throat. 'Tell them straight away. Everything else can wait . . .'

It was full dark and snowing hard by the time they dismounted in the covered stable-yard built behind *The Two Towers*. A glance from side to side as their horses were taken in hand by the liveried ostlers was enough to give an indication of the clientele the place attracted. Aldric whistled thinly through his teeth at the several town carriages drawn up in a neat row under the sheltering roof of the yard. Some were sedate closed coaches, two others were the sort of transport merchants hired to convey – and impress – business colleagues, but it was the gleaming low-slung two-seater at the end of the line which attracted his attention.

Built as much for ostentatious speed as for comfort, it was a young man's vehicle of the kind only ever built to order, and only ever ordered to demonstrate the style, the taste and above all the wealth of its owner. The coach-building and lacquerwork alone would have taken a craftsman half a year, and the thoroughbred horsepower which drew such elegance was bound to be equally worthy of admiration. More so, to Aldric's mind.

It was inevitable that he would head straight for the stable-block itself, claiming a concern for Lyard's and

K'schei's comfort that was in truth no more than one young man's curiosity about another's high-powered horseflesh. He wasn't disappointed, because there was an eight-legged king's ransom munching hay in the wide stalls. Aldric fussed and petted over the pair of softly questing noses for a moment, then let them get back to their eating.

'Content again?' asked Kyrin, watching him rub the hay between his palms and smell it.

Aldric glanced at her. 'Good hay,' he said.

'Yes, I'm sure it is. And you've checked to make sure there's nothing in here that matches Lyard.'

He grinned at her. 'That obvious?'

'Every time. At least you're feeling better.'

Aldric dusted the hay from his fingers and smiled. 'I'm getting my appetite back, at least. But I'll still hold you to that drink. Let's get in.'

There was some sort of clerk seated inside a booth under the sweeping curve of the main staircase, who sniffed disdainfully at the sight of the inn's latest guests. Certainly they looked disreputable enough: the big gilt-framed mirror that formed the entire side wall of the entrance lobby reflected a couple wearing long furred and hooded overrobes, black with soaked-in meltwater except for the places where there was still solid snow. There was slush-mud on their boots. The battered saddlebags slung over their shoulders – money had changed hands and the stuff from the pack-horses was being carried for them – weren't exactly the richest or most stylish form of luggage, and both they and their bags smelt faintly of wet horse.

'Yes, can I help you?' the clerk said, not troubling to stand up and at the same time conveying the fervent hope that he wouldn't be able to do anything of the sort.

'A room, a private bath and hot-food-and-drink, all for two,' said Aldric, pushing back his hood with his free hand. The clerk said nothing straight away; instead he looked pointedly at the heap of snow which had slithered to the floor and now sat there, melting fast. Aldric cleared his throat equally pointedly. 'Is there a problem?' he asked.

'I really think that you should read our list of charges, sir,' said the clerk, staring hard at the state of their clothing. He pulled a board from beneath his counter and held it out, not quite between finger and thumb but managing to convey that impression succesfully enough. 'And . . . these are fixed charges, sir. That means no haggling; *The Two Towers* does not encourage haggling.'

'Oh.' Aldric took the board and looked at it, then said, 'Oh,' again.

'The tavern on the corner of Bridge and Central will probably be more to your liking,' said the clerk with an air of finality.

'Why?'

'Well, sir, the prices are—'

'Higher? I doubt that.'

'No sir, quite the rever—'

'Don't assume, my son,' said Aldric, feeling suddenly very much older than the puppy snapping from behind the safety of his desk. 'It can affect your health and job prospects.' Reaching inside his overrobe, Aldric pulled out the Guild Freyjan money-purse and held it for a moment with the Guild's unmistakable crest an inch from the end of the clerk's nose, then dropped it with a crude but highly satisfying slam and a puff of chalk-dust into the middle of the charge-board. 'Hard cash,' said Aldric, his face expressionless. 'Want to find out just how hard?'

The clerk looked at the purse, then opened it and peered inside. He blinked twice and swallowed, not daring to try biting one of the coins, if indeed that was what had been meant, and he was inclined to doubt it, then summoned up a sort of smile. 'Uh,' he said. 'No. I mean yes. I mean thank you, sir, but you can pay when you leave, sir. Enjoy your stay in Drakkesborg, sir . . .'

Everything the Freyjan Guildsman had said about *The Two Towers* was true – including his warning about the prices. Kyrin was able to understand more clearly why

169

Aldric had acquired such a quantity of cash, for their accommodation and meals for the next week would take a sizeable bite out of it. At least they were getting what they paid for. She had never seen such luxury, not even when they had been hauled into the presence of Alba's King Rynert that time in Erdhaven. His home-from-home and part-time palace had been furnished in the classic Alban style of understated elegance, whereas there was nothing understated about *The Two Towers*. It shouted opulence at the top of its voice.

There seemed to be a competition between the bedroom and the bathroom as to which could shout loudest; the bathroom probably won on grounds of sheer sybaritic exuberance. Kyrin had thought the tavern three nights ago had come close to crossing the border between elegance and excess, but it seemed either that the *Towers* had never heard of any difference between the two, or had forgotten it superbly. There was no nonsense here about wooden tubs, no matter how fine the wood might be, or water-coppers heated by the same fire that warmed the room. The water for *this* bathroom, they had been informed in proud and enthusiastic detail, came from the cellar furnaces that kept the whole inn warm, and in unlimited supply. The centre of the floor was all bath, sunken into it and ringed with baskets holding sponges and fine soaps in block form and in handsome ceramic jars. Its fittings were either solid gold or some other metal so heavily gilded as to make little difference, and for those who preferred steam-baths in the fashion of the Eastern Empire and – Kyrin grinned and made straight for it – the far North, there was a timber cubicle and an iron rack loaded with sleekly river-polished granite rocks that could be heated in the room's own fire. Aldric, of course, tried both; and when they emerged from their respective baths they tried the bed as well.

Whether or not it was the brief altercation with the clerk downstairs or any of the various other distractions of the past hour, Aldric was quite recovered from the stomach-flutters born of his first venture into surgery by the time a liveried servant brought the night's bill of fare for their inspection. There was fish, both fresh and smoked; five meats; two sorts of roasted bird; vegetables fried, boiled, steamed, and baked in a sour-hot sauce; pastries with two savoury and three sweet stuffings; four soups; seven cheeses; and a sufficient variety of different wines to leave even Aldric lost for choice.

After making their decisions during a lengthy, amiable wrangle with each other and the servant – who had opinions of his own and was not afraid to share them – they changed from their rakishly-wrapped towels into fresh clothing and sauntered down to the tavern's dining-room, set comfortably far away from the noise and smoke of the public common-room. Aldric nodded equably to the clerk as they passed him, pausing long enough to make some softly-spoken enquiries before arranging to rent a carriage after dinner.

'What for?' Kyrin asked as they took their places at the quiet corner table Aldric had requested. There was a bottle packed in snow already waiting for them; it seemed that the desk clerk was apparently trying to put right his earlier mistake by being more than just knowledgeable and obliging.

'After-dinner entertainment,' said Aldric, lifting the chilled bottle and pouring wine for each of them. 'And behaving entirely as two wealthy people such as we appear *would* behave.' He swirled his own glass thoughtfully under his nose and sipped; then seemed to forget what he was about to say, gazing instead into the middle distance with a dreamy expression on his face. A moment later he shook himself just a little, and gave the shy half-smile that might go with learning all was well with the world after all. 'Anyway, we're visiting the theatre. And this is as fine a Seurandec as I've ever drunk. If it's a bribe from that clerk, I think we'll forgive him.'

Kyrin, amused, had watched his little byplay with the wine, well aware it was for the benefit of various watching eyes. No wine could be that good. Except that this wine was . . . 'Which play – as if I had to ask? *The Prince*, wasn't it?'

'Of course. And that's *Tiluan the Prince*.' He glanced sideways as plate-bearing servants made their way towards the table. 'Oh, God be thanked. Food!'

By mutual consent all attempts to talk were suspended for the next few minutes, at least until the first fine edge of a noble hunger had been blunted. Dinner began with a dish of several smoked meats and fishes, arranged in a handsome pattern and then glazed with a thin piquant jelly of red wine and bitter oranges; then came the grilled freshwater crayfish tails, the veal in cream and white wine sauce with morels, the bacon-stuffed potatoes roasted in herb butter and the half-dozen other items they had ordered. Both were grateful that they had thought to make an additional request – for small portions to offset the variety of the food.

It was Kyrin who first broke the companionable silence with more than the softly-voiced exclamations of pleasure that might occur at any dinner table and so scarcely qualify as conversation. 'Aldric,' she said, 'what plans have you made? Or haven't you made any at all?'

The wine-glass lifting to his lips paused for a beat and then returned untasted to the table. He smiled, the sort of pleasant smile that would be adequate response to almost anything; except that it went no further than a mouth which shaped it by a deliberate movement of muscles and left his eyes cold, cold, cold . . .

'Hit,' he said flatly. 'One point to the lady. How long have you known?'

'Since now.' Kyrin shrugged. 'It was no more than a guess.'

'Best you know . . . so you can start to understand.'

Aldric tried another smile and still his facial muscles seemed unwilling to carry the expression. He pushed his plate aside, appetite fading as fast as the smile. 'I've been hoping for some wonderful idea. I hoped that maybe coming here, starting to make all the proper moves, playing the part without a script, would produce some flash of brilliance, something foolproof.' He shook his head, pressed fingertips to head in imitation of deep thought and grinned, a wry expression that seemed much more at home than anything humorous. 'Not a damned thing – except such a bloody case of the shakes I'm surprised you never noticed.'

'Not such a bloody case as you thought. You covered well. You think terrified, but you don't act it. And you tried – you did your best.' Kyrin stretched luxuriously; despite the intensity of the murmured words, they were both taking care to maintain the pretence of a young couple with too much money, enjoying it and all that it could bring. There was a deal of released tension in that stretch, but she wasn't about to say so here and now. 'Now we can leave.'

'Without the Jewel?'

'Let the Warlord keep it. Let Gemmel get it back himself. When he put that spell into your head he took away whatever duty you owed him, and when he took it out he gave you back your free will. You don't owe anybody anything any more.' She stopped talking abruptly and took a mouthful of wine, trying to cool the angry heat that was building in her words. 'Except maybe . . . you owe yourself a life. Start living it.'

Aldric sat quite still for a long time, and it seemed to Kyrin that she could see the thoughts swim in his eyes like fish – except that these thoughts were black fins cutting through grey water. Then he blinked and the image was gone. 'Tonight,' he said, 'we'll go to see the play.' He got to his feet, drawing Kyrin up with him. 'And then tomorrow we'll go home.'

Lacework patterns of frost obscured the windows' leaded panes, and icicles hung from the snow above them in a ragged fringe, like fangs in a gaping white-gummed mouth. Dark clouds drifted across the moon.

Inside was colder still, and darker. *Woydach* Voord could feel the blood thickening and freezing in his veins despite the charms of warmth and nourishment and guard that ringed him. The candles had gone out, choked in their own stinking grease, and he hadn't dared leave his protective circle to relight them. Voord had seen what happened to people who were rash enough to make that mistake, and had no desire to experience the same rending at first hand. His own hand hurt him, throbbing alternately hot and cold along the marks of its mutilation. All the other injuries had faded to a background murmur of discomfort, but here in this place the old wound pained him as if newly inflicted. Voord was on his knees at the centre of the circle, a weaving of curves and words, of angles and symbols and letters inlaid in black on the white marble floor of his most private chamber. In the intermittent, frost-muffled moonlight, it lay on the surrounding pavement as stark as ink on paper. Slow coils of spicy incense smoke echoed the shapes that made the circle . . . then, shifting subtly on unfelt currents in the icy air, made mock of them instead.

There was a heavy droning that filled all parts of the room, a sound like bees in summer – or flies around a ten-day corpse. It swelled and receded in slow waves of sourceless noise, then faded slowly, slowly, until it was gone. Voord stayed where he was for a long time, making absolutely sure, sweating even as he froze. At long last he stood up – a movement that seemed more like one long shudder – and looked about him. There had been starless void beyond the circle, and Presence. Now he was alone in a circle at the centre of the room, hemmed in by shadows and by smoke-skeins that smelt of spice, of incense . . . and of roses.

Voord raised his hands with their palms pressed together – or as near together as the talon of his crippled hand allowed – then parted them, stepped across the circle's outermost perimeter and closed his hands again. It was a simple enough charm, to preserve the integrity of the protective patterns – and forgetting it had killed so many sorcerers that Voord was determined not to be the next unless he was quite sure that death was permanent.

And It had told him death was not . . . not yet, anyway. If he expended more power, then perhaps . . . If he gave It more gifts and sacrifices, then perhaps . . . If and perhaps; that was all he heard, nothing more certain than *if* and *perhaps*. Neither was enough for Voord to gamble the little power he still had at his disposal. He husbanded that, spending it as frugally as – Voord thought of his mother, years dead – a widow trying to feed her children. *If* and *perhaps*. Too many ifs for one uncertain perhaps. Get the equation wrong . . . and learn what Hell is really like.

He bowed towards the empty darkness, always mindful of his manners even when nothing was there – or seemed to be there. The courtesies were due, witnessed or not – but once they were completed Voord didn't linger. There was always the risk that until it had completely dissipated the aura of sorcery – and more especially of Summoning – lingering in the small dark chamber might attract other things than it was intended to, like wasps to honey. Now that he was outside the circle, if something like that were to happen he would as soon be out of the room as well. And preferably the city, the province and even the War-lord's Domain itself . . .

And once again, Tagen was waiting for him outside the door. Voord closed it, locked it and secured the key on its chain around his neck before he said anything at all. An awful jolt of fright had gone through him at the sight of the bulky silhouette backlit by the lanterns in the corridor outside, for with the smells of incense and roses still in his nostrils it had been only natural to think for just an instant that Something *had* been attracted . . . and even recognition didn't take away the fear at once. Tagen was a friend, a companion, a confidante, all those and more;

175

but there was and always had been an air about him which suggested the not-quite-natural, the sensation felt by others that was inadequately defined when men earned the title *Terrible*. Then Tagen saluted, and smiled, and the image was gone.

'I thought my orders were that I was not to be disturbed when in my workroom,' said Voord. 'Wasn't I clear enough?'

'Sir, I know that. So I didn't disturb you at your work; I waited.'

Voord looked at him, then up and down the corridor. It was icy down here, for except the lanterns there was no other source of heat; and the still more intense cold flowing out of his workroom had left long glittering fans of frozen air around and under the door – one of the reasons why a sorcerer didn't leave his spell-circle until certain it was safe to do so. However, Tagen's comfort was not his foremost concern: it was what the man might have heard. 'Did you wait long?'

'Until you were done and came out, sir. Your orders said *under no circumstances*, and that means never.'

Voord shrugged, dismissing the matter with the realisation that whatever his henchman might have overheard, it would have been done by the Commander and that would make it all right. Tagen was slow rather than simple; but disciplining him for the normal small infractions or too-literal interpretations of commands – which would be done without a second thought to any other soldier – seemed always too much wasted time. As well discipline a dagger when it cut one's finger. 'All right. Explanation accepted. Now, *why*?'

'Good news, sir. Two guards – they were on the Shadowgate duty shift between the hours of Hawk and Serpent this afternoon. Hault has them upstairs. In the Hall.' Tagen shouted the last words, because Voord was already running for the stairs.

★

'Yes, soldier, I know about the description sheet, there's no need to describe it,' said Voord impatiently. He stared at the two troopers, wanting to grab them by the fronts of their undress tunics and shake what they had to say out of them, rather than waiting while they took turns at making the most of their brief importance. At least their chattering had given him the chance to get his breath back; but now he'd had enough. 'I was the one who had it sent out, remember? Get to the point.'

'Yes, sir. A little before the bells struck for Serpent, Karn and me, we went off-duty at Dog; we were going for a drink and then to see the play, but he'd left his smokes behind.'

The soldier Karn held up a pipe and drawstring pouch for proof – then saw the expression in the *Woydach*'s face and gave his companion an elbow-nudge of warning. Voord noticed it and smiled thinly, a smile that was all teeth and cold, cold eyes.

'You're very right, Guard-trooper Karn. Because if I need to order Guard-trooper Volok to hurry up just one more time, I'll forgo the command and have the information beaten out of you. Do you both understand? Good. I see you do. Now talk! *Sch'dagh-veh hoh'tah'!*'

Trooper Volok's face had drained of any colour given it by the drinks he and Karn had consumed before going back to the Shadowgate to find Karn's forgotten pipe. He jolted through a rapid full-honours salute and slammed to rigid heels-together eyes-front parade attention before daring to say another word. All the stories told in barracks about *Hautheisart* Voord had taken on a new edge with the discovery that he was now Grand Warlord, and Volok was very scared indeed.

'Sir! We-admitted-two-people-who-might-be-the-state-eriminals-on-the-recent-warning-sheet-they-are-now-in-the - city - and - have - not - left - it - to - the - best - of - our - knowledge-at-least-not-by-the-same- gate-they-came-in-by *Sir!*' he said all in a single breath.

'Very observant,' said Voord, not troubling to keep the

satisfaction off his face. 'I'll remember both of you.' The troopers managed to maintain eyes-front – just – but there was a hint of a flinch about the way Karn stiffened his back like someone waiting to be flogged. Voord chuckled, feeling in rather better humour. 'Favourably, that is. Hault, pay them a bounty of ten florins apiece; it might remind them that it's worthwhile keeping their eyes open – and their mouths shut. Dismissed.'

When Hault and the two troopers had gone out, Voord glanced at Tagen. 'State criminals?' he asked.

'I didn't know what other charge to use, Commander. And they're your enemies and you're the State, so . . .'

Voord concealed his groan behind a cough. 'Yes, of course. Well done, Tagen. And thank you for the compliment.' He stood up, feeling the wounds ache again and not caring just this once. 'Turn out the Guard. Close the gates and seal the city. Start a search from the walls inward . . . and bring what you find to me . . .'

EIGHT

'*Tiluan the Prince*, now. How could you be sure of finding a performance? There must be lots of other plays playing in a city as big as this . . . ?' Kyrin adjusted her balance against the slight sway of the coach and quirked her brows quizzically at Aldric.

'It's the size of the city that counts. At this time of year there's bound to be some company somewhere playing *Tiluan* as well as all the others.'

'Time of year? Surely it's not a religious play? Not with men in towels, dropping them everywhere . . .'

'That performance was by me. Just me.'

'Mmm. I still like the bit with the towel; they should put it in the real play.'

'Ask them and maybe they will.'

'I might. I just might . . .'

In a city as large as Drakkesborg, Aldric had known there would be at least one theatre performing the seasonal dramas, and the clerk of *The Two Towers* had directed him to the most well-known and splendid and now the most modern as well, the new Old Playhouse, recently refurbished and made *New* at great expense to house the Lord Constable's Men. He and Kyrin spent the short journey looking through the sheaf of pamphlets and hand-bills which all the theatres printed at this time of year to entice customers through their doors. Comical; historical; tragical; and all the subgenres, admixtures and complicated bastard children that resulted from combining them together.

' "*The Claw Unsheath'd*, by Reswen and Lorin",' read Kyrin, laughing as she made sure to give a good delivery to all the emphases, ' "being a very Pretty Fine new Fantastical Satire, where Cats are shewn large as Men, with

179

Marvellous new Masks and Costumes *never before seen*! Also Musick, Songs and Dances wrought *for this play only*!!" ' She fluttered the sheet of paper at Aldric and grinned. 'This has to be a joke!'

'No. But it *is* a sequel . . .' Aldric unfolded another pamphlet, this one with four pages and coloured illustrations, all very splendid – which to a cynical mind might suggest that the play it advertised needed all the support it could get. 'Whereas this . . . !' He seemed unable to decide between wry amusement and genuine anger. ' "Count your country and yourself fortunate. *Lord Urick's Revenge*, or *The Alban Tragedy*, by Gaufrid ar Meulan." '

'What's wrong?' Kyrin was making a very good attempt at keeping her face straight, but it wasn't really working. 'Did you *know* this Urick person?'

'Hardly; it's not even an Alban name – though I'll concede it's close, very close. The enticement, I'm afraid, continues at some length. "A Play play'd in the True and Actual Costumes of that Land with Swords, Harness and etcetera all recreat'd in the Barbaric Splendour of that People. Together with such Musick, Songs and Dancing as are us'd commonly in that Land, played by Proper skill'd musicians, brought Here with their very Instruments at Much Cost and No Small Peril to the Company.

' "There will be in this Drama three strong Castles besieg'd with Real Siege-Engines, to be seen upon the Stage shooting Fire as in Life; a Battle of Two Hosts; a great Sea-Storm, with Thunder-and-Lightning made by Herran d'Win, Thundermaker to the Lord Constable's Men; Lord Urick's Concubines, seen clad in the Flimsy Garments of such Lewd Females and play'd by Real Women; and many other Delights." '

'Is that what they really think of you . . . ?'

'It's the popular image, which counts for the same thing in the long run.' Aldric looked once more at the pamphlet and its gaudy woodcuts, then folded it up and creased the folds down to a razor edge with nails that were far more ready to tear the offensive thing to rags and tatters. 'Never mind. We're not going to see that, regardless of the "Real Women in Flimsy Garments". At least Osmar uses words instead of' – he spat the word like an insult – 'spectacle.'

'The Playhouse, sir, milady,' said the coachman. 'Play's not started yet, so no need to rush.'

Translated as, no need to hurry off without giving me a few coins extra, thought Aldric without malice as he helped Kyrin back into her furred over-robe. *And why not?*

'Well driven, man,' he said aloud, dropping an extra couple of coins into the coachman's hand. 'Now get yourself into a tavern and have some ale to keep out the cold, then collect us here after the play.'

'Sir, yes sir,' said the coachman, saluting with the butt-end of his whip but quite unable to take his eyes from the soft golden glint of the two quarter-crowns resting in the palm of his glove. Whoever or whatever his passenger might be, he had just been tipped maybe half the value of the whole carriage for one short ride. The coachman fought a brief and silent battle between avarice and conscience, before conscience – reluctantly – won. 'Sir, you've given me—'

'What I meant to give you. Just don't talk about it, in case the lady's . . .' Aldric gave him a conspiratorial wink. 'Ahem. Never mind that. Go get your drink, and be here later.'

'Yes *sir!*'

'Why?' asked Kyrin. She had seen the gold change hands where silver would have sufficed and was understandably curious.

'Because,' he said. 'That's all.'

Kyrin smiled. 'That's enough – for me at least.'

Aldric glanced sidelong at the departing coach, not smiling. 'And for him, I hope. Shall we go in?'

The good citizens of Drakkesborg had long been used to soldiers on their streets. The city was not only the capital of the Warlord's Domain but had for a long time been a garrison town in its own right, so that the sounds of drum and trumpet and the business of military routine went almost unnoticed . . . until the routine changed. As it was changing now.

Because of the many barracks within the walls and the consequent need for a degree of both security and military discipline, Drakkesborg's gates had always been shut at night from the striking of the hour Fox at ten o' clock to the hour Horse at six the next morning, but those with the proper papers could still enter and leave without restriction through the smaller posterns. Except that this night, the great iron siege-screens were in place and locked before the half-way strike of Dog at seven, sealing the entire city like a corked bottle. Neither papers nor bluster nor bribes were enough to obtain entrance for those outside; and use of the same methods by those trying to get out resulted only in quick, quiet arrest.

After the rioting earlier in the week, followed only this morning by a vigorous restoration of order, no one was concerned by the presence of the constables or the urban militia, even though both now wore light armour beneath their uniform tunics and carried hardwood truncheons in full view as a deterrent to anyone thinking of resuming such nonsense. If anything they were a comfort to the law-abiding majority, a reminder that their right to walk the city streets without harm was being protected, but the men who joined them as the evening drew on were not a sight that held the least reassurance.

Some were in full battle harness and bore gisarms instead of staves. They had shortswords, still sheathed but with the red tapes of their peace-bindings unsealed, and their armour bore the mailed-fist insignia of the Bodyguard, down from the citadel itself. Elite troops to be sure, but still only soldiers. It was the others who sent people hurrying to clear the streets: those whose rank-robes showed no rank at all, only the jagged black and silver thunderbolts that marked them as *Kagh'Ernvakh*.

Getting behind a door and locking it was of little use,

for as the formation of armed men moved forward in an iron ring that encircled the city perimeter, every building that they passed was searched. The regular law enforcement officers had all their entry warrants ready, and somehow contrived to leave the places that they had examined as neat if not neater than when they came in; but the Bodyguard and the Secret Police went in where they pleased, whether that was through a door or through a window – or even through a wall if the notion struck them as amusing – and left devastation in their wake.

Privilege was no protection. The most privileged person in Drakkesborg was the Grand Warlord who had commanded this operation, and neither rank, money nor the names of friends in high places were of any use. Occasionally such attempts were made to sway the intrusive troopers, but as at the gate those making the attempt were either ignored or put under close arrest on any one of half-a-dozen charges.

No matter how ruthless they were, it was a slow business. Drakkesborg's position as first – or second-wealthiest city in the Empire might have been subject to question, but that it was by far the largest both in buildings and in population had never been in doubt. Slow or not, progress was made and small successes scored; the suddenness of the security raids caught several criminals red-handed in the middle of their preferred crimes, and with no need for a court to judge a guilt which was apparent to all, justice was swift and bloody.

It was, as young *Tau-kortagor* Hakarl of the Secret Police observed to his men, a bit like lifting up a rock and finding something nasty underneath that needed to be squashed. His squad did its own fair share of squashing before they reached the Merchants' Quarter and Hakarl thought to find out what the Guilds themselves might know . . .

Oren Osmar's *Tiluan the Prince his Life and Triumph* was recognised as a classic throughout the Drusalan Empire, and was perhaps the most enduringly popular of the Vrei-jek playwright's works. Because most of its action took place during the Feast of the Fires of Winter when the days reached their shortest and began to lengthen again, it had been performed at the Winter Solstice since its writing almost three centuries before, in guises varying from masques to musicals.

According to the pamphlet in Aldric's hand, this present revival was based not on Drusalan translations but on the Jouvaine-language original. Having read that same original some two years earlier, and knowing the current state of political turmoil within the Empire, Aldric doubted this production's vaunted 'accuracy' at once. In the present climate an Imperial audience would hardly appreciate either the plot or the sentiments it expressed – all about fealty to a Lord rather than to his chiefmost Lieutenant – and especially not this audience.

Their entry vouchers had been assured by a runner sent from the *Towers*, and as they were shown to their seats another sheet of paper was pressed into Aldric's hand to keep all the rest company. This, on a superior quality heavy paper, carried the usual things that wealthy theatre-goers might want to know: the names of the Lord Const-able's Men and of their characters, a useful if over-lengthy synopsis of the plot, a briefer and more restrained descrip-tion of the effects that had been levered in between Osmar's words – though the programme didn't express it in quite that way – and where, from whom and for how much food and drink could be acquired.

There was an unsettling number of soldiers in the audi-ence, wearing either undress uniform or their best civilian clothes, but all labelled clearly by their neatly – if exces-sively – close-cropped heads. Aldric's own hair was not long recovered from just such a military crop, and though Kyrin either didn't notice them or made a point of not registering their existence, he felt uneasy until it was clear that both their seats – while commanding an excellent view of the stage – were shadowed by a pillar and by the

184

balcony above it. The nasty sensation of being watched was probably a result of nothing more than hindsight-aided wariness; but this was augmented by the idle glances turned towards him by so many of the Empire's military, any of whom might through the workings of an unkind fate have recognised him from past events. He didn't feel truly comfortable until the house-lights were hoisted into their dark-shades and the play began.

Events on stage were more than enough to distract anyone's attention, with plenty to entertain the senses as well as – Aldric sniffed, exchanged a pointed glance with Kyrin in the gloom and smiled thinly – *ymeth* and other substances in use to dull them.

The audience's own small entertainments aside, *Tiluan the Prince* had been brought up to date with a vengeance. There was one scene, the Betrayal, which should have been restrained and intimate, as terrifying as a whisper in a darkened room. Instead it took place during the gold and scarlet glitter (the Emperor's colours, a fact not lost on any of the audience still in possession of their senses) of a court ceremony, contrasting outward splendour against inner corruption. The overt political comment did not go unnoticed, drawing whistles and jeering laughter as the scene reached its conclusion – which, to Aldric's mind, suggested it had worked quite well enough.

Trumpets in the wings and among the musicians blared an elaborate fanfare as first the lamps and then the curtain opened up again. Figures in armour fantastical as that of insects strutted to and fro beneath their gilded banners, declaiming the famous well-known speeches that each drew their own separate applause:

It pleases me to see the joyful season that is Autumn.

the actor playing Overlord Broknar was saying,

For it swells the fruit upon the trees
And makes the harvest rich and tall.
And it pleases me to hear . . .

★

Gibart d'Reth had been a Guildsman for forty of his fifty-seven years. He enjoyed it; there was a certain sense of satisfaction in watching, helping and, as time passed, controlling the extraordinary sums of other people's money that gave a merchant guild its power. The power rubbed off. Few men were as respected as the Guildsmen, and few Guildsmen so respected as those of Guild Freyjan's House in Drakkesborg. There was a degree of amiable rivalry between his House and its opposite number in Kalitzim, but on the whole Gibart felt that he was the senior Master in the Empire. Certainly he saw more money in the form of cold, hard cash than Ascel in Kalitzim could ever hope to do. If he wasn't bound by the near-religious secrecy of the Guild, he could tell such tales . . .

Drakkesborg was like that. There was enough luxury for any man to enjoy, especially if like Gibart d'Reth he was a bachelor as well as wealthy, but beneath the surface the city was simmering with plots and intrigue. Senior officers in all the arms of service had far more gold to hand than on their rank insignia, and were working busily to have it moved away from any area of trouble – which in the present climate meant right out of the Empire. And then there were the ordinary matters of business, which were sometimes far from what a layman merchant would regard as normal practice. Gibart smiled at the thought and closed his last ledger of the night. He put it, with all the others, into an iron safe with powdered clay packed tightly between its double skin as a protection against fire, and turned the first of the three keys. This was a ritual performed every night, more important by far than simply locking away the Guild's gold. There was not sufficient gold in all the Empire to buy those ranks of dull blue covers – or more precisely, the transactions recorded between them. He put the second key to its lock—

—Then dropped it at the sound of a crashing in the corridor outside. The key made a sound like a tiny metallic laugh as it bounced under the immovable mass of the safe, something that would normally have made Gibart swear at the prospect of the grubbing about with a bent piece of wire which usually followed such a fumble, but he was past worrying about such petty everyday annoyances. Sounds of violence in a Guild House after dark meant one thing only.

The door of his office was kicked open, so hard that it was vibrating like a drum as it shuddered to a halt, and three men stepped inside. Or rather two men, dragging what looked like a side of raw beef between them. Gibart came surging to his feet, mouth open to yell something about the outrageous liberty of entering a Guildsman's presence in this fashion; but he froze half-way as he recognised the side of beef.

It – *he* – was Kian, Guild House Drakkesborg's chief guard; and the horrified Gibart could identify him only by his size and by the Freyjan crests marked on his tattered gear. Not even the man's mother would have known him. Gibart could only stare wide-eyed and realise for the first time what that saying really meant.

'He didn't want to let us in,' said one of the two men bracing Kian by the elbows, and as he spoke both of them removed their support. The guard swayed forward and his head struck squarely in the centre of Gibart's desk before he rolled limply to the floor. 'Even though we told him that this was official business.'

'What the hell are you doing here?' roared Gibart d'Reth, finding his voice at last. 'And who gave you the right to act like—'

The riding-crop of plaited leather that slashed a weal across his cheek was just one more of the several shocks Gibart had suffered in the past few seconds; but it was the first one that really hurt. He clutched his face and flopped back into his chair, too stunned by the impact and the anguish and the suddenness of it all even to protest.

'I told you,' said the man who had spoken before; he was very young. 'Official business. That means the *Woydach* himself gives us the right.' He grinned, his teeth

187

very white against his tan and the shadows within his helmet, and reached out to stroke the tip of his crop lightly across the other side of Gibart's face. 'You don't object to that, now, do you?' Gibart said nothing; only his eyes moved, following the crop as it weaved to and fro before them like a plaited leather snake.

'Wise,' said *Tau-kortagor* Hakarl gently. 'Now,' he pulled a crumpled sheet of official-yellow paper from the cuff of his glove, smoothed out the creases more or less and held it up for Gibart to see. 'Read this description and then tell me: have you seen this man . . . ?'

> . . . *the song of the birds*
> *Who make their mirth resound through all the woods . . .*

'Broknar' was over-acting just a touch, his gestures too flamboyant and his voice too determinedly thrilling, but at least it cut through the chords of exciting music so that everyone could hear what was after all the best known speech in the entire play.

Just so long as he doesn't sing, thought Aldric with a mirthless smile. The smile faded almost as soon as it appeared, for he was beginning to hear something very wrong in the treatment of this crucial speech – something very wrong indeed, and a wrongness that was of a piece with the unsubtle use of colours on the stage.

Tiluan's colours were the red and gold of the Emperor – that much he had noticed already, and thought no more than some satirical observation; but 'Broknar', leader of the group of lords who seized the country from its prince, not only wore the Grand Warlord's black and silver but was speaking the words of a hero.

The historical Broknar had been a usurper who with his companions had misruled the land and brought it to the edge of ruin before remorseful suicide had restored order, and had been treated as such in Osmar's original play. Here he was portrayed as a wise, experienced military man who had *rescued* the land from an immature and wilful tyrant. The whole play was a propaganda for the *Woydachul*, and for a policy of war. Just the sort of thing that would appeal to the young hot-heads amongst the lords and officers of the Warlord's Domain; they wouldn't object to a war, no, not at all, for the sake of its drama, its romance, its excitement – and the rapid promotion that comes with filling dead men's shoes.

Aldric stared at them, actors and audience both. He still remembered – how could he forget? – riding past the battlefield of Radmur Plain, not quite nine months ago. *Righteous Lord God, was it really so short a time?* Enough to begin a new life of his own, but not enough and never enough to restore the tens of hundreds of lives cut short on those bloody pastures.

It had been before the burial parties started work and he had seen a mile-wide meadow strewn with men and horses, all bloating in the warm Spring sun. He had smelt them, too. Even the mere memory of that ripe stench was enough to make him wrinkle his nose. A whiff of it here would drown out the scent of *ymeth* and of perfume, and put paid to such nonsense as was being ranted from the stage. Or would it . . . ?

And it pleases me to see ranged along the field
Bold men and horses armed for war.
And it pleases me to see my foemen run away,
And I feel great joy when I see strong citadels besieged,
The broken ramparts caving in among the flowers of fire,
And I have pleasure in my heart when I behold the hosts
Upon the water's edge, closed in all around by ditches,
With palisades of strong stakes close together . . .

Kyrin's mouth quirked in distaste and she turned to look at Aldric to ask if this was really, truly, the rest of the speech she had heard him quote with such good cheer and laughter. Her question was never asked, because the expression on his face provided her with answer enough.

And once entered into battle let every man
Think only of cleaving arms and heads,

For a man is worth more dead than alive and beaten!
I tell you there is not so much savour
In eating or drinking or sleeping
As when I hear them scream . . .

Aldric stared coldly at the rest of the audience, not feeling superior but just more bitterly experienced. Though most were drinking in the ringing words, several – the more imaginative – were looking apprehensive, and one or two almost queasy. *Oh Light of Heaven I would love to make you sick*, he thought savagely. *All of you. You might be less enthusiastic for this sewage then.* The images were there, rising unbidden from the dark corners of his mind like drowned men in the first thaw: a raven with an eyeball on its pick-axe beak; the putrid seethe of maggots; grey wolves whose pelts were slimy with the juices from some mother's liquefying son.

' "I would speak to thee of all the glory that is war," ' quoted Aldric softly.

'You've seen it, haven't you?' Kyrin said. 'You know what it's really like.'

'Yes, I've seen that *glory*.' He seemed almost to be tasting the flavour of the word. 'Duergar Vathach used the Empire's way of making war; he brought it to Alba with him. Burnt villages, dead children and the sound of women weeping. Crows and buzzing flies and the air so thick with death that you could taste the stink. Sweet, and sickly, and foul.' He knuckled tiredly at his eye-sockets, all the warmth of wine and food quite gone and only a leaden coldness left behind. 'I know indeed. All too well. Kyrin, when this scene ends, we're going – back to the *Towers*, to pack our things. I want to leave the city at first light tomorrow.'

'To go home?'

'Home. Or wherever. I just want away from here.'

'Sir, may I speak privately with you?'

'Not now, Holbrakt.' Hakarl paused on the threshold

190

of *The Two Towers*, a mink baulked at the door of a chicken-run, and glanced back at his serjeant. The man's expression – what could be seen of it – was worried. 'Or is it as important as you make it look?'

'Yes, sir. I fear it is.'

'Damn you!' Hakarl's voice was calm, controlled, without animosity in the curse. 'All right, then. You, you and you,' Hakarl pointed with his crop, an odd accoutrement for a foot soldier but one he found most useful nonetheless, 'get in there. If he's there, call me *at once*. If he's not, ask – nicely, at first.' The *tau-kortagor* smiled so that his men could see it. 'But don't stop asking until you get an answer.'

He left them to their own devices, however inventive and worth watching those might become before the information was obtained, and turned back to Holbrakt. The serjeant still looked like someone with griping in the guts, far from comfortable with whatever it was he had to say.

'What's the matter, man? Your belly hurt?'

'No sir, my neck. As if there was a headsman's axe resting across it.' Hakarl watched him but said nothing. 'I mean, sir, the Guild Houses and what was done in them.'

'I did wonder . . .'

'Four Guilds will hold you responsible, *Tau-kortagor*, sir. They will—'

'Do nothing.' Hakarl cocked his head sideways and listened as the thuds and grunts and cries of an impromptu interrogation reached his ears. 'Particularly when I bring these criminals before the *Woydach*. That's the way to be forgiven, Holbrakt; forgiven for anything.' The rhythmic thudding from inside the inn stopped and there was silence; then a sound of breaking glass and an instant afterwards a high, shrill scream suddenly cut off.

'But you killed two Guildsmen and tortured three—'

'I, serjeant? Why all this *you* that I keep hearing. What about *we* and *us*, or did I merely imagine seeing you and all the others? You didn't falter when there was a chance

191

of finding gold coins piled up on the shelves. Was that what you expected, serjeant?' Hakarl flexed the whippy crop between his hands and smiled. 'Was that why you didn't make your little speech until now, eh? Well, they don't keep their cash like that these days, as I could have told you had you asked.'

Holbrakt took a step backwards, skidded on the frozen snow beneath his heel and almost fell. *Tau-kortagor* Hakarl laughed at the man's discomfiture. 'That's right, serjeant. There's no sure footing any more, and we are all of us in this together . . . which some realised before you chose to say it.' He tapped the crop against his boot and looked pleased with himself. 'That's why Meulan needed only a suggestion and not an order before he went back to fire all the Guild Houses that show . . . ah . . . signs of interference. Rioters and looters, Holbrakt; they always take advantage of any confusion in the city. Am I not right . . . ?'

'Yes, sir.' The words came out grudgingly, but they came out nonetheless. 'You are, sir.'

'Then remember it. Ah, good.' Hakarl turned to face his three troopers as they emerged from the inn. One of them was flexing his fingers and blowing on bruised knuckles, the others were wiping blood-smears from their truncheons. 'What news?'

'Sir, we have him. Both of them. They're in The Playhouse even now – watching *Tiluan*, if you please.'

'I do please. Very much. Because the play's no more than half-way done by now, and because we've bloody got them . . . ! Well, come on, *move!*'

And when I hear them fall among the palisades and ditches,
Little men and great men all one on the bloodied grass,
And I see fixed in the flanks of the corpses
Stumps of spears with silken streamers,
Then I have pleasure in the downfall of my enemies!
Great Lords and soldiers of this great Empire,

Pawn your mansions and your cities and your towers
Before you give up making war upon all who oppose you!
Swiftly go now to the great Grand Warlord and tell him
He has lived in peace too long!

As the scene intensified the stage lights dimmed as tinted shutters were drawn across them; but as the symbolic darkness fell Aldric stiffened in his seat and his eyes went very wide, trying to make use of the remaining glimmer of red light and thus make sense of what they saw. His stare was fixed on one man's face, an Imperial officer glimpsed in profile just as the stage beyond went black. There had been something about those adze-carved features, a strange familiarity that sent a nervous shivering all over his skin, as if God had spoken his name and not with favour. It was a face which raised questions, the kind of questions that needed urgent answers.

'Up,' he snapped to Kyrin. 'Up and out, right now.'

'Now? You said at the end of the—'

'Don't argue with me. Do it.'

Kyrin's eyes went wide and her face paled, for though she had heard him use that flat and deadly tone of voice before it had never, ever been directed at her. It was only when she saw how the anger and mild disgust on his face had been replaced with something very close to fear that she began to understand. They got to their feet quickly, quietly and with minimum inconvenience to those around them.

'Play faint,' Aldric whispered, fanning Kyrin with the playbill as he laid a comforting – and concealing – arm across her shoulders to force her head downwards and out of sight. 'I'll help you out.' They managed to work their way clear of their own seats and along the row for a few feet – and then the scene ended, and so did their escape.

Neither Aldric nor Kyrin had expected anyone else in the Playhouse to stand up just as they did, clapping their hands and shouting for a reprise of the most raucous part of the speech. Although there was enough applause to cover the movement of a troop of horse, there was also enough movement in the audience itself to prevent that troop of horse from taking more than two steps in any direction. They managed those two steps as the cheering died down a little, only to be trapped again when the actor playing 'Broknar' returned to the stage.

The man held up his hands for silence, and waited patiently during the few minutes while the mannerly resumed their seats and went quiet – then for the few minutes further while they shushed their less courteous or more drunken neighbours.

'My lords, my ladies and good people all,' said 'Broknar', making his obeisance to all into a single splendid gesture, 'I pray you, let the play continue to its true conclusion; for the company do promise that they shall both reprise and re-enact while yet in costume when all the action's done, being certain that more will be demanded than just the words of this poor player. Enjoy our play – and of your mercy, make way for the lady that she may recover and return ere we begin again.'

Aldric flinched and felt his stomach give a lurch like something pushed abruptly off a roof; but, trapped too far away to return to their seats, somehow they both contrived to remain within their roles. Kyrin put one hand to her face and forehead again, concealing any expression that might betray her, while Aldric inclined his head to acknowledge the actor's thoughtfulness – and to conceal his features from whoever might find them of interest. But neither, now the focus of benevolent attention, moved quite fast enough.

The Imperial officer Aldric had spotted as the last scene ended glanced once incuriously in their direction; then again, far more intently, and stood up to see them better. Aldric saw his eyes and his mouth move, and he knew that what the man had said was '*You . . .*'

Aldric was able to go one better, if 'better' meant having a name go howling through his head rather than vague sounds of recognition forming on his lips. Warship commanders needed shore leave as much as lesser mortals, and it was likely that most would try to spend the winter holiday somewhere they could be assured of entertainment – like the capital of whichever region of the Empire had their allegiance. But whatever had brought *Hautmarin* Doern of the battleram *Aalkhorst* to The Playhouse on this night of all nights, Aldric hoped that it was choking on the laughter of its dismal joke.

There was no real enmity between Doern and himself, but after their last and so far only encounter the *hautmarin* would want to know what business brought the man he knew only as a mercenary – and a sorcery-enravelled one at that – to the heart of the Warlord's Domain. It wasn't every battleram commander whose ship had helped destroy one of the flying demons known as *isghun*, and even the wildest optimist wouldn't dare to hope he had forgotten it already. Aldric was not an optimist – at least not in a situation such as this. The only hope he entertained was that Doern had read only blank non-recognition from his face rather than the startled concern that was really there – and it was a hope dashed almost at once, when the *hautmarin* yelled, 'You there, *stop!*'

That Doern would know nothing of which he could suspect them was never any obstacle to an Imperial officer; flight was guilt until proved otherwise, and their departure from the theatre would already have seemed flight enough. At the same moment they broke free of the audience who hemmed them in, and ran. Kyrin, aware of it as much as Aldric, was playing her part to the hilt in an attempt to give their haste another reason. With one hand to her forehead and another flat across her stomach, she projected such an impression of a pathetically sick lady of quality that the crowd who might have tried to block someone with a sword parted to let her through.

Hautmarin Doern and the two other men who were presumably his First and Executive officers were trying to follow, but like all the other military men in the Playhouse they were in civilian clothes. It was a small point, but where the people around them would have scattered in obedience to the orders of a Fleet uniform, now they merely continued to resume their seats or even actively obstruct the passage of a trio whose actions they regarded as being no more than rude. Sparing a second at the door to glance behind him, Aldric saw just enough of Doern's difficulties to create a sort of smile. Then Kyrin's hand was pulled from his own as she was seized, dragged through the door and out of sight. Aldric's smile dissolved in an oath and he kicked the closing door wide open, plunged outside . . . then froze.

There were eight men standing across the entrance of the theatre, all in the thunderbolt-slashed black of *Kagh'-Ernvakh*, the nominally-Secret Police. A ninth lounged nonchalantly against one of the uprights that supported the entrance awning, tapping a riding-crop against his booted leg and looking very pleased, for all that he and his men seemed out of breath. 'You see, Holbrakt,' he said smugly to the tenth and last man, the one standing beside him who was holding Kyrin by the elbow, 'I knew that we should double-time it here before the end of the play. And once again, am I not right . . . ?'

'Yes, *Tau-kortagor* Hakarl, sir.' From his tone the other soldier didn't seem especially happy to make the admission. 'You are, sir.'

'Well said. And you' – the junior officer Hakarl straightened himself and levelled his riding-crop at Aldric – 'are the man the *Woydach* wants.'

Aldric ignored the threat implicit in the crop and stared instead at its wielder, not much liking what he saw. So this was the face of the new order in Drusul, the face of the New Imperial Man whose destiny it was to rule and be obeyed. It was scarcely an appealing prospect. 'Why me?' he asked.

'Because the *Woydach* said so should be good enough for you, *hlensyarl*. Good enough for you and your woman both.'

Hakarl's words made Aldric shiver; this was becoming

too much like the episode at Ivern's steading. It required a conscious act of will to keep his right hand away from Widowmaker's hilt. No sense in starting trouble yet; there would be time enough for that when the moment came. 'And why the rough handling? We're guests in your city, *Kortagor*, not criminals.'

'My orders say otherwise.' Hakarl made a quick motion of encirclement with the thonged tip of the crop. 'Take him.'

Isileth Widowmaker came out of her scabbard with the sort of eager metallic singing that gives even the most battle-hardened soldier pause for thought, and these men were not combat troops no matter how the term was stretched. Their more usual opponents were unarmed men and women, confused beyond the capability for rational thought by being woken from a sound sleep in the small hours of the morning by the noise of their house doors being kicked in. The sight of a longsword poised in the hands of someone who looked all too eager to use it produced an immobility that made nonsense of Hakarl's order.

'*Sh'voda moy, Kagh'Ernvakh*,' said Aldric, and for all that he spoke softly there was a deal more authority in his voice than there had been in Hakarl's. Widowmaker levelled in exactly the way that the young officer had levelled his riding-crop, her gleaming, bitter edges giving extra weight to the gesture. Aldric tracked her point from face to face, slowly, as if he was letting the blade have first sight of her prey. '*Hlakhan tey'aj-hah, ya vlech-hu taii-ura! H'nach-at slijeii keii'ch da?* Or as we say at home, who's first?'

'The woman!' snapped Hakarl and chopped his hand downwards.

There was another quick scrape of drawn steel – then Holbrakt shrieked hoarsely and fell over as Tehal Kyrin put the serjeant's own stolen shortsword through his left lung. She stepped back, whipping blood from the blade with a quick sideways slash that – deliberately – sent a spatter across Hakarl's glossy boots, and said, 'Not quite. Who's next?'

'What are you going to do?' asked Hakarl mockingly. 'Fight the whole city garrison?'

It was a question that had occurred to Aldric and Kyrin already. Before blood was spilt they might have had a chance to talk their way out of this situation, although with the Warlord's personal involvement – if the young *tau-kortagor* spoke truth at all – that was always unlikely. Now, with one of the Secret Police choking in the snow, it was downright impossible . . .

Then everything happened at once. Hakarl, still not convinced that what Kyrin had done was more than lucky accident, snapped the lash of his crop at her eyes with one hand and with the other ripped his own sword from its sheath into a thrust at her throat; the theatre door burst open as Doern and his two companion officers finally reached the exit and jerked back into the Playhouse again as three feet of *taiken* split the still-swinging door in half from top to bottom; and in the momentary shift of Aldric's concentration all eight of the remaining troopers leapt at him . . .

Straight into the arc of a longsword's focused strike.

The snow went scarlet and began to melt as blood gouted steaming across it from two troopers whose concerns were more immediate than their bad landings. Two more, crumpled at the end of long smeared skid-marks, were no longer concerned by anything at all. The four who remained fell back in confusion at losing half their number to a single cut.

Aldric snarled silently at them. There was the pain of what felt like a pulled muscle in his shoulder, brought on by the strains and stresses of the impact, but otherwise nothing at all – no reaction to killing two men with a single blow and most likely mortally wounding two others. That would come later, when he had time for it. Right now his training and his reflex responses were all that mattered. More of this and he and Kyrin might – do what? Fight the whole garrison indeed? Run? Hide? Where . . . ?

During the brief lull he had enough time to glance across to where Kyrin matched cut for cut with Hakarl. She skidded for one heart-stopping instant on the snow, only to flick out her free hand and rip the riding-crop from his grasp before snapping it back across his eyes in a reflection of his own opening attack . . . but a reflection that moved slightly faster than the original. Hakarl's screech at his blinding was a muffled squawk, gagged by the wide blade that rammed up underneath his chin and almost took his head off.

Aldric saw her pull the shortsword free and look down at the corpse a moment, then turn towards him. He saw her eyes go wide and her mouth open in a cry of warning . . .

. . . But he didn't see *Hautmarin* Doern, or the make-shift cudgel descending on to the base of his skull. And after that all the world's lights went out.

NINE

A storm-wind came shrieking out of nowhere into the Hall
of Kings in Cerdor, and a spout of blue fire sprang up
before lashing itself into oblivion; when all was over and
silence had returned, Gemmel leaned against Ykraith the
Dragonwand and smiled a little wearily. 'It is done,' he
said. 'There will be peace in Alba, at least for a little time.
Now the matter of how long it lasts will rest with both of
you, and all of them, and what you have to say to one
another.'

Lord Dacurre said nothing, merely inclining his head
a touch in gratitude and more relief than he was prepared
to let the enchanter see. Lord Santon, younger and if not
more sceptical then certainly less controlled and infinitely
more curious about the ways of wizards, leaned forward
across his table and its carefully weighted paperwork and
stared. 'How? You can't have spoken to all the lords in
Alba! You were only gone a day!'

Gemmel and Dacurre glanced at one another and, their
differences temporarily set aside, exchanged the sort of
rolled-eyes look of despair that all old men with youthful
relatives must employ at some stage if they wish to keep
their tempers. For all that Hanar Santon was a high-clan
Alban lord, he was also the same age as Aldric Talvalin –
but lacked Aldric's four years of experience in why people
shouldn't ask users of the Art Magic just that sort of
damn-fool question.

'The *how* is my affair, my lord, and so is the time I
took to do it.' Gemmel's hesitation just before he spoke
made it quite clear that what he was saying now was not
what had first crossed his mind, and Dacurre was grateful
for the other man's restraint – such as it was. 'I much
regret that talking to full-blown Alban clan-lords – that

is, of course, *other* Alban clan-lords – is never something I prefer to take long over. They're all so . . . honourable.' He said it as if the word was a sticky sweetmeat lodged in a hollow tooth, and for all that Aymar Dacurre knew that he, too, could take offence if he so desired, the old man hid a smile behind his hand instead.

'What did you say to them?' Dacurre asked when his features were once more under some control. 'And what did they say to you?'

'Respectively, a little and a lot,' said Gemmel. 'And none of them offered me a chair, nor a drink, nor anything to eat despite the distance I had travelled . . .'

Dacurre went somewhat pink at having to be reminded of the oldest obligation due a lord of any standing – that of hospitality to guests. He rang the small bell on the desk in front of him with quite excessive vigour, and when the ringing was answered by two sentries and three servants – all of whom gaped to see Gemmel somewhere he shouldn't be without their knowing it – issued a rattle of orders that sent all five of them scurrying in different directions.

While Gemmel took first his seat and then some food and wine, Dacurre leafed through his files to find whichever papers might prove useful. There were very few. Alba's past rulers had made few provisions for being assisted in their work by the dubious class of wizards, sorcerers and enchanters. At least, unlike the Drusalan Empire, there were no laws on the statutes involving guilt for actually talking to one of them – and if there were, neither Dacurre nor Santon had seen them, and right now did not wish to.

Though he hid it better than the younger man, Dacurre was as curious about Gemmel as Santon seemed to be – a curiosity that today was based on something rather more solid and immediate than the whys and wherefores of the Art Magic. Aymar Dacurre was more concerned with the enchanter's clothes. On the few other occasions when their paths had crossed, Gemmel had been dressed in commonplace Alban garments – shirt and tunic, boots and breeches, jerkin and overmantle – quality work and weave, but none of them worthy of a second glance and certainly not the fanciful robes that sorcerers were supposed to wear. Only the ominous presence of the Dragon-wand had ever marked him out as different before; that was, until today. Now, under the furred overrobe that was the same concession to the season made by everyone, he was wearing what Dacurre could only think of as some kind of uniform – and one which, colours apart, was too like that of the Imperial military for comfort.

There was a high-necked shirt beneath the tunic, and he was wearing boots and breeches; but though the garments could be named, their austere cut and their material were unlike anything Dacurre had seen before. Everything was a blue so dark that it was almost black, with insignia in a silvery metal at the shoulders, cuffs and collar; except for the leather of boots and belt which *were* black and of an impossible glossiness. There was a flapped weapon-holster on the left side of the belt, supported at a cross-draw angle by a strap that ran across and down from the opposite shoulder, and at first glance it appeared to hold nothing more outlandish than a *telek*. Then Dacurre got a slightly better look and realised he wanted to know neither what the weapon in the holster really was, nor where it had been made.

'You came into the presence of *ilauem-arluthen* dressed like that?' Always, always, Santon could be relied on for the unsubtle question. Dacurre flinched slightly, more from personal affront than out of any fear of Gemmel's reaction, and quelled the younger lord with a glare.

For his part, Gemmel sipped his wine and studied both of them over the rim of the glass. 'It's almost like having Aldric here, don't you think?' he observed mildly. 'And in answer, Lord Santon, yes I did. Since I was making a formal call, so to speak, I chose to dress formally; it's only polite.' He set the wine-glass down, considered refilling it, then pushed both glass and carafe aside, sat back in

202

his chair and made a steeple of his fingers in a mannerism unsettlingly reminiscent of the dead King Rynert.

'As both of you are probably well aware, the so-haughty members of the ex-Crown Council were not exactly pleased to be addressed with the words I felt that all of them needed to hear. Words not unlike those you used to me, Lord Santon, and which proved so . . . effective.' Gemmel didn't smile; he wasn't making a joke, and had neither forgotten nor forgiven the way the younger lord had trapped him with a net of words into performing this mission when he had so many other things to do. 'Especially when those words were spoken by the *pestreyr* sorcerer who had obtained the fealty – some two or three who thought themselves witty said fouler things – of Aldric Talvalin by some sort of wizard's trick. Lord Ivar Diskan of Kerys was one who thought to elaborate on what an unmarried older man might want from one much younger.' This time Gemmel did smile and Dacurre, seeing it, would have preferred that he had not. 'His sight will return, in time. And in the meanwhile, Lord Dacurre, he has developed something of a willingness to talk about peace. So have they all, even the ones who didn't . . . ah . . . provoke me.'

Gemmel stood up and closed his overrobe about him, hiding the strange uniform and the stranger holstered sidearm. 'Their couriers are heading for Cerdor even now, and I am heading for the Empire.'

'Where?' asked Dacurre, rising from his own seat. 'Maybe we can help you . . .'

'You, help me?' That Gemmel didn't laugh out loud was only out of courtesy. The mocking laughter glittered in his eyes just the same. 'No. I shall start at the centre, in Kalitzim, and work outwards from there. The Emperor's sister owed Aldric the favour of a life and I intend to collect the debt. Just remember this. What I said before holds true: I lost a day thanks to the pair of you, and if that lost day has hurt me and mine then I shall hurt you and yours. Revenge, my lords. You Albans know the word, I think . . .'

There was a sound like thunder and a blue-white flash like lightning that made both clan-lords blink; and then there was a short sharp bang as air rushed in to fill the space where Gemmel Errekren had been . . .

Voord had achieved something like a sound sleep for the first time in many nights, only to be woken from it by a polite, persistent rapping on his bedroom door. Two seconds before he became sufficiently aware to mumble, 'Yes, what?' in a tone of entirely justified irritation, there was a shortsword out of its scabbard and in his hand. At times he wondered what it had been like to sleep easily and to awaken unafraid; but even the recollection of those times had been forgotten long ago.

It was Tagen again. There had been a time when Voord would have expected him to be there, but he had tired of handsome young men with heavy muscles and was growing still more tired of finding this particular example of the breed lurking outside his doors at all hours of the day and night. Indeed, he was growing simply weary . . . of constants: constant fear, constant plotting, constantly keeping two steps ahead of the knives that sought his back whether they were simply political or real steel. And most of all he was weary of being in constant pain. Giorl had done her best, but that best was based on ordinary medicine rather than the ailment which infected him. As he sheathed the sword and beckoned Tagen in, Voord realised that what he wanted most from life at this moment was an ending to it. The one thing that he was denied . . .

'Good morning, sir,' said Tagen. 'A very good morning indeed. We have them both.'

Voord blinked, the significance of the words eluding him for a moment. Then he remembered and made himself smile, since that was evidently what was expected of him. Yet he knew that just now he didn't care. There had been nights when he had lain awake beside the sleeping body of whoever had been sharing his bed, staring at the ceiling and wondering what his imagination could create for Aldric Talvalin if and when there was ever the opportunity for such a diversion. There had been nights, too, when his lovemaking or his sleep had been sweetened by those same dreams of atrocity-to-come. But this night, with the opportunity for making dreams reality placed in his grasp, all that he could think of was trying to recover the stillness and the rest that Tagen's arrival had stolen from him.

'Then have them placed somewhere secure. I'll see them later in the morning.'

Tagen stared, plainly astonished at this lack of eagerness. Voord returned the stare with a gaze as blank and expressionless as that of a lizard on a stone. Right now he was unwilling – no, unable – to share Tagen's bottomless capacity for violence. The gilt wires twisted through his flesh were hurting him, and the cuts and gashes they held shut were hurting him, and even his head was hurting him as well. Looking more speculatively at Tagen, he wondered whether spreading the pain would not in fact reduce his own – or at least take his mind from it for just a little while.

'Do as I command, Tagen,' he said. 'Then come back here.' The thought faltered, faded, and one hot and hurtful memory was replaced by another just as hot, just as painful, but far more recent.

'No. Instead of that, I'll come with you. Help me dress. This is supposedly official business, so it had best be uniform.' Voord sat up, slid sideways and got out of bed, moving as carefully as an old, old man for fear of ripping open one of his wounds. The burnt flesh of his legs stung him as if to emphasise his recollection of what had brought them to such a state, and he glanced down at the wrapping of ointment-smeared bandage which had been all Giorl could do. There had been Dragonfire and raw, unfocused power in the courtyard of Egisburg's Red Tower. He had been within an instant of becoming no more than a silhouette etched into the stones at the base of the Tower, but with shape-shifting and the speed that granted him, he had escaped . . . all but the pulse of force that leapt from the spellstone in Talvalin's hand, blue fire, white fire, heat and light and noise . . . and, inevitably, pain.

'What about their gear? Was everything brought here?'

'Everything; even their horses are stabled in the Guards Cavalry block.'

'Good.' Voord spoke with the neutrality of mild interest, taking care not to betray what was forming in his mind for fear that Tagen would object and, given sufficient time, work out some way to thwart the plan. 'And them: have they said anything yet?'

'The girl, Kyrin, alternates a sullen silence with inventive oaths. The man Aldric is still unconscious.'

'Unconscious? I said that neither was to be harmed.'

'There was a brawl during the arrest, sir.' Tagen began talking much faster; he knew of old that coldness in Voord's voice, and had no desire to be the recipient of his rising anger. 'The Alban had a sword with him, and the woman stole one during the fight. By the time he was knocked out four *Kagh'Ernvakh* men were dead and a fifth isn't expected to last the night.'

'Just now I don't care about *Kagh'Ernvakh!* The clumsy fools had their orders. Which of them hit him?'

'A Fleet *hautmarin* called Doern, sir – in the city on leave over the holiday. He was in the Playhouse where the arrest took place. It seems he knows the man Talvalin from somewhere else; he's been asking questions . . . and mentioning the use of sorcery.'

'Has he indeed? All right.' Voord stamped into his boots and waited while Tagen knelt to buckle them. 'Then this afternoon I'll have this quick and observant *Hautmarin* Doern presented with a fat bounty and a promotion for assisting in the capture of a dangerous enemy of the state. That should convince him how important a catch he's made; and how pleased with him *I* am.'

'And once he leaves the fortress, he's to be "robbed and murdered", sir?'

'Not this time. It would look overly suspicious.' Voord hesitated, considering, then glanced down at Tagen and patted him on the head as he might have done a dog or a precocious child. 'All the same, put someone on to him while he remains in Drakkesborg and have them report back twice daily. If Doern finishes his leave and returns to his ship, well and good; but at the first indication that the gold or the rank-tabs haven't shut his mouth, I promise that I'll let you kill him.'

'Sir!' The boots dealt with, Tagen sprang to his feet and saluted, all bounding energy and quivering eagerness. Had he a tail, he would have been wagging it. 'What about Talvalin and his woman, sir . . . ?'

Good dog, Voord thought, coming very close to saying it aloud. 'In my good time, Tagen. I'll let you know when that time will be, never fear. But I think I should take a look at them first, don't you?'

Kyrin had drifted in and out of an uneasy doze since they were brought to the fortress. Between cat-naps she stared through the gloom of the poorly lit cell towards the pallet where Aldric had been laid. Shackled by one wrist and one ankle to the bed on the opposite wall, stare was the most that she could do.

Kyrin had had only the briefest chance, in the snowy bloodstained darkness outside the theatre before the pair of them were dragged unceremoniously away, to make sure that his skull had not been fractured. Certainly there was a lump the size of her fist, and without light there was no opportunity to check for pupil dilation or any of the other signs of concussion. Aldric's head was notoriously hard – he had said as much himself – but Kyrin doubted it was hard enough to take the sort of impact that Doern had delivered and still remain intact.

What concerned her most of all was the gentleness with

which they had been treated. After the deaths of four of their comrades, she had feared rough handling at the very least from the remaining Secret Police. Instead, the worst that it could have been called was unmannerly. It suggested either that they, or more probably Aldric, were being held as bargaining counters for the Empire to gain some sort of concession from Alba – or that there was much, much worse to follow.

The cell door opened and two guards carrying lanterns came inside. Now that there was light, she was surprised at how spacious their confinement really was. Apart from the massive door and the wrist-thick bars on the little green-glazed windows, it didn't look too much like her idea of a prison cell. No chilly damp, no sodden straw on the floor, no stinks except for the smell of oily metal that wafted from her manacles every time she moved and a faint, sourceless almost medicinal odour; and no rats. That, too, wasn't much of a comfort, and for the same reason; after all this softness, how hard would the truly hard become?

Their lanterns hooked to metal fixtures in the wall on either side of another door she hadn't seen before, the guards glanced towards her and as they went out again exchanged some remark that made them both laugh. It was an unwholesome laughter, the sort that went with the image of several drunken men meeting one woman in a lonely alleyway. Kyrin shivered and tried to put the thought out of her head by wondering what was behind the other door; only to discover that the sort of suggestions her mind was putting forward were even worse than thinking about the laughter.

'I bid you welcome to Drakkesborg, Tehal Kyrin,' said a suave voice, 'and I bid you welcome to my house.'

Kyrin's head jerked up to see two other men standing in the doorway of the cell; she had been so lost in her own thoughts that she had neither seen nor heard them come in. One was a young man, big and broad-shouldered, with a face she would have called handsome had it not been for the shuttered eyes that gave his expression a disturbing vacancy. It looked not so much as if he was concealing what went on inside his head; rather, that nothing went on there at all except what he was ordered to do. And the most likely source of those orders was standing right beside him.

'I know you,' said Kyrin softly, trying not to be frightened of the man she had last seen aiming a *telek* at her face: the man who had killed Dewan ar Korentin that time in Egisburg, when Dewan took the dart meant for her. The man Aldric had called Commander Voord, and therefore the same man who had – Kyrin was suddenly very conscious of the bed beneath her – raped Kathur the Vixen two months past in Tuenafen.

'Good,' said Voord, and pressed one hand over his heart to give her a small mocking bow. 'I have a certain reputation; it pleases me to see it spread.'

'Your reputation!' Kyrin's mouth twisted in a sneer she didn't even try to hide. There was most certainly nothing she could do to make their situation any better, and probably nothing to make it any worse. 'As a murderer and a traitor—'

'And most recently as Grand Warlord.' Voord was unruffled by the insults, and even smiled faintly at her recitation of what he probably considered virtues. 'Which makes all the rest a little insignificant.' Then he turned from her and looked at the big man who stood at his side. 'Tagen, you told me their gear was brought here, too. Where is it?'

'Sir, he's an Alban *kailin-eir*, one of their clan-lords and for four years before that he was an *eijo*, a landless warrior who lived by his sword. Until we check every piece of clothing and equipment for concealed weapons, I don't dare take the risk of leaving anything where he might—'

'That stuff doesn't concern me; where's his sword?'

'That would be the worst thing of all to—'

'Enough. I ask again, where is it?'

'In the armoury with everything else. It needs checking too, just in case there's more to it than just a sword.'

Voord's head snapped round and as his eyes met Kyrin's, he smiled. She had betrayed no reaction at all to his words, but evidently he had sensed something . . . or it amused him to let her think so. 'I don't know about the rest of it, but you may well be right about the sword. Have it brought in here.'

'Here? Now . . . ?' Tagen was aghast. 'But, sir, you know what this man is like! Bringing a weapon anywhere near him would—'

'Tagen, shut up. He's unconscious and hardly likely to stir for a long while yet. So do it.' Voord glanced around the cell, considering. 'Bring one of the armourers with you – and whatever materials he might need to fix the weapon to that back wall.'

Tagen hesitated for maybe one whole second, as close to disobedience as he had ever been, then shrugged instead of saluting and left the cell. As Voord watched him go out Kyrin could see an odd expression on his face: anger that his authority had been challenged, mingled with shock that the challenge had come from this of all sources.

'What's wrong, Commander Voord? Was your dog threatening to bite?'

Voord shot her a quick angry look, but paid no further heed to the remark. Instead he walked over to where Aldric lay and gazed thoughtfully down at him, then put out his hand – the unmaimed right – and laid its widespread fingers across the Alban's face.

'Leave him alone, you bastard!' Kyrin yelled, jerking forward to the full length of her chains and lashing out at Voord with one futile fist.

'Make me,' said Voord, and smiled. 'Did he ever tell you about a certain use for the drug *ymeth*?' Kyrin glowered but said nothing. 'To get inside a man's mind, to learn what he knows, what he thinks – and what he fears. Useful things like that. Nothing held back, nothing hidden, nothing lied about. I need no drugs, not when he's like this.' Voord took a deep breath and his fingers tightened until they seemed about to sink into the skin of Aldric's face.

Kyrin had been expecting Aldric to cry out, or to try to pull his head free, or to do *something*. Instead he did nothing; even the quick, shallow rhythm of his breathing remained unchanged. Voord, however, turned his own head and gazed at Kyrin with such lascivious amusement that she blushed scarlet and looked away. 'Yes, indeed,' said Voord. 'Nothing hidden.' Then he glanced back at Aldric with the suddenness of one finding exactly what he was looking for, and laughed as he released his grip. 'Good,' he said softly. 'Welcome to your nightmare . . .'

Tagen was back in a matter of minutes, with Widow-maker held in both hands and slightly away from his body as if he didn't want even the scabbarded blade to come too close. The armourer was at his heels, a stocky, silver-bearded man in a leather apron with a canvas bag of tools and equipment hanging from one hand as though a permanent part of his anatomy. He glanced incuriously from Voord to the shackled prisoners and then back, plainly seeing nothing until he was told what he was supposed to see.

'You brought all you need?' asked Voord.

'I did, my lord.' The armourer fished noisily in his bag for a moment before holding up a piece of forged metal for Voord's inspection. 'Two of these clamps, three strips of steel, ten masonry spikes and my best hammer. Do you wish the weapon capable of being drawn, or not?'

'Emphatically not. I want the whole thing immovable. But also I want as much of it on view as can be managed – you understand?'

'I had already suspected as much, my lord. Hence the clamps, one for point and one for pommel, and the steel stripping to hold the crosspiece and the scabbard snug.'

Voord looked quickly at Tagen, but guessed that wherever the armourer had gleaned his information it hadn't been from that source. Tagen was still looking too worried about the whole proceeding to have realised yet what was in Voord's mind. But the woman knew; she was glaring hatred at all three of them, blue eyes venomous as those of a basilisk. Voord smiled back at her, quite unaffected by her gaze. 'Yes, my dear,' he said. 'Expressly to frustrate the pair of you . . . and especially him.' He jerked his head towards Aldric, and his smile went thin and nasty as he patted the innocent blue-white crystal that was the *taiken's* pommel-stone. 'This . . . Ah, this sword's the only thing that makes him what he is. We'll see how he fares when he can see it and speak to it, but can't get at it . . .'

Aldric's eyelids fluttered, squeezed tight shut and then ventured open. 'I think I'm going to be sick,' he announced in a fragile voice, and abandoned any attempt to sit upright.

He closed his eyes to blot out the sight of two of everything, wishing fervently that he hadn't opened them at all. It didn't seem to matter that he was lying flat on his back and looking nowhere except straight up; the entire world appeared to be making a slow spiral progress through his throbbing head, with exactly the same effect as watching the real world do the same thing from the deck of a heaving ship. It made him want to heave as well.

There was a sound like little bells jangling in his ears and mingling most unpleasantly with the thumping of his own heart, every beat of which sent another dull spike of pain jolting from the back of his neck to the backs of his eyes. There were a few minutes just after he moved when he thought that he might die; and then a few more when he fervently hoped he would.

'You were hit on the head,' said a voice like Kyrin's, sounding very far away and almost drowned out by the noise of those damned bells. 'I suspect that you have a concussion.'

'I suspect nothing of the sort,' said Aldric. Even his own voice sounded far away, and he had to pronounce each word carefully to make sure that it was the right one. 'I *know* I have a concussion . . . and that I was hit on the head. It's happened before. Either that or the Playhouse fell on me.'

'Aldric, we're in trouble,' said Kyrin's voice, sounding frightened as she began to explain exactly what the trouble was.

He listened to the words without really hearing them, trying instead to track the swirling world and make some sense of it. Although he had passed into something more like deep sleep within two hours of Doern's cudgel-blow, the brain-rattling effects of the impact required rather more time than just a night's sleep before he shook them off. Shook off, indeed, was scarcely the proper word, since Aldric knew from past experience that if he tried to shake off even a speck of dust tickling his face, he would regret the sudden movement for a long time afterwards. Only the name *Voord* managed to pierce the purple fog filling his mind. It was a name he knew from . . . Dizziness or not, his eyes snapped open.

'Say that again; the last part, about Voord.' Aldric didn't want to hear it, because that would mean it had to be true and wasn't just another part of the foul fever-dreams that were troubling his sleep.

'What I said was, Voord has somehow become the Grand Warlord. And he's the one who had us both arrested.' She looked over at him again, lying quite flat and still as if posing for the carven effigy on a tomb-lid. After the arrest, *Kagh'Ernvakh* troopers had searched them both. They had found three small knives on Aldric: one strapped to his left wrist, a second down his boot and the last – a tiny push-dirk – hung from two loops at the back of his tunic collar. After that, they had taken away all outer garments made of fabric thick enough to hide a blade. For the first time in her memory Aldric was in total black, without the touches of white or silver or of polished metal which had been his – conscious or otherwise – nods in the direction of melodramatic dress. That sombre uniformity of non-colour, and the blow against his head, gave his face the bone-white pallor of someone two days dead.

Aldric closed his eyes again and this time not just through sickness, unless it was a sickness of the spirit. Without the life and movement granted by those eyes, his face became that of a corpse; it was an image and a premonition that made Kyrin shiver.

'I'm sorry,' she said.

'Sorry? For what?'

'For coming here. For getting involved when you wanted me safe. I'm sorry for all of it. But I told you: where you go, I go. To the end of all things.'

The fetters clinked as Aldric moved his hand slightly, dismissing the matter. He smiled wanly up at the ceiling and shook his head, both sadly and with pride that anyone should think him worthy of such love, then lay quite still and shivered as that head-shake brought the nausea quivering back into his stomach.

'I know how much you want to hurt him, Commander, and I know how much he deserves to be hurt. But what I cannot understand is why you would do anything so dangerous as putting his sword in with him. Putting it *into* him would be—'

'Too quick, Tagen.'

Woydach Voord finished his breakfast, a syrup of white poppies in brandy and a piece of bread, then pushed the cup aside while his mouth twisted at the taste of the stuff on which he had been living for what felt like years. He looked enviously at Tagen's mug of beer and at the fried blood-sausage on his plate. Voord's nostrils twitched; there was thyme in it. *All forbidden now*, he thought. *One more reason not to stay here longer than I have to . . .*

'Much too quick – although I appreciate the irony of it

214

all. And I have another use for Talvalin. What do you think that he would do if he got loose, knowing who I am and what I've done to him and his in the past few years?'

'Sir, he'd try to kill you!'

'And do you think that he'd succeed?'

'Not while you're under my protection. Otherwise . . . almost certainly. Except that you can't die of wounds any more; they only hurt you.'

'They always hurt me, Tagen.'

'I wish that I could do something to help, Commander – but all I know is killing.'

Voord looked at him for a long, silent moment. 'You could help me, Tagen,' he said, 'by not killing.'

'Sir . . . ?' The big man was confused; it was as peculiar a request as Commander Voord had made of him in all the years that they had known one another, and Voord was well aware of it. '*Not* killing, sir? I . . . I don't understand.'

Voord had hoped, uselessly it seemed, that Tagen would take his meaning straight away. Evidently not; the leaving-alive of an enemy until that enemy has done what no friend could was far too subtle for this particular *kortagor* of Guards. As well expect an arrow to understand why it must remain in the quiver.

'Talvalin,' said Voord, slowly and carefully so that his meaning was quite clear, 'must remain alive until after he has killed me.'

'What!' Tagen came out of his chair so hard and so fast that beer and sausage both went flying. The clatter attracted accusing stares from all across the Food-Hall for the half-second needed to recognise who had made the noise – and who was sitting with him. After that the only thing that it attracted was servants to clean up the mess and to replenish Tagen's plate.

'After you are certain I am dead, you can kill him as slowly and in whatever way you wish.'

'Commander, are you drunk? Or would you rather I called a physician?'

'No to both. I haven't been well drunk in over a month; I don't dare for fear I fall and do myself yet another irreparable mischief, and I'm sick of the constant need for a physician within call. Do you understand me at last, Tagen? Do you begin to realise how my days are no longer anything to live, but just to be endured? *Do* you?'

Tagen sat very still; what he knew and what he understood was that when Voord's voice took on that particular shrillness, it was safer to be somewhere else – and he had nowhere else to go. As Voord watched him, he could see a kind of comprehension beginning to form in the big man's mind as he tried to relate the Commander's trouble to the sort of life he led himself.

Not to take a woman now and then, because her bites and scratches would never go away; not to ride a horse for fear of the broken limb that wouldn't heal or the broken neck that would leave you still alive but useless; not even to fight someone for the joy of it in case they killed you and you didn't die . . . He broke off his nervous, submissive stare at the table, straightened his back and looked at Voord instead. 'Yes, my lord *Woydach*,' he said, using the new and proper title for the first time, 'I understand completely.' He rose, saluted and walked away.

Voord watched him go, wondering just how much Tagen really understood at all. Had he been fully convinced of that understanding he might have asked the big man – the only person in the whole world whom he could trust – to take Talvalin's sword and do the necessary killing himself. But only if he could have been sure . . .

Because if the sword alone couldn't do it, then the spellstone certainly could. Voord recalled the thrill of mingled shock and pleasure he had felt when he discovered barely half an hour ago that someone – Talvalin most likely – had put the two together into what should be a single, supremely potent weapon. And tomorrow, the twentieth day of the twelfth month, was the beginning of the Feast of the Fires of Winter, when night and darkness were at their most powerful. By the twenty-first, the Solstice itself, he would know if his planning had been successful – or more hopefully that success would be manifest in his knowing nothing any more. Now that Tagen had been dealt with – and it had been both easier and much more difficult than he had expected – there remained only the prime mover: Aldric Talvalin himself.

His own reflection, his image in a smoking mirror. That was one of the many, many reasons why Voord hated the young Alban so very much. Mirror-reversed from right to left though it might be, and invisible to others, Voord could see it. What Aldric Talvalin was, Voord Ebanesj might well have been . . . except that he was not.

They were most alike in one very particular characteristic, the one that was most useful to Voord now. Give either sufficient reason to do so, and they would rip the world apart to gain requital for an injury. Voord's methods were crookedly subtle, but Aldric Talvalin could be just as implacable and far more savagely direct in avenging any violation of his personal honour-codes. It was a matter confirmed by written records, both here in the Empire and most likely in Alba as well. That vengeful streak was a quality of which Voord approved, though he himself had never let something so abstract and valueless as honour control the way he acted.

There was just one risk: that if Talvalin guessed how he was being manipulated, and that killing his enemy would not be vengeance but a kindness and a gift, then he would be just stubborn enough to withhold the final cut. Therefore he would have to be brought to such a white heat of hatred that the risk did not exist.

Voord reconsidered the word *violation*, and liked it.

Aldric and Kyrin had learned at last where that other door led to, and Kyrin's worst terrors were made manifest in the white-tiled room beyond. Some of the equipment there was so elaborate that they could only guess at operating principles, but the function of each and every device was invariably plain enough. They had been designed and built solely to bring pain, or to hold securely while the pain was brought by someone else.

They sat on opposite sides of the room, leather straps around their wrists and ankles holding them in wooden chairs that were far more ordinary than the ugly, ominous metal seats which squatted empty here and there.

Not all were empty; one held the clerk from *The Two Towers*, or what the past two hours had left of him. No questions had been asked, none of the babbled confessions to various petty crimes had been paid any heed, for that was not the function of this particular exercise in cruelty. Before it had begun, the gloved and aproned chief torturer had studied both of them dispassionately as they were strapped down and informed them that Voord had ordered an entertainment for their benefit. 'I am Giorl,' she had said. 'The *Woydach* orders me to show you what it is that I do.' And she had said nothing more, but had shown them far more graphically than any words.

It was sufficiently appalling to learn that what they were witnessing should be done to another human being merely to impress them; the revelation that the principal architect of this fleshly dissolution was a woman came close to unmanning Aldric entirely. It was grotesque beyond belief; torturers were hooded, hairy, subhuman brutes, not a pleasant-faced woman who looked more as if she should have been at home with her children than here putting a near-surgical skill to this perverted use.

'Enough,' said Voord's voice from the door. 'Finish with him.'

The woman Giorl glanced over her shoulder as if to ensure the identity of the speaker, then nodded. 'As you command,' she said, and extinguished what life remained with a single incision underneath where her Subject's right ear had been. 'The rest of you, clean up,' she said to her assistants, stripping off her stained gloves and dropping them into a waiting hand. 'My lord, if you no longer need me I'd like to go home. Until she regains her strength I want to be close to my daughter.'

Aldric and Kyrin gaped at one another across the room as this ultimate obscenity sank in. That the woman should do this was bad enough, but that she should then wash off the blood and slime and go home to a child with the smell of someone's excised guts still warm in her nostrils . . .

'All right, Giorl. And thank you for coming here at such short notice.' Voord gave her a perfunctory salute. 'How is the child anyway?'

'Improving. Whoever did the surgery lacked finesse, but I'd have thanked a pork-butcher for doing it then, just so long as it was done. Good day, my lord.'

'Just one last thing, Giorl . . .'

She hesitated, watching him, waiting for whatever was in his mind this time. Voord moved aside so that the exit was clear and inclined his head a little, manners as polite as any Jouvaine courtier.

'The rest of this is all for me. Don't come back until you're called – do you understand me?'

Giorl glanced at her recent and most definitely captive audience, then back at Voord. Her face was devoid of all expression. 'My lord, as always, my understanding of your wishes is quite perfect.' She bowed, brushed past him and was gone.

Voord watched her go, appreciating the delicacy of her snub, then gestured with both hands so that the four Bodyguard troopers behind him came into the interrogation room. 'Take them out of those chairs,' he said, 'and put them back to bed.' He was immediately conscious of the effect his choice of words was having on the two prisoners, and augmented it with a slow, lecherous smile at Kyrin as he reached out to cup her chin in the claw of his left hand. She spat at him, then flinched in anticipation of a slap as the hand jerked back from her face. Instead Voord merely patted her cheek in light reproof of unlady-like behaviour, although Kyrin would have preferred the slap; there was something dreadfully promissory about this uncharacteristic gentleness, and she had seen what had been done to Kathur – an employee rather than an enemy – for far less reason.

'This is between you and me, Voord,' said Aldric, trying to keep his voice quiet and reasoned while at the same time struggling uselessly against the buckled straps that held him down. 'Let her go. She has nothing to do with either of us.'

'Oh, but she does. You love her. When I hurt her, I'll hurt you, and when she's been all used up, why then I'll still have you. I am the master here – time you both began to learn it.'

'Then you'd best learn this as well.' Kyrin and Voord both recognised the terrible calmness with which Aldric spoke, but only Voord was truly pleased to hear it. 'The whole of this world isn't big enough to hide in. There'll be nowhere far enough for you to run.'

'Fine, stirring words, Aldric Talvalin – but slightly misplaced, considering your present position. Get them into their cell.'

The guards carried out his command with all the swift economy of movement that comes with long practice. Both Aldric and Kyrin gained the negligible satisfaction of landing a few telling blows with fists and feet, but against men wearing half-armour and heavy leathers it was mostly wasted effort. The order executed, all four soldiers saluted and left the cell without needing to be dismissed. There was a distinct impression that Voord had told them in advance that he was to be left alone, which to Kyrin's mind meant one thing only. The bed beneath her felt more like a torture-rack with every passing second, and as she stared at Voord like a rabbit confronted by a weasel it took all her force of will not to be sick.

'Well now,' said Voord, folding his arms and leaning back against the door, 'this *is* cosy.'

Aldric, flung unceremoniously face-downwards on his pallet and chained that way by the one guardsman who had taken knuckles in the face rather than on the helmet, said something venomous that was muffled by the crumpled bedding and then coughed as dust caught at his throat.

Voord stared at him. 'I don't know why you want me to go to Hell, Aldric; this is Hell enough. Except that all of it's for you. I can't begin to explain how long I've waited to offer you just this sort of hospitality. And I can't begin to explain how much of a thorn you've been in my flesh these past years. Fist Duergar—' – Aldric choked on another cough and stared in disbelief – 'then the Geruaths, and finally Princess Marevna. Oh yes, I was involved in all of those, and every time you blundered in and ruined subtle plans you sometimes didn't even know existed. I could forgive a little if you were a true opponent – but not when your interference was driven by nothing more than your petty personal motives! Father of Fires, that a stratagem three years in the making should come to nothing because of some sword-swinging Alban lout who hadn't the grace to be killed with the rest of his clan of bloody barbarians!'

Voord's voice had risen almost to a yell, but stopped just short of it as he shook his head and pulled himself back under control. There were flecks of spittle on his lips, and his face was red. 'But then, I can attend to that unfinished business at my own pace now,' he said more quietly, panting slightly. 'And in my own fashion. Slowly . . . slowly and with imagination.'

He looked briefly at Kyrin, caught her staring at the gilt wires twisted through the flesh above his eye and below his chin, and straightened up so that the metal strands glinted in the light of the lanterns. 'You wonder about these?' he said in response to a question no one had dared to utter. 'Another memento. Your lover is very good at causing pain. Even I could learn from him – and he will learn from me.' He walked over to one side of Aldric's bed and stood there for a long while, staring. Then he reached down with his crippled hand and stroked it slowly and gently down the entire length of Aldric's spine.

His free hand pressed against the back of Aldric's head, pushing his face down into the pillows for a long and choking moment before releasing him to gasp for air. 'The learning starts now.' Voord spoke with an Alban accent which had not been there before, a careful, deliberate simulation of someone else's voice from long ago and far away. He could as easily have handed over one or both of them to Giorl the torturer, but his subtle mind with its fondness for equally subtle stratagems had seized on this as being far more effective.

The *Woydach* gazed at him through hooded, unreadable eyes, and though nothing could be taken from Voord's still features, the manner in which he now spoke was enough to set Aldric's skin crawling as the more brutal threats had been unable to do. It was too . . . He crushed the memory at once, but still wasn't quick enough.

It was too familiar . . .

'Yes, indeed,' said Voord, and smiled. 'Welcome to your nightmare.'

It was over. Voord was gone, the cell door slammed shut and locked behind him, but not so soon that the laughter from outside hadn't drifted in. All that remained was pain, and shame, and the feeling of being unclean.

And the tears on Kyrin's face that said how much she understood . . .

TEN

'Why did you do it? Why not just give both of them to the torturer?' Tagen was intrigued by what he had watched through the spy-hole in the cell's outer door, so much so that just this once he had set aside all the respect he had for Voord and gone straight to the point with his questions.

Voord sipped at another cup of the brandy-and-poppy tincture, no longer caring about the taste. His exertions of the morning had strained several of the wired wounds, so that the flesh had been cut like cheese and several wires were beginning to unravel. There was another session with Giorl in the offing, and while he didn't relish the prospect he no longer cared very much. Not when he felt so pleased with himself. Voord was glowing.

'Talvalin was expecting torture, his woman was expecting rape. What I did was the only thing neither was prepared for; neither had their defences ready.' Voord's eyes widened and he clapped one hand to his side, holding it there and whimpering. An ooze of fluid darkened the fabric of his shirt, and the sharp ends of a length of wire poked through the weave in the middle of the stain. When the spasm passed, he drained his cup at a draught and refilled it from the green glass bottle on the table. 'And it was a private horror of his own. Oh, there were all the other fears, of loss and pain and death – both his own and the woman's, which is worth bearing in mind – but this was special. It might have been a pleasant memory of his youth for him to look back on' – Voord grinned viciously and raised his cup in a mocking toast – 'except that someone he thought he knew took it and him and turned the whole thing foul. And now neither of them know what to expect from me, except that it will always be far worse than anything they can imagine. I think that Talvalin will be more than ready to take any chance we give him . . .'

Tagen muttered something under his breath, still far from happy with this death wish of Voord's even though the reasoning behind it was plain enough even to him. 'Then what about the woman, sir?' he asked. 'Will she be left until . . . until afterwards?'

'Mostly.' Voord's eyes were a little glazed as the drug and the brandy began working their brief effect. The respite would be short – it always was, and had been growing shorter with each passing dose. Giorl had warned him that the poppy-syrup liquor was known to be addictive, but for any one of several reasons Voord felt he had no need to worry about that risk. He shook his head to clear away the mists that threatened to fill it completely, and looked back at Tagen. 'Mostly, but not altogether. You and your four men go down to the cell and move our two guests back into the interrogation room.' Tagen got up, eager to begin, and Voord rapped the table for attention. 'You will not, I emphasise *not*, harm either of them just yet.'

'But sir, you said—'

'Move them. Nothing else . . . yet. But you can make it plain to both that she'll be next. When I give you permission, you and the others can do whatever takes your fancy – but only when I allow it. And I don't want her killed, or disfigured, or permanently maimed, otherwise escaping will lose its appeal for both of them and Talvalin won't try as hard as he might do when there's everything still to gain. Do you understand what I mean?'

'Yes, sir. I think so, sir.'

'Then go do it – and remember, only threats and promises until I say otherwise. Dismissed.'

'Sir!'

Voord watched as Tagen hurried off, wondering what the big man would say if he knew that his Commander was even now considering which of the Bodyguard troops were least efficient and most expendable. After Tagen's

224

squad had done to Kyrin whatever it was their unpleasantly fertile minds could conjure up, Voord's plan was that Aldric alone be moved back to the cell – by two guards of sufficient clumsiness for his savage efforts to break free to have a better-than-even chance of success. And after that . . .

Voord had seen the Alban in action before, and knew well enough that once loose and with a weapon – any weapon – in his hand, he was more than a match for any but the most capable swordsman in the Guard. Neither of the soldiers that Voord had in mind was anything like good enough. There was another matter needing some attention in the little private room near the interrogation chamber; the room with the spell-circle set into its floor. And after that, it would be only a matter of waiting for his release to come through the door.

He swallowed more of the pain-easing drink as the effect of the last mouthful began to fade and the lines of fire began once more to mark out his wounds, and thought of how good it would be to end the hurting once and for all. He would welcome oblivion as any other man would welcome recovery from sickness, smile at the Alban as he swung his sword, open his arms to embrace the descending blade. And then Voord thought of the way that Aldric had looked at him, and despite his eagerness to die he shivered . . .

'Aldric . . . ?' Kyrin spoke the name for what had to be the hundredth time, and again heard no response other than the too-quick, too-shallow rhythm of his breathing. He hadn't moved since Voord finished with him and went out, not even to rearrange his clothing because with hands shackled at shoulder-height and ankles secured to either upright of the cheap little bed, there was no way in which he could have reached. All that he could do, and all that he had done, was to lie still to avoid the pain of moving

225

and stare at the wall with an unreadable expression burning behind the eyes which blinked too slowly.

Oh my love, thought Kyrin, *oh my dear one, I wish that you would say something. Anything. Not just lie there and watch it all inside your mind, over and over and over again.*

She began to speak, very softly, not calling his name any more but telling one of the old stories of her people as she might have done to a child awakened frightened in the night. Kyrin didn't know what good it would do, whether he was hearing what she said – or even whether she was doing it not for his benefit but for her own, to take her mind away from the time when the door would open and it would be her turn.

'Long, long ago and far, far away in the frozen Northlands, there was a hunter who went out one day to hunt, and as he wandered near to the shores of the cold Northern Sea he heard a crying and went to see what made the sound. And there among the rocks and the grinding bergs that surged up and down on the icy swell, he found the cub of a white bear and the bear's mother dead and drowned beside it. So the hunter thought at first to kill it, but it cried so sorely that his heart was touched and instead he took the little furry creature home to be a pet and a companion if it lived . . .'

She spun the tale out and out, weaving into it shreds and threads of other stories so that it grew more fantastic and seemed to take on a life of its own. That had always been the way with the old tales, so that a travelling storyteller could spin an entire evening's entertainment – thus ensuring his bed and board for the night – from a single original idea. But unlike the storytellers back home in Valhol she was not to be allowed to finish without interruption, because she was only three-quarters through the tale when the cell door clanged open and Tagen's squad of guards came in.

Aldric turned his head just enough to look at them, but his blankness of expression did not alter; he remained shut up within himself, seeming neither able to see nor to hear anything except whatever was going on within his head, refusing to react to the crude hands dressing him or the cruder jokes made while they did so. As they hauled him upright, Kyrin got her first chance to see his face in other than shadow – and by comparison with the man she knew he looked like a house where nobody is at home. And then she saw the quick, almost imperceptible glance that he shot towards the back wall of the cell, and towards the *taiken* that was shackled there just as securely as he had been shackled to the bed.

There was just the glance and nothing more; it was gone again almost at once, and if she hadn't seen it so clearly Kyrin would have doubted that the somehow shrunken figure who slumped between the soldiers had such a speculative, calculating look left in him. She wondered what hope or plan or seized chance lay behind it; and indeed, as the guards dragged him from the cell into the torture chamber next door, whether there would be enough left of either of them to make use of any granted opportunity.

They came back for her a few minutes later, all hot hands and stale breath and hungry eyes as they unlocked the chains and told her what it was they were going to do once *Woydach* Voord had learned whatever it was he wanted to know. Kyrin shut her ears to the stream of dirt; most of it was coarsely repetitive and not overly original, and the fact that they kept using the word 'later' allowed the tremulous flutter in her belly to relax a little. That 'later' would be respected, if only out of fear, for only one of the five dared more than an elaborate fumble around her crotch while setting the chains aside, and he was promptly snarled at by the big *kortagor* called Tagen.

And then they were alone again, strapped to the only ordinary chairs in the interrogation room that was empty of everything but the hulking inanimate machinery of pain, left no doubt to think of the last time they had sat in these same chairs and what they had witnessed. Left to wonder when Voord would come in, and what would happen the next time the door opened. And to wonder whose turn it would be then.

Ryn Derawn filled his wife's glass with distilled grain-spirit for the third time in ten minutes and watched uneasily as she stared at the clear juniper-scented liquid like a wise-woman reading futures from a bowl of water, then – also for the third time in ten minutes – drank down the potent stuff in a single swallow.

'I'm still not convinced,' said Giorl to her husband, 'no matter what you say. If I was wrong, then the consequences for you, for me, for the children, for all of us . . .' She shook her head, dispelling the images, and held out her glass for yet another drink.

'No. You've had plenty for now, and I haven't had half enough for this to make any more sense.' Ryn put the tall stoneware bottle to one side and smashed its stopper into place with the flat of his hand. 'Giorl, no matter what you do up at the fortress you've never needed to hide behind this stuff before. These two new prisoners . . . You must have *some* suspicions, or you wouldn't even have mentioned them.'

'All right. All *right*! So I'm wondering.' Giorl looked at her empty glass one final time, then thumped it down on to the table and stared instead at Ryn. 'And I'm scared to give room inside my head to what you've just suggested. Whoever they are and whatever they did, they're his now. Voord's . . . to do with as he pleases. And there's nothing I could – or would dare – do about it!'

'If they're the ones I think, they saved Mal's life – you said that yourself. If they hadn't been here she would have died long before I could have found you.' Ryn sat down beside her and put one arm around Giorl's shoulders. 'That wasn't all you said. Do I have to remind you – or didn't you mean any of it at all?'

'Oh, you bastard . . .' Giorl's taut features crumpled, she leaned her head against him and Ryn felt the first sob

228

go jolting through her as she began to cry. He felt wretched too, wishing that neither of them had brought the matter to discussion; but he knew also that he would never have looked at his beautiful, kindly, learned, lethal wife in quite the same way again if he had kept silent.

All he wanted was for Giorl to take him inside the Warlord's citadel for sufficient time to see the two captive foreigners that she had spoken of. Nothing else. Just so that he would know enough for his own peace of mind. Ryn hadn't yet decided what he would do if they really were the young couple with the talent for impromptu surgery. He almost hoped that they were not – that he could look, and shake his head and go away again . . . and try to forget what it was that awaited them. He knew little enough about what was done in the Underfortress when Giorl wasn't acting as consultant surgeon to various high-ranking personages, and that little he had discovered had been more than enough to prevent him from trying to learn more. For her part, Giorl didn't talk. That was what had made her outburst today so startling, when she had come through the door of the house shaking all over – and not from the cold – and had drunk down the first of those brimming glasses before trusting herself to speak.

Not that his response had calmed her down. When she described the people for whom Voord had ordered a demonstration – and Ryn was grateful that she hadn't described what *that* had involved – she had been hoping for a denial. He knew her well enough by now to read something so simple from her face, and he was angry now that he hadn't told a lie; except that she knew him just as well, and would not only have been in her present state but also something worse because of his attempted deceit. Truth, Ryn decided, was the least painful of the several painful courses open to him. Assuming that *Woydach* Voord did not become involved . . .

'Put on your outdoor boots and get your overmantle. We're going to the fortress.' There was still the thickness of recent weeping in Giorl's voice, but once she had straightened her back and wiped the tears from her face all other traces of uncertainty were gone. She had spoken calmly, with determination and the serenity born of a decision made and now unshakeable. Almost unshakeable; for when Ryn hesitated she smiled minutely at him and made small shoo-ing movements with both hands. 'Do it, love. Quickly. I'm running just a step ahead and if we don't move now, at once, it'll catch up with me.'

Ryn looked at her quizzically but received no further elaboration. He stamped into the fur-lined boots and pulled on his heavy, quilted overmantle without asking anything aloud, and it was only as they left the house and walked out into the slowly falling snow that the question moved out of his eyes and became words.

'What are you running from?' He thought that he knew the answer already, but he had to hear it from her just so that he could be sure. The silvery mist of Giorl's exhaled breath was between their faces as she glanced at him and then turned her head away, still smiling that same small fixed smile, and Ryn knew his guess had been right.

'My own fears,' she said softly, and looked up towards the grey clouds as though a shadow had passed across the unseen sun. 'Of course . . .'

The candles in the ice-encrusted room were burning blue, their flames stirring the sluggish drifts of incense smoke and sending them in spicy-scented tendrils up to the crystalline ceiling. There was a buzzing, the sound of glutted flies, and there was the sonorous rise and fall of words from where Voord knelt once more at the centre of the circle and spoke to That which listened to him only through lack of any other worshippers.

'. . . O my Lord O my true Lord O my most beloved Lord O most favoured Bale Flower O Issaqua Dark Rose Dweller in Shadows I pray thee and beseech thee hearken to thy faithful servant who begs most humbly take away this Gift of life from me and grant me peace . . .'

He could smell the roses now, an overwhelming perfume which blurred his mind in a way that the poppy-syrup never could. The candle-flames began to shrink and for all that it remained snow-shot day beyond the shuttered, curtained, frozen windows, a darkness deeper than mere nightfall flowed like ink into the room. Voord began to hear the sweet, sad, wordless music that was the Song of Desolation, and with that hearing he began to tremble. The warning words of the charm written into one of his grimoires came back to haunt him; but he had ignored that warning so many times now that the haunting was little more than one ominous memory among many.

Issaqua sings the Song of Desolation
And fills the world with Darkness . . .

In that Song there was a loss and a betrayal, the sense of being discarded that was all part of the smashing of altars and the tearing down of shrines, or worse, their re-consecration in the names of other Powers with no right to dwell there. When his dabbling in sorcery began, so many lost years ago, Voord had been delighted by the ease with which demons responded to his Summonings; it was only as time passed and he learned more that he discovered the truth behind their eager attention. The deities of an older race were reduced to the demons of the new, diminishing thus down through successive generations until they were forgotten. For all their past majesties, they were often as pathetic as lost children – grateful for any attention at all, even idle curiosity, rather than re-consignment to oblivion.

Issaqua the Bale Flower hung before him in the icy air, a wavering nimbus of reddish-amber light – like that from heated iron – that formed unstable curves suggesting the whorled petals of a monstrous rose. He bowed very low, stood up and stepped out of the circle without any of the precautions he had always been so sure to take before. They were redundant at this late stage; and in the Presence of Issaqua, there would be nothing of a lesser stature that he needed to fear. The light throbbed slowly behind him, illuminating nothing but itself, and Voord felt his boots crunch in the hoar-frost that had formed from the moisture in the air as he walked to the door. The dry coldness ground into him, searing his mouth and nostrils as he breathed, chilling the metal wires that held his flesh together until they seemed to burn instead.

Tagen was outside, standing at parade-rest a diplomatic distance down the corridor. As Voord emerged in a pearly cloud of freezing vapour, the *kortagor* came to attention and saluted. Voord nodded acknowledgement, then sagged backwards against the rimed timbers, exhausted. *Soon now, very soon . . .* he thought, looking at the big man through eyes that refused to focus properly. *A long race, but almost run . . .*

'I was coming out to tell you—'

'That we can attend to the woman, sir?'

Oh eager, eager, my hound. 'Yes. I will be in here, Tagen . . . waiting. Make certain that Talvalin knows. Now go. Gather your squad. And, Tagen . . .'

'Sir?'

'Be thorough.'

'Ryn? Well, tell me.'

Ryn Derawn backed slowly away from the small shuttered peephole let into the door of the interrogation room. It was only when Giorl touched him that she realised how her husband had begun to tremble. He stared at her and his lips moved, but no sound came out.

'It's the pair you thought, isn't it?' she hissed, shaking him, trying to restore some sort of coherence. Ryn nodded. He had gone chalk white, not so much with fear of where he was or recognition of Aldric and Kyrin, but because of his first look within the harshly white-tiled environment where his wife did most of her work. He had never seen a torture chamber before, except in old woodcuts, and hadn't been prepared for the air of cold

232

efficiency that flowed from the place like mist. Most of the apparatus was too mechanically refined for him to guess its purpose without explanation, but there had been enough pieces whose operation was all too obvious for his stomach to turn sick.

'Yes,' he managed to say at last. 'I was hoping not, but . . . there they are: the ones who saved Mal's life.'

'And what are we going to do? Let them go and end up where they are now?' Giorl was always deadly practical where cause and effect were concerned, and never more so than when the matter in question was serious. This was as serious as any in her life, and already she regretted giving way to Ryn in the first place. 'We'll have to get out of here before someone sees us,' she said, the hand which had touched his shoulder in comfort tightening to pull him away. 'There isn't anything that we—'

'Cut them loose,' said Ryn. He shrugged free of Giorl's grasp and turned towards her. 'We needn't help them escape – but we can give them the same chance at life that they gave Mal.' He grinned crazily. 'Cut, and go away, and let them survive if they can do it by themselves. Please, love! Do it – it's only right!'

Giorl stared at him and at the wildness in his eyes. This wasn't the Ryn she knew, but a man fired by a Purpose. She had seen many such, whose various Purposes had brought them no further than the room beyond the door and to what was done there. Then she shrugged, a quick dismissive twitch that agreed with none of his reasoning and just barely with his plea, and went past him into the interrogation room.

Though his face somehow managed to remain immobile and unreadable, Aldric's stomach turned over when the woman torturer Giorl came through the door, lifted a knife from one of the wall-mounted clips and walked towards him. He stared at her for just a moment as she approached, then through her and beyond her as if she did not exist. At least Voord wasn't here yet; though doubtless he would arrive before the show really began in earnest, grinning and wearing that self-satisfied expression Aldric wanted so much to shear right off the *Woydach*'s face. It seemed as though he would no longer have the chance to do it – not in this life, anyway.

Then Ryn Derawn stepped quietly into the torture chamber just behind her and pulled a second knife from the same row of clips. Aldric made a supreme effort to keep any giveaway flicker from his eyes, wondering first how Ryn had got in here and second if he knew exactly where to plant the knife. When Giorl said, 'Hurry up, for the Lady Mother's sake,' and said it unmistakably to Ryn, he thought for just one horrible instant that his mind had given way.

If you go mad, is part of the madness in not knowing it?

He had asked that question years ago, so many years that he couldn't remember if there had been an answer. Certainly there was no answer now, only utter confusion. Seeing the two of them together made no sense, especially when the man he recognised and the woman he feared – and feared enough to admit it even to himself – not only knew each other, but set about the same hurried task of sawing through the heavy bullhide straps that held his wrists and ankles to the wooden chair.

Cutting was the quickest method, or at least not the slowest. The buckles securing each strap had been threaded through with heavy wires which had been plier-twisted shut, like gross copies of the little golden threads that he had seen – and felt – decorating Voord's face and body. Unpicking them would have needed armourer's tools and more time than Ryn and Giorl seemed to be willing to take. Aldric flinched once or twice when the blades, designed to cut through less resilient skins than these, skidded on the leather or the wires and sliced him instead. He made no sound the whole time, not so much through stoicism as not trusting himself to speak, because by then he had seen the looks and the quick nervous

234

smiles that his two rescuers exchanged – and they were the same looks and smiles which passed between himself and Kyrin . . .

It was impossible to bear, and when his right hand came free with the sting of another accidental cut that became the rending snap of whittled leather giving way, he resisted the first and still near-reflex reaction – which was to seize Giorl by the throat and not let go until she had at the very least thrown away her knife – and merely asked, 'Why?'

'A debt,' said Giorl, gasping slightly as she had to saw with a delicate instrument whose edge was now quite spoilt with all this clumsy work. 'You're owed one life.'

'Whose?' He looked at Ryn. 'Your daughter's?'

'Our daughter's.' It wasn't Ryn who said it but Giorl, and the laconic statement shocked Aldric far more than if she'd run one of her spiked probes into his ear instead of speech. Again his stomach did that violent shocked somersault and with as much or better reason.

Maybe going insane is just a way to make the world make sense, he thought, and almost giggled. *Because I don't want to take much more of this* . . . The bubble of crazed laughter welling up inside him turned to a sob that was actually painful; but then he ached all over anyway, thanks to Commander Voord. The cold-eyed, long-jawed face smiled down at him in his imagination, and with the pain was quite enough to jolt him back to something like sobriety, where giggles had no place and sobbing was for later.

The only sound that Aldric wanted to hear in the next while was the liquid ripping of Widowmaker's blade in flesh . . .

'Yours, too?' he said to Giorl in a voice that surprised him with its calmness. She nodded and continued cutting. 'Then that means he's your husband?' Another nod, more impatient now; the strap on his left ankle was giving trouble and by now her knife was just a flattened piece of metal with no indication that it ever had an edge at all. 'And that means you,' said Aldric to Ryn with all the

235

pedantic care of a child getting some fact explained just so, 'are married to the chief torturer of Drakkesborg.' Ryn nodded. 'Why didn't you mention it before?'

'Was it so important?' Ryn said defensively. 'Would it have made a difference to what you did for the child?'

'I . . .' Aldric began to say and stopped, suddenly unsure. The tugging and hacking at his bonds continued and across the room – half-hidden by one of the more elaborate machines – he could see Kyrin trying to get a glimpse of what was happening. *Of course it wouldn't have made a difference* was what he would like to have said, but wondered now if that was true. A sick child was a sick child was a sick child, in any language of the several he knew; but to know what one of that child's parents did for part of a living – let alone that it was the *mother*, for sweet pity's sake! – and to guess, as he guessed now, what sort of cutting might have been keeping Drakkesborg's best cutting-surgeon from doing something to help her own daughter . . . He shrugged, not caring now that the movement would hurt scratched and bitten shoulders, and told the truth. 'I don't know. Probably yes, if I'd known beforehand. Neither of us would have gone near the house. But we didn't know, and,' another shrug, 'it wasn't so very important anyway.'

'A very pretty confession, Alban,' said Giorl, ripping away the last shred of leather strapping from his leg by main force rather than with the useless knife. 'I couldn't have got a better out of you myself.'

Aldric looked at her for a few seconds, then curled his lip. 'That was a poor sort of joke,' he said.

Giorl looked at her knife, made the beginnings of a motion to throw it disgustedly away and then slipped it into a pocket of her overrobe instead. 'Someone might notice,' she said to herself, then glanced at Aldric with a far from humorous quirk to her mouth. 'I don't joke about my work . . . any of it.'

'Then you *are* a surgeon – Ryn wasn't just using—'

'An imaginative figure of speech? No, he told the truth. The acceptable half of it, anyway.'

'But *why?* Why do you . . .' Aldric was at a loss for some way to phrase his question that would not be dangerously rude; he hadn't forgotten that there was still a belt of wire-reinforced leather holding him to a chair far too heavy to be lifted, that Kyrin was still strapped into another chair, and that the woman he spoke to had obviously been persuaded to come here by her husband and against her own better judgement. The combination of factors made for a deal of delicacy when it came to choosing words, and he was grateful when Ryn came to his rescue in a manner just as real as the cutting of any number of restraints.

'It's a job; someone has to do it. My wife does it.' The man was smiling, but it was a mechanical curving of the lips that came nowhere near his eyes. 'Maybe sometime soon she won't have to do it any more . . . and then she'll be able to stop. Satisfied?'

Aldric nodded silently. He hadn't missed the emphasis Ryn had laid on certain words, and though there was certainly an interesting story behind how a pretty woman, a mother and a much loved wife could become what Giorl had become, it was no story that he had any wish to hear. He lifted his hand free of the halves of the last strap and stood up; then brought both hands together and bowed, giving honourable obeisance to them both for any number of reasons. He watched as the couple took up new knives and went to free Kyrin, waiting just long enough to see the relief wash the uncertainty out of her face . . .

Then he turned, forcing down any reaction to the pain which lanced up into him at every step, and walked back as quickly as he dared towards the cell . . .

Isileth-called-Widowmaker hung upon the wall of the cell, with her weapon-belt wrapped interlacing-style around her scabbard. That style, *hanen-tehar*, showed proper respect for the ancient longsword; but it was respect shown only to mock for instead of being laid across a sword-stand she hung vulgarly point uppermost, crucified upside down.

Aldric looked at the steel strapping and the hammer-forged clamps that were as thick as his own wrists. She was as securely shackled as he had been, and as helpless to resist the hands which had left the smeary marks of fingers everywhere; but she was eager to be free and about the business for which she had been made.

He could feel the killing-hunger radiating from the blade as he might have felt heat radiating from a fire; it might have been his own feverish imaginings, but Aldric doubted it. This *taiken*'s name and reputation had not come from daydreams, and his own respect had always borne the merest unadmitted thread of caution. Many things might happen to a weapon in twenty centuries, and most of them had happened to this sword; but it was widely believed that no good could come from a blade with so ominous a name as *Widowmaker*. Aldric had stopped caring what was said; what the faceless, nameless *They* said, and always had to say, about a hundred dispar-ate matters that were not and never had been any of their concern. Four years now he had slept with this cold mistress by his side to guard him, and she had never failed him yet.

Aldric reached out one hand to Widowmaker, and felt the familiar cool harshness of braided leather and black-lacquered steel solid and reassuring against the callouses of his right palm. He closed his hand around the grip, feeling the hilt-loops squeeze against that familiar angle-joint on the index finger where it hooked over for better control. But she remained where she had been placed, not even moving in her irons, fulfilling the function of that placement, teasing and frustrating him like any object of desire held tantalisingly just out of reach . . . but not quite far enough.

Had she been truly out of his reach, as she had been

238

before, Aldric would have been more concerned; had he been stronger in both mind and body, it would have concerned him less. But he had outrage instead of health, anger instead of caution and fear not only for himself but for the others outside instead of any cause more just. Those substitutes for rightness, as so often happened in this far from perfect world, would have to suffice. Their less worthy cousins, vengeance and hurt pride, had been enough before.

'*Abath arhan*,' said Aldric quietly, the words familiar as his own name now for all that he still had no memory of learning them. Warmth of hand and words of power wound together on the longsword's hilt and worked their magic. There was a sound, a sonorous thrum so deep that it was more felt in the marrow of the bones than heard, and the Echainon spellstone that he had set as pommel-stone into Widowmaker's hilt left off its pretence of being no more than a polished dome of crystal and came back to life.

It began as no more than a thread in the heart of the stone, twisting like a flaw come to life; and then the blue flames spilled out in a great globe of cool radiance that flung Aldric's shadow up and across the farther wall and ceiling. Fire licked upwards from the *taiken*'s pommel, lapping his fingers and Widowmaker's hilt with lazy tongues like those of sleepy tigers. Aldric brought them fully awake.

'*Alh'noen ecchaur i aiyya, r'hann arhlaeth.*' The words of the spell, if spell it was, came from his mouth in a tangle of syllables that bore no relation to Alban or any other language spoken in the world of men, and the spellstone and the sword responded.

The blast alone should have killed him, for it ripped stones from the walls and tiles from the floor and flung them like catapult missiles from one end of the cell to the other, leaving Aldric standing in a scoured space that smoked and spat as though just drawn from the heart of a furnace. It had been a furnace hot enough to melt proof

239

steel, for the straps and clamps and rivets which had held Widowmaker to the shattered wall glowed rose and white and fell in thick trailing drops like honey to the blackened floor as they let the sword come free. The light that filled his vision faded down through purple and orange to a dazzled near normality, but as the reverberations of the contained thunderclap became no more than a jangling echo in his ears, Aldric heard the slam of a door flung open and then the shouts of angry men.

He drew in a breath and turned, feeling the smooth slide of joints and muscles which no longer hurt. The breath came hissing out again through teeth close-clenched in a feral snarl as he heard a voice he knew among the babbling outside. Voord's henchman Tagen was out there, making threats. Aldric buckled Widowmaker's weapon-belt around his waist and stalked out of the cell.

Kyrin hadn't believed her eyes when Ryn came through the door behind the torturer. She hadn't believed her ears when he told her what was going on. But she had believed her sense of touch when the brutally tight strapping on the chair began to fall away. She let no surprise show on her face at the revelations of how strange the family of Ryn and Giorl Derawn seemed to be, disarming Giorl's own terse and acid observations with equally sharp comments of her own. It made the interrogator-surgeon look oddly at the knife she held, then stare at Kyrin even more oddly still.

'Ryn told me about you both,' she said. 'Not just about what you did, but about what you were like. He was wrong about only one thing: when he said your gentleman friend didn't talk much.' Without a smile, or indeed the slightest hint from her emotionless features, it was difficult to decide if Giorl had made some sort of joke, or was expressing irritation, or was merely passing the time of day until she was done and could leave.

'We can't, and won't, help you to get out of this fortress,' she continued, slicing efficiently at leather and with less success at metal wire. 'That's your problem and his. I have a family to take care of, and playing some sort of hero isn't part of it. At best you'll get away; at worst, find yourselves a cleaner death than the *Woydach* has in mind. Because if you're back on those frames when I come in to follow orders, I'll do exactly as I'm told to do. I can't do anything else. Understand?'

Kyrin shivered slightly and made a vaguely affirmative noise. She understood exactly. Giorl had the classic surgeon's mind: too classic by a long way, if the opinion of an ex-physician's aide was worth anything – which it was not – and if she dared to offer it aloud, which she didn't. To Giorl, work was the bringing together of metal implements and human flesh, to heal on one side and to hurt on the other. She had managed to lock away the different end results in some dark place at the back of her mind, and now regarded what she did as something more akin to mechanics: removing a part that no longer worked, closing an accident-created hole . . . or testing until something cracked.

'Understood. Thanks for telling me. I hope—'

Whatever it was she hoped was lost in the vast wash of light and noise that blew the fragmented, burning access door of their cell clear across the torture chamber. And then the other, outer door slammed open in the ringing silence after the blast, and *Kortagor* Tagen came in.

He was not alone. There were three other men behind him, all in the undress uniform of *Kagh'Ernvakh* and all wearing expressions in which shock shared equal space with the last vestiges of lust. Tagen hesitated in the doorway for a heartbeat's duration, and in that brief time whipped sword from scabbard with such speed that his right fist seemed to sprout steel in the instant of its clenching. There was no shock on his face, and while his expression might have passed for lust it was a lust for slaughter.

'Treacherous bitch,' he said to Giorl, and he said it in a calm, pleased voice. 'You and your husband, both traitors.

241

Both helping enemies of the state. The *Woydach* will want to deal with you personally – but we'll have the rest right now . . .' He grinned and started forward, with the rest of his squad close on his heels.

'I think not,' said Aldric's voice behind them, and the door of the torture chamber shut and locked with clicks as small and final as a coffin-lid coming down. 'In case you're wondering,' he continued, as Widowmaker sheared off both key and handle, 'the only way out is through my cell. You're all welcome to try.'

There was an interesting silence during which the loudest noise was the echo of the severed key falling to the tiled floor, and then Tagen lost his temper. Had he paid any attention to Voord's carefully explained lessons in pressure and leverage, he might have earned himself and his companions some few minutes more of life by trying to hold Kyrin as a hostage for their release.

Instead he leapt at the young man who was only another victim after Voord was done with him, an enemy whose time to die had come at last – and who smiled coldly as he sidestepped Tagen's rush to let him meet a blur of blade instead . . .

'*Hai!*'

Tagen's leap continued straight into the wall, but the top of his head and most of its seldom used contents were already all over the floor behind him.

Aldric snapped blood and a few flecks of brain-tissue from Widowmaker's blade, quite well aware that the movement sent a sinister swirl of azure fire up and around his hands as he brought the weapon back to low-guard centre. 'Next?' he said. The first wild flaring of rage had died away by now, enough at least to let his skill return; but his anger remained, fuelling the skill and giving him Voord's own potential to be cruel. Raked, banked fires burn hottest, and the heat within him was such that none of the Warlord's Guard would leave alive while he lived to stop them.

None did.

Giorl and Kyrin looked at the bodies, and the contents of bodies, and the pieces of bodies, and listened to the blood that was already dripping audibly down the torture-chamber's drainage gutters. Ryn was staring at the wall behind him, and had already been sick twice. It had taken perhaps three minutes, and that only because Aldric had been in no great hurry.

He wiped Widowmaker clean with a strip of cloth torn from the front of Tagen's tunic, which through the manner of his dying the big man had not soiled, then picked his way through the carnage as delicately as a cat in wet grass. The *taiken* glinted as he raised her blade in salute to Giorl and her still-nauseated husband. 'If not for you,' he said, and didn't trouble to say the rest. They had all seen, and all heard, and anyway words whether of thanks or of thanksgiving seemed somehow inadequate right now. 'Lady,' this to Kyrin, 'are you unhurt?'

She held up a wrist nicked twice during the freeing of it and shook her head. 'Nothing else. You?'

'Not even that. You know the spellstone well enough by now.' Widowmaker whispered thinly as he slid her back into her scabbard, and he glanced around the chamber looking for other things than the ragged corpses. 'Where does Voord go to play, if not here?' he wondered aloud, and gazed equably at Giorl.

She met him stare for stare, and after a few moments smiled. 'If he's dead, I'm free,' she said, and smiled an honest smile which looked a little clumsy through lack of use. 'Look for him in the room under the gallery. There'll be no guards anywhere in this wing of the fortress, not now. Not after . . . whatever it was exploded in the cell. When something like that happens – and it does, now and again, thanks to the *Woydach* – those who want to live long clear out until they're told it's safe. Down the corridor outside, then left, left again and down. And when you cut his heart out, do it slowly, just for me.'

Aldric blinked, his own feelings about Voord seeming mere annoyance beside the coldly cherished hatred of this small woman. Again he found himself wondering what story she could tell, and again, despite the lack of compunction with which he had executed the Guardsmen – there being no better or more appropriate word for it – he didn't want to know whatever nasty truths were there. Instead he stepped back to let Giorl get past him, acknowledged Ryn's feeble smile with one equally half-hearted, and watched as they made their way to the cell's sidedoor, and through and out of sight.

'Kyrin,' he said as she peeled the last pieces of cut strapping from her arm and leg, 'there was something said about the rest of our gear in the armoury. In the corridor outside. If she's right, the place should be deserted. Help me arm.'

Tehal Kyrin, Harek's daughter of Valhol, stood up and dusted herself down, then looked at her lover and her husband-to-be. 'Only,' she said, 'if you then help me . . .'

Giorl had been right: the corridors and passageways of the Underfortress were deserted. Aldric and Kyrin found their gear strewn about the armoury in various stages of disrepair, but it had been the kind of articles – like clothing – most easily pulled to pieces which had suffered the greatest damage. There had been little mere 'investigation' could do to *an moyya-tsalaer*. The Alban Great Harness had evolved over centuries to withstand more than the curious pokings and proddings of Drusalan Secret Police. There were no secrets to be extracted from the gleaming black-lacquered metal, other than that a man encased in such carapace was safe from all but the most determined attack.

Aldric felt a deal more comfortable once he was inside it; and more at ease with himself, in a far more subtle way, when his *tsepan* Honour-dirk was back in its proper place pushed through his weapon-belt, rather than hanging from straps as a self-preserving imitation of less worthy weapons.

The black dirk had not been beyond arm's length since he had received it from Lord Endwar Santon more than four years ago, except for those times when it had been taken from him by force. All but one of those thieves were now dead. Santon was dead too, in the honourable act of *tsepanak'ulleth* before witnesses, to atone for his failure in the campaign against Kalarr cu Ruruc. He had been a grim, courteous man who had conducted his entire life as if knowing that the fixation with honour that ruled it would also govern its ending.

Aldric had been one of the witnesses to Lord Santon's suicide, and for all his own respect for the old Honour-codes and no matter that he wore his own dirk as a mark of rank, he was secretly glad that within himself there was nothing so – fanatical was the only word for it – which would make him put his *tsepan* to its ultimate purpose. It had threatened often enough: to preserve his own endangered honour, to resolve the intolerable conflict facing him whilst on task for Rynert the King – when to obey was to be shamed and to refuse was to be dishonoured – even to reprove Rynert for the stupidity of his actions. But there had always been a way out that kept the dirk's blade from his chest – provided he looked hard enough. His dark moods aside, Aldric loved life too much to regard the leaving of it with anything but reluctance.

He was conscious of Kyrin watching him as he picked up the *tsepan*, and was half-inclined for the sake of her already-jangled peace of mind to slip it down inside his boot, or give it into her keeping, or do any of the number of things which would be consonant both with honour and with giving her a crumb of comfort. He shook his head, a gesture only for himself and imperceptible inside the helmet. That would have to come later, after he had dealt with Voord. And after that both sword and dirk could be retired to a handsome weapon-rack on the wall of some small house, and he and Kyrin would forget their duties owed to honour and to vengeance and to the simple requirements of keeping alive when they moved in such lethal circles as this, and they would live their lives for each other instead of for everyone else. That was a dream, indeed; but he and she both had seen so many nightmares become real that there was no reason to doubt reality might have some room left over for the small and ordinary. He hoped so, anyway; it would be a sick world otherwise.

'Ready?'

'Ready.' Kyrin piled up her hair inside one of the Empire's own *seisac* helmets and settled it until it felt at least not actively uncomfortable. 'If being ready is being scared sick.'

Aldric glanced at her and smiled coldly, knowing exactly how she felt. 'It is,' he said, and meant it.

The room where Giorl had told them they might find Voord was itself easy to find, whether he was inside it or not, and the look of the door alone was enough to raise Aldric's armour-protected hackles. Its timbers – on the outside – were sheathed in a finger's thickness of clear ice – and there were wide white fans of frost on floor and walls around its edges. Neither of them cared to think how cold the room itself would have to be.

Kyrin stopped in the corridor outside, well away from that sinister portal, and was reluctant to take a step closer until someone with the authority to do so told her on oath that it was safe. One look at Aldric's face was enough. He might have had the experience and the consequent authority, but he wasn't about to start telling any lies.

He had talked a little – surprisingly little, for a man who tended to be garrulous in company he liked – about some of his previous encounters with the Old Magic and with the High. It had made uncomfortable listening, and Kyrin had been grateful not to have a part in any of the stories . . . until now, and the still more uncomfortable discovery that she was a part of this encounter with the darkness whether she liked it or not, unless she turned and walked away right now, and came to terms with staying away for always.

She was in love and filled with joy at being so – but she was human enough, and frightened enough, to weigh what she felt for Aldric very carefully in the balance against the chance of such a death as she dared not imagine. Then she drew her Jouvaine *estoc* from its scabbard slung across her back and poked thoughtfully at the ice, and said, 'Well, how do we get in?'

The way that Aldric looked at her, and the crooked smile he gave to her bold words, made Kyrin wonder briefly just how much of her hurried calculation had been visible across her face. 'I have a key here for all locks,' he said, and leisurely unsheathed Widowmaker.

Her blade came from the lacquered wood with a soft whispery song of steel and arched over into one of the ready positions Kyrin had seen him practise with nothing more dangerous than a length of polished oak. It was a length of polished metal now, and the lanterns in the corridor flashed back blue-white from the weapon's edges. '*Isileth'kai, abath devhar ecchud*,' Aldric said to the sword, focused for the taking of a single breath and swung full force at the door.

'*Hai!*'

Widowmaker smashed into the nailed, ice-encased timbers in the downward diagonal cut called *tarann'ach*, striking thunderbolt. The door boomed its bass reply to the high vibrating shriek of the *taiken*'s impact and then – perhaps made brittle by the intense cold – made a harsh high crack unlike the rending of wood and exploded into a shower of burnt and burning splinters. The few smoking fragments which remained on the hinges swayed slowly to and fro like hanged men, and there was the scent of lightning on the icy air.

Lightning . . . and roses.

Voord Ebanesj stood quite still in the centre of the pattern at the centre of the floor, and waited. He had waited for a lifetime, if a lifetime is how long it takes to suffer more pain than a man has any need to bear. His shirt and trews were stained with foul matter which had been leaking stealthily out of him since the silver-gilt stitches of his injuries had pulled through the flesh and left each wound like a mouth – mouths that smiled with ragged open lips, and exhaled the heavy stench of gangrene.

It had begun when he had been preaching his theories to Tagen and feeling so very pleased with his own cleverness. Why then, he didn't know; all need to know the reasons behind happenings was lost in the limitless world of pain caused by the happenings themselves. Voord had cried with the agony at last, made all the noises he had heard in the white-tiled bloody chamber, even pleaded for release to a tormentor three weeks beyond hearing him. Yakez Goadec ar Gethin had gone willingly and open-eyed into the darkness to give his sorcery such power, and there was nothing on the breathing side of the gulf of Hell that Voord knew could stop it. Except perhaps for the spellstone of Echainon, mounted in the pommel of Aldric Talvalin's hungry sword.

The door of the chamber blew apart in a billow of smoke and sparks and slivers of charred wood went skittering across the frozen floor. The smell of burning fought with the perfume of roses and mingled briefly in an amalgam that was like the scent of funeral cremation.

Aldric stepped across the threshold, and his sword was burning blue.

Voord looked at him, not making any move. He had never seen the Alban in his own armour before, only that loaned to him by the Drusalan Empire, and had never realised just what an air of menace the Great Harness gave its wearer. Talvalin was just a silhouette against the doorway, blacker than the shadow that stretched out before him, but as the candles within the chamber were caught and flung back from the lacquered surfaces of helmet and plate, mail and lamellar cuirass, he glittered in the darkness as if coated in frost.

The Alban paused just inside the room, his breath pluming grey in the cold air, and looked from side to side as if searching for something. 'No guards, *Woydach*?' he asked. 'Now that was most unwise.'

Voord looked at him, not making any move. He could hear the soft lament of the Song of Desolation, and sense the coming of Issaqua as a man might sense the sun's position through an overcast of cloud. And he could sense that Talvalin was not especially impressed; instead the armoured man was reacting with what looked like familiarity to the ikon of the misty rose that hung in the air at Voord's back.

'Oh, Voord, Voord, you'll have to do better than *that*.' The too-controlled voice with its hateful Elthanek burr was mocking him and making light of everything he held in esteem. 'I've pruned roses before, in Seghar. You might know the place . . .'

Voord's mouth quirked at the inference. Sedna ar Gethin again, no matter how distant the connection. He stared balefully at Aldric. 'I know it,' he said, 'as I know you.'

'As you know your own reflection,' said Tehal Kyrin, stepping into view behind Talvalin, unharmed, armoured and carrying a bared sword. 'Because you and he are each other seen in a dark glass. But he had all that you lacked – and still does. That's why you hate him so, Commander Voord. Deny the truth, man.'

Voord glared hatred at her and shrugged in resignation though the movement sent agony lancing through him. 'What truth?' he said. There was a buzzing in his ears as the Song of Desolation faded, becoming no more than the sound of an insatiable hunger waiting to be fed with what he had promised it. 'The only truth is that which brought you two here with weapons drawn. Killing is truth. So kill me.'

It was an invitation which needed no repeating. Voord

saw the black-hilted longsword shifted from a single- to a double-handed grip, and saw, too, the expression on the Alban's face as he took three steps forward and one to the right. The pupils of his eyes were as wide and dark as those of a hunting cat, and there was no mercy in them.

'As you wish,' said Aldric. Widowmaker rose to poise behind his shoulder for an instant, and then came scything down.

'*Hai . . . !*'

Aldric snapped one step sideways and froze in low-guard ready position for an instant, then relaxed. The form *achran-kai*, the inverted cross, comprised two strokes – one horizontal through the target's upper chest and the second a vertical directed at the crown of the head. He had never yet needed to complete the second cut, and he did not need it now. If the horizontal sweep connected, it was not a cut from which opponents walked away.

Its impact had thrown Voord off his feet so that he lay on his back, arms and legs widespread. For all that he had been opened like a sack of offal there was hardly any blood on the *taiken* blade, as if the dead man's body had none left to spare. Only a small and stealthy puddle formed beneath the Warlord's body as it stared through sightless eyes towards the ceiling.

And then Voord's corpse reared from the bloodied floor and screamed a dreadful blubbering scream that came less from its mouth than through the huge straight slit across its chest. Issaqua the Bale Flower expanded with that awful undying shriek as a man's chest might expand upon inhaling some sweet scent, and as its own reeling perfume flooded the icy air the demon rose swelled out to the monstrous proportions Aldric had seen before in Seghar.

Almost as if it's feeding on his pain . . . The Alban stared grimly from devourer to devoured, then shook his head and spat sourness from his mouth. *No, not almost. Of course it is . . .*

He staggered as the marble pavement underfoot rose and fell in a motion like that of a massive wave, flexing the inlaid tiling until it shattered. Part of the chamber's outer wall cracked across and across, then fell down with a slithering crash so that snow came swirling in. Two great chunks of stone tumbled in as well, looking like gross snowflakes until their impact against the armour guarding Aldric's legs – for no snowflakes could crush proof metal quite like that. He barely noticed, for the perfume of the rose grew more and more intense until their senses swam with it as though with *ymeth* dreamsmoke . . .

Voord continued to scream. Aldric looked once, then winced and turned away. And still the screaming went on, and on, and on . . .

'He's dead!' Kyrin's voice came hard to his ears, fighting through a sound like a million buzzing flies. 'He's dead! You *killed* him – so why won't he die . . . ?' She was near to screaming-point herself. '*Aldric!* Leave him. Take me away from here!' She tugged at the icy metal that sheathed his arm, trying to drag him towards the door. Great white flakes of snow slapped against her face, and Voord's howling hammered at her sanity. 'Finish it! For sweet mercy's sake, kill him and get us out of this place!'

Aldric remained where he was, staring at Issaqua, the scent of roses in his nostrils and the sounds of dying in his ears. 'Kill him?' he said, the words more read from his lips than heard. 'How? With what? Widowmaker can't. Not then, not now. He's a toy now, for that *thing* to play with. It needs to have a death . . .'

Kyrin saw the pallor in his face within the shadows of the helmet, saw the anger and the revulsion and the shame, and suddenly she was afraid – afraid for herself, but most of all afraid for him. 'Use the sword again, and this time use the spellstone too,' she said quickly and too loudly. 'Do it now.'

'No.' Aldric swung Widowmaker up from where her point was braced against the snowy floor, and stared sombrely at the weapon's long blade. 'Not that way, and most especially not with this.' The grey menace hung about the

251

taiken still, flowing like a chill air from her bitter edges, a need for slayings that was at once terrible and yet no more than a sense of purpose and an awareness of function.

'Enough killing for you,' he told the sword gently, regretfully. He went down on one knee and braced Widowmaker flat across the other, closing his left hand on her naked blade a span down from the point. The edges bit at once so that his own blood, steaming slightly in the winter air, mingled with Voord's on the shining steel . . . as if they were becoming brothers rather than merely reflections of each other.

As he leaned in to the work and the blade arched back on itself, whatever else he might have said was changed to a quick, shallow gasping. Widowmaker twisted in his grasp like something living, something trying to break out of a strangling grip. Like something trying to stay alive . . . Aldric's face went white as bone, and sweat dripped from it almost as swiftly as blood ran from the sword.

Then Isileth, called Widowmaker, snapped in two.

Aldric tried to release the broken shard of blade locked in his fingers, biting back an anguished whimper as sinew and tendon refused to obey him any more. The palm of his left hand had sheared clean away, and all that remained of his Honour-scars spattered blood across the broken milk-white marble of the floor. While the remnant of the hand . . .

Had become a twisted claw like Voord's.

The piece of sword-blade came free at last and fell with a harsh belling to the ground near his feet. It was a clumsy, messy, painful business trying to open laced lamellar armour with one hand, but he managed at last.

Voord's screams were growing ragged now, but there was still no sign of an end to his long dying, if while Issaqua remained there would ever be an end to it. Worst of all, he was denied even the refuge of insanity, for there was still intelligence in his bulging, bloodshot eyes when

Aldric steeled himself to look that way. Enough intelligence at least to recognise what the eyes saw, and enough scepticism not to believe it.

Kyrin believed it. She saw the black *tsepan* leave its sheath and Aldric kneel awkwardly in First Obeisance on the churned, snowy, bloody floor, and believed implicitly not only in what she saw but that it would be carried through. She began to cry the bitter tears of loss, yet made no move to prevent Aldric from completing what he had chosen to do.

'It needs to have a death,' he had said, and without needing explanations Kyrin guessed his hope – that a death offered willingly would tip the scales. He had taken responsibility for Voord, for what had happened to him and – for all she knew – for what the *Woydach* had done to them both. It was his choice, and his right.

The *tsepan* went in beneath his breastbone at a steep angle, and Aldric's face was wrenched into a grimace of pain. Blood poured out through his fingers and as he coughed, darkened his teeth and chin. He swayed a little, and only now that strength of will was of no more account did he look towards Kyrin, pouring all into the look that he would have said aloud had he been able.

Voord's screaming stopped abruptly.

In that silence, Aldric Talvalin smiled at some small private victory; then he slumped on to his side as gently as if falling asleep, and lay still . . .

I miss her. I wish she was here, too. But you always pass the door alone.

Alone and naked. Aldric wore nothing but the marks collected over the course of a quarter-century. Most were not even welted scars, merely the pale traceries of wounds that were all the spellstone of Echainon left in the wake of its healing. Only the puncture beneath his breastbone was worthy of note, and that because it was where his life had drained away.

Nothing can ye bring, and nothing bear away; skin was thy sufficient dress in the beginning and sufficient shall it be at the end; naked come all into the world, and naked all depart . . . And it was in the face of this truth, written in the oldest of old books, that the corpses of dead clan-lords were clad in their finest before their bodies were committed to the fire . . . Aldric would have laughed aloud except that laughter in this place seemed less than proper.

It was dark beyond the door, that Door which the books said only ever opened in one direction, only admitted and never released. The air, if air it was, felt neutrally warm against his bare skin, and still, and very quiet. It was the sort of place where if voices were heard at all they would be mannerly murmurs and nothing louder. But there were no voices. No other people. Only himself . . . and one other.

That other's eyes were squeezed tight shut, so that he might as well have been alone. Aldric wondered why. He thought that he might know this other man, if he could just recall his name, and any companionship would be better than none at all. By the look of him he would have tales to tell; the long straight slash of a sword-stroke had ripped his bare chest from one armpit to the other, there were other brutal scars on face and body and something had mangled his left hand until it was no more than a claw of bone and leather.

Just like Aldric's own . . .

'Voord,' he said, remembering at last. Remembering all of it. The *Woydach*'s eyes opened and Aldric smiled at him as calmly as he would at his best friend. Or at Kyrin herself. *Oh God, how I miss her. But she understood what it was I had to do. She understood me. That's why I miss her so much.*

'Talvalin . . . ?' Tentatively the smile was matched and mirrored, until at last it reached Voord's eyes and warmed them as they had not been warm this dozen years. All at once those eyes flinched away from Aldric's steady gaze,

254

as if embarrassed – or ashamed. 'Talvalin, finish with me. Do it now . . . while I have the courage.'

Aldric's left hand, crippled now and cradled in his right, was clenched shut in an attempt to contain the blood-flow in his fist. It wasn't successful. When he reached out to touch Voord's forehead with fingertips that left dark smears in their wake, there was no mockery in what he did. It was simply that there was blood everywhere. His blood . . . this once, his blood alone. '*Woydach* Voord,' he said, not caring that titles of rank were no more carried here than the badges and regalia that marked them, 'I think it's been done already.'

Voord stared in disbelief at the blood and the evidence of pain. 'You . . . you did this. For *me*?'

'Voord,' Aldric said softly, not knowing his once-enemy by any other name and here no longer needing to know, 'it counts for very little. What value is a gift that's easy to give? Killing has been the easy way for both of us; it always was. Living in peace – with the memories we share – would have been the hard part. That alone would have made it worth doing . . . for both of us. A pity that we missed the chance.'

No matter what Kyrin had said, while they lived neither would have been able to accept the other as a brother beneath the skin. There was too much hatred and brutality between them for anything that might have led to understanding or forgiveness. And now, for all the words that might be said concerning dark and light, right and left, good and evil, none of it had any value any more.

There was a smell of lancemint leaves in Aldric's nostrils and just for a moment that clean astringence made his gorge rise, made him – almost – thrust Voord away as the memories of lancemint-sweetened breath and the last time he had smelt it came flooding back, heavy with pain and self-disgust and loathing for the man who might have been a friend. Then he saw the tears streaming down Voord's face and the old hurts twisting at his features, and knew that this time and for always he had won.

Lancemint leaves. And roses . . .

As that too-sweet, too-rich perfume cut sickeningly through the sharp scent of mint, Aldric blinked rapidly and for the first time paid some small attention to what surrounded him.

At first there was nothing. Utter nothing. No shape, no colour, no sound, neither above nor below nor before, nor behind, nor to either side. Only the stillness and that cool warmth which was neither pleasant nor unpleasant, no more felt against his skin than skin is felt against the flesh beneath it. Skin which for no reason at all was hackling like the back of a frightened cat . . .

And then the reason became all too plain. Voord began to scream again, and this time his screaming was edged with the knowledge that he was beyond even the release that comes with death . . .

Kyrin cradled the body on her lap and stared down at its still face. There were no more tears, not now; she had been shocked beyond weeping when the *tsepan* drove home, when the blood flowed, when Aldric really, truly gave up his own life as honour's price for an enemy's clean death. There had always been the hope that the gesture alone would be sufficient, right up to the moment when he fell over and the quick, shallow movement of his breathing fluttered to a stop.

Aldric's eyes were closed and his features without expression, almost conveying the illusion of sleep until illusion was destroyed and the reality made plain by the black dirk jutting from his chest. Already he was growing cold and there was no colour in him; all the colour had leaked out on to the floor, as red as . . .

As roses . . .

Kyrin pulled the borrowed helmet from her head and flung it clattering clear across the room. She would hate the colour and the scent of roses for the rest of her life. As grief gave way to awareness of the eight guards staring through the still-smouldering doorway, she realised that *the rest* was measured now in seconds. Their lord was slain and his assassin was beyond their reach, but whether impelled by loyalty or by more mercenary motives these were men who wanted to kill someone – and she was the only one not dead already.

Her own long stabbing-sword was belted at her hip, but at first Kyrin gave it only passing thought. The cooling dead-weight across her thighs had taken away whatever desire she might have had to prolong an inevitable and now enviable end. Kyrin was not fond to live. At long last, and too late, she began to understand Aldric and the Albans.

Without the helmet they could see she was a woman, but at least there would be no nonsense this time about keeping her for later, 'for dessert'. They were too enraged. They would carve her as the main dish on revenge's table, and it would be quick – perhaps too quick even for pain, although in her heart she knew that thought was foolishness.

Kyrin closed her eyes and shook her head. Nothing made sense any more, and shaping a decision from the confused whirl within her mind was as lifting some great weight. Oblivion. Peace. To go where Aldric was. To die . . . that would be good. But to die well. Maybe it would be better to go out fighting after all. She owed these bastards so much – they and what they represented.

'Soon, my loved,' she said, letting Aldric's body slide gently to the floor as she came to her feet and unhooked the sheathed *estoc* from her belt. 'Very soon. Wait for me . . .' Kyrin raised the sword level with her face, one hand about its hilt and the other on its scabbard. The guards fanned out, watchful and suddenly uncertain, eager to slaughter her and at the same time reluctant to make the first move. There was too much of death and desperation in this room to leave any space for error. Kyrin could feel it.

She forced herself to smile at them across the *estoc* blade as she slowly drew it from its scabbard, and saw at least one flinch as she dropped the empty scabbard to the ground beside the empty husk which had been her lover. That one had made the connection, and knew she had neither reason to live nor fear of dying. In his career he would have seen many such, and none left free to swing a blade would have gone alone into the darkness. Kyrin met his eyes, concentrated on him and made her forced smile grow tight and cold and predatory. He was afraid . . . that left seven who were not.

The seven poised their swords and came for her in a single rush.

The release that was death gave only a surcease to the pains and terrors of the flesh. Those were past and done with, an ugly memory and no more. What remained for Voord was worse. Far, far worse. He had died in debt, with what he owed still barely collected . . .

And dying was no escape from demons.

The cool un-warmth on Aldric's skin was suddenly swept away by an iciness that ground through to the marrow of his bones and the very core of his spirit. Darkness became dawn, and was flushed by an unwholesome light that was the livid colour left by blood settling through the tissues of a days-dead corpse. All of that dark untrammelled world contracted in upon them, until the boundary of what had been infinity was the inside of a mirrored sphere as wide as the room in which their bodies lay. A boundary as wide as the gulf between the living and the dead.

Issaqua crossed the boundary, following its prey.

For all that the demon was hunger incarnate, it still smelt of roses. The perfumes carried with it a reeling drunkenness that even here set the senses swirling like strong wine, but that was the last remaining trace of the Bale Flower which Aldric had seen twice before. In the here and now beyond death, where all was made naked and unadorned, there was no place for the foul-fair semblance of a monstrous blossom. No need for anything at all but truth at last – a truth that was reason enough to set Voord screaming.

Issaqua's shape had warped from the softness of rose-petals into a thing of fangs and drool and chitin, the glistening armoured bulk of its first, worst child. It was a shape that Aldric knew of old, from dreams that lurked beyond the gates of sleep and from a reality that was worse than any dream. It was a shape that he could name: Warden of Gateways, Herald of the Ancients. *Ythek'ter auythyu an-shri.*

The Devourer in the Dark.

Ythek Shri swung its eyeless armoured head to study them, and Aldric felt that unhuman consideration sweep over him like a gust of winter wind. There was a promissory recognition in the demon's gargoyle glower, a recollection of the Devourer's last meeting with this puny scrap of living meat which had dared give it defiance – and worse, had won. It stepped forward with that raking grace he knew so well, stalking on triple-taloned claws across its own curved and distorted reflection that was thrown back and back again from the mirrored limits of the world. Aldric held his ground and returned the demon's regard with as much composure as he could summon. He had made no pacts, owed no debts, and the Law of Balance that lay behind all things extended even here. Ythek Shri could not harm him.

Voord . . . was not so lucky.

Kyrin stared at the oncoming swords with less fear than she would have believed. They glittered coldly in the wintry light streaming through the shattered wall, and were for all that threat no more than her keys to the door that kept her from Aldric's side. Sharp keys, and painful, but of no more concern to her now than any of the other means to an end that she had employed in her brief life.

259

She laughed, a grim sound that was more than half a sob, and met them half-way across the room with the cut that the Albans called *tarannin-kai*, twin thunderbolts, a horizontal figure-eight that jolted either side in flesh and sent someone's fingers pattering across the floor. The charge broke, guardsmen scattering in every direction – and Kyrin pirouetted like a dancer, cut backhanded and felt first impact and then a spray of wet heat. She was not fencing in the Jouvaine style she had been taught but fighting for her life – or at least a good death – in the ruthless Alban fashion which Aldric had favoured, where any move that failed to draw blood was wasted. A return cut clashed on the forts of her sword, and as the force of the stroke glissaded uselessly against her hilt she counterthrust hard into an unguarded shoulder. The meeting steel rang and grated. It was not the harsh wild belling of Widowmaker's hungry blade, only the shrill chime of common metal – but metal that was hungry enough without two thousand years to teach it appetite. Kyrin's boot slammed up to drive the air from a guardsman's lungs before her sword ripped out the little that remained. For that first frenzied minute their fear of her desperation was as good as a weapon – and then a blade bit into her side and all fear and hesitation vanished.

Kyrin cried out, a sound that was more shock and outrage at the violation of her flesh than any reaction to pain – the pain of such a injury would come later, had there been a later. She clapped her hand against the spurting wound, missed her balance for an instant and almost at once took another cut that opened her thigh from hip to knee. This time, Kyrin could not help but scream as she reeled sideways and fell down on to the broken marble paving of the floor.

Everything went black and when her senses came wavering back, the first to return was taste as the tang of blood and oily metal flooded her mouth, dribbling from the smeared sword-point resting against her lips. Kyrin stared up at the soldier whose boot was under her chin.

There was no pity in the man's face, nor in those of his companions. As the blade pressed downwards and clicked against her teeth, Kyrin clenched them uselessly and shut her eyes.

Aldric watched with revulsion as Voord cowered in the presence of his nemesis, then turned, screaming – always, always screaming – in an attempt to flee. It was useless; here, where all places were the same place, there was nowhere for him to run without the glinting black bulk of the Devourer there already, waiting. As the once-Warlord stumbled to a terror-stricken halt for the tenth or the hundredth or the thousandth time, Issaqua the Shri grinned at him with a mouth that was the mouth of Hell.

It made a slavering noise, and its great triangular head split wide apart like the petals of a flower – except that no flower possessed such a ragged infinity of dreadful teeth. The spikes and blades of those fangs dribbled glutinous saliva as they ground together with a sound like shears, and strings of vile slime dripped on to Voord's upturned face. His shrieks rose to an incoherent squeal that was beyond screaming as Issaqua stooped down from its fifteen feet of height and opened its crooked claws in a rending embrace that ended only when Voord came to pieces . . .

And was restored, to do it all again for as much of eternity as the demon desired.

Aldric stared in horror for a long second while the mangled fragments which had been Voord became Voord again and tried again to escape. Except that here there was neither escape by flight nor escape by insanity any more than there was escape by death. Issaqua's talons clashed shut on nothing, mocking him by missing as he flinched frantically aside, then opened wide and reached for him again.

They jarred to a halt as Aldric blocked the way.

He had seen what had happened to Voord – what even

now was happening again to Voord – and was consumed with a fear that was as far beyond earthly terror as he was now beyond life. Fear and honour had fought together for the longest of times, and yet it seemed only the barest instant before honour won. Aldric had not driven his *tsepan* into his chest, had not given up that life, freely and without bargains, to preserve Voord from torment only to see it happen now.

The Devourer's monstrous head jerked backwards as if it had been burnt. It reared up hissing to its full height and snarled like torn sheet steel. There was intelligence in that sound, but it was not the sort of intelligence which could be bargained with. Voord had made that mistake and was paying for it now. He had forgotten that Issaqua was a demon and its processes of reasoning were uncluttered by pity, or mercy, or remorse. There was only the Law of Balance, a logic cold and hard and unforgiving as a razor's edge. Cause and effect, action and reaction. Guilt and punishment.

It was all that kept it from doing to Aldric as it had done to Voord, and somehow, from somewhere, he knew. The icy aura of fear which hung around Ythek Shri did not fade, but rather it ceased to chill his flesh. Voord was behind him, cringing on his knees like a beaten dog and whimpering so that Aldric's stomach turned sick inside him. There was nothing now, neither fear nor threat nor past hatreds, that would make him step aside and allow Issaqua to reach its prey, for all that the prey was lawful and condemned to this by his own actions. To do so would make his death a worthless gesture and no freely-given gift at all.

The Devourer's fanged maw gaped, drooling, and made a softly bubbling hiss that was heavy with malice. Only the Balance stood between Aldric and an eternity of anguish, the Law that not even one of the ancient powers could flout with impunity. And yet, for all the bindings and restrictions that hedged it, Ythek, Issaqua, the Herald, the Devourer, was subject to at least one all-too-human failing: a failing Aldric had seen too many times, in himself and others. It was rage, that very special single-minded rage which comes from being flouted, mocked, denied, defied. The rage that makes fools of the wise and strengthens the weak. The black and brooding fury that blinds to all thought of consequence.

The pallid, deathly light began to fade, taking on the colours that Aldric had seen once in the petals of a rose – crimson and black and purple as a bruise. Issaqua's spiked and jagged bulk melted back into the shadows as night returned to the world beyond death's door. Yet the demon was so much darker than the darkness that Aldric could still see it as a silhouette, a hole ripped in the very structure of things through which all light and hope of rebirth were leaking out. The heavy reek of roses clogged his nostrils and the sound of the Song of Desolation was in his ears – and in his head, repeating like some grim litany, were the words of the prophecy he had read in Seghar; only words then, but a threat now. Or a promise.

> *The setting sun grows dim*
> *And night surrounds me.*
> *There are no stars.*
> *The Darkness has devoured them*
> *With its black mouth.*
> *Issaqua sings the Song of Desolation*
> *And I know that I am lost*
> *And none can help me now.*
> *Issaqua comes to find me*
> *To take my life and soul.*
> *For I am lost*
> *And none can help me now.*
> *Issaqua sings the Song of Desolation*
> *And fills the world with darkness.*
> *Bringing fear and madness*
> *Despair and death to all . . .*

From out of the darkness, in a blur of fangs and claws that were as black as a wolf's throat, Issaqua came for him.

★

263

Kyrin lay on her back with a boot across her throat and the point of a sword in her mouth. Fresh blood, her own blood, was trickling from the cuts the guardsman's sword had made in her lips, but its point was still poised on her teeth and no further. All it needed was a little pressure and the blade would come crunching down, but that pressure was withheld. She still lived.

A hot wind burned one side of her face, and from its source came a glow of light that she could see even through her closed eyelids. Someone swore, and all of a sudden the blade was gone from her teeth. Kyrin's eyes snapped open. The soldiers still surrounded her, but she was no longer the centre of their attention. She took the only opportunity that she was likely to get and rolled frantically sideways towards her own discarded *estoc* as fast as her wounds allowed. Aldric had always said that there were good and bad ways to die, and what had threatened her was one of the worst. He had not lived long enough to make her Alban by marriage, but rather than be butchered on the floor she could at least be Alban enough to die in their way – quick and clean on her own sword's point.

The rings and bars of the *estoc*'s hilt rattled as she grabbed at it, reversed it – and then blade and hilt together clashed against the broken flagstones as a foot clad in a long black boot kicked the weapon from her hand and stamped it tight against the floor.

'No need for that,' said Gemmel Errekren. 'No need at all.' He lifted his boot from the sword and reached down to help Kyrin to her feet, driving the Dragonwand into the stone floor for her to lean on but never once taking his eyes away from the guards. None of them had moved: the manner of his arrival amid fire and lightning had seen to that, and his appearance now was enough to confirm their caution. Kyrin glanced sidelong at him and herself felt the beginnings of that very special skin-crawling unease which comes when the familiar turns strange. She had barely grown accustomed to him as a sorcerer, even one who refused to dress the part; she had no terms of reference at all for whatever he was now.

What Gemmel wore now was without doubt a uniform, and one which by its cut and colour was intended to be ominous, but more ominous by far was the weapon he had cross-drawn from a flapped holster and now held in his right hand. Her first glance made her think it was a *telek*, but her second and all other glances told her that it was nothing of the sort. It was more massive than the Alban spring-guns, and tiny lights glowed red and blue and green like jewels against the steely sheen of its metal. Gemmel's thumb shifted something, two of the red lights turned blue and the sidearm began to sing a faint, high, two-toned song to itself, a thin humming that was to Kyrin's ear as sinister a sound as any demon-born Song of Desolation. 'Is that magic?' she ventured.

Gemmel glanced at the thing in his hand as if he had never seen it before. 'No,' he said. Then he looked from beneath his brows at the guards and smiled crookedly. 'But whatever happens, *they* won't know the difference.'

There was a shimmering exhalation of waste heat from the black fins running the length of its heavy barrel, but other than that haze-dance there was no suggestion of movement. Gemmel was holding the weapon as if shooting in formal competition at a target, shoulder and arm and hand all one straight line, but the barrel remained as unwavering as if clamped to a bench as it swept across the five guards who were still a threat.

The soldiers looked at one another, then at the elderly man and the injured girl who was as good as dead already, and without saying a word began to fan out. Gemmel watched them in silence, but there was a glitter of cold amusement in his eyes as he saw his firing arc grow slowly wider. '*Teyy'aj hah!*' the enchanter said at last. It was a simple, blunt command to stop, but a half-hidden something in the back of his voice made the Drusalan imperatives more brutal than even they normally sounded. '*Kagh telej-hu, taii'ura!*'

The guards only grinned and began to move faster. One of them raised his sword and poised it behind his head for a downward stroke. 'I suggest you don't,' said Gemmel. His voice was bleak, and Kyrin felt the hackles rise on her neck at the sound of it.

'Listen to him, you fools!' she snapped desperately. Even though she knew that she was the last person the soldiers would heed, the warning was something she had to give. The attempt to save lives had to be made.

Gemmel's hand came down lightly on her shoulder. 'Save your breath, lady,' he said, 'and your concern. This is their choice.'

'Their choice,' echoed Kyrin softly, and shivered.

That was when the guardsman farthest to the left made his move. The man might have been nettled by the sound of two victims expressing a sort of pity for their slayers, or he might just have reached that one point on the floor from which his attack could best be launched. For whatever reason, he raised his sword and charged with a guttural war-shout – that became a scream in the instant he realised that he would never reach the old man fast enough.

Gemmel's arm came around with all the smooth speed of a battleram's turret mounting, and the weapon at the end of that long arm matched the soldier's scream with a screech of its own. Focused energy blasted across the intervening space in a sweep of heat and light that ripped into the man's chest and flung him backwards in smoking pieces.

The sidearm had begun to fire an instant before it came on target, and Gemmel had held its trigger-grip closed right through the weapon's traverse. By the time he released it, a long horizontal stripe of the wall was glowing white and the rough-hewn granite all along that line of heat had slumped out of shape like wax in a furnace. The air was darkened briefly by a billow of greasy grey smoke that smelled horribly of burnt pork, and when it cleared

Gemmel had the undivided attention of everyone in the room.

He stared at the surviving guards and tracked the shrouded muzzle slowly across them just to make sure that they understood. The men went white and the sound of four shortswords being dropped to the flagstones might have been confirmation enough, but it was only when they picked up their wounded companions and scurried from the room that Gemmel let his hand and its lethal burden drop back to his side. Slowly he returned the sidearm to its holster and secured the flap. His face was without expression, as blank as a sheet of paper, but Kyrin had seen it in the first instant that Gemmel had let himself look full at Aldric's body, and at the black *tsepan* hilt jutting from it, and she knew . . .

'So you killed yourself.' Gemmel dropped heavily on to one knee and put out one hand to touch the cold face. 'No one else could.' The hand was shaking. 'Why, my son? Oh, why . . . ?'

'For Voord,' said Kyrin miserably. 'He did it to let Voord die.'

Gemmel's head jerked up and the glisten of unshed tears in his green eyes hardened to the brilliance of flawless faceted emeralds. He drew a quick, deep breath and came to his feet in a single movement, no longer a grieving old man but a sorcerer fired with hope. Kyrin felt a surge of new strength in the hands which came out to grasp her upper arms. He managed not to shake her in his eagerness, but all the energy of that shaking was contained in a single softly spoken word. 'Explain . . .'

There was nothing left of Aldric's world but the promise of pain in a glitter of talons and teeth. Without thought and without hope, his instincts took over and his empty right hand lashed out at the heart of the hungry blackness in an attempt to block. Without a sword in that hand the gesture was useless, but long years of practice had made some kind of defensive counter as much a reflex as pulling back from a fire.

And then the hand was empty no longer. A light that was the hot transparent blue of an alcohol flame ran down his arm from where the cut was born, up in the heavy muscles of shoulder and back, almost as if the power that would have propelled a sword had become visible. It flared out from his fist and formed a blade – no more than the shadow of a blade, as all things here were shadows – but when one unreality slashed across another in a sweeping stroke that left an arc of fire in its wake, Issaqua the Devourer reeled back screeching.

Aldric glanced quickly over-shoulder, making sure that he still stood between Voord and the demon. The once-Warlord was on his feet, watching wide-eyed as the Alban who had been his enemy defended him from the demon which had been his ally. From the expressions fighting for precedence on his face, the Vlechan's confusion was absolute.

None of Voord's old certainties made sense any more. That any man should willingly have died for his sake was hard enough to comprehend; that it should be *this* man, and that the gift should go on beyond pity and into forgiveness, was almost more than he could bear.

Aldric knew; he had been there, seconds and a lifetime ago, when he had knelt and drawn his *tsepan*, and realised not only what he was finally about to do but why. It had been the last of all the reasons he had ever considered and yet, strangely, the most honourable of them all.

He shook his head, then stared at his own poised right hand; the arm, his whole body, were naked no longer, but instead were encased in a familiar metal skin, *an moyya-tsalaer*, his own Great Harness. It was as it had always been, jet-black, so that as he moved his limbs they glittered darkly. Like Ythek Shri. Too much so for comfort. For all that the armour looked to have been wrought of smoke instead of steel, he had no doubt that it would be just as effective as the sword.

That, too, was still gripped firmly by his mailed fingers, and its shape was without doubt that of a *taiken*. It was as if Isileth Widowmaker, being broken, had come with him into death and had waited only to be summoned to his time of greatest need. The longsword or – by its colour – the Echainon spellstone set into its pommel. Both, maybe. Singly and together they had preserved his life often enough, had been almost as much a part of him in the past year as his own heart and hands. Why not then preserve his soul from harm . . . ?

Aldric watched Issaqua coldly from beneath the shadowy peak of a shadowy helmet. What was, was. Thinking grimly that it would have amused Gemmel to see him dismiss the mystery, Aldric questioned no longer, did not pause to wonder any further about the *why?* or *when?* or *how?* but instead closed the distance in three swift steps and cut again.

'*Hai!*'

Teeth glistened amid a webbing of saliva as the demon's maw gaped wide – then went on gaping, wider and wider as both of its lower jaws fell away. Issaqua bellowed, vomiting up a thick silvery blood like molten metal as it scrabbled at the ruined mask of its face, trying to restore the smashed pieces to their proper configuration. In some dispassionate part of Aldric's mind it seemed strange that the Devourer could so easily repair its careful dismemberment of Voord so that it could pull him apart again, and yet could not heal itself.

A strange hope began to take shape, that instead of fighting this long fight down through eternity he might actually finish it – finish with Issaqua once and for all and finally be at peace. Kill it, if killing was possible here beyond the door of death. Maybe it was. Maybe this was the only place where the unkillable could truly die. Slain by the already-slain.

Aldric laughed harshly through the wild whirl of his own thoughts. His sword had twice cloven the demon's substance, yet when the great hooks of its talons came raking towards him they were blocked by something more than just the smoky carapace that was the memory of armour. That merely gave an outward form to his true protection. He was already dead – and unlike Voord he could not be harmed or torn or tormented, because even now in his willing defence of a helpless victim he had done nothing to deserve retribution.

It was Issaqua's attempt to rend him which had broken the Law and upset the Balance, and he held the bladed consequence burning blue in his right hand. Aldric hefted the un-weight of the shadow sword and watched the Devourer rear up to its full height, more than twice his own. The coldness of its hatred burned him and despite his confidence all the old fears came whimpering back. If he had misjudged, if he was wrong about this, if *auythyu an-shri* laid hold of him – then eternity would be a long, long time to scream.

There was a flickering of half-seen movement. Too fast. Far too fast. Aldric snapped around and the sword came up, but long before he even saw what it was something had seized his left arm in a grip like white-hot metal. And behind him, with the sound of despair that comes only when hope is offered and then snatched away, Voord began to shriek . . .

Gemmel was working with a feverish speed that Kyrin had never seen before. He had taken Ykraith the Dragon-wand out of her hands and spoken to it under his breath in that quick, slipshod monotone which always made her think of priests babbling over-familiar litanies, then thrust its spike into the stone floor beside Aldric's body. As Kyrin watched, he repeated the procedure with Widow-maker's hilt-shard, driving the broken blade into the marble flags with an ease that gave the lie to its impossibility.

'Why can't you let him be?' she said wearily. 'This is a waste of time.'

Gemmel straightened up with a jerk and stared at her, and for just an instant Kyrin discovered what it felt like to receive a flicker of real rage from those deep-set emerald eyes. She flinched as if he was about to strike her, then the old enchanter forced a smile on to his face and the moment was gone. 'Then it's my time to waste, lady. Isn't it?' He stepped back from the corpse and beckoned her closer. 'Come here. Now.'

She stood at the crown of Aldric's head, looking down at him. Gemmel had withdrawn the *tsepan* and returned it to its scabbard, and had rearranged his dead son's limbs and clothing so that the ugly wound was hidden. Had it not been for the ivory pallor of his skin, Kyrin might still have believed that Aldric was only sleeping and might be wakened by the touch of her hand. Gemmel watched her for a moment; then he said, 'Call him.'

Kyrin was not in the habit of swearing, especially at people so menacing as Gemmel Errekren, but she swore now – bitterly and with the tears newly stinging at her eyes. For all that she called him filthy things which would have drawn a reaction even from Aldric himself, the enchanter took her oaths without a flicker of response. 'Call him.'

'He's not asleep,' wailed Kyrin softly, 'he's *dead*!'

'I know.' The flat response silenced her as nothing else could have done. 'But you told me the reason and the manner of it. There is a Balance in these matters, Kyrin, and for these few moments it's still weighted on his side. So do as I bid you and *call him*!'

'I . . . Yes.' Kyrin stared at the pale, still body and tried to forget that she had seen a knife go into it and all the blood and life go out. She put from her mind all but the times when he had dozed off fully clothed, all the times when he had looked as he did now, all the times when a word or a touch was all she needed to make his eyes open and his mouth smile. 'Aldric. Oh my loved, can you not hear me? Aldric, dear one, come back to me . . .' Gemmel was beside her, watching, and she turned to him in despair and hope of sympathy. 'It isn't working. Nothing's happening. It isn't working . . . !'

'Hush, now. You wouldn't have brought him back from the corridor outside, and he's farther away than that. Call him again and keep calling him until . . . until I tell you to stop.'

'And then . . . ?'

'And then watch, and learn, and become wise. *Abath arhan, Ykraith, hlath Echainon devhawr ecchud. Aih'noen ecchaur i aiyya.*'

Kyrin felt the air turn thick, like honey. Power thrummed in it so that little sparks ran crackling down her hair and sleeted from the tips of her fingers. The spellstaff and the broken *taiken* became the uprights of a doorway, one that had no lintel and no door save only a slow rippling like the near-invisible haze that rises from a heated surface. It was quite transparent, yet things seen through it were not quite the same as things seen around the sides. They were . . . changed. A whirl of snow from the darkening sky outside gusted through the shattered wall and roof, and Kyrin saw the doorway fill with stars. Then there was only a scattering of snowflakes that settled on to Aldric's face and had not heat enough to melt.

'Take his hand,' said Gemmel. There was the sound of effort in his voice, and it took on an edge of urgency as Kyrin bent towards the cold hands crossed on the cold breast. 'No! Through the door. Reach out and bring him home.'

Kyrin did not hesitate, but extended her hand towards the shimmer and into it, and through it. The hand vanished from sight as if she had thrust it into ink instead of a surface that seemed as clear as glass. The junction of wrist and doorway was as straight-edged as the stroke of a razor, and there was a freezing instant of horror as she realised this was what an amputation would look like. Then something solid and metal-cold brushed against her fingertips, something laced and buckled. She closed her grip on what could only be the wrist-plates of an Alban

lamellar battle armour. There was a sudden wrench of
resistance and Kyrin cried out, pulling with a desperate
strength that had no thought for what else might be
brought as well . . .

His sword was half-way through a savage downward sweep
when Aldric wrenched the descending blade to a dead
stop, for what was locked around his armoured sleeve was
no demonic claw but a human hand and wrist which had
pushed through a shimmering shear plane in the very air
itself, a hand that burned but only with the heat of living
blood. He felt his throat thicken and tears sting at his
eyes as he recognised the ring on its third finger: heavy
gold, with a square face that was plain except for the
chequered diagonal of a clan-lord's youngest son – the
ring that he had set on Tehal Kyrin's finger as a love-
token until they could find a better.

Kyrin's hand began to pull him through the walls of
death and back towards the living world, and in the same
moment Issaqua took a single raking stride forward. Once
he was gone, it would have Voord all to itself. The *Woydach*'s renewed wails of terror dinned in Aldric's ears and
made his skin crawl. Everything was going to be worthless
after all. Unless . . .

His left arm had been drawn through almost to the
shoulder when Aldric threw himself against the slow,
steady pull and lunged towards Issaqua. It lacked all grace
and control and was more the limb-flail of someone falling
from a horse, but it brought him just close enough to cut
tarann'ach, a vertical stroke with all his focused force
behind it that split the universe in two blue-blazing pieces.
His whole body jolted, and he didn't know whether it was
with the impact or with being brought up short in his
tracks by a frightful jerk on his outstretched left arm.

The demon's armoured shape stood quite still for a long
second with only its great crooked claws flexing like a

spider's legs – glowering, unhurt, as impossible to dismiss as a bad dream.

Oh God, what does it take to kill you . . .

A silvery line as straight and precise as a geometric exercise appeared down the centre of the demon's huge triangular head. It slumped a little and ceased to be symmetrical, then sagged sideways and fell apart in two sheared halves. Issaqua, Ythek Shri, the Devourer in the Dark, quivered once all over and toppled silently forward in a long, long fall that flared into hot blue light and drifting ashes and never reached the bottom . . .

Kyrin's hand came back through the doorway with a sudden rush, and the haze between the lintels winked out of existence. There was nothing now except a staff carved with the outlines of a dragon and the black hilt of a broken sword. Nothing at all . . . her hand was empty. She stared at it, not wanting to believe that what her eyes said was the truth. The ring on her finger, Aldric's ring, glinted coldly in the cold light and mocked her hopes.

Gemmel was watching her. He did not speak, and Kyrin was glad of it. There were no words left to him that would mean anything more than the most feeble of excuses. She tried not to blink, for fear that the tears would start again. 'I told you.' Her voice was quiet, without any hint of blame. 'Can we go now, please?'

'Not without my son.'

'I would have carried him,' said Kyrin simply, 'but you can help me, if you want.'

'No.' Gemmel made no move. 'Wait!'

Kyrin felt anger at the old man's stubbornness boil up slowly through her grief. She could understand how Gemmel felt – did she not feel the same? – but not why he persisted in this useless charade once they had both seen how he had failed. There had to come a time when he accepted what she had known in her heart all along, that Aldric was dead and no sorcery or talk of Balance set awry would bring him back. To do otherwise lacked dignity, and that was all Kyrin had left. 'Wait?' she echoed. 'You've done all that you thought you could, old man – more than that, you made me believe it, too. You made me see him die all over again . . .'

'Did I? Then I ask your pardon for it.' Gemmel shrugged, dismissive more than apologetic. 'But had you trusted more and doubted less, it would not have happened. Look, Kyrin . . . look again – and see him live.'

Kyrin looked . . . and at first saw nothing. Aldric lay as still and pale and dead as when she laid his body on the ground. Then something moved, a thing so small that at first she did not realise what it meant. No more than a bead of water on his brow, as unremarkable as sweat or rain . . . or a snowflake that had only now begun to melt.

Aldric's eyes snapped open, then as quickly shut to squinting slits until they grew more accustomed to the winter dusk that was a blinding glare after the blackness beyond the gate. For long seconds after that they stared unfocused at the ceiling, while vague dark figures moved to and fro and voices spoke through the ringing silence in his ears. The breath came back into him in a single long shudder and he tried to sit up; then let that first breath come gasping out again as the hurt muscles of his stomach suggested *not just yet*.

There was more pain in his left arm, a silver needle of it stabbing up from the hand he had braced against the floor – a hand whose palm he was suddenly afraid to look at. Now that memory came rushing back like the spray of that wave of pain, he was more than willing to lie still and try to make some sense of what had no sense in it at all. 'I was dead.'

'You were dead.' That the first voice he heard should have been Gemmel's, and agreeing with him, was of a piece with the rest. That it should have been edged with irritation in an attempt to hide any softer emotion was also quite in keeping. 'Pig-headed self-sacrificial tradition-bound honour-fixated . . .' Gemmel paused, clearing his throat with unnecessary vigour. Seen upside-down, his smile was a peculiar thing, but even so it went a long way towards taking the sting from what he said. 'Don't make a habit of suicide, Aldric. It's usually permanent.'

Always give as good as you get, when you're able . . . Aldric grinned the tight little smile of someone receiving unnecessary advice. 'I'll bear that in mind, *altrou*.'

Gemmel snorted and stalked around to stand beside him, where he leaned on the Dragonwand and stared down critically. 'Can you stand?'

Aldric thought about it. 'I think so.'

'Then take my hand.'

'I . . . Your pardon, Father, but there was another hand – the hand that brought me back. Please. Kyrin was here.'

'She still is, my loved.' Kyrin knelt down beside him on the shattered marble of the floor amongst the snow and the blood, and reached out as she had done before across an infinitely greater distance. 'I told you once, Aldric: where you go, I go. We go together, or not at all.'

Aldric looked at her left hand – long-fingered, ringed with gold and perfect – and shuddered when he thought of the claw that Isileth's edges had made of his own. At last, reluctantly, he raised it. There was no claw. The hand on his wrist showed hardly any sign at all that its palm had been carved off – except that where the Honour-scars had been was now all new, unblemished, slightly tender skin.

Kyrin had seen the look and the hesitation, and knew why. She took his hand in hers and helped him to his feet. 'They're gone. All the duty and the obligation went with them.' She touched a fingertip lightly to his chest, and to the small white triangle where a *tsepan* had gone home to the full length of its blade. 'The only Honour-scar that matters now is here.'

'Now, and later,' said Gemmel. 'Much later, and well

away from here.' He bounced something on the palm of his hand, a thing of gold and greenish crystal which Aldric had known for several months by no more than description, before he saw it clasped around the neck of *Woydach* Voord. The Jewel, that had been the cause of so much grief. 'Before he wants this back.'

Aldric and Kyrin gazed distastefully at it and then, as the import of the enchanter's words sank in, stared at the place where the Grand Warlord's corpse had been. Voord was standing up . . .

'These things happen,' said Gemmel, very dry. 'But then, I understand you couldn't kill him anyway?'

'I tried.' Aldric shrugged, watching the unsteady figure in the sword-slashed clothing. 'But I couldn't.'

'You tried to help him die . . . and instead helped him to live.'

'You know that well enough,' said Kyrin, and gave the old man a warning look from underneath her brows.

'I do. Yes, indeed. But I'd as soon not put too much pressure on his gratitude. Not after this' – he tucked the Jewel into one of the pockets of his tunic and out of sight – 'and especially not now that he owes you what can never be repaid. I doubt he takes kindly to the debt.'

'He's got his life back,' said Kyrin, 'and ought to be satisfied with that.'

They walked carefully together towards the ragged hole that sorcery had torn in the wall, breathing the cold clean air of winter as it gusted through, and then Aldric hesitated. 'What about Widowmaker?' he asked.

Kyrin glanced sharply at him, and for a second her expression was that of a woman whose lover asks after the health of an old mistress. 'It's just a sword, and a broken one. Leave it.'

'It still deserves better than to be left here.'

'I don't . . .' Kyrin shrugged and smiled briefly, dropping the dispute. 'Go and get her. We'll,' with a warning look at Gemmel, 'stay here.'

As he searched for the point-shard, meaning for safety's

sake to replace it in the longsword's scabbard, Voord watched him through glazed, hooded eyes. The *Woydach* was breathing, but as Aldric reached out carefully for the still-sharp blade it occured to him that Voord was somehow different, as if he had not been restored whole and entire. There was a lack of lustre about the man, as if some inner spark was missing; he might be upright, but he was still dead inside.

Aldric's fingers closed on the length of chilly metal, and he realised that Widowmaker, too, was changed. There was no longer the tingle of hungry menace which he had associated with the *taiken* for so long. It was as if all the killings of the past two thousand years had never happened. She had returned to what she had been in the beginning: Isileth, 'Star-steel', an elegant weapon made by the finest swordsmith of all swords in all times and places from metals that had fallen from the sky, for no other reason than to test his skill. Kyrin would like that.

Aldric heard the scuff of feet behind him, overlaid too late with Kyrin's cry of warning. Something massive hit him in the back, punching through the lamellar armour as if it wasn't there and doing something to his lungs that made him cough. He staggered forward into arms which had not been close enough to save him. There was perhaps two feet of steel in Widowmaker's hilt, and by the feel of it most had gone inside him. There was no pain, only a dull sensation of being pulled off-balance by the long blade standing out between his shoulders, and a sickly awareness of his own stupidity as he turned his head.

Voord was smiling now, as he had not smiled before. It had been brooding hatred which had made him seem so dull and dead – hatred at being saved, which was bad enough, and saved through pity and an enemy's sense of honour, which was far worse. Only with requital for that ultimate of insults had the spark of his life returned.

'Burn the bastard!' Aldric heard Kyrin spit the words in a voice so vicious that it had almost ceased to be her own. For the first time in her life she had learned what it must be like to suffer Voord's soul-spoiling hatred for any other living thing. He felt Gemmel draw his sidearm from its holster, and his ears filled with the high shrill whining that meant death.

'No . . . !' He grabbed for the weapon and weakly tried to pull its muzzle out of line, but might as well have tried to bend a bar of iron.

'*No?*' Gemmel plainly did not believe what he was hearing.

Aldric coughed blood-spots on to the old man's immaculate uniform. 'No. Didn't go through . . . all of that – not just so you could kill him. D-dying isn't *that* much fun.'

He saw understanding in their faces, felt the pistol's long barrel drop from aim and smiled with relief. His head lolled forward as if it weighed a thousand pounds, then dragged upright again as he shook the encroaching darkness from his vision and grinned savagely back at Voord. 'Poor sort . . . of revenge anyway,' he said, taking care to speak distinctly. 'No imagination any more.'

Woydach Voord glared at them in loathing with all satisfaction drained out of his face, knowing beyond doubt that whether Aldric lived or died the sweet taste of his victory had turned irrevocably sour. He began to screech something that none of them bothered to heed. Kyrin and Gemmel heard only the frightened urgency in Aldric's voice: 'Like death. N-not worth repeating. Once is . . . is enough. But I'm dying, Father . . .'

'Easy, my son,' said Gemmel. 'I know.' He raised the Dragonwand above his head and braced his new-found children close against his side. Power blasted down from the spellstaff and swirled about them so that they stood at the heart of a twisting column of ice-blue flame. 'I know. We're going where I can help you. Home . . .'

Aldric watched their faces, heard their voices, until all faded. All sound was lost. All sight was swallowed up. All the world faded; and went black.

The fire faded and went out, and they were gone.

GLOSSARY

achran-kai. (Alb.) 'inverted cross'; a double cut in *taiken-ulleth* in which the blade, often striking from the scabbard, follows first a horizontal path at chest or eye level and then a vertical downward path, both to strike a target directly in front. If the first cut is delivered with proper force, focus and accuracy, the second is not usually required.

altrou. (Alb.) 'Foster-father'; also a title given to priests.

an-sherban (Drus.) Patronymic of members of the Sherbanul dynasty, present rulers of the Drusalan Empire.

arluth (Alb.) 'Lord'; ruler of lands or of a town.

aypan-kailin (Alb.) 'Cadet-warrior'; a youth undergoing training in the military skills of sword, horse and bow.

coerhanalth (Drus.) 'Lord General'; Commander-in-Chief, most senior of all Drusalan military (as opposed to political) ranks.

coyac. (Jouv.) A sleeveless jerkin of fur, leather or sheepskin.

cserin. (Alb.) Child of a clan-lord, and in line of succession to the title.

cymar. (Alb.) Long over-robe for outdoor wear.

eijo. (Alb.) 'Outlier'; a wanderer or landless person, especially a lordless warrior.

eldheisart. (Drus.) 'Commander'; Imperial military rank.

elyu-dlas. (Alb.) 'Colour-robe'; formal crested garment in clan colours.

erhan. (Alb.) 'Scholar'; especially used of one who travels in the course of his/her studies.

eskorrethen. (Alb.) The coming-of-age ceremony at age twenty, when a warrior is confirmed in his status and in any ranks, styles or titles to which he may be entitled. His hair, grown long for the purpose, is tied back in a queue (originally the handle by which his severed head was carried if he fell in battle); oaths of loyalty are taken before religious and secular witnesses; and if he is *kailin-eir* (q.v.) and thus of a rank to warrant it, he is given a *tsepan* (q.v.) which is used to cut the Honour-Scars in his left hand. These three scars are a permanent reminder of his blood-oath of honour and duty to Heaven, Crown and Clan. From that time forward the *tsepan* must always be within arm's length, and when in public his hair must be tied back in a queue.

estoc. (Jouv.) A sword with a slender single-edged blade, sometimes slightly curved but more usually straight, whose fencing style makes more use of thrusting than does the Alban *taiken* (q.v.)

glas-elyu Menethen. (Alb.) The Blue Mountains, a range in North-Western Alba.

hanalth. (Drus.) 'Colonel'; Imperial military rank.

hanan-vlethanek. (Alb.) 'Keeper-of-Years'; a Court archivist.

hautach. (Drus.) 'Sir'; literally 'High One', used when acknowledging the commands of a superior officer.

hauthanalth. (Drus.) 'Over-Colonel'; Imperial military rank.

hautheisart. (Drus.) 'Lord-Commander'; Imperial military rank.

hautmarin. (Drus.) 'Ship-captain'; Imperial naval rank equivalent to *hautheisart*.

hlensyarl, hlens'l. (Drus.) 'Outlander'; a foreigner or stranger. This can mean someone from a different province, city or even village, but is always a person of whom to be suspicious.

ilauan. (Alb.) 'Clan'; a noble family, linked by name and bloodline. All members of a clan are related to a greater or lesser extent, but only the *cseirin*-born (q.v.) may rule, and then only in line of succession.

ilauem-arluth. (Alb.) 'Clan-lord'; the head of a noble house, ruler of its lands and commander of its forces.

inyen-hlensyarl. (Drus., from *hlensyarl* q.v.) 'Alien-foreigner'; someone from another country, and therefore always considered a potential enemy. The present political situation within the Drusalan Empire has done nothing to amend this, and increasingly the word has taken on the connotations of insult.

kagh'ernvakh. (Drus.) 'Honour's-Guardians'; the Imperial Political and Secret Police.

kailin. (Alb.) Warrior, man-at-arms, especially when in service to a lord.

kailin-eir. (Alb.) Warrior nobleman, of lesser status than *arluth* (q.v.)

kortagor. (Drus.) 'Lieutenant'; Imperial military rank.

kourgath. (Alb.) The Alban lynx-cat, proverbial for ferocity out of all proportion to its size; also a nickname.

margh-arluth. (Alb.) 'Horse Lord'; one of the Alban warrior nobility whose clan lands are found mostly in Prytenon and Elthan.

mathern-an arluth. (Alb.) 'Lord King'; literally 'lord above other lords'; formal title of the King of Alba.

matherneil. (Alb.) 'Kingswine'; the sweet white vintages of Hauverne in Jouvann, rare and expensive in Alba because of small vineyards and restrictive export tariffs.

moyya-tsalaer. (Alb.) 'Great Harness'; full battle armour, with helmet, lamellar cuirass, armoured sleeves and leggings. Shields are uncommon, normally carried only during formal combats.

281

pesoek. (Alb. dialect, Cernuan and Elthanek.) 'Charm'; a lesser spell, or a conjuring trick performed without true magic.

pestreyhar, pestrior. (Cernuan, Alb. dialect.) 'Wizard' or 'sorcerer'; literally, one who creates power with words.

pestreyr-pesok'n. (Cernuan, Alb. dialect.) 'Petty-wizard'; a conjurer, one incapable of using true power, an employer only of insignificant charms or sleight-of-hand. (*pesoek*, q.v.)

purcanyath. (Cernuan, Alb. dialect.) 'Enchanter'; literally a spell-singer.

seisac. (Drus.) A distinctive form of helmet with (usually) a high, conical crown, deep neck-guard and cheekplates and a peak through which may be slid a nasal bar.

slijei? (Vlech.) 'Understand?'; interrogative imperative of an officer completing the issue of an order to subordinates. The word carries an element of promissory threat.

slij'hah! (Vlech.) 'Understood!'; standard response to the interrogative imperative.

taidyo. (Alb.) 'Staffsword'; a wooden practice foil, usually of oak or a similar hardwood.

taiken. (Alb.) 'Longsword'; the *kailin*'s classic weapon, a straight, double-edged cut-and-thrust blade in a hilt long enough for both hands but sufficiently balanced for only one. When in these trained hands, a properly forged and polished *taiken* (the word 'sharpened', with its suggestion of prior bluntness, is not encouraged) delivering a focused strike can shear through most forms of composite armour. The body of the armour's wearer has never been considered an obstacle.

taiken-ulleth. (Alb.) Generic name for all schools and styles of *taiken*-play.

taipan. (Alb.) 'Shortsword'; a short, sometimes curved, often richly mounted weapon which is usually restricted to wear with the formal *elyu-dlas* (q.v.)

tarann'ach. (Alb.) 'Striking thunderbolt'; a cut in *taiken-ulleth* in which the blade follows a diagonal downward path to strike a target directly in front.

tarannin-kai. (Alb.) 'Twin thunderbolts'; a cut in *taiken'ulleth* (q.v.) in which the blade follows a horizontal figure-eight to strike two targets at right and left.

tau-kortagor. (Drus.) 'Under-lieutenant'; the lowest Imperial military rank.

taulath. (Alb.) 'Shadowthief'; secretive mercenaries, available for hire through devious routes for the purpose of spying, sabotage, blackmail and assassination; they perform all those politically necessary duties forbidden to *kailinin* by their codes of Honour.

telek. (Alb.) 'Thrower'; a personal-defence sidearm which projects lead-weighted darts with considerable force (over short distances) from either a box or rotary magazine by means of powerful springs.

tlakh-woydan. (Vlech.) 'Lord's-Protectors'; the Grand Warlord's Bodyguard Regiment, stationed in Drakkesborg Barracks.

tsalaer. (Alb.) 'Harness'; the lamellar cuirass worn without armoured sleeves or leggings, often under clothing as a concealed defence. (All parts of *an moyya tsalaer* (q.v.) may be worn separately, as need dictates.)

tsepan. (Alb.) 'Small-blade'; the Honour dirk of Alba was originally a weapon carried into battle by its owner as a mercy knife, for others or himself. (It was and still is considered dishonourable and vulgar to finish off a fallen *kailin* with a *taiken*, for all that he may be killed outright with one while still on his feet.) As the requirements of honour, duty and obligation came to be observed with ever-increasing stringency, the *tsepan* became instead a means whereby a warrior could recover lost honour (or at least evade the consequences of its loss) by killing himself. This was an acceptable form of self-punishment, and meant that other penalties, notably forfeiture of lands or titles, were withheld. With a few notable exceptions, the practice has fallen into disuse.

tsepanak'ulleth. (Alb.) The act of ritual suicide.

vosjhaien, vosjh'. (Vlech.) Father, 'papa'.

woydach. (Drus.) 'Grand Warlord'; while the title appears exclusively military, it also carries political connotations. The Grand Warlord of the Drusalan Empire was originally responsible for foreign affairs, frontier security and the overseeing of any policies of expansion put forward by the Emperor. More recently the post has been that of military dictator, with the Emperor as no more than a figurehead.

woydachul. (Drus.) The Warlord's faction in the Empire.

woydek-hlautan. (Drus.) 'The Warlord's Domain'; all those provinces of the Empire which through policy or conquest regard the *Woydach* rather than the Emperor as true head of state.

ymeth. (Drus.) 'Dreamsmoke'; a common recreational narcotic, used also as a soporific before surgery and as an adjunct to certain forms of sorcery.

A Selection of Legend Titles

☐	Eon	Greg Bear	£3.50
☐	Forge of God	Greg Bear	£3.99
☐	Falcons of Narabedla	Marion Zimmer Bradley	£2.50
☐	The Influence	Ramsey Campbell	£3.50
☐	Wyrms	Orson Scott Card	£3.50
☐	Speaker for the Dead	Orson Scott Card	£2.95
☐	Seventh Son	Orson Scott Card	£3.50
☐	Wolf in Shadow	David Gemmell	£3.50
☐	Last Sword of Power	David Gemmell	£3.50
☐	This is the Way the World Ends	James Morrow	£4.99
☐	Unquenchable Fire	Rachel Pollack	£3.99
☐	Golden Sunlands	Christopher Rowley	£3.50
☐	The Misplaced Legion	Harry Turtledove	£2.99
☐	An Emperor for the Legion	Harry Turtledove	£2.99

Prices and other details are liable to change

ARROW BOOKS, BOOKSERVICE BY POST, PO BOX 29, DOUGLAS, ISLE OF MAN, BRITISH ISLES

NAME...

ADDRESS..

....

....

Please enclose a cheque or postal order made out to Arrow Books Ltd. for the amount due and allow the following for postage and packing.

U.K. CUSTOMERS: Please allow 22p per book to a maximum of £3.00.

B.F.P.O. & EIRE: Please allow 22p per book to a maximum of £3.00.

OVERSEAS CUSTOMERS: Please allow 22p per book.

Whilst every effort is made to keep prices low it is sometimes necessary to increase cover prices at short notice. Arrow Books reserve the right to show new retail prices on covers which may differ from those previously advertised in the text or elsewhere.

Bestselling SF/Horror

☐ Forge of God	Greg Bear	£3.99
☐ Eon	Greg Bear	£3.50
☐ The Hungry Moon	Ramsey Campbell	£3.50
☐ The Influence	Ramsey Campbell	£3.50
☐ Seventh Son	Orson Scott Card	£3.50
☐ Bones of the Moon	Jonathan Carroll	£2.50
☐ Nighthunter: The Hexing & The Labyrinth	Robert Faulcon	£3.50
☐ Pin	Andrew Neiderman	£1.50
☐ The Island	Guy N. Smith	£2.50
☐ Malleus Maleficarum	Montague Summers	£4.50

Prices and other details are liable to change

ARROW BOOKS, BOOKSERVICE BY POST, PO BOX 29, DOUGLAS, ISLE OF MAN, BRITISH ISLES

NAME...

ADDRESS...

....

....

Please enclose a cheque or postal order made out to Arrow Books Ltd. for the amount due and allow the following for postage and packing.

U.K. CUSTOMERS: Please allow 22p per book to a maximum of £3.00.

B.F.P.O. & EIRE: Please allow 22p per book to a maximum of £3.00.

OVERSEAS CUSTOMERS: Please allow 22p per book.

Whilst every effort is made to keep prices low it is sometimes necessary to increase cover prices at short notice. Arrow Books reserve the right to show new retail prices on covers which may differ from those previously advertised in the text or elsewhere.

Bestselling Thriller/Suspense

☐ Skydancer	Geoffrey Archer	£3.50
☐ Hooligan	Colin Dunne	£2.99
☐ See Charlie Run	Brian Freemantle	£2.99
☐ Hell is Always Today	Jack Higgins	£2.50
☐ The Proteus Operation	James P Hogan	£3.50
☐ Winter Palace	Dennis Jones	£3.50
☐ Dragonfire	Andrew Kaplan	£2.99
☐ The Hour of the Lily	John Kruse	£3.50
☐ Fletch, Too	Geoffrey McDonald	£2.50
☐ Brought in Dead	Harry Patterson	£2.50
☐ The Albatross Run	Douglas Scott	£2.99

Prices and other details are liable to change

Bestselling Fiction

☐ No Enemy But Time	Evelyn Anthony	£2.95
☐ The Lilac Bus	Maeve Binchy	£2.99
☐ Prime Time	Joan Collins	£3.50
☐ A World Apart	Marie Joseph	£3.50
☐ Erin's Child	Sheelagh Kelly	£3.99
☐ Colours Aloft	Alexander Kent	£2.99
☐ Gondar	Nicholas Luard	£4.50
☐ The Ladies of Missalonghi	Colleen McCullough	£2.50
☐ Lily Golightly	Pamela Oldfield	£3.50
☐ Talking to Strange Men	Ruth Rendell	£2.99
☐ The Veiled One	Ruth Rendell	£3.50
☐ Sarum	Edward Rutherfurd	£4.99
☐ The Heart of the Country	Fay Weldon	£2.50

Prices and other details are liable to change

ARROW BOOKS, BOOKSERVICE BY POST, PO BOX 29, DOUGLAS, ISLE
OF MAN, BRITISH ISLES

NAME...

ADDRESS...

....

....

Please enclose a cheque or postal order made out to Arrow Books Ltd. for the amount
due and allow the following for postage and packing.

U.K. CUSTOMERS: Please allow 22p per book to a maximum of £3.00.

B.F.P.O. & EIRE: Please allow 22p per book to a maximum of £3.00.

OVERSEAS CUSTOMERS: Please allow 22p per book.

Whilst every effort is made to keep prices low it is sometimes necessary to increase cover
prices at short notice. Arrow Books reserve the right to show new retail prices on covers
which may differ from those previously advertised in the text or elsewhere.